THE FINEST PRINT

ERIN LANGSTON

PRAISE FOR FOREVER YOUR ROGUE

One of the most utterly gorgeous character transformations historical romance has offered up in some time.

— THE NEW YORK TIMES BOOK REVIEW

Wonderfully constructed from start to finish, with high notes of grace and humor, Langston has written a novel that romance fans will treasure.

— LIBRARY JOURNAL, STARRED REVIEW

Smart, sexy, and powerfully grounded in history, written in clean, clear prose - this book is the definition of a Desert Island Keeper.

— ALL ABOUT ROMANCE

A simmering, swoonworthy story that takes you to places both excitingly new and reassuringly familiar.

— PASTE MAGAZINE

Sweet, sizzling with breathtaking chemistry, and so superbly written that the book will stay with you long after you've closed it.

— MARVELOUS GEEKS MEDIA

This book is dedicated to writers, journalists, and all creators who put ink to paper and papers in hands. Time and again, in ways big and small, telling and disseminating our stories has been a labor of love, perseverance, and bravery.

And for Pete—
My partner, my friend. Thank you for always being my good news.

<h1 style="text-align:center">The Travers and Sinclair Families</h1>

circa Spring 1848

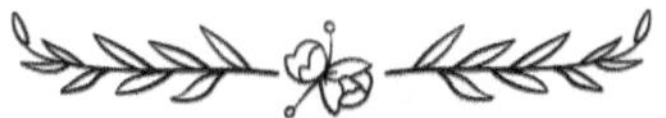

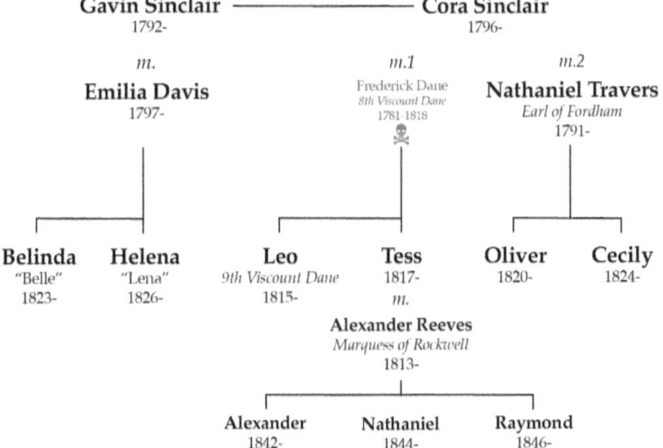

PROLOGUE

March 1844

London

THERE WAS A VERY good chance Belle Sinclair was ruining her life.
There was an even better chance she was doing so in vain.

By the time she walked out of Scotland Yard today, her circumstances would be both better and worse, and there was no telling which would withstand the test of time.

She wasn't wearing the ring; it was safe in a little silk pouch in the concealed pocket of her skirts. She'd removed it two days ago, twisting it off her finger and enclosing the skin-warmed band of silver in her fist.

Now she put the pouch on the desk and slid it across the roughly hewn wood to Detective Sergeant Lawrence Duncan, who watched with mild bemusement.

He lifted the pouch, opened it, spilled out the ring. A small metallic clatter sounded as it spun twice.

Duncan chuckled. "You cannot be serious, Belinda."

She stared at the ring, fighting a frightened impulse to snatch it up, to squash it on her finger, to keep her feet walking the path they'd agreed to walk.

But then she looked up to encounter his knowing smirk.

He didn't believe she could go through with it, which was precisely why she had to.

"I'm quite serious." Her voice sounded far softer than intended.

She swallowed hard and imagined herself in front of the gilded mirror on her dressing table, where she'd practiced this conversation a dozen times in the last two days. Her reflection—finely boned face, wide hazel eyes, barely tamed waves of tawny hair—was always composed. Her reflection did not entertain nerves, because it had none. She needed to be the same—dispassionate, assured, the embodiment of Belle Sinclair in the mirror.

And she had to do it from the warm side of the glass.

Duncan picked up the ring and slid it on his pinky. He held it to the sunlit window in his tiny office, examining it as if he had never seen it before.

"I presume this is because of the incident with your journal?"

"It was my manuscript," she corrected hoarsely. She was unable to think of it. All those lost pages. Words she loved, words she nurtured.

Words she could never, ever get back.

She looked at him, no longer seeing his sleek pomade and polished veneer—only the man of two days ago, his face twisting as she retrieved her ruined pages from the puddle of his upended teapot. Duncan's ugly outburst had been a sobering shock and yet, somehow, entirely expected. It confirmed that her mounting unease was warranted, that she had taken the measure of him after all.

In truth, her revulsion didn't stem from his treatment of her manuscript—his outrageous jealousy over her busy pen—but from the malice lurking behind his calculated composure. She curdled, recalling how he tossed her a napkin, bluntly censuring her distress. *Come, Belinda, let's not make a fuss.*

Now she blinked away from him, supposing nothing said so much of a man's character than what he would and would not make a fuss about.

"You do realize you have no other prospects?" Duncan spun the ring on his desk with casual confidence. "I'm the only man who offered for you. And not to be crude, Belinda, but I might remind you, a broken engagement will harm you *far* more than it will me."

She resolutely squashed a blurry memory of his hand on her knee. If he thought to trap her with the small liberties she'd cautiously granted him, he was wrong about what would harm her.

"I have the prospect of myself," she said, holding her fists tight in her lap. "Of my family. Of my writing—"

"Your writing is not only trite and meaningless, it's a liability," he interrupted tersely. "I'm due to be named *Inspector*. Superintendent one day. Christ, Belinda, the only thing you had to be was convenient."

She stared at him, grateful he'd admitted it. She knew he valued her for her family connections, just as she knew she was meant to value *him* for his own merits—without question, Duncan was competent, respected, and highly ambitious.

How different things might have been, if he'd also been *good*.

"I am not a convenience." Her throat ached with feeble resolve. "Nor can I become so. It's not what I want."

"Indeed, you are not."

Duncan spun the ring again. She watched it rotate on the table, fast under his finger. Her cheeks grew tight, a sure sign she was close to tears—which was infuriating, because she wasn't sad…not precisely.

"Is Justice Sinclair here?" He glanced at the door.

At the mention of her father, Belle's courage rebounded. "He's here."

Her father was waiting in the corridor outside. When she finished, he would step in to conclude the business of a broken betrothal. He'd done just so, many times over, in his career as a barrister. Papa wanted to attend this meeting with her, but Belle asked to come in alone. She was determined to undo her own near-disastrous mistake. God knows she would require the same fortitude in the days to come.

Duncan huffed one short laugh. "So this is it, then?"

She reached out to put her hand atop the spinning ring, setting it squarely on the desk in front of him. She wanted nothing about this moment to be in flux.

"This is it." She had more to say. But she couldn't. She wanted to go home. She wanted to curl in her bed and rest her aching head on her mother's knee. "Thank you for your time, Sergeant."

She left the office, an awful levity rising within her, a bubble of emotion about to burst. All of the hard things would come now, the rumors, the whispers. Mess, all of it a mess. A mess her parents had cautioned of even as they handed her a broom. *If you have reservations*, Papa told her, *so do I*. But then he looked at Mama with a grim resolve that settled in Belle's bones.

"Belle." Her father was pacing the dingy corridor, his dark blue eyes somber as he took her in. "No. Not here."

She was breathing too fast; her face was wet. She quickly dragged her knuckles across the damp ridge of her cheekbone.

Papa glanced behind her, then put his hands on her shoulders. She looked up at him. She was twenty-one years old and had just upended her life over a bad feeling. And her father had let her do it. She couldn't imagine ever feeling as grateful as she did right now.

"Eyes dry," he said, his voice low. "The way you walk out of here matters, Belle. There is no world in which Duncan will make this easy for you. I'll be quick, but you should wait outside."

Belle nodded, pitching with painful relief.

Swiftly, she descended the staircase and crossed through the back hall. It wasn't until she stepped out to the street that she remembered her careful rehearsal, the impassioned, well-articulated remarks Duncan would never hear.

But now, standing in the cold, cold blue, she found her eyes were indeed dry, and she was fiercely glad she'd remained silent.

Belle had no idea what the future held. Her words might be all she had.

And she would not waste a single, precious one.

1

April 1848
London

…When you dock in Liverpool, arrange for locomotive transport to London via the North Western Railway to Euston Station. (If your funds allow, I recommend a first-class carriage—anything less is markedly uncomfortable!) Send your itinerary to my offices at this address, and I will meet you beneath the Doric Arch, timed to your arrival in London.

—Excerpt, letter from Mr. Hubert Gabler to Ethan Fletcher, dated February, 1848

"Careful now, Mr. Fletcher, you'll want to watch for mud."

Ethan lifted his boot from a sluice of sludge, then raised one dark eyebrow at Mr. Gabler, his avuncular new lawyer. No, his *solicitor*. Apparently, the specific nature of Gabler's work demarcated him a solicitor in England, as he first announced via letter, then again when he greeted Ethan at Euston station. Ethan didn't give a damn what Gabler was called, only that he was waiting as promised. As it were, it had taken a quarter hour to disembark from the locomotive, secure his luggage, and determine where the hell to find the Doric Arch. He might very well have left again if the portly solicitor hadn't been bouncing anxiously beneath it.

"Come, Mr. Gabler, we both know this isn't mud." Ethan gave an experimental sniff and instantly regretted it when the choking stench hit his nostrils.

The two men jostled through the crowd and exited the railway station, leaving behind the seething locomotive. The chaotic bustle of the platform spilled into the street, where porters grappled with trunks, trading curses as they sidestepped disoriented passengers and harried pedestrians.

"Welcome to London." Gabler's nose wrinkled above his bushy mustache. "Fear not. Conditions will somewhat improve by the time we arrive on Fleet Street."

Ethan frowned, trying to absorb the gobsmacking tableau of this new city while maintaining a semblance of nonchalance. Some of this maddening urban crush was familiar to him; Boston, after all, was bursting at its seams. But he'd cut his teeth in Boston. It's where he had his last kiss from his mother, his first kiss from a girl. He knew to avoid the Charles Street side of the Common. He knew he best be at Quincy by quarter to dawn if he wanted to secure breakfast at his favorite pushcart.

He didn't know what to make of the behemoth unfamiliarity of London. The world had turned to fog, and there was no telling what was shrouded beneath the thick gray cloak.

At least it was a stationary gray cloak.

For sixteen days, Ethan Fletcher had been moving, but rarely by means of his own two feet. He'd been forced into idleness—relying on other men to transport him first across the Atlantic, then across England—all while he sat, restlessly anticipating whatever the hell awaited him. He wasn't used to sitting still; nor was he used to the immediate, oppressive *filth* of London. Looking at the thickly smeared cobblestones beneath his feet, he was almost sorry he'd finally run out of conveyances.

Boston to Halifax, Halifax to Liverpool, Liverpool to London. Two weeks of hellishly confined space, beginning on the lurching *Hibernia*, where his cabin was about as spacious as a coffin. It had been impossible to comfortably stretch the full length of his broad frame across the so-called bed; after some unfortunate bruising during a particularly rough storm, Ethan had finally hauled his pallet to the floor. But the steamship was pure luxury compared to the second-class carriage on the locomotive from Liverpool, which had a roof but open sides. Ethan shared a bench with a mother and her three small children, the younger two of whom he'd covered with his overcoat when afternoon rain blew through the compartment.

By the time he disembarked at the Euston railway station to meet the mysterious Mr. Gabler, Ethan was so grateful to be on solid ground, he almost didn't notice that ground was covered in…well. *Some* of it might have been mud.

"This will do," Ethan said to a pair of porters. The lads heaved his trunk to the dirty street and waited expectantly. Ethan dug for his wallet, fumbling with the unfamiliar coins. He exchanged his money in Liverpool, but the harried cashier had done a piss-poor job explaining the currency.

"Here." Gabler plucked a coin from the jumble in Ethan's palm. He wanted to ask what, exactly, he'd just paid but opted to stay ignorant for now. This damnable voyage had substantially cut into his savings, and so far, all he'd got for his sum was a sour stomach, a wet coat, and shit on his boots.

"I've secured transport." Gabler ushered him along the teeming street. "Just here."

Ethan eyed the congested line of carriages and hansom cabs. "It's too far to walk?"

Gabler shook his head. "Much too far, especially with luggage. The station is outside the city center, Mr. Fletcher."

Right. Ethan sighed and hefted his trunk.

"Very well, Gabler. After you." He rolled his shoulders, the muscles in his forearms straining to accommodate the cumbersome bulk of the trunk. "I have to say, I'm curious to see the promised improvement of Fleet Street. Unless we're signing papers in your office?"

Gabler's jovial expression noticeably dimmed. "I think we should perhaps start with your lodgings, get you settled. I took the liberty of sending a woman to clean the residence above the shop. A bath and a beer will improve your spirits, don't you think?"

Ethan shortened his long stride to allow the solicitor to keep pace. "Gabler, I've traversed half the damn globe to secure a wholly unexpected but decidedly welcome inheritance. I know I look like a bedraggled brute, but I assure you, now I'm here, my spirits are just fine."

Gabler blinked. "Did you…ah…not receive my letter? I know it took an age to locate your whereabouts, but—"

"Of course I got your letter." Ethan shifted the trunk. "How else would I know where to meet you today?"

"Not that letter."

If Ethan wasn't very much mistaken, his new solicitor visibly gulped.

"My *second* letter."

Ethan stopped in the middle of the street. No fewer than four drivers shouted at him, but he paid them no mind. What he'd just told Gabler was no exaggeration—he'd come to London to seek his future, and he was putting his grimy boots nowhere except the threshold of his new printshop.

"What second letter, Gabler?"

Gabler shook his head and pointed to a vacant cab. "A bath, a beer, then business, Mr. Fletcher. I think we'll both be better for it."

And just like that, the smell of his boots was the least of Ethan Fletcher's problems.

~

The first letter—the only letter Ethan gave credence to—arrived February 18, 1848, a day typical in every regard except for the fact it altered the entire course of his life. In the weeks following, the letter had been his constant companion; by now, it was so well-creased, it was nearly torn in two. The correspondence had arrived at the Washington Street office of the newspaper, addressed in heavy, elegant script to *Mister Ethan T. Fletcher, % Printing-Office, Boston Sentinel,* and a bevy of colored-ink handstamps charted the letter's course across land and sea until an agitated clerk dropped it on Ethan's desk.

He'd nearly missed it. He'd been in a foul mood, intent on drowning his frustration in a liquid supper at the Commonwealth. His parvenu editor had assigned him to attend yet another salon on the south slope—why anyone needed weekly updates of the Beacon Hill elite, Ethan couldn't begin to guess.

But then the clerk delivered the letter, and Ethan had been reading it ever since.

Good thing too. Regardless of what Gabler now said from behind the safety of his mahogany desk, Ethan knew damn well exactly what that letter stated.

"You wrote to me six weeks ago and told me in English plain enough for us both to understand that"—here, Ethan jabbed the letter as he recited Gabler's message verbatim—"*Robert Gaines, the recently departed brother of Marina Fletcher, has left to you, Ethan Thomas Fletcher, the son of Marina Fletcher and sole living relative of the aforementioned Robert Gaines, the entirety of his estate, consisting of a dwelling-house, shop, and materials of a printing office, located at No. 62 Fleet Street, London.*"

He stared at the solicitor, his gaze hard. If Gabler thought a bath, a beer, and the gentility of a London office would protect him from a throttling, he didn't know the first thing about Ethan. He'd bloodied his knuckles for far less than a brutal Atlantic crossing and the promise of unprecedented financial freedom.

"Did you not write those words, Mr. Gabler?"

"I did." Gabler shifted, nervously placing his hands on the desk.

"To be sure, I most certainly wrote that…but you see, Mr. Fletcher, I sent a *second* letter informing you there has been an unforeseen issue with your uncle's estate—let me see, I expected it to reach you a fortnight ago—"

"A fortnight ago I was boarding a steamship to meet you at a goddamn Doric Arch, per the instruction in *this* letter."

Gabler's mustache twitched.

In fear, Ethan hoped. He closed his eyes and drew three slow breaths. "Gabler. Are you telling me I quit my employment, ended my lease, spent hard-earned money on passage…and I *didn't* inherit my uncle's business?"

"You did. You did inherit it." Gabler leaned forward earnestly. "Nothing in question there. Your name is in the will. *You* own 62 Fleet and all materials therein. Gaines Print Works is yours."

"Then what the devil—"

"What we didn't know—as your uncle's solicitor, I'm quite disappointed to say I truly had *no idea* of this arrangement, the whole affair shocked me, absolutely *shocked* me, Mr. Fletch—"

"Gabler."

The solicitor shook his head. "Your uncle was a good man but a terrible *business*man. Apparently in recent years, he'd become woefully slipshod with his accounting. He was losing clients—the Law Society had canceled their contract—and it seems he had a cards problem, to boot. He was in debt, Mr. Fletcher. Horribly in debt."

"Personal debt?" Ethan worked his jaw. "Or business debt? Because bankruptcy—"

"Bankruptcy is a criminal offense here and carries a prison sentence." Gabler looked so glum, Ethan almost felt bad for the man for having to deliver this news. "Which is likely why your uncle turned to a money lender."

"A money lender." Ethan was now repeating words and phrases at random.

"A creditor, if you will. Mr. Charles Howe. Howe is…well, he has a reputation. He'll lend to anyone, but his terms are punishing.

He lent Mr. Gaines a great sum of money. And your uncle put up 62 Fleet as collateral."

"My uncle is dead," Ethan said flatly. "*I* didn't accumulate any debt. I didn't even know the man."

"It doesn't matter." Gabler sighed. "If Gaines had gone through a bank, perhaps we'd have some room to navigate this, but he signed a promissory that's clear as crystal. If Howe is not repaid in full by the fifteenth of June, *he* owns your business."

"June fifteenth…of this year?"

At Gabler's nod, Ethan's stomach churned. It was the first week of April. Mid-June was in just over *ten weeks*.

"How much did Gaines owe?"

Gabler paused. "Ah…with interest, the remaining sum of the debt is just over one hundred pounds sterling."

Ethan's fists clenched as an odd sort of numbness spread through his chest. It was the sensation of something catastrophic happening outside his control.

"The exchange rate for the pound sterling is…what?" He rubbed his temples, trying to recall the rapid-fire discussion in Liverpool. "Just under five dollars, is that right?"

Gabler reluctantly slid a paper across his desk. "Thereabouts. I asked my banker to calculate the sum in your currency. The amount you owe to clear the debt is approximately four hundred eighty American dollars."

Ethan stared.

"Do you perhaps have that sum, Mr. Fletcher? If you do, this would all be—"

"No," Ethan interrupted hoarsely. "No. I do not." He thought of his accounts, wobbling after his travel to London. "I don't have even a fraction of that right now."

He rose to his feet, needing to move. "Damn." He paced the length of Gabler's office like a restless bear. "How in hell is it possible to inherit *less* than nothing? Do you understand the risk I took to come here? I left *everything,* because I was about to own a print works—a *solvent, functioning* business. I thought I might finally establish my own newspaper. No more scraping by, no more taking whatever my superiors will give me, no more proving myself at every turn—"

Ethan broke off, his face heating in embarrassment. Gabler didn't need to hear his woeful tale of a poor boy who grew up to be a slightly less poor man.

He gritted his jaw, forcibly shifting into action. "What are my choices, Gabler? Buy, sell, forfeit?"

"Well, on that front, the matter is quite simple." Gabler steepled his fingers. "You can pay the debt by the fifteenth of June, or you can, at present, relinquish the business to Howe. My second letter intimated you *might* prefer to remain in America to keep clear of the whole mess, given the constraints." He winced. "Of course it's too late for that."

Ethan pinched the bridge of his nose. If Gabler's second communication had reached him, would he have stayed in Boston, stagnant at the *Sentinel*? He couldn't say. And it hardly mattered. Gabler was right. He was here now, and his future dangled in front of him.

But to seize it, he needed to scrounge up a sum equivalent to *two years* of his previous salary.

It jarred to the point of physical pain.

"What's stopping me from selling the shop?" Ethan paced toward the window. "Is there a reason I can't offload the property and pocket the proceeds?"

"Unfortunately, you can't sell 62 Fleet while ownership is tangled up with this creditor," Gabler sighed. "You'll sign your name to the deed, but the deed is what Gaines promised Howe. If you sell, he could lay claim to the proceeds. You'd end up losing the shop with very little revenue to show for it…"

Ethan stared out the window as Gabler rambled on. Across the street, a small family made their way through the crowd—mother, father, distractible little boy. He watched their uneven progress, ponderously running his hand over the dark beard shadowing his jaw.

"Your uncle was fortunate he wasn't sent to debtor's prison, given the state of the accounts. *Truly*, Mr. Fletcher, it was only a matter of time…"

The boy suddenly lurched far too close to the congested street, and the mother responded faster than Ethan's startled pulse. Her arm snapped forward to catch her son by the wrist, holding him safe against her. At the sight of their joined hands, Ethan's fingers curled around the windowsill in exquisitely sharp recollection—the rough plane of his own mother's knuckles, perpetually abraded by the salt she scrubbed across the boardinghouse floor.

The last time he felt those familiar calluses was the curdling July morning when she left him at Russell's printshop. She kissed Ethan's forehead hard, her face pinched with desperate regret as she explained he was now to work as a printer's devil, he was to expect nothing but a meal and a mattress, he was to learn a trade and not come home. Her brittle-thin retreat was forever linked to his first whiff of the ink vats, a noxious nightmare from which he gradually understood she wasn't coming back. From that day on, the only hands he could rely on were his own.

"Mr. Fletcher?"

Ethan slowly turned to Gabler.

The solicitor shifted uncomfortably. "If I understand correctly, you cannot afford to lose the business, nor can you afford to purchase it. What, then, do you aim to do?"

Ethan squared his shoulders. What did he aim to do? The same damn thing he'd always done. Against all odds, he pulled through, didn't he? He'd leveraged the brutal years of his apprenticeship into steadily advancing work—compositor, pressman, foreman. He'd filled every position at the paper, tirelessly doing all that was required of him before asking to do more. The week after his twenty-seventh birthday, he'd been made special reporter—an *impossible* coup considering where he started—and for the last two years, he'd been striving to parlay that opportunity into something more, something of his own.

And here, *finally*—his chance.

"Think of it this way, Gabler." He thrummed with renewed

determination. "I can't pay the creditor *yet*. Nor do I have to. I have ten weeks."

"One hundred pounds in ten weeks?" Gabler looked uneasy. "Is it possible for a printshop to turn that kind of profit?"

Ethan smiled grimly. "I suppose we're going to find out."

2

In the Constabulary was a Notice Board: missing persons, missing property, and in one memorable occurrence, a missing parrot (the bird in question was expeditiously located in a ruby-encrusted birdcage at a pawnshop near Whitechapel, unharmed but for its unfortunate proximity to such a garish enclosure). Day in, day out, the Notice Board was afflicted with scraps—desk clerks pinning up and constables tearing down, until it was nothing but a vertical jumble of lost things everyone forgot to notice at all.

Everyone, that is, except Clementina Bloom.

—Excerpt from The Sensational Cases of Clementina Bloom ~~Prologue~~ *Chapter 1 (Draft 2)*

BELLE SINCLAIR'S nickname preceded her, a fact which had always felt significant. She was Belle before she was Belinda; she was Belle before she was born.

Having the diminutive of her name selected prior to her first greedy breath served as a reminder her existence was anticipated. She was as meant to be as her parents' unlikely introduction—

which, according to family lore, transpired one long-ago evening at the Belle, a coaching inn where a penniless governess upended a tankard of beer over the head of a lonely barrister.

Because Gavin and Emilia Sinclair were sentimental, they'd contrived to name their first child after the establishment. And thus, she became Belle, though her mother insisted on Belinda as a formality. She'd never been quite certain what the plan was if she'd turned out to be a boy.

"—Miss Sinclair." Doyle, her favorite guard at the Old Bailey, interrupted her narrative with an indulgent shake of his head. "You told me this story three times before."

"Ah, but it's an important story, Doyle." Belle leaned against the paneled wall of the corridor. "My name has *meaning*. I don't take the thought of changing it lightly, even for a nom de plume."

Behind her, the muffled but distinct drone of the defense counselor rumbled from the courtroom. Court was in session, which on a slow afternoon might see Belle discreetly tucked into the back of the spectator gallery with her journal. Unfortunately, the courtroom was crowded today, so she'd decided to wait with Doyle in the passage between the judge's parlor and the Old Court while her father patiently doled out justice.

"You hear back from that fancy journal then?" Doyle lowered his thick gray eyebrows. "They accept your story?"

"No." Belle bit her lip. "Nothing from *Blackwood's*. Yet. But I want to be prepared, should the occasion arise." She frowned, fiddling with her hair. A pin was askew, buried somewhere in the thick waves. "You know, men don't need to think of such things. They can be whoever they like. Even themselves. Take Mr. Dickens —he certainly doesn't need to debate the merits of publishing under his own name. Except when he used Boz, I suppose."

"Well, Dickens is a good name," Doyle mused.

"Yes, it is," Belle allowed. She found the hairpin and neatly tucked her light brown tresses into place beneath the short brim of her bonnet. "Charles Dickens is a very good name. Then there's Mr. Poe."

"No," Doyle said emphatically. "Don't start."

Belle ignored him, rummaging through her basket for a battered copy of *The Ladies' Companion.* "I was recently revisiting 'The Mystery of Marie Rogêt.'" She flipped through the journal. "Goodness, Doyle, there's something *visceral* about it. Did you know Edgar Allan Poe based this story on a true, unsolved case? Mary Cecilia Rogers—she lived in New York, and they called her the 'Beautiful Cigar Girl.'"

Doyle considered. "Now that is a good name."

Belle nodded her agreement. "I thought the same. Perhaps a missed opportunity for a title, just between us. Regardless, what Poe did is fascinating—he used *factual* details of a crime, writing about it even as the investigation was ongoing." She dropped her voice to a whisper. "Miss Rogers was found floating in the Hudson River."

Doyle signed the cross and looked askance at Belle. "You shouldn't talk such, Miss Sinclair. It ain't right for a lady—"

"The police *never* found out what happened. All signs point to *murder.* And then Poe turned it into one of his C. Auguste Dupin mysteries." She raised one slender eyebrow. "You know, that's essentially what I've been attempting to do. It has me thinking."

"You don't need any more thinking." Doyle shook his grizzled head.

"My father's docket alone—these trials are ripe fodder. We're here day in and day out, Doyle. Why else, if not for inspiration?"

"I know why I'm here all day," Doyle said dryly. "It's nothing to do with *inspiration.* As to why a pretty, clever girl like yourself sits around this hovel with a graybeard like me—"

"Don't speak so about my beloved," she teased lightly. "The Old Bailey is not a hovel."

It wasn't strictly true, but she cherished the hours she spent here with her father. When he wasn't at the bench, the two of them would sit in his judge's parlor, working in companionable silence— he, reviewing briefs; she, copying trial notes into her journal. Better still were the early evenings when Papa would put away his papers, pour her a scant finger of whisky, and ask for her thoughts—*Had the witness been led by counsel? What did she think of the plaintiff's presentation of evidence? Had she gleaned any useful information for her manuscript?*

Court personnel, like Doyle, thought it a strange habit, but for Belle, nothing was more familiar. These parleys were born in her childhood, in the years when Gavin Sinclair had been a young barrister building a busy practice from the first floor of their town house. So long as she didn't cause disruption, Belle had been permitted to play beside his desk. She used to sit against her father's shins and covertly observe the dark skirts of frightened women seeking his measured counsel. Her imagination was first sparked on the worn carpet of her father's study, and it had been crackling ever since.

She still shadowed her father, but her view expanded with his reputation. As a common law judge at the High Courts, Papa divided his time between Westminster and the Old Bailey, where Belle was privy to entire proceedings of the criminal court. She found it endlessly fascinating, a veritable testament to man's best and worst instincts. Even in recent years, when the gallery was too crowded for comfort, she would listen from the corridor, enthralled by the endlessly delicious knots of crime. She couldn't stop the machinations of her brain; she couldn't stop the scratch of her pen.

In her father's world, justice was sadly not always served. But in the world of her creation, she could change that. Her greatest aspiration was to bring a tale of courtroom mystery to life. If only she could find a literary magazine whose greatest aspiration was to publish the gruesome musings of the unmarried twenty-five-year-old daughter of a respected judge.

Her ruminations were interrupted by dear old Doyle, loyally fretting over her social calendar. "But, Miss Sinclair, you don't want to be here all hours, do you? Surely, you got friends?" He narrowed his eyes, as if doubting the truth of his notion. "*Lady* friends, I mean."

"Well, I have Helena, of course." Belle shoved *The Ladies'*

Companion into her basket. "And Cecily…though my sister and cousin tend to ration my discussion of the criminal court."

"As they should." Doyle crossed his arms. "I should do the same. I'm telling you, this business ain't proper."

"Propriety has never been much of a concern to Belinda Sinclair."

Belle prickled with cold shock as the smooth, derisive voice echoed down the corridor.

No.

Absolutely not.

Doyle's eyes widened in warning, but there was no need to alert Belle who approached. She knew that voice, just as she knew she had no desire to see its owner.

After all, she'd managed to avoid doing so for four years.

Detective Sergeant Lawrence Duncan. No. Detective *Inspector* Lawrence Duncan. To her infinite chagrin, she'd heard he received his blasted promotion sometime after reassignment to Nottinghamshire.

Belle turned around to see the lanky man stalking toward them and warily smoothed her dark green skirts.

"Inspector Duncan."

He came to a stop in front of her, his aggressively polished boots a clipped staccato on the floor. She stared at those boots, wondering if he ever got them dirty. It would be just like him to expect his constables to build his reputation.

"I…I heard you were returning to London," Belle finally said, constitutionally unable to wait him out. "I didn't realize you were already here."

He looked her over in a way that set her teeth on edge. "Asking after me, Belinda?"

"Hardly." She swallowed. "The superintendent mentioned it to my father, I believe."

Duncan, for his part, seemed perfectly at ease in this situation. His superior calm made sense; he loved nothing more than putting her off-kilter.

"You know, it's quite fitting one of the first people I would happen upon today is you, Belinda. You've been on my mind this afternoon."

Belle steeled herself. "Is that so?"

"Quite." Duncan propped one arm on the wall beside her, and Belle was immediately reminded of his habit of leaning too close while he talked, as if sniffing out what wasn't said in order to steer the conversation in the manner he wished. "Your hair is coming loose."

Damn. She half reached up to adjust the blasted pin but blanched at the thought of doing anything at his suggestion. Let her hair come loose. She hoped a dozen people walked by to see him in conversation with an unkempt woman. It would be his worst nightmare brought to life.

"I've just come from a bookstall on the Strand." Duncan watched her closely. "I was looking to purchase some paper and reacquaint myself with London's latest."

He paused. Belle wanted to both meet and avoid his gaze.

"Is that so?" she repeated. She needed to stop saying that. She needed to stop saying any words to him at all.

"Indeed. The shop had a marvelous selection of fiction in addition to the news. I perused the offerings in great detail."

She stared over his shoulder at the closed door of the Old Court. It was terribly unfair the very same man who ensured she was uncomfortable in a crowded courtroom was now making her uncomfortable in the corridor outside of one.

"It's the funniest thing." Duncan cocked his head. "I didn't see *your* novel anywhere. In fact, the bookseller hadn't heard of you. I wrote your name out for him...but no. *Nothing.* As though you don't exist."

And just like that—as instantaneous as the nick of a razor blade—the old wound opened. Shame blossomed, seeping through the dressing she'd carefully applied for the last four years.

She looked down, acutely aware of Doyle behind her. There was a slow tickle along her scalp, her hairpin again sliding free. It fell to the floor with a tinny echo of defeat.

Her neck reddened as she took a half step back. "Well—"

The sharp bang of her father's gavel reverberated from the courtroom. The sound spurred her to action.

"If you'll excuse me, Inspector." She tightened her grip on her basket. "I don't have time to chat. I have a busy afternoon, and I didn't expect to see you here today."

"I should say the same, Belinda. The Central Criminal Court is no place for a lady." Duncan's lip curled. "But it seems some things never change. Including your penchant for doing whatever you please."

She had no argument.

The only thing that pleased her was to be left alone.

BELLE HAD PLANNED to meet her father when he finished for the day, but after her disconcerting run-in, it was inconceivable she would wait idly in the judge's parlor. She needed to move, she needed to… be *somewhere*. Away from here.

She packed up her things, deciding a brisk walk would serve her well. It was a bright afternoon, unseasonably warm for early April, and sitting in the sun with a tale of murder and mayhem would surely put this whole unsavory business out of her mind.

The walk along Fleet toward the Inner Temple Garden indeed loosened the knot in her stomach. Leaving behind the noise of the street, she checked over her shoulder before slipping through the wrought iron gate. She skirted the formal courtyard and made for a secluded bench tucked into a knot of sleeping rose bushes. In a matter of weeks, these walkways would be crowded with blooms and visitors who came to enjoy them. But today, with the bite of March only recently retracted, there was naught but the sound of the barges on the Thames.

Glancing about to ensure she was alone, Belle pushed back her straw bonnet and tried to settle in with Poe's gripping mystery. But it was no use. Her thoughts were still wholly ensnared by a grim tale of her own making. Oh, how she *wished* she'd handled Duncan with more aplomb. Couldn't fate have at least allowed her the dignity of running into him when her hair was nicely fixed and the man at her side hadn't been seventy years old?

She listlessly turned a page, reminding herself that, in a way, the scandalous denouement of her betrothal had benefited her. She had a measure of freedom now. Thanks to Duncan's rumormongering, Belle was decidedly a spinster. And with no presumption of modesty to protect, she no longer required a chaperone the way Helena did. Even so, she preferred to keep to her desk or the courthouse. She knew people found her peculiar, but she'd found her own ways of maneuvering through it.

But for all that, she was determined to make something of herself.

Any day now.

She sighed in frustration and set her reading aside. It seemed she couldn't even appreciate Poe today.

"Damn," she muttered, her foul mood returning in force.

"Could it be someone in this godforsaken city is having a worse day than I am?"

Belle startled; she hadn't realized anyone was in this section of the garden. There, across the path from her, was a man in a dark coat. *Blast.* This garden was meant for barristers and their clients.

"I'm awaiting Mr. Nichols," she lied promptly, naming the defense counselor she'd heard at the courthouse. "He's presently in the Old Court, arguing for a landlord who was overcharging his tenants by ten shillings a month. There's really no way he can win, the prosecution produced at least a half dozen lease agreements—"

She broke off as his accent registered—the flat vowels of his warm baritone identified him as American, and something about the way he leaned against the cobbled wall confirmed it. This wasn't an Inner Temple barrister looking for news of Nichols's failed stratagem.

"Go on." The man lifted the corner of his mouth. "I'd love to hear more about Nichols and his landlord. Misery does, in fact, love company."

"That's all I know." She frowned. "I'm actually not meant to meet him. I only said that because you startled me."

"I didn't mean to." He tilted his head toward the new-budding trees, looking up into the starkly blue sky. The stretch revealed an inch of corded throat, briefly visible between the dark beard of his jaw and the collar of his shirt. "I honestly wasn't sure I was allowed to wander in here until I saw you reading."

"The garden is meant for the barristers of the Inner Temple," she admitted.

"Figures." He rubbed the back of his neck. "I saw the river, then the green, and I couldn't stop myself from cutting through. I think this is the first moment of quiet I've had in this city."

She found her curiosity piqued. "Are you new to London?"

He leveled her a look. "Are you a barrister of the Inner Temple?"

"Hardly." She fought a small smile. "Sometimes the gates are open for clients, so..." She raised her shoulder. "I stay out of the way, and nobody makes a fuss."

A refrain that governed her life.

"Hmm." The man looked around the garden. "I might adopt your strategy. God knows I need somewhere to escape..." He gestured vaguely. "London."

Her smile widened. "So you *are* new?"

"That I am."

He folded his arms and regarded her, and she felt she had no choice but to do in kind. He was half-propped against the wall, so it was difficult to discern his height, but there was undeniable power in his build, a certain fluidity in the way he crossed his arms, pulling his coat across the expanse of his shoulders. Even if he'd been English, there was no mistaking him for an aristocrat. His clothing was neat but inexpensive, his tie loose around his neck. His face was half-shadowed by a dark beard that, despite being out of fashion, suited him very well.

To her alarm, he addressed her at the same moment she was appreciating his beard.

"Are you reading *The Ladies' Companion*?" He motioned to the journal on her lap.

"Ah, yes," Belle said in surprise. The publication wasn't easy to come by in London. Her cousin Oliver had procured it from one of his American investors. "Are you familiar with it?"

"I recognize the typeface." The man shrugged. "I worked for a year at a letter foundry in New York. Snowden's typesetter was a bit of a bear."

"Oh." She had no other response to a sentence containing such density of foreign concepts.

"I wouldn't think it circulated here," he mused. "I half want to congratulate it. I have a new appreciation for anything that survives an Atlantic crossing." His hat was slanted over his brow, obscuring his eyes, but she sensed a perceptive stare all the same.

She blinked, sharply aware they were alone.

"It's not a subscription. I've had it for a few years," she found herself explaining. It was strange, that someone would be interested in what she was reading. Interested in her at all. "My cousin had an associate send it to me. There's a serialized Poe story I've been reviewing…"

She straightened in abrupt excitement, just now registering he said he'd lived in New York. A hundred questions came to her as she recalled Poe's unsolved inspiration.

"Come to think of it—"

She broke off. None of her hundred questions were appropriate. She'd been desperately close to asking this stranger what he knew of the density of the Hudson River. She could practically hear a barrage of warning voices—her mother, her sister, Doyle the guard —urging her to seal her lips.

"Are you a student then?" He tilted his head. "Or…a critic?"

"Pardon?"

"You said you were reviewing a story? I assume you would have a reason for doing so."

She blushed. The notion that this man thought she might have a legitimate professional reason for studying Poe was a wonderful novelty.

Bolstered by this small confidence, she considered telling the stranger she was a writer. But then he might inquire where she'd been published, and she would have to admit she'd so far compiled nothing but rejection letters.

"I'm just…a connoisseur, I suppose," she said lamely.

He waited, but she did not elaborate.

"You're a puzzle, is what you are," the American finally observed. "I've never met a connoisseur with so little to say about their interest."

She smiled. "If you must know, literature. Gothic in general, but especially horror, crime, mystery. I'm a bit voracious for intrigue."

If he found her answer disagreeable, his face hid it well. But he didn't ask her any more questions, and she didn't know how to extend the conversation. Too late, it occurred to her she could have benefited from describing nearly any other genre of literature.

Seeming to mistake her quiet for discomfort, the man raised his palms.

"My apologies. I'm still addled from a hellishly long journey and some dismal news awaiting me upon my arrival yesterday." He grimaced. "I've clearly intruded on your solace."

"I think we might overlook it, just this once," she said, charmed by his casual irreverence. "Much can be forgiven on the first pleasant day of spring."

At that moment, a gust of wind blew the loose ribbons of her bonnet, sending the satin ties sliding along her neck, where her hair was still only half minding its pins. She scrambled for her hat, laughing in surprise, again feeling the slow tug of the stranger's stare.

This time, she held it.

For one brilliant moment, everything lifted in the enterprising breeze—her hat, her hair.

Her spirits.

"I appreciate your graciousness." The man pushed away from the wall—a long, broad ripple of dark trousers, dark coat, dark beard—and nodded to her. "I'll leave you to your reading, madam."

She wasn't certain what made her do it. All around her, the air was cloying and damp, sweetly scented with hopeful growth, and it suddenly seemed imperative to make something clear.

"It's *miss*."

"Come again?" He turned and looked at her from under his hat.

"You called me *madam*." Her cheeks turned pink from more than the sun. "I'm not married."

To her immense surprise, the American finally raised his hat and smiled, hitting her with green, green eyes and a beautiful flash of white teeth against his dark beard.

She heated unexpectedly, grappling with a surge of instantaneous recognition. *This was it.* The face of every man she'd ever read about that made her heart skip—princes and pirates and heroes, both dashing and dastardly. She hadn't realized until she turned into a human candlewick: *he's* what they all looked like.

"Well, thank you very much, *Miss*."

"What…are you thanking me for?" Her voice sounded strange to her ears.

He tipped his hat. "The first good news I've had since I arrived in London."

3

THE RECORD OF TITLE TO LANDS, No. 181
By deed dated 3 April 1848, the hereditaments of 62 Fleet Street in the City of London were transferred to the undersigned.

Ethan Thomas Fletcher
Parish of St. Bride's, London

As HE MADE his way back through the gardens, Ethan enjoyed a small measure of relief. His situation was dire, but at least it wasn't so dire he couldn't be cheered by a pretty face. Few things in life were more restorative than flirtation.

He ambled back toward Fleet with his hands in his pockets, still smiling over her doe-eyed surprise. He'd been too forward with her, but really, what was the harm? All morning, he'd been consumed with work, sifting through his uncle's accounts while a teasing slice of sunlight crept through the windows and across the uneven floorboards of the printshop. Finally, he permitted himself a break, itching to see what life was like in his new corner of the world.

And what he found was a welcome sight indeed.

The first thing he noticed as he drew up to the cobbled garden wall was the bend of her bonnet, and—*well*. Such simple pleasure in such a small curve. Had any sight in this gray city been as welcome as the graceful arc of this woman's neck? Still, he might have kept walking had she not cursed. The sound of a bald oath in that soft, cultured accent was too alluring to ignore.

He couldn't take the chance such a lovely neck was in distress.

When he came around the path, he found her curled on the bench in an evergreen dress, and he could tell just by looking at her, a man like him should do nothing more than look. Her curse notwithstanding, she was clearly refined—the fabric of her bodice cut so close, even his inexpert eye could appreciate the craftsmanship in how it clung to the slender lines of her arms. Her head was down, her hat pushed off her face, and the hair unspooling from her bun gleamed two shades darker than the finely braided straw of her bonnet.

Green and gold.

And that sweet, *sweet* curve of her neck.

Thank you. Ethan directed the words to whatever deity's apology for these hellish circumstances came in the form of a beautiful woman holding a familiar book.

Maybe the next apology would come in the form of one hundred pounds sterling.

When he reached the top of the street, he oriented himself within the winding, illogical maze of his new neighborhood. Spying a secondhand bookshop in a side alley, Ethan paused. If he had time to flirt, he had time for a reconnaissance mission. He had just about ten weeks to execute a plan for paying off the debt.

He was ready to work.

It had been two years since he operated a printing press, but when he inventoried his workroom that morning, he'd been filled with a blooming sense of purpose. As he curved his calloused palm around the sculpted-eagle weight of the gorgeous Columbian press, it all returned to him. How his body stretched with the laborious rhythm of the lever, how his muscles gradually thickened with each roll of the type form. God, he'd once been so *fast*, the hours blurring as his shoulders burned.

Ethan was no stranger to the hard work of printing—but it typically required having *something* to print.

He entered the dusty bookshop, scanning an array of publications on display. Papers, pamphlets, periodicals. He asked for one of each—a reckless selection, but if he were going to continue this foray, he needed to see what was what.

"Five pence?" He frowned at the cost of *The Times*. "Is that usual for a newspaper?"

The proprietor nodded brusquely. "Just about."

The *Boston Sentinel* was a penny paper, intended to be read by the working class, which was why Ethan chafed at his editor's shortsighted coverage. There were a number of more expensive weekly publications in America, but penny dailies were what most people could afford. When Ethan said as much, the bookseller shrugged.

"Stamp duty," the man said by way of explanation. "Publishers pay a news tax."

"How much is the tax?"

"A penny per paper for news. Paper duty on top of it. Drives prices up." He looked over Ethan's shoulder, as if to summon a less inquisitive customer. "Anything else, sir?"

Ethan jerked his chin toward a stack of densely printed serials, notable for a garish illustration of a caped man at the gallows. "This one is priced a penny?"

"No news tax on it." The bookseller tied up his publications. "It's a story paper."

"*Varney the Vampire*." Ethan raised an eyebrow. "A penny blood, I presume?" He'd heard about the sensational stories of lust and gore.

"They're horrid." The man grimaced. "But you won't hear me complain. I won't have any left after the lads come round later."

Ethan's mind ticked back to the woman in the garden—*horror, crime, mystery.* He'd thought it an odd preference, but now he considered the gruesome etching on the penny blood. It would be a damn shame to run into her again and have nothing to talk about.

Ethan lifted the serial. "I'll take one of these as well."

He strode with his purchases back to No. 62, mulling over the disconcerting information he'd gleaned from the bookseller.

Hell. There was no way around it; the news tax was punishing. Not one of Ethan's readers in Boston could afford a five-cent paper. He'd bet a healthy portion of his precious savings most of London's working class couldn't afford it either. Information had value, something those in power knew all too well.

It didn't sit right with him. Not only would it be too expensive to establish a newspaper here, it would be too expensive for his desired readers to purchase.

Damn. Damn. Damn.

He pushed open the door to the printshop, fighting with the string of a tinkling bell above the doorframe. The bell was entirely unnecessary; in the last two days, not a single client had stopped in.

"It's only me," Ethan called to the back as he disentangled himself from the threshold. "We need to do something about that damn bell, Tobias."

A sturdily built Black man emerged, wiping his hands on his apron. "I'll have Sam take a look at it," he replied amiably.

"It will give him something to do," Ethan groused. "Business being what it is."

"I have him distributing type sorts." Tobias folded his arms, surveying the dusty front office. In the afternoon light filtering through the big windows, the small space felt decidedly lackluster. "He can clean in here next."

Tobias and Sam Porter, father-and-son pressman and apprentice, were the only two remaining employees at Gaines Print Works. When Ethan asked why the Porters stayed when the compositor and other apprentices moved on, Tobias only lifted one heavy shoulder. "Somebody had to finish the outstanding job prints. Not that there are many."

It had been Tobias's blunt assessment that first got Ethan thinking. If they couldn't rely on external business to turn a profit, the obvious alternative was to publish something new of their own... wasn't it?

He tossed his purchased publications on the rickety desk. "Do you have a moment, Porter?"

"I have as many moments as you need until six o'clock." Tobias had made it clear Mrs. Porter expected both of her men home for their meals; Ethan sensed he wouldn't fare well if he crossed her. "What have you here, sir?"

Ethan shucked his coat and dropped it over a bench. "If a printer needed to turn a profit quickly, what, in your professional opinion, would be the best way to do so?"

The pressman leaned on the doorframe. "Not job printing, that's for certain. At least not the way your uncle did it." He hesitated. "If I may..."

"Go on." Ethan waved his hand. "You won't offend me. I never even met the man."

The only thing he knew of Robert Gaines was that he'd owned a printshop. His uncle's trade had always loomed large to Ethan's mother, who left London when she was nineteen years old, on the arm of an American sailor. To hear Marina Fletcher tell it, she regretted leaving her brother every day of her too-short life. It's likely why she apprenticed her son to a printer before he was shoulder high.

"You can be honest with me, Porter. Your honesty is, in fact, imperative."

Tobias grew thoughtful. "Your uncle was too particular about his work. There can be money in job printing—timetables, business cards, invoices...the single-page bits and bobs, if you're familiar."

Ethan nodded. He'd worked a jobbing press in his day, though by the time he'd become a journeyman, he was almost exclusively focused on newspapers.

"Well, your uncle wanted illustrious commissions." Tobias shook his head. "He turned work away. Then work stopped coming...and then, of course, there was the paper debacle."

Ethan rubbed his temples. He would circle back to that last statement in a moment. He didn't need another debacle right now.

"So job printing requires rebuilding a clientele," he muttered. "And with small runs, we won't see much revenue."

"At least not quickly," Tobias confirmed.

Ethan rifled through the sample papers he'd purchased. "From what I gather, a newspaper is out of the question?"

"Entirely out of the question," Tobias said flatly. "Stamp duty aside, we'd need a whole different outlay. A steam press, perhaps. More staff, at the very least."

"Job printing is too irregular. The news is too expensive." Ethan set the newspapers aside. "What we need, Porter, is something both consistent and cheap."

A clatter sounded from the back, followed by Sam's colorful curse.

"Language," Tobias boomed. A pause. "Are you all right, son?"

"Dropped a bloody frame." Sam came into the office, rubbing his knee. "But all the type's distributed, sir."

The boy approached his father, and Ethan couldn't help but smile at the pair. Sam, a lanky lad of sixteen, was as tall as his father but half as broad and twice as talkative. In most cases—Ethan's included—apprentices left home when they began learning their trade. His uncle was clearly partial to unconventional business practices, but in this regard, Ethan was glad for the atypical arrangement. Having both Porters lent an air of stability to this otherwise unsteady operation.

Sam glanced over the publications on the desk, his brown eyes growing wide at the sight of the gory illustration splashed across the penny blood. "Say, is that this week's issue?"

"I believe so." Ethan picked up the serial and contemplatively flipped through it. "Do you read *Varney the Vampire*, Sam?"

The boy was ready for him, launching into a long, complicated recounting of some family who seemed, in Ethan's opinion, to have worse luck than him, given their penchant for unholy run-ins with the titular vampire.

"Last week, Varney was hanged," Sam said passionately. "He's been killed before—I think this is maybe the third time—but the doctor is going to resurrect him." He longingly eyed the serial. "And it looks like he has. Can I see it…just for a moment, sir?"

Ethan handed over the paper and grinned at Tobias. "It's a real shame he doesn't like it."

"I wouldn't say it's the most wholesome subject matter, but at least it keeps him reading." Tobias shrugged. "And not just him—the lads on our street lap this up like a cat with cream."

Ethan looked over at Sam, now fully engrossed in Varney's possible revival. But the vampire wasn't the only one coming to life. Ethan's pulse was racing in the way it sometimes did when he realized he still had another step between his back and the wall.

He was possibly having a ludicrous notion.

"Bookseller said the same," Ethan said slowly. "I can see the allure—it's sensational, certainly. It's also affordable. Affordable to buy…" His voice lowered. "Affordable to print?"

He glanced at the workroom, where two iron presses squatted indolently.

"You're thinking a penny blood," Tobias mused. "It's certainly an idea."

"Yes. But is it a *good* idea?" Ethan rolled his cuffs. "Or a neutral idea?"

"I'm trying to decide if it's a bad idea," Tobias said, his voice warm and deep. "It would kill your uncle twice over. There can be profit in penny fiction, but there's no prestige. I take it you aren't a proud man, Mr. Fletcher?"

Ethan laughed, booming and full-throated. "Porter, I slept on the floor of a ship for two weeks. I assure you, pride is not my weakness."

Tobias rubbed his chin. "In that case…"

A dozen considerations jostled for precedence. Eight pages an issue, one issue a week, one penny each, minus the cost of material, labor, distribution. Ethan had no sense what sort of print run they could sustain, let alone how to compete in this market.

Then again, there was what he *did* know—the bookseller couldn't keep penny bloods in stock; Sam couldn't turn the pages fast enough.

No tax on fiction.

"Fletcher?" Tobias appeared taken aback by the sudden force of Ethan's concentration.

"There's still the paper duty to contend with." Ethan rattled through drawers, trying to locate a pencil, trying to keep his expectations in check. "There will be a cost to starting anything of our own. It might not be feasible."

"Oh, paper's not a problem." Sam laughed. "Not precisely. Tell him, Father."

Ethan narrowed his eyes. "What about paper?"

Tobias sighed. "Follow me."

PAPER. Dozens and dozens of reams of paper stacked along the walls of the storeroom.

"I told you we don't have a paper problem," Sam said, delighted at the shock on Ethan's face. "At least not a paper *quantity* problem."

"How…how many reams?" Ethan ran a hand along one shelf, incredulous. From what he'd seen in his uncle's books, the cost of a taxed ream of paper was nearly twenty-four shillings. "Why in *hell* wasn't he using this? Do you have any idea what this is worth?"

"It's worth nothing," Tobias said. "Gaines's troubles started when he made a bad investment with a paper mill. This is all damaged. Pulp paper, practically disintegrating. He couldn't use it for his job prints."

"But he already paid the duty on it?" Ethan glanced up. "We own this supply outright?"

Tobias nodded confirmation, and Ethan's blood surged.

"Can it be printed on?" He bent, slitting open a ream with his pocketknife. The paper was discolored, the quality uneven. Tobias was right; this couldn't be used for business documents.

But for a one-cent serial…

This paper was a sign. It wasn't the capital he'd expected, but perhaps it was the capital he needed. His idea took root, spreading, sprouting. In this dark, musty storeroom, Ethan's lungs filled not with the smog of London, not with the grease and ink of the printshop, but with bright, grassy *hope*.

"We could do this," he breathed, staring at his beautiful, damaged, free-and-clear paper. "We could publish a penny blood. We have the material. Between the three of us, I wager we have the labor."

"Cheers." Sam looked between Ethan and Tobias. "So…who's going to write it?"

4

Clementina had been the courthouse maid for long enough to under-stand a trial was naught but a performance. And on stage today? Augustus Foote, playing the role of Defense Counselor with all the dread of an unprepared understudy. It was little wonder he was nervous. Foote was defending Miss Allegra Carter, and three weeks ago, Miss Allegra Carter poisoned the Magistrate.

Of course, she had good reason.

—Excerpt from The Sensational Cases of Clementina Bloom
Chapter 3 (~~Draft 2~~ Draft 3)

WHEN BELLE ARRIVED BACK at Lincoln's Inn Fields after her afternoon in the garden, she was greeted by the familiar sight of Mrs. Bowers hovering at the door. The comings and goings of various Sinclairs were a source of constant consternation for the punctual housekeeper.

"Good evening, Mrs. Bowers." Belle untied her bonnet and hung it neatly on one of the many pegs studding the front hall.

"This came for you today, Miss Sinclair, but I don't advise you dawdle with it." The housekeeper sounded vaguely reproving as she handed over a letter. "Your family is about to dine."

Belle grasped the letter, the embossed stationery heavy in her fingers. She'd instantly recognized the seal.

Blackwood's Edinburgh Magazine.

She thanked Mrs. Bowers and slipped into her father's empty study, her heart racing. *Blackwood's* was both an unlikely prospect and her last one. The magazine frequently published horror fiction. And they sometimes published women. Granted, they didn't usually publish both at the same time…

As she scanned the letter, her stomach plummeted.

Miss Sinclair,

Thank you for your letter, dated 9 February. Enclosed, please find the chapters you included, returned in full to you with a recommendation that Blackwood's Edinburgh Magazine decline to publish at this time. While your submission shows promise, there is some concern about the Subject Matter and Authorial Reputation.

She closed her eyes.

Another rejection.

Likely her final rejection. She had no other outstanding submissions.

Damn. Damn. Damn.

Belle had been writing *The Sensational Cases of Clementina Bloom* for the last four years—writing, rewriting, submitting, resubmitting. Her pile of rejection letters was half as thick as the blasted manuscript. Her gruesome tale of courtroom mayhem didn't fit anywhere. It seemed nobody knew what to do with it—except to tell her to change it.

Much like Belle, herself.

She quickly stuffed the letter in her basket, refusing to contemplate its ramifications before dinner. She looked herself over in the mirror above the mantel. Her family was waiting, and her father, for certain, could read her mood on her face. If she was going to cry, she would need to either do it very quickly or much later.

Papa's bracing refrain from the day she left Duncan worked its way to the surface—not that it had a long way to travel. His hushed advice had bolstered her through many a sore spot in recent years. She drew a deep breath.

It matters how you walk out of here.

Satisfied she was appropriately composed, Belle made her way to the dining room. She paused at the threshold to watch Papa pour wine. Her family always dined *en famille* and sometimes with a rotating and random assortment of guests—relatives or law students or the occasional progressive-minded MP. She was relieved that tonight, the table was set only for four.

"Hello," she said, stepping into the dining room.

"Belle." Mama swept her into a sweet-smelling embrace. "There you are. Come, sit, darling. You've been out all day, you must be famished."

"Doyle told me you departed early." Papa's dark blue gaze was as perceptive as always. "I assumed you'd be home before me."

"I took a long walk," Belle said evasively. "It was such a nice day, I thought I'd read outside."

"Speaking of walks..." Lena, always good for distraction, thrust a dish of haricots verts in her direction. "Here, dear, I'm all finished with them, so take what you'd like. Now, you won't *believe* what happened at the milliner's..."

Belle settled into her seat and let the conversation wash over her, wondering how long she could avoid participating. She did not wish to talk about her day, a goal at odds with family dinner. Mama, mindful of her quiet husband and eldest daughter, had long insisted on fairness—everyone shared, everyone listened. It wasn't that Belle was opposed to conversing with her family, but she didn't welcome the prospect of reliving twin embarrassments inflicted by Duncan and her latest rejection letter.

"Belle?" As if reading her thoughts, Mama turned to her with a bright smile. "How was your afternoon?"

Belle paused with her fork halfway to her mouth. Was there *anything* she could safely share about her day?

A flash of green garden, green eyes, a slow, *slow* smile…

She coughed.

"She's blushing." Lena leaned forward, her eyes alight. "Belle! What aren't you telling us?"

"She's not blushing," Papa said.

"She does look a bit pink," Mama countered. "Did you get some sun today, darling?"

"Fine." Belle speared a potato and pointed it at her younger sister, struggling to maintain a straight face. "If you must know, Doyle called me pretty."

"Doyle, the elderly guard?" Lena's laugh met Belle's. "Let's hope he has a grandson with a chiseled jaw."

"Helena." Their father slid Lena a look as he neatly cut his roast. "Might you refrain from discussing chiseled jaws at the dinner table?"

"Oh, Papa, we're only teasing." Lena squeezed their father's hand. "I still think there's something Belle isn't telling us."

Belle pushed her vegetables across her plate. The news would come out eventually. "All right." She cleared her throat. "I do, in fact, have something to tell you. But before I do, I want you to please believe I am perfectly fine."

Mama set down her fork. Lena leaned forward.

Belle kept her eyes on her father, who perhaps remembered the blistering fallout better than anyone.

"Lawrence Duncan has returned to London."

"Do you know what would make you feel better?" Predictably, Lena had barreled into Belle's bedroom the moment they were excused from dinner. Now she was pacing behind the dressing table while Belle readied for bed.

"I feel perfectly fine." Belle dragged a brush through her long hair.

"Fine. It will make *me* feel better. Come to Lady Beaumont's ball on Friday."

Belle gave her sister a sharp look in the mirror. "I will do no such thing."

"I don't want to go alone."

"Cecily will be there."

"No. She and Aunt Cora are visiting Tess this week. Speaking of..." Lena paused, apparently willing to defer her crusade for Belle's social life to share family gossip. "Cecily said Tess has been a *complete* beast this time around. She can't keep anything down but lemon bars. It's even worse than it was with Nathaniel, and it was plenty bad then." Lena tilted her head mischievously. "Though Cecily also told me we needn't be overly sympathetic. Tess admitted her husband is most *enthusiastically* provisioning more than desserts."

Belle smiled. "You're terrible."

Lena squashed beside her at the dressing table and pressed their cheeks together. Helena had inherited the brightest features from both their parents—their father's blue eyes, their mother's flaxen hair. Belle, for her part, was all Sinclair. She had the same tousled curls as her father, though her light brown hair and hazel eyes were hers alone. When she put her face beside her sister's, Belle sometimes felt muted, as though the water colorist had meant to dip his brush one more time. But she'd always felt generally content with her appearance. The way she looked to others wasn't the problem; it was the way *she* looked at the rest of the world.

"You really won't go to the ball?"

"Was I even invited?" Belle asked skeptically.

"Well..." Her sister hesitated, confirming Belle's suspicion.

Lady Beaumont was the sort of woman who preferred the ladies on her guestlist have unimpeachable reputations and polite interests. Belle, as an aspiring crime novelist with a broken engagement, was not likely to ever be asked to grace her ballroom.

"Lena."

"If you ask Aunt Cora to write to Lady Beaumont, she would do so in an instant," Lena said in a rush. "No society matron in her right mind would deny a request from Lady Fordham."

Belle sighed. Lena was right. Aunt Cora—Papa's younger sister and a fixture of the *ton*—would happily maneuver on her behalf. But Belle wanted no such attention.

Though the Sinclair family's connections granted them access to the fashionable set, she'd never fared well at upper-crust dinners and dances, as evidenced by her only offer coming from the respectably middle-class Duncan. Belle hadn't minded. Her eccentric interests were more suited to her father's professional circles anyway.

Not that it mattered now.

"Aunt Cora is *not* begging an invitation for me," she informed her sister. "I'm perfectly fine."

"You've said that four times tonight," Lena said quietly.

"It's nothing a ball will fix," Belle admitted, setting down her hairbrush. She crossed to her writing desk and retrieved the letter from *Blackwood's*. Sighing, she turned to her sister. "I've been turned down. Again."

"Oh, Belle." Lena pulled her sister down to sit beside her on the bed. "I'm so sorry, dearest. Did the publisher say why?"

Belle passed her the letter.

"This is it?" Lena skimmed the short rejection. "Drat."

Lena's solidarity was lovely, especially considering she herself had not read Belle's manuscript. Not for lack of trying—Helena, as it turned out, had no stomach for bloodshed.

"It's a better rejection than the last dozen," Belle said glumly, flopping back on her bed. "Mind you, *Subject Matter* and *Authorial Reputation* are capitalized. Apparently, they wished to clarify that point specifically." She sighed. "Poor Clementina. She should have been written by a man."

"These well-to-do magazines do seem to be flummoxed by your feminine wiles," Lena observed. "Or possibly your lack thereof."

"How wretched." Belle pressed her fingers over her eyes. "You know, I thought having my novel published would go some way toward soothing the sting of my ruined prospects. It might be time to admit it's having the opposite effect."

Lena made a soft sound of protest and tugged Belle to sitting. "You aren't ruined, Belle."

"Duncan knows it." Belle winced, recalling the uncomfortable meeting. "Of course he would relish the notion that I've made no gains in my aspirations, even as his own career has blossomed without me. He was *insufferable* today."

"More insufferable than usual, you mean?" Lena pulled a face. "Because from what *I* recall, you suffered plenty."

"Don't remind me." Belle's stomach clenched. "Goodness, he's a vainglorious brute, isn't he? I lost at least six months of work when he dumped that teapot on my pages."

Even now, she could scarcely bear to think of it. Of all the things he took from her, the very first draft of Clementina hurt the most.

"You know, Belle, I understood why you ended it." Lena gently touched the ends of Belle's hair. "But I never understood why you agreed to marry him in the first place."

Belle looked down, fiddling with the hem of her night rail. "There were things I once admired about him," she said slowly. "Of course, that was before I understood those things were only what he wanted me to see."

She looked at her sister, contemplating how best to explain why she let things go on for too long.

"Do you recall when Papa won the Briggs trial? When everything started changing?"

"By *changing*, you mean we had money?" Lena laughed. "Yes, I don't think I could forget."

"Mama took us to the cobbler for new boots. It was so important to her. She wanted it to be perfect, you know how she is about spending, she's still so careful, even now. But my measurements must have been off, because those boots only *mostly* fit."

"They pinched," Lena nodded. "I remember. You had a blister but wouldn't tell anyone."

"I didn't want anyone to know." Belle frowned. "I was embarrassed the boots turned out to be wrong. I *wanted* them to fit...but everything chafed. And my foot was my foot. I couldn't change it." She shook her head. "I could only change the boots."

"Darling." Her sister smiled sympathetically. "I can say with certainty, even those pinching boots were a better fit than Duncan."

Belle sighed and tossed the rejection letter aside.

"It wasn't only that he didn't want me to write, it was that he held me in so little regard. He didn't want me to do *anything*." She wrinkled her nose. "Well, that's not entirely true. He wanted me to help him rise."

Lena lifted her eyebrow, and Belle rolled her eyes.

"I don't mean that in the way you're thinking, you little minx."

"Don't you?" Lena teased.

Belle flicked her shoulder. "You really are terrible."

Lena laughed and kissed her forehead. "I'm sorry you had a trying day, darling. It's a load of rot, top to bottom—Duncan, *Blackwood's*. I hope you at least enjoyed the sunshine." Lena looked her over. "Your cheeks *are* a bit pink."

"I did enjoy the sun." Belle tugged the end of Lena's plait. "Now you need to go to bed, and so do I. I had a very trying day, as you said, what with all the humiliation and rejection."

Lena tutted and stood. "Put it all out of your mind," she said firmly. "Your luck is going to turn, I'm absolutely certain of it." She paused, smiling deviously. "And when it does, think how satisfying it will be to see Duncan eat crow."

Belle fought a smile. "That's not why I want to succeed."

"Of course it isn't." Lena winked. "But it certainly won't hurt."

5

Outstanding Submissions (April 1848)

The Ladies' Cabinet

The Court Magazine and Monthly Critic

Messrs. Chapman & Hall

Lloyd's Entertaining Journal

Messrs. Bradbury & Evans

Bentley's Miscellany

Fraser's Magazine

Blackwood's Edinburgh Magazine

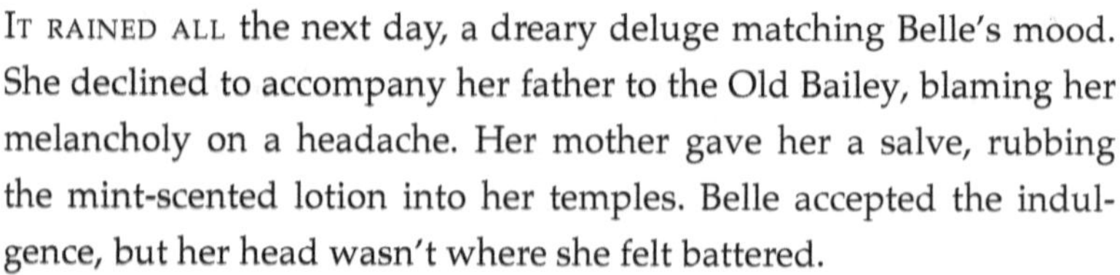

IT RAINED ALL the next day, a dreary deluge matching Belle's mood. She declined to accompany her father to the Old Bailey, blaming her melancholy on a headache. Her mother gave her a salve, rubbing the mint-scented lotion into her temples. Belle accepted the indulgence, but her head wasn't where she felt battered.

She'd tried to make light of her situation with Lena—*humiliation and rejection*—but the truth was Belle felt utterly stagnant.

Nothing was happening.

Nothing was changing.

And she'd had enough of it.

So on Wednesday, when a weak spring sun crawled from beneath the clouds, she again set out for the garden. In her basket was her fourth draft of *Clementina Bloom.* It was her least favorite version of the manuscript—something had gone wobbly in the third trial—but if she were going to do what she knew she must, she preferred to do it to draft four.

As she settled in with her work, she couldn't help furtive glances about the gardens. She'd given away her secret spot to a mysterious stranger, and yes, it briefly occurred to her he might *perhaps* be here today.

The prospect of seeing the American was certainly not the reason she declined Lena's offer of company, nor was it the reason she once again donned her braided straw bonnet. She simply happened to like this hat, and she had no time today for Lena's impassioned ruminations of chiseled jaws.

Besides, she didn't even know if the American *had* a chiseled jaw. It was impossible to tell with the beard shadowing his face.

She sighed and raised her pencil over her draft, feeling far more sentimental about this than she ought. But if she wanted the book-stalls on the Strand to carry her stories, it was high time she addressed the obstacles of *Authorial Reputation* and *Subject Matter.* Belle had no idea how to change the tenor of her stories, but there was one adjustment she *could* make.

With resignation, she scratched out the title page and looped a new one.

THE SENSATIONAL CASES OF CLEMENTINA BLOOM
A novel by ??? Surname

She stared at the page until disgust blurred her vision. She often felt like she didn't fit anywhere, and now her own journal confirmed it.

"*Damn,*" she muttered, staring at the question marks where her first name used to be. "Damn it to—"

"Is it a particularity of London that all garden benches include a woman in distress?" His deep voice floated behind her. "Or am I merely lucky?"

She jumped and looked over her shoulder as he approached.

For an instant, Belle reeled in dizzying incredulity that he was actually here. And he somehow looked even better than she remembered—the same casual tone of voice, the same broad figure, the same dark beard…shading a very obviously chiseled jaw.

"I'm not always in distress," she protested, setting down her journal as he came around the bend.

Then he proved her a liar, because instead of leaning against the wall, he came right up to where she sat. Belle stared at him, marveling at the long shadow he cast, her pulse skittering in a way a physician would certainly find distressing.

"May I?" He gestured toward the opposite end of her bench.

Belle tried to imagine herself making a wise choice. *No, sir, I'm sorry, but it would be unseemly for us to sit together.*

She raised one shoulder, peering at him from under the brim of her bonnet. "I suppose."

"That's fortunate." He lifted the corner of his mouth as he sat. "Because I came here looking for this bench, and I very much hoped you'd be at the other end."

Belle stilled, shocked by his forwardness. "I beg your pardon?"

"I hoped to find you again," the American said frankly. "I was thinking about what you said two days ago."

What had she told him two days ago? That she wasn't married? It had been a rare moment of boldness. Leave it to providence to ensure she'd be mortified for it. This is precisely why polite society had rules—so strange, bearded Americans didn't proposition eccentric spinsters in the middle of the Inner Temple Garden.

"Sir." She straightened. "You have the wrong impression."

His smile widened. "You don't even know what I'm impressed about."

A flutter ticked in her throat as she mutely crafted and rejected no fewer than a dozen rejoinders before retreating to banality. "Why were you trying to find me, then?"

He didn't seem to notice the blush choking her. Rather, he was intently studying the manuscript on the bench next to her. "Is that one of the macabre stories you are a connoisseur of?"

"Ah." She glanced down at the pages. "Of a fashion. *Wait—*"

He reached for the manuscript, and she all but lunged to slap her palm atop it. He paused, one large hand extended between them. He turned it over, as if calming a skittish colt. "Apologies. I shouldn't have presumed. Might I look at this?"

She regarded her journal. Her name was no longer on it. Even if it were, this man didn't know her name. He couldn't possibly tell she was the author, so what harm was there in letting him look? Outside of the publishers who routinely rejected her, she hadn't permitted anyone to read her draft. It was a rather languishing experience; writing was meant to be read, wasn't it?

She managed a nod. "You may look."

He lifted the journal and unhurriedly flipped through it. She fell silent, simmering with nerves and regret. The slide of his thumb over her pages was a terrible intimacy. He paused at intervals, scrutinizing text while Belle compulsively smoothed her skirts and pretended this stranger wasn't skimming the worst version of her manuscript.

"*Hell.*" He leaned forward, stroking his beard, his expression one of either intrigue or horror.

She craned her neck, noticing he was on chapter nine. "Ah. I recommend you work up to that part." She winced; chapter nine was not for the faint of heart. "The bloodstained robe has a logical explanation, but it's best read in context."

He turned to face her fully, but he wasn't looking at her with concern or discomfort. Rather, his handsome face was illuminated with odd intensity.

"This is grisly." He pointed at the page. "And it's damn clever."

Belle stared at the journal in his hand, her ears ringing. A rush of pride and disbelief radiated from her chest, all the way up to a smile she tried very much to keep to herself.

Grisly. Damn clever.

If he did in fact intend to proposition her, he was making a strong case for himself.

But no, she had no idea who he was. Nor why he was assessing her manuscript.

"Excuse me, mister…?"

"Fletcher," he murmured, still reading with stark concentration. "Ethan Fletcher."

"Mr. Fletcher. You never said—why were you hoping to find me?"

Her question snapped him to attention. He closed the journal and laid one arm across the back of the bench.

"You said you were interested in a genre of literature that, as it turns out, might solve my problem." He nodded to her journal. "*That* genre, specifically."

"What problem?" She couldn't imagine what sort of problem could be solved by any of the events in chapter nine.

At her probing expression, his half smile returned. "Between us? I'm having a hell of a time with my new business. But I think I'm nearly at a solution. When one has a plan, it's hard to feel miserable."

"I suppose." Belle considered. "As long as the plan is a good one."

The man genially tipped his hat. "Truer words, miss."

His voice lowered on the last word, a rumble that dropped straight to her belly. She heated, wishing this bench was much longer. Or much shorter.

"What's your line of business?"

"I'm a printer. Or at least, I'm trying to be." He cocked his head. "I have, however, found myself with a dearth of material to publish."

Belle froze.

A tingle crept over her scalp, the fine hairs at the back of her neck prickling with awareness. "That's unfortunate," she said slowly. "To be a printer with nothing to print."

"Indeed. Most unfortunate." His verdant gaze was still sharp on her face. "That's why I wanted to find you. I was hoping, given your interests, you might have a name for me. A contact, possibly."

"What sort of contact?" Her throat was very dry.

"I need a writer."

A writer.

He stood and pointed to her journal. "Is this published?"

"Ah, no." She swallowed. "It's not."

"Do you know the author?" He squinted at the crossed-out title page. "This Mister Three-Question-Marks Surname?"

He seemed to take her poleaxed expression to mean she was unable to disclose the identity of the author in question.

"Well, if you are ever so inclined, I would very much appreciate you giving him my name. That's Fletcher—let me write it down—I'm at Sixty-Two Fleet…" He patted his pocket, looking for a pencil.

"Wait." Belle scrambled to her feet, clutching her journal, scarcely able to believe the force of her conviction. This was patently insane behavior. She knew nothing about this man. Only that he'd read her pages, and he seemed to like them. Which was more than she could say for any other man with a printing press.

He paused, and she stood taller.

This was it. *This* was the change she required. Right here, with green eyes, in this garden.

"My name is Belinda Sinclair." Her voice was hoarse. "Belle. I'm Belle Sinclair. And I do in fact know the author."

She slowly, slowly extended her hand. He grasped it, her slender fingers fitting securely within the warm, calloused breadth of his palm. He squeezed lightly, and she squeezed back.

"And now, Mr. Fletcher, you know her, too."

~

Mr. Fletcher's casual ease shifted to action the moment they shook hands. Before she'd quite wrapped her mind around her own bravado, he was walking away, saying something about his printshop, a glint in his eyes that made it vexingly difficult not to follow him.

"*You* wrote this?" He glanced at her, and she hastened to match his purposeful stride. Her corset and petticoats made it rather difficult to keep pace.

"Yes."

"You wrote *all* of this?" He looked skeptical. "Even the…ah, incident in chapter nine?"

They rounded the corner to Fleet and came to a halt in front of a shabby door.

"Yes." She bit her lip. "I wrote all of the incidents, in all of the chapters."

He raised an eyebrow. "Did you now?"

"I did." She let herself look up at him, as long as she wanted, because if he were assessing her by virtue of chapter nine, he was likely forty seconds away from declaring her an aberration, packing up his green eyes, and slamming this door in her face.

But he merely laughed and gestured her forward. "A puzzle," he muttered, skating his gaze over her. "Just as I said."

Fletcher unlocked the door to No. 62, a corner building studded with grimy windows. He paused in the threshold to straighten a faded wooden shingle proclaiming the business Gaines Print Works. Belle took in the peeling paint on the sign, fairly certain Clementina Bloom had solved a crime in an establishment just like this.

She trailed him inside and glanced around the shop. The space was long and narrow with a big-windowed front office featuring a creaky floor and an assortment of mismatched furnishings. Two doors opened off the office; through one, she spied a wedge of the bright and spacious workroom, through the other, a steep staircase leading to the second floor. Everywhere she looked was dust and disarray. The desk in the corner was piled with papers, and the row of bookcases sagged under mountains of parcels and ledgers. A length of rope was strung along one wall, a few neglected pages fluttering from it like paper shirts drying in the breeze.

"It's...ah..." She broke off awkwardly, not wishing to be rude. "It's quite...unpretentious."

Fletcher flashed her one of his slow, bemused smiles. "Oh, most assuredly. Pretension is one of many things we lack."

He moved to the desk, lifted the chair from behind it, and swung it around with a flourish. "Here you are, Miss Sinclair."

She cautiously lowered herself to the seat.

He looked about for another chair, saw they were all under piles of detritus, and sat on the edge of the desk instead.

His thigh was very close to her. She looked at the dark wool of his trousers for one harrowing breath before pulling her focus to the desk, where she was greeted by the lurid illustration of a bearded man stealing into a woman's bedchamber.

Wonderful.

"A penny blood?" She gestured to the paper. "I wouldn't have guessed you partake."

"Are you opposed to them?" He watched her curiously. "It seems these should align with your interests."

Belle shrugged. Had he brought her here for a chat? She thought they were meant to arrange publication of her novel. "I would say I'm largely indifferent."

"To reading them?"

She frowned. "Why, yes. What else would I do with a penny blood aside from reading it?"

"Ah." He rubbed his neck. "I was thinking you might...write one?"

"What?" She could hardly stifle a laugh. "You mean stories of highwaymen and bandits and ghosts?"

"The very same."

She looked at him with chagrin. "I don't write penny bloods. I am a *novelist*."

"Is that so?" he asked dryly. "Such certitude for a woman who, not ten minutes ago, used punctuation as her moniker."

"Well, that was a bit of a low moment."

"Look." Fletcher sighed. "We're going about this backward. Let's establish a rule—as I said before, there's no pretension in this shop, and nor will there be in this conversation."

"What do you mean?"

"I'll tell you what I want, you tell me what you want." Fletcher tilted his head, and she watched a muscle in his jaw work back and forth. "I inherited this business, but as you can see, it's floundering. I need to turn a profit. Quickly. Penny fiction is reliable, fast, and cheap. I have everything I need to do it. Except a story."

"But…" She faltered. She looked about the shop, taking in the disrepair, then back to the paper on the desk. "You *aren't* interested in publishing my novel? *That's* what I want. I can't find a publisher, and I would very much like to finally get these words out of my blasted journal."

He was already shaking his head. "Even if I had the time and expertise to produce and bind a novel, I can't afford it. Not to mention our paper is poor quality." He shrugged. "Make no mistake, I'm not a proper publisher. What I *can* do is print and distribute a weekly serial. I've worked in papers for most of my life."

This information settled as a disappointing weight in her stomach. "I see."

"I imagine this is not what you expected, Miss Sinclair, but my aim is sincere. Penny fiction has potential. I think your pages do too," Fletcher said. "I think given our shared frustration, we might arrive at a shared benefit…if you're amenable to compromise."

Belle eyed him warily. He was possibly on to something. There was no doubt penny bloods had become wildly popular in recent years. They were far cheaper than literary magazines or triple-deckers—the three-part novels cost more than some men's weekly wages.

"My pressman told me some penny bloods circulate upward of

ten thousand copies each week," Fletcher said casually. "It's one way to get your words out of your journal."

She sickened at the memory of Duncan's snide barb—*I didn't see your novel anywhere.* Unfortunately, the oaf had been right. Penny bloods might be a far cry from respectable literature, but right now, Clementina wasn't any kind of literature at all.

Belle straightened. Ethan Fletcher thought she was *grisly* and *clever*. The least she could do was hear the man out.

"How would it work?" she said slowly. "If we did…*this*?"

She unthinkingly indicated the story on the desk, which was regrettable, as now they were both looking at the illustration of an impending ravishing.

"Well." Fletcher pointedly slid the serial away from her. "I'm not entirely certain yet. Tell me more about your manuscript. This Clementina Bloom, she's an investigator?"

"In a manner of speaking." Belle brightened. "She's a courthouse maid, and she takes it upon herself to look into cases that were unsatisfactorily decided at trial. She sees everything, but nobody notices *her*. She helps women right wrongs, finds the real culprit and whatnot. And misadventures unfold along the way."

"That's a fairly expurgated description of what I read." He cocked his head. "Involving substantially less arsenic."

"Well…the circumstances tend toward the dramatic," Belle admitted. "I want it to be exciting, you know."

"So it *could* be pieced up," he mused. "If you added more cases and…*misadventures*, as you call them. We could serialize it. One issue per week, eight pages an issue."

She looked at him doubtfully; her story would need a great deal of restructuring to work.

"For how long?"

"I can promise to publish for ten weeks."

Ten weeks.

Ten weeks of guaranteed publication. Her heart leaped in nervous excitement.

"When would you start?"

"Immediately," he said, his hand once more moving over his beard. "I'd want something out by Saturday."

"*Saturday?*" Belle laughed. "That's three days from now. It's impossible—"

"It doesn't matter if it's possible," he said bluntly. "It's what has to be. I don't have time to delay."

"Why?" She narrowed her eyes. "You keep saying that—no time for a novel, no time to delay."

"Because." He rolled his neck. "My creditor has me in a noose."

"*What?*"

"Not literally," he said hastily, his green eyes widening at the look of horror on her face. "Apologies, that was an exaggeration. I must have been unduly influenced by the events in your manuscript."

"You have a *creditor*?" Belle's voice dropped to a whisper. She glanced around the shop uneasily.

"Well, I don't keep him here." Fletcher pushed away from the desk and moved to the streaked window. "I'll just visit him weekly and deliver all my earnings."

"You mean to say you're..." She trailed off uncertainly.

"In debt? Yes." His tone did not invite questions, though Belle found herself with plenty.

"How..." She furrowed her brow. What sort of trouble had he already found for himself? "You said you've only been in London for a few days."

"It seems my uncle left me with more than a printshop," Fletcher explained curtly. "The debt is his, and this shop is collateral. If I don't clear what he owes by mid-June, I'll lose my business."

"Oh." She watched him pace, selfishly relieved Ethan Fletcher wasn't an irrepressible wastrel who couldn't be trusted to run a business aboveboard, even as she sympathized with his frustration. "That's very unfair, Mr. Fletcher."

"Indeed." He hesitated. "And on that subject, I'm afraid I can't afford to pay you the full going rate. I have a small staff, and I'm already forgoing my own salary to pay theirs."

Belle frowned. She wasn't concerned about payment, but she *was* worried about legitimacy. Could she truly agree to this? Ethan Fletcher had never published fiction before. He was new to London. He was in debt. Not to mention, if word got out she was writing a penny blood, she would be even more of an outcast than she already was. There wasn't a single mitigating factor in the mix.

And yet.

This wasn't the opportunity she'd been hoping for, but it was *an* opportunity. And despite her reasonable misgivings, she couldn't deny Fletcher's offer felt fearsomely, wonderfully *exciting*.

Hadn't she thought it, just that morning? She *needed* change. She couldn't go on this way, trying to make the wrong boot fit. Perhaps for ten weeks, she could wear a different shoe.

But if he was going to clarify his terms, she needed to as well.

"I don't require payment," she said slowly. "I *do* require partnership."

"No." It was his turn to frown. "I can't take on a business partner. I just told you, I have no funds—"

"Not in that way," she said. "I'll defer compensation altogether, but I *won't* forfeit decision-making. I'm assuming a measure of risk with this endeavor—to both my creative and personal reputations. I'm not going to simply hand this journal over to you and step aside."

She drew in a breath.

"I'm willing to try this, but I need to ensure it meets my standards, that I have some degree of security. So, yes, I expect to be your associate."

"Partners." His jaw was working again, bunching beneath the shadow of his beard.

"Yes."

She lifted her chin, and his gaze followed, charting a shockingly bold path across her throat, her mouth, her eyes. It took him a very long time, and all the while, a faint thrum built somewhere deep behind her sternum.

"Fine." Fletcher said, his voice pitched low. "I suppose I can agree to that. And if you're in agreement as well—"

"Not yet." Belle raised a finger. "We haven't finalized the last of it. What happens at the end?"

"The end?"

"After the ten weeks," she said. "If you pay off your creditor? If you don't?"

"Honestly, I haven't the faintest." He exhaled slowly. "At the very least, I hope to have more than we do now."

She looked around the derelict shop. "All we have now is a story and a press."

"True." He smiled, a wide, brilliant arc of possibility, and Belle fell straight into it. "It's more than either of us had before."

6

––––––––––

Mr. Fletcher,

Thank you for calling at my esteemed establishment; it's always a pleasure to put a face to finances. I'll give you this much—you're a fair sight more enterprising than your uncle ever was. However, after reviewing your proposed strategy, I regret to inform you I will not be altering the terms of the debt. I'm not in the business of doing men favors unless it's the kind they can pay for.

I will expect your first payment next week, or the deed to the property at any time you wish to relinquish it prior to the fifteenth of June.

In Friendship,
Charles Howe

THAT NIGHT, Ethan couldn't sleep. He wasn't used to lying awake—at the end of a hard workday, he typically stripped down and tumbled straight to the mattress, where a deep slumber already waited for him.

But tonight, he found nothing in his bed but agitation.

Sometime after midnight, he gave up, rising and wandering to the small parlor in his new residence above the printshop. He started a fire in the grate and wondered what the hell was wrong with him.

Perhaps he simply didn't feel like *himself* here. Not in 62 Fleet, which didn't feel like it belonged to him. Not in London, where he didn't feel like he belonged.

This particular melancholy was unusual. Ethan wasn't sentimental about the places he lived. In recent years, home had been a rented apartment where he slept and shaved. As a boy, home was a boardinghouse, full of strangers and strain. When Ethan's father was at sea, times had been hard; when his father was in port, times had been harder.

So no, *home* wasn't a nostalgic sort of place.

But when he was young, there had been a small stretch of summers when his mother sent him to his father's sister in New Bedford. He used to sleep on the rickety porch and slurp oysters, bold and briny. On their evening strolls, his aunt pointed out the widow's walks, spinning fantastical tales of women who watched for whaling ships to return from the misty Atlantic. He used to eye the rooftop lookouts and doubt anyone could miss a sailor.

He poured a measure of whisky, idly wondering if he would ever see a widow's walk again. There was nobody in America scanning the horizon for him, but if he failed here, he would have to return anyway. It wasn't lost on him that his aspirations were wholly dependent on a ticking clock, a stash of damaged paper, and the deranged journal of a woman he'd met twice in a garden.

But what a journal.

He stared at the lambent flames and rubbed his thumb along the start of a speculative smile. Enough woolgathering; Belle Sinclair was a far more productive contemplation. Hell, it was remarkable, wasn't it? Meeting her again, stumbling upon the fact she was in sore need of the one and only thing he could provide.

He wasn't the only one chasing a dream, and the notion somehow bolstered him.

For the first time in his life, he had a partner.

He tipped back his whisky, his chest burning from the liquor and another burn besides—the faint flush clinging to her cheeks, the threads of gold in her light brown hair, the warmth in her hazel eyes.

And beneath all the luster hid the most dazzling prize of all—

A thoroughly grisly little brain.

Hadn't he thought it, the first time he saw her? *Green and gold.* She was lucky. She was gilded.

She was his only good news.

Belle Sinclair was going to save his sorry neck.

He could feel it.

"I NEED AN ADJECTIVE, SOMETHING ATMOSPHERIC," Ethan called from the workroom, where he was setting type. "Five letters. Four with an M or W. That'll do for an even column."

He was a quarter-inch short, which wasn't the worst of his current problems but annoying all the same. Cast metal spacers would justify the column, but using too many prevented a snug line.

What he really needed was an additional *word*.

He glanced over his shoulder to the office, where Belle Sinclair had spent the day revising pages for what Ethan was bound and determined would be a Saturday print run. Unfortunately, she seemed equally bound and determined to be a lovely little headache.

He couldn't see how he'd lost control of this endeavor so quickly. In his mind, the manuscript needed only a few alterations to be adequately parsed up as a serial. In *her* mind, every tweak was a grievous and cataclysmic shift. The woman treated her pages with the care and ferocity of a mother bear.

"Which page?" Her voice drifted to him from the office.

Ethan eyed the diagram of the eight-page arrangement, absently running his hand along his cheek. He'd finally shaved that morning, and his face felt both familiar and wrong. Like the printshop felt with a lady slinking about.

"Page five...damn, no—sorry, it's five for me. It's...ah..." He scanned the fair copy he'd tacked above the composing case. "It's *your* page seven."

"Never mind, I can't keep track. Context will suffice..."

"The magistrate's study." Ethan squinted. "His...life? Wife? I can't read your writing—it's all cramped in the corner. I'd say, judging by the preceding sentence, either of them is in danger."

"Risky?" She appeared in the threshold, the lithe slip of her fine blue skirts dragging across the dusty floor. "Dicey? Dodgy?"

His fingers skated over the sorts, sliding each letter backward into the composing stick. "Dodgy works."

"Read it back."

"Belle—" He kept dropping proper forms of address in favor of expediency. He appreciated her tidy name; it made things that much simpler.

"Read it back." She folded her arms and regarded him sharply. "If dodgy wasn't there before, there may be a reason."

He skimmed the typeset lines, instinctively reordering the backward sentences into the mirror-image they would print.

"The shock of moonlight illuminated a new danger. Clementina eased into the study, slipping under dodgy cobwebs and over creaking floors."

"*That's* what you wanted an adjective for? Cobwebs?" She was, predictably, again at his elbow. "Cobwebs cannot be dodgy."

He looked at her indignant, upturned face and experienced the mixture of exasperation and pleasure he'd been grappling with all day. A loose curl of golden-brown hair had escaped the neat coil at her nape, and there was ink smeared on the bridge of her nose. There was something elementally satisfying about the way her loveliness was breached by hard work, work she was doing for *him*. But so too was there aggravation in her proximity, because he didn't have time to be mapping ink stains on her skin. Nor did he have time for yet another argument about adjectives.

"Why in hell not? I certainly try to dodge them."

"Yes, *you* are doing the dodging. But you've modified the cobwebs to be of questionable character, which they aren't. Now the whole sentence reads wrong—it's supposed to be eerie, nearly spectral—"

"Fine." He set down the composing stick and flattened his palms on the worktable. "I'll rephrase. I need a four- or five- word adjective to describe morally upstanding cobwebs that won't detract from the spectral nature of the magistrate's moonlit study."

She glanced down the length of his arms. His sleeves were rolled, and the soft brush of her stare was as sharply tactile as the splintered wood beneath his hands. He inhaled. The air around her was infused with the light scent of mint. It clung to her hair, her skin. Ethan had spent decades in print works, and the most obvious smell had always been ink vats, white grease, sweat.

Mint was far better.

And also far worse.

"What about..." She closed her eyes in concentration. *"Clementina slipped into the darkened study, lifting her hand against a shroud of cobwebs as the floorboards creaked in warning—"*

"No." He shook his head grimly. "Absolutely not. You've just changed every word. I'm not having it. We are not revisiting the horror that was the composition of page three."

"Page three was much better after we revised."

"*You* revised. You revised not once, not twice, but *three* times, all while pacing about back here, not listening to any of my suggestions."

"But it turned out better." She lifted her chin. "You said so."

"Doesn't sound like something I'd say."

"You did say it, sir." Sam Porter popped out of the storeroom, where he was supposed to be completing a long overdue inventory, not eating an apple and eavesdropping, which was the course he'd evidently taken. "You said 'Damn if this doesn't work. Look sharp, Miss Sinclair—'"

"Thank you, Sam," Ethan said pointedly. "Very good, very timely insertion. Unlike when I needed help greasing the presses."

"I thought my father was on it." Sam grinned. "I didn't know he was still out."

"I, for one, appreciate it, Sam." Belle turned to Ethan with an arch smile. "See? *Better.*"

She wasn't wrong—page three *was* better after her exhaustive rearrangement. Her mind had a remarkable way of working sideways, and she seemed to write as fast as she thought. But locking the thought in a type frame was another matter entirely. Over the last four hours, he'd gleaned two certainties: Belle Sinclair could pen one hell of a murder, and she was *excruciatingly* particular.

Over her shoulder, past the accursed curve of her neck, a clock hung crookedly on the wall. It was five minutes behind Ethan's pocket watch, but even this pathetic timepiece served a purpose. He hadn't a minute to spare. Not for this. Not for anything.

"Fine. It was better." Ethan raised an eyebrow. "That being said, I'm establishing a new rule—you are not permitted to be precious about your pages. No more revising at the stick. Once I've set the type, we're working in inches alone. Which is to say, I will make it explicitly clear if I need more from you, or if I have enough to fill the frame."

She blinked. "But what if I think of something—"

"No." He inclined his head. "Part of our arrangement is the implicit understanding that you allow me to do *my* job."

"Your job is to print it," she said matter-of-factly. "My job is to produce it. A partnership, you see, requires two people doing two jobs. If you're going to start inserting dodgy cobwebs everywhere, we have a problem, Mr. Fletcher."

"Of course we have a problem." Ethan leaned against the worktable and gestured around the shop. "This entire operation is a problem. It's a problem that I've been here five days and have yet to turn a profit. It's a problem that I've officially put my name on the deed to this sinking ship. It's a problem that you won't just give me your damn manuscript without fussing over every single blasted paragraph. So certainly, why not add my misuse of adjectives to the list?"

"Well." She had the decency to look guilty for about ten seconds. "When you put it that way, I can see my problems are not the same as yours, but please don't think I have no problems at all."

She, too, leaned over the table, her golden gaze somber.

"You know why I'm fussing, Mr. Fletcher. Your so-called sinking ship is all I have on offer. But I wrote a novel, not a serial, and it needs to be reworked." She shrugged. "It's a process. I need to *think*. I need to—"

"The *only* thing you need to do is stop hovering and start writing." Ethan straightened and came round the worktable. "At this very moment, Tobias Porter is circulating news that on Saturday, we're publishing a brand-new serialized mystery."

She emitted a soft cry of surprise as he gently grasped her shoulders and spun her away from his composing case.

"A partnership is two jobs, is that right? Then allow me to tell you mine, Miss Sinclair. We'll start with a lesson on serial publishing." He marched her through the workroom to the desk in the office, his legs brushing the hem of her skirts. "To distribute Saturday morning, we need to finish assembling five hundred copies by tomorrow night."

He found a dried steel pen and eyed her as he flicked his tongue to the nib.

"To assemble five hundred copies by tomorrow night, I need to lock the frame by the end of today."

He lifted her right hand and slotted the pen in her palm.

"To set the type today, I needed pages from you *yesterday*," he breathed. His fingers curled over hers, guiding her to grip the pen. "Which is to say, I very much need you to produce them."

"Ah." She was staring at their joined hands, color high on her cheeks. "That's rather presumptuous of you, Mr. Fletcher."

"My apologies." He squeezed lightly. "Are you left-handed?"

"No." She pulled the pen from his grasp. "My hand is not the problem. It's just…what you described is not how I work. I've tried to keep pace with you all day, but Clementina Bloom is on her fifth draft. I can't tell an entire story without—"

"You're not telling an entire story." He dropped to his knees beside the desk in an attempt to locate the source of its incessant wobbliness. It had to be driving her mad, writing on such an uneven surface. "You're telling eight pages of a story. Or at least, that's what you're supposed to be doing. In reality, you've spent most of the day tripling my work." He shoved an old newspaper beneath the back left leg, which was a scant inch shorter than its counterparts.

"It's hard to write, knowing you're back there making it all... official," she admitted. "It makes me feel a bit off-kilter."

Ethan grasped the desk, testing it with a firm shake. It lurched only marginally. *There.*

"No need to feel off-kilter. I've fixed the desk." He stood and pulled out the chair for her. "You should have no trouble staying put and giving me three more pages of fair copy."

She finally sank to her seat, a maneuver he wished to encourage. He needed to finish typesetting so Tobias could ink upon his return, but there was no point until he was certain she wouldn't pop up behind him like England's most managing jack-in-the box.

"You've plenty of material to work with, from what I've seen," he said bracingly. "Just choose something. Choose chapter nine. That ought to be sordid enough."

"No...chapter nine requires that we've met the Contessa's husband, and I've yet to introduce him. I'll find something in my notes." She raised her hand, halting his protest. "I'll find it *quickly.*"

He watched her page through her journal, unable to stop the question that had been tugging at him all day. "How do you do it?"

"Hmm?"

"Where do you find these crimes?" He appraised her. "Surely, you aren't inventing all of it?"

"Some I invent." She paused, making a note. "But I also rely heavily on trials at the Old Bailey."

"The Old Bailey?"

"The Central Criminal Court." She half smiled. "My father is a judge."

A judge. Damn if that didn't explain a few things.

"I wondered how you were so intimately familiar with the inner workings of the court." He shook his head. "I have to say, I'm relieved it's not due to your own arrest."

"Not yet, at least." She resumed examining her notes. "Oh, look—there was a poisoning in Brixton last week. The maid claimed she thought it was sugar." She glanced up at him. "Although you told me I should rely less on arsenic."

He shrugged, walking backward to the workroom. "At this point, add all the arsenic you'd like. Write a damn advertisement for it. Believe me, I don't care what's on those pages, as long as it's scripted in your hand." He eyed her significantly. "Until you start, I can't finish."

"Don't you dare use *dodgy* for the cobwebs," she called after him. "Use...*viscid*." There was a pause, and he could practically hear her self-congratulatory smile. "Viscid is a good word."

Ethan chuckled, conceding her point as he turned back to his composing stick. *Viscid* indeed worked for page four, so that left only the front copy. Which reminded him...

"I need a name," he shouted. "For the title page."

"*Secrets of the Old Bailey*," Belle and Sam answered in unison.

Ethan sighed. Belle and Sam had debated half the morning about what to call the penny blood—Belle was unwilling to give up the title of her manuscript, so they landed on *Secrets* instead.

"No, for *you*. How do you want to be credited? Miss Sinclair? Belinda Sinclair? Three-Question-Marks Surname?"

He'd expected a laugh, but there was no response, the shop quiet but for the sound of Sam whistling in the storeroom.

"Belle? Did you hear me?" He sifted through the sorts. "I need a name, sweetheart."

"Ah..."

Her voice sounded odd, and he immediately regretted his teasing endearment. It was a rude habit, drawn from the uncivilized pressroom of the *Sentinel*, where a rotating cast of female secretaries assisted with clerical work. He couldn't keep track of all the new faces, but they'd all answered to his cheek in kind, so it seemed harmless enough.

But Belle Sinclair wasn't his secretary. And she certainly wasn't his sweetheart.

Against his better judgment, he strode back to the office to apologize. She was sitting at the desk where he'd left her, but her concentration had faded to a look of deep discomfiture.

Damn.

"Ah. Listen—"

"You would publish under *my* name?"

Ethan stopped short in the threshold. "Am I...not supposed to?"

"It's just..." She faltered. "Actually, I'm not sure what it is."

He managed to bite back impatience, though the effort was significant. "Do you think you might know what it is soon?"

She had a lovely way of frowning, her brow creasing in deep introspection, as if every one of life's befuddlements deserved careful attention.

"I always imagined I'd publish with my name, but I've never actually had the opportunity before. And...you know, my family. My reputation." A small spasm ticked in her jaw. "There's much to consider."

"Does your family not know you're a writer?"

"They know I write, yes." She bit her lip, plainly caught in some internal battle. "I haven't told them about our new endeavor, but they know about the manuscript."

"Then what's the problem?" Ethan regarded her shrewdly. "Yesterday, you were champing at the bit to start work on this serial. Today, it's been one thing after another stopping you."

"I'm not certain." She shook her head. "You see, I've gone from one extreme to the other. Using my name when I was theoretically writing a novel is one matter. Intentionally publishing a penny blood is another. Putting my name on it...well, it feels a bit *permanent.*"

"And you don't know if you want to be permanently attached to a penny blood." Ethan read between the lines. Her wince confirmed his suspicion.

"I do wish to be taken seriously," she said in that soft way of hers. "I don't yet know if this is serious."

He supposed he could be offended, but he wasn't. His goal was to print a newspaper, not a story paper. Tobias Porter had asked him if he were a proud man, and he wasn't, not precisely. He'd do what it took to clear the debt, but then he wanted to forge a new path.

Tobias's warning rang in his ears—*there's no prestige in penny fiction.* Belle coddled this manuscript like it was a damn child. Her hesitation to slap her name across the stained paper of an untested publisher was, perhaps, only natural.

"We can use an alias," Ethan offered. "Would that suffice? Or..." He glanced at the clock. Tobias was likely out for another hour. He couldn't ink right now. "Why don't you think it over? Once it's done, it's done, so it better be done right. Take a walk, clear your head. Just let me know what you want by day's end."

"Now there's time for a walk, is there? Time for thinking?" she asked mildly. "I thought I was meant to sit and produce fair copy of three more pages."

"I did say that, didn't I?" Ethan propped one arm in the doorway.

"Not even five minutes ago," she confirmed.

"How beastly of me. You shouldn't listen to me. I only know half as much as I pretend to."

"In that case, I suppose I can listen to you half the time." A small smile played at the corner of her lips. "But not about arsenic."

His grin stretched, beckoning hers, and—*damn*, there it was again, that spark, that small absorbing heat, as though their mirrored smiles were kindling. The whisky burn once again stirred inside him, and he knew by the answering flare in her hazel eyes, she saw it happen.

He cleared his throat, absently running a hand along his newly smooth jaw.

"You shaved, I see." Her gaze followed his fingers.

"Yes."

She observed him for a long moment, and he couldn't help but wonder what she saw. Likely nothing more than a man with everything askew—his tie, his business. He suddenly resented all of it. He wanted her to behold not things as they were, but things as they could be.

He could fix his damn tie. He could fix his damn business.

He could make something fit for her name.

She lowered her eyes and found a fresh page in her journal. "I'm partial to it, you know."

"The poison? Or the beard?"

"Ah." She pressed her thumb to the nib of her pen. "What fun is it if I tell you?"

She was teasing him, and he wanted to like it—he wanted her to be the girl on the bench, the girl he'd met twice, a random and distant flirtation. But in that moment, with the sun slanting through the grimy windows and casting her in a shadow so bright he could see nothing but shine, Ethan's thoughts turned hazardous.

This wasn't a one-day arrangement. She was *working* with him. She would be here all the time. Here, in his printshop, at his desk, bossing him about, smelling faintly of mint as she dropped her pretty little accent into his ear.

Belle Sinclair was going to save him, all right.

If she didn't kill him first.

7

Secrets of the Old Bailey, Vol 1., No. 1
What Happened in the Study

Clementina eased into the study, slipping under viscid cobwebs and over creaking floors. She had only one chance to take what she needed, for the Magistrate's wife was in grave danger. She found the desk and jostled open the top drawer.

There it was. The emerald ring, just as she'd suspected.

Unfortunately, it was still on the severed finger of the Magistrate.

On Saturday morning, Belle's eyes flew open with the sun. She stretched beneath her heavy counterpane, grimacing at a dull ache in her shoulder and neck, residue of a wicked headache that seized her the day before.

The headaches were unpredictable—she could often go weeks without issue, but sometimes if she wrote for too long, there would be sudden hell to pay. The first warning shot was always in her right shoulder, the revolt clawing up her neck and scalp, the muscles gradually bunching and yanking sideways until it seemed her head would sever from the rest of her. Once the headache took hold, she was rotten for anything else, forced to wait for knots to unknot and tension to ease. She loathed laudanum, how it turned her woozy and disagreeable, but she'd had no choice but to resort to a tincture yesterday afternoon.

She felt sick twice over as she lay abed—in her aching head and in her frazzled nerves, for she had no sense of what was transpiring at the shop, whether Fletcher and the Porters were on schedule for publication. But last night, he'd sent word via messenger, and Harriet, the housemaid, brought it to Belle with her evening tea.

We've finished.

She pulled the note from beneath her pillow, studying the long slant of his terse scrawl. It had felt like a dream, the first moment she saw him at his composing case, his dark head bent in careful concentration as he nimbly arranged type, type he would later ink, ink he would later press to paper. Her words were no longer hidden in her journal but were laid bare in Ethan Fletcher's hands. He was holding them, he was making them real. He was doing it right in front of her.

And today he'd placed five hundred copies around the city.

She climbed from bed and quickly dressed, fastening the bodice of a floral spring gown, then coiling her disheveled curls at the nape of her neck. She felt better now she was up and moving. Her headache had dissipated with a night's rest, and not a moment too soon.

She had to find a newsagent.

She hurried down the staircase, buoyant with anticipation. What if there were no papers left? She might never get to see her own story—

"Belle?" Mama's voice floated from the parlor, and Belle paused at the foot of the stairs. "Are you going out, darling?"

Belle eyed the front door with longing but dutifully poked her head in the parlor, where she was greeted by a wall of fragrant color. Mama held a giant bouquet of white ranunculus in one arm, attempting to find a place for it on the sideboard with half a dozen other arrangements.

"Goodness, have we opened a florist shop?" Belle hurried over, moving an armful of purple hyacinths out of the way. She inhaled the cloying scent of crowded blooms and sneezed three times in rapid succession.

"There was a card with those," Mama said, poking through the stems. "I think from Mr. Marsh…unless he was the tulips."

Belle surveyed the crush of blossoms. "I take it Lena had a successful showing at Lady Beaumont's ball?"

"That she did." Mama maneuvered the ranunculus to the back of the sideboard. "This is a rather garish display, isn't it?"

"They look lovely." Belle plucked a tulip from a vase and tucked it in her mother's bun.

"Of course they do. Flowers are meant to be lovely." Mama put her hands on her hips. "Whether the promised affection lasts longer than the bouquets remains to be seen."

Belle fought to keep a straight face. As a former governess, Emilia Sinclair had spent many years in the homes of wealthy gentry, and she was well-acquainted with all a shiny veneer could hide. She was famously unimpressed by Lena's suitors, especially after Belle's own disastrous courtship.

Belle lifted a creamy notecard from the tulips. "Mr. Turner's messenger must have arrived at the florist with the sun," she observed. "I wonder if the poor man even slept."

"Mr. Turner?" Mama thought it over. "He *was* rather unsteady on his feet by the end of the evening. I imagine he stumbled head-first into bed."

"No, I meant his *messenger*." Belle smiled mischievously. "Heaven knows I'd be sleepless if I had to deliver a note about 'the potency of Helena's blue orbs.'"

"Belle." Mama laughed. "Be nice." She read the card and cringed. "At least be nicer than this note. We can't let Lena see it. The poor man will never stand a chance."

Belle ran her fingertip over the waxy leaves of the nearest bouquet. "Is Lena still asleep?"

"I'm afraid so. Your sister, understandably, enjoyed the champagne more than she enjoyed the gentlemen," Mama confided. "I've just brought her a cool compress, but I expect she'll be the one with a headache today."

"I hope she had more fun earning hers than I did." Belle chuckled. "A headache born of swishing skirts and crisp champagne arguably has more merit than day-old pain of slouching behind a desk."

She flashed briefly to Ethan Fletcher's dark head kneeling beside her skirts, his broad shoulders flexing under his shirtsleeves as he fixed the rickety desk. He had indeed turned everything straight and steady, except for the lurch in her belly, which had only worsened.

"I'm sorry, darling." Mama furrowed her brow, seemingly unaware of the heat creeping up Belle's neck. "It was unspeakably rude of Lady Beaumont to leave you out. Lena and I should have declined."

"Absolutely not." Belle shook her head. "I've been left out for years, what does it matter now? Lena is twenty-one years old, at the cusp of life. I won't see her missing out because of me."

Mama looked pained. "Belle—"

"Don't be sour on my account," Belle warned. "I had flowers once too…you know, before."

Before a pride-injured Lawrence Duncan let rumors swirl about her. Before he downright *encouraged* rumors, then waltzed off to a new post. Her chest grew tight, slammed with an unwelcome echo from the past.

"I remember," Mama said softly.

Understanding settled between them. Of course her mother remembered when the flowers came; so too did she remember when they stopped coming. Mama took Belle's dwindling prospects in stride, but that didn't mean she was unaffected.

"I don't even care for bouquets." Mama frowned. "I nevertheless wish some of these were for you."

"Mama..." Belle reached for her hand. "You do know I harbor no grudge toward Lena, don't you? These flowers don't offend me. I don't want you to fret."

"I'm not fretting," Mama protested. "I simply want both of my daughters to be happy."

I'm trying to be. Belle brightened at the thought of the vendors who might, at this very moment, be selling her story. Her course had been corrected; she was finally on her way.

She was going to be fine.

"Not everyone needs champagne and dancing, Mama. After all, *you* never planned to marry. You had a life and work of your own."

Mama was quiet for a moment. In the midmorning sun filtering into the parlor, she looked very young—exactly like Helena, though far more somber.

"That's true. I did have work of my own. But, Belle..." Mama hesitated. "My independence was no honeyed life. I was unbearably lonely. Marriage wasn't my plan, but it *was* my dream."

"Oh, Mama," Belle said fondly. "So sentimental, so early on a Saturday."

"Indulge me." Her mother gently cupped her cheek. "What I mean to say is this—*you* can have whatever dream you want, be that a family of your own or an entirely unforged path. Or both. Or neither." Mama laughed, her dimpled smile returning in earnest. "As long as you understand it's your choice, not your fate. Don't let anyone else decide what's closed off to you."

An uncomfortable pinch seized behind Belle's ribs. It was a wonderful notion, but not one she fully ascribed to. She was a black sheep in more ways than one; choices were a luxury no longer on offer.

"I suspect my bouquet days are long behind me," Belle said quietly. "I prefer to think of what's in front of me."

They locked eyes—brown, hazel—and Belle suddenly felt she looked a bit like her mother, after all.

"Very well, darling." Mama planted a swift kiss on her forehead. "Now, then, what is in front of you today? The courthouse?"

"Eventually," Belle said. "I'll meet Papa there later."

"Oh?" Her mother tilted her head. "Where, then? Shall I accompany you?"

"You needn't worry. There's a new publication I want to find," Belle hedged. "Nothing exciting, I fear."

As expected, her mother didn't press. Belle's routine was peculiar but reliable, and her parents granted her the courtesy of privacy. Not that she required it; she was nearly always writing, researching, or with her father. She was a perfect spinster—out of the way, out of trouble.

Most of the time.

"Give Lena a kiss from me when she finally comes round," Belle said, securing her bonnet.

"I certainly shall." Mama returned to futilely arranging flowers.

"And please, do not let her read the cards until I've returned." Belle twinkled. "I'd hate to miss out on the fun."

SHE WOULDN'T LOOK for the penny blood until she was close to the shop. There was no telling where Fletcher distributed, and it wouldn't do to pointlessly raise her hopes. But as she passed a stall on Fleet, she couldn't resist skimming the displayed publications— and once her eyes snagged on a familiar title page, her feet followed.

Oh.

SECRETS OF THE OLD BAILEY

A Tale of Mystery and Crime

Written in Weekly Parts by Irascible Nell

After vacillating between excitement about the serial and a fierce desire to avoid further scrutiny, Belle decided to publish under an anagram of her name. It had taken far too long to rearrange *Belle*

Sinclair into anything that resembled a pseudonym, but Fletcher had finally cracked it. *Irascible Nell.* It was still *her*, but only the part of her she wanted the world to see.

She stared at the scrambled letters of her name until they blurred under a wash of warm, disbelieving tears.

It was real.

The wizened newsvendor eyed her oddly as she dug for a handkerchief and dabbed at her face with a small, helpless laugh.

"Don't mind me." She waved away the old man's concern. "I… ah. I know the author."

"Of the new story paper? He a friend of yours?"

"Something like that." Belle tucked her handkerchief away, offering the man a watery smile.

"Good morning, Roberts."

A deep, decidedly American voice floated over her shoulder, and Belle jumped about two feet off the ground.

"And to you as well, Miss Sinclair. I'd say I'm surprised to meet you here, but it seems impossible to do anything *but* meet you."

She flushed before she could even turn around, a half second too slow at banishing the memory of the pleasurable shape of his frown. In the last two days, she'd only permitted herself sideways thoughts of him—the slope of his shoulder bending at her knee, the veins in his forearm as it pressed the door jam, the fissure in his green eyes when he barked orders from the workroom.

"Good morning—" She pivoted stiffly and looked up at him, her words dying in her throat at the sight of his shadowed jaw. He was growing his beard again. She stared, assailed by a shocking rush of heat before directing her focus to the relative safety of his ear. "Mr. Fletcher."

"How are you today?" His eyes flicked over her. "Are you feeling better?"

"Quite," she confirmed. "The headaches are a painful nuisance but are usually relieved by some rest…"

She trailed off, refusing to contemplate whether it was typical for a man's beard to be so dark, so fast. He'd been clean-shaven on Thursday. Surely, she hadn't imagined it.

Well, she *had* imagined it, quite a bit...which is how she knew she was right.

"How are we selling, Roberts?" Fletcher's question snapped Belle back to herself. She looked to Mr. Roberts with avid interest.

"A fair few copies, Mr. Fletcher." Roberts nodded thoughtfully. "Though, if I may be blunt, there's a great many more to go if I'm to stock it next week."

Belle's rising hope skidded to a crashing halt. It hadn't even occurred to her that newsagents and booksellers may not wish to carry the serial week to week. Now she could see the risk was plain —these shops were buying wholesale, and they would want the copies to move.

She glanced quickly at Fletcher, waiting for him to step in to convince Mr. Roberts sales would surely increase.

"I figured as much," Fletcher said instead, narrowing his green eyes. "What about hourly circulation?"

"That's doing better," Roberts said. "You're getting eyes on it, if not sales."

Belle stared between the two men, neither of whom seemed remotely perturbed.

"What's the issue, in your mind?" She studied the penny bloods next to hers, wondering if the lack of an illustration was a problem. She'd tried to convince Fletcher to hire an artist, but to no avail. "Why is it not selling?"

"It's selling some." Fletcher folded his arms. She watched the shoulder seam of his dark coat shift with the movement. The garment wasn't tailored well, and yet, somehow, it was only doing him favors.

"Mr. Roberts, is it?" Belle turned to the newsvendor. "Why do you suppose this serial isn't selling? Because it needs an illustration?"

"It's too new," Fletcher said easily. "There's no audience yet."

Belle ignored him. "Mr. Roberts?" she prompted politely.

"Too new," Roberts confirmed. "There's no audience yet."

Her spirits sagged. "Well…how are we to get an audience if people will only read it if there's already an audience?"

"Time," Fletcher and Roberts answered in unison.

Belle hadn't stamped her foot since she was a little girl, but she could very well understand the impulse right now. After all his lofty espousing of the need for expediency, Ethan Fletcher better not dare talk about taking his time.

"*Time*?" She whirled to face Fletcher. "You said there was no time. Wasn't that part of your lesson on the mechanics of serial publication? The one you delivered as you *manhandled* me to your desk?"

A gasp came from behind him as a trio of dowagers passed.

"Nobody was manhandled," he assured the scowling women. Sensing Mr. Roberts's keen stare, Fletcher sighed and drew Belle to an alley.

"Apparently, we need to establish a second rule—don't get me arrested. Unless you know how to break me out. Which, come to think of it, would not surprise me any more than finding you skulking around every corner of London."

"How are you acting so cavalier right now?" She glanced over her shoulder as a pair of young men approached the stall. "Wait… oh. Look! They're picking up Clementina…"

"I'm not cavalier. I'm realistic. This is only the first week. We'll gradually increase the print run, and ideally, we'll be printing at capacity by mid-May."

Fletcher's explanation of sales trajectory was lost to her, seeing as the lads were ignoring Clementina in favor of a long-running serial about a bandit.

"Oh blast! They've put it aside."

"Once we establish a good routine, some of this will become much easier. I can make templates of the front copy, and we can even do a reissue, if we plan ahead—"

"Do you suppose I should offer to purchase it for them?"

"God, no." Fletcher shook his head, finally conceding she hadn't taken in a word he'd said. "You are to do nothing of the sort. Do you propose to haunt every bookstall in the city, buying copies of your own story?"

She wished the prospect didn't sound so ludicrous. Or so tempting.

"But we only printed five hundred copies," Belle said anxiously. "If those copies don't sell, what will we do?"

"Belle, it's been a day. Not even a full day—it's been a *morning*." He shrugged. "The serial will be available throughout the week, and people will find it. Or they won't. If they continue not finding it, we'll try something new."

"Something *new*?" Her face grew hot. "How can you say that?"

"Because you asked me what we're going to do." Fletcher was looking at her as though she had two heads. "If you ask a question, I'm going to answer it. Do I strike you as the kind of man who hems and haws and needlessly flatters?"

He didn't strike her as that kind of man at all. Ethan Fletcher had been nothing but unflinchingly honest, which is why she was about to cry in the middle of the street.

She couldn't *believe* this. Only an hour ago, she'd thought she was finally on the way to success—even if it was small, even if it was secret. Now she was coming to learn she couldn't even manage to sell penny papers.

"Listen," he said, seeming to sense her distress. "It might not come to that at all. We need to see what happens."

It was maddening, how rational and detached he was.

"It's an experiment for you," she said slowly.

"A bit, yes. Trial and error. Sometimes we try, sometimes we err. Then we try again."

"To make the serial better?"

He appraised her, working his jaw. "To make the serial *sell*."

Her stomach sank. For the last four days, ever since they struck their deal, Belle thought they were aiming to accomplish the same goal. Now she was all upside down, because she could see she'd been a fool. Fletcher had told her, that very first day, this endeavor was his means to an end.

For Belle, temporary or not, this might very well *be* the end. She may never be published again after June, and she desperately hoped to make the most of it.

"This…this isn't an experiment for me," she said, hating her fluster. "This is my life's work. I've gone down a very difficult path for this manuscript."

"*You've* gone down a difficult path?" Fletcher raised a skeptical eyebrow. "Sweetheart, this isn't a game you want to play with me. I won't deny your work might be challenging, but I'm sure the comfort of your down pillows and expensive skirts will ease the sting."

Belle flinched, taking a half step back. Fletcher had no idea what he was talking about. Memories shifted beneath the surface, where she never let them rise. The *not caring* could be exhausting, could consume everything, if she let it.

I'm sorry, Belle. My mother said you can't come to the wedding…

It's unseemly. You understand…

Have you heard about Sinclair's daughter?

Fletcher was staring at her, and she quickly composed herself, hoping the pink lining of her bonnet hid just how red her face had become.

"This isn't a productive conversation," she finally said, hugging her stomach. "Clearly, we cannot compare life experiences."

"Clearly."

"What is your strategy?" she asked briskly, glancing back at Roberts's stall. "Aside from time?"

"Tobias and I have a distribution plan."

"I didn't see any records at the shop." Belle had been at that desk all day Thursday with nary a plan in sight.

"It's more…implied," he allowed, pushing back his hat and tapping his temple. "You don't need to worry about it. You need to keep writing and leave the rest to me."

"Ethan." He'd vexed her into rudeness. To be fair, he also had a tendency to be rather rude himself, what with his liberal use of her first name and inflammatory application of the word *sweetheart*. "I'm not leaving *the rest* to you."

"Hmm." He looked aggravatingly amused. "I wasn't aware you had a choice."

She wanted to shake him by his admittedly beautiful shoulders.

"Then I suppose you have my payment?" Belle tilted her chin, holding her ground. "Because as I recall, I agreed to forgo compensation as long as I was your *partner*."

His sudden laugh took her by surprise. It was warm and rich, flowing from his chest to hers.

"All right, then, come along."

"Where are we going?" Belle was again trailing after Ethan Fletcher.

"If you want to talk strategy, I'm due to meet with Porter at the shop. I hope you have sustenance in your fancy little basket because it's going to be a long afternoon."

Belle drew to a halt. She was supposed to go to the courthouse later. Her father would be waiting for her.

"I don't think I can," she started to explain. "My father expects me."

"Such a good girl," he observed dryly. "Hold, please."

To her surprise, Ethan turned not in the direction of 62 Fleet, but back to Roberts's stall, where the young men were purchasing a bandit story. Ethan approached the pair, angling his broad frame behind them.

"You'll want this one as well," he said casually, lifting *Secrets of the Old Bailey* from the stack and setting it on their pile. "I'll spot you the penny."

"What's this?" the boy puzzled.

"Take a look." He clapped the lad's shoulder, but he was looking at Belle. "I heard the writer is beautifully gruesome."

The expression on his face was unreadable yet wholly compelling. She couldn't look away. But when she did, her eyes fell to her own story paper.

Clementina, in a boy's hand.

They had done that. She and Ethan.

They had done it together.

"Fine," she found herself saying, hastening to catch up to him. "Fine, yes. I'll join you."

"Oh?" He slid her a look. "What about your father?"

She hesitated.

Yes. What about her father? If she was to spend more time at the shop, she would need to devise an excuse. Perhaps she could say she joined a writing club? A publishing program? Some rationale that allowed her to explore this endeavor while still maintaining her privacy. She knew her family loved her, but it only made the prospect of yet another failure that much more unbearable.

Ethan was eyeing her expectantly, but Belle couldn't voice her complicated wishes. She longed to lay claim to something she was proud of, but public scrutiny had left her with bruises that still ached. She wasn't certain how much more of herself she could give away. For something she loved…maybe.

But not for a ten-week *experiment*.

"I'll sort out my father," she resolved. "If you're planning, *I'm* planning."

"Is that right?"

"I can't have my new publisher folding to a creditor," Belle said firmly. "I'm only just getting started."

He loosened another big laugh, and though there was nothing amusing about the situation, she found herself smiling in return.

When they started down the street again, he let her walk a half step in front of him.

8

———————

Accounting Ledger of E. Fletcher
Week of 8 April 1848
Secrets of the Old Bailey Vol. 1, No. 1
Earnings less expenditures—13 shill.

Remaining debt owed—£99

∼

"WHAT THE HELL is on my desk?" Ethan stomped into the shop late Monday morning, disagreeable after paying his first deposit to Howe. When he'd left an hour ago, the desk had been usable. Now it was half-covered by pink and yellow flowers.

"Present company, Fletcher," Tobias Porter murmured, nodding toward Belle, who was standing on a chair and sorting through a crate on a shelf. Ethan looked up at her. Today she wore a pale yellow that brightened the strands of gold in her hair.

"Oh." She waved aside Tobias's concern. "That's hardly the worst he's said in front of me."

Belle nimbly climbed from the chair and straightened the vase of enormous blossoms on the desk. "To your question, these are tulips.

I brought them from home. I thought they would improve this place a bit."

"Who's Mr. Turner?" Sam asked, lifting a creamy note card from the bouquet.

"Hmm?" Belle picked up a broken oil lamp and turned in a slow circle, as if unsure where to put it. After two rotations, she gave it to Ethan.

"The flowers are from *Mr. Turner*." Sam spoke around a mouthful of pastry. "Says he had a nice time at the ball—"

"Let me see." Ethan snatched at the card, but before he could ascertain what Mr. Turner and his damn flowers had been doing with Belle Sinclair, she plucked it away and handed him a broom. He moved the lamp to his other arm.

"You can sweep over there," she instructed. "Tobias kindly moved the bookcase."

"These scones are delicious, Miss Sinclair," Sam said appreciatively.

"I'm glad to hear it, Sam. I'll be sure to tell Mrs. Bowers you enjoyed them."

Ever since she'd arrived at the shop that morning, Belle had been single-minded in her pursuit of organizing the place. Ethan and the Porters had been directed into one chore or errand after another—moving furniture, cleaning the storeroom, and apparently, eating freshly baked scones.

"The place is looking cheerful," Sam announced. "It's nice to have a secretary around."

"Miss Sinclair isn't a secretary." Ethan frowned. "She's my writer."

"You're my publisher," she corrected.

"It's the same thing." He turned to face her, anticipating a challenge in her hazel eyes.

"Not quite the same."

"You're parsing words." Ethan folded his arms, digging in. When she turned contrary, she had a tendency to lift her chin, a stubborn little arc that exposed the alluring line of her neck.

"And you're obfuscating them."

"Such vocabulary."

"I've been studying." She tossed him an arch glance. "I'd hate for your pages to run short, after all the fuss you made about working in inches."

His gaze drifted over a faint flush painting her throat. "Inches should no longer be a problem."

"Fletcher?" Tobias said pointedly. "Might you help me move the bookcase?"

"Actually, let's put it in the opposite corner, I think," Belle said, snapping her attention from Ethan. She gestured to her handiwork. "I want you all to see this."

For her part, Belle had spent the morning tacking a series of tabulations and calendars to the wall. Ethan supposed it made sense to move to a vertical workspace, seeing as the desk was half-covered by Mr. Turner's blasted flowers.

"What have you here?" He set down the broom and the lamp and came to stand behind her. The light scent of fresh mint floated from her hair.

"Since we're tidying our space, I thought we might tidy our plans. Specifically, that they might live somewhere outside of your head."

Ethan glanced over her array of charts.

"This takes into account the distribution stratagem we devised Saturday," she said, pointing to the first two weeks on her list.

"Coffeehouses," Tobias confirmed, slinging a rag over one big shoulder. "Lending libraries. We need eyes more than we need sales right now. Get enough people talking…"

"And you'll get them spending," Ethan finished. "Eventually."

Tobias marked a date halfway through May. "Somewhere around here, we'll need to start buying paper. The tax will eat into our profits, considerably."

Belle knit her brows. "This all depends on a fairly steep increase. Several thousand copies a week."

"Which is impossible," Sam said around another mouthful of scone. "Isn't it?"

"Not at all," Ethan said confidently. "Other penny bloods do it every week."

"Other penny bloods are about bandits and vampires." Belle bit her lip. "Not a courthouse maid. *And* they have illustrations."

She brought up the damn illustrations approximately once every other hour.

"Belle, we've been over this. I can't afford an artist," Ethan said. "So for now, the courthouse maid, it is."

All four of them silently looked at the tacked-up plans.

"There's not much room for error," Tobias admitted.

Ethan stared at the wall, the numbers telling a story as grim as Clementina Bloom. But he was used to circumstances bending away from his will and having to find a way to meet them head-on at the other side.

They'd set a plan in motion; his responsibility was to keep it moving.

"We only need to worry about one week at a time," Ethan announced. He took a pencil from a little enameled tray Belle had unearthed and made a note on her tabulation sheet. "One issue down, nine to go."

As if reading his mind, Belle slid past him and lifted her bonnet from the stand in the corner. "Come along, then."

Ethan looked around the shop. "Come along who?"

"You." She tossed her journal to Tobias, who caught it handily. "Tobias can start typesetting the pages I have ready. You and I are going on an exploratory mission."

"For…what exactly?" He narrowed his eyes. "And where?"

"For more stories," she said decisively. "We're going to the Old Bailey."

"And I need to be there?"

"You're my publisher."

She finally did him a favor and tilted her chin. *So damn sweet.*

"I expect you'll want to keep me in line."

"THIS STREET once demarcated the western border of the city," Belle said brightly as they approached the impressive brick edifice of the courthouse. "It had a fortified wall, which is, of course, where we derive the word *bailey*."

He sidestepped the swing of her basket. "Are you writing a serialized mystery or a tour pamphlet?"

"Come now, Ethan," she chided. "Don't you care to learn about your new environs?"

"No." He followed her to the arched front entrance. "I'm still not convinced I will remain in this infernal city."

"Hmm." She frowned. "I don't think London is so bad. Now over there, you see the Bail Dock. In medieval times, the layout was different. The wall had spikes on top to prevent prisoners from escaping."

He regretted asking the question before it left his mouth. "Did it work?"

"That depends if you're on the side of the prisoners or the spikes," she said soberly.

Fortunately, before she could elaborate, they were swept up in the bustle of the Central Criminal Court.

Belle led the way through the harried crowd and approached a gray-haired official. "Good afternoon, Doyle. Is my father at the bench?"

"G'day, Miss Sinclair." The man jerked his chin toward the doorway behind him. "He's sitting in the Old Court. If you want in, you'd best hurry." The man turned a critical eye to Ethan. "It's a shilling for the gallery, sir."

"It is not, Doyle, and you know it," Belle admonished. "It's a ha'penny."

Ethan scowled. "That's an outright racket—"

"Enough. You don't need to pay." She placed a hand on Ethan's arm and turned back to the guard. "He's with me, Doyle."

Both Ethan and Doyle stared at her gloved hand, which had no business looking so good resting on his forearm.

"He's with you, is he?" Doyle asked suspiciously. "Says who?"

"Says me." Her thumb moved fractionally along his broadcloth sleeve, etching a furrow of desire so shocking she might as well have dragged her finger down his stomach.

Christ.

If she meant to placate him, she was doing a terrible job.

Doyle's glare dug deeper. "When we talked about you finally getting some friends, Miss Sinclair, this ain't what I had in mind, precisely."

Ethan pulled his gaze from her hand to her face, which was turning pink.

"Thank you, Doyle," Belle said hastily. "Mr. Fletcher is here…as an associate. And," she added, "shame on you. You know my father doesn't want you collecting fees for the gallery."

"He's the only one." Doyle shrugged. "Fine, fine, go in. It's bedlam today."

"Is it?" She dropped Ethan's arm and peered past the guard. "Oh, drat. It's nearly full-up."

Through the open door of the courtroom, Ethan could see a steeply raked gallery filled with men.

"I'm sorry, Miss Sinclair," Doyle said. "I can help you find a seat."

"No, no. Don't concern yourself, Doyle." She sighed. "I'll go round the side."

She turned from the courtroom and moved toward a passage to the left. "This way," she called to Ethan.

"Aren't we going in?" He angled his body to allow two men to pass. "I can't imagine someone won't give you his spot. You're a lady, after all."

"Ah, no." Her face shuttered. "Being a lady is no boon in the Old Court. And…" She faltered. "Well, I prefer not to draw attention. If I can, I come early, tuck myself into a back corner, and stay put."

"And if you can't?"

"I listen from here."

She led him down another paneled corridor. The crowd siphoned off as they drew deeper into the courthouse. She stopped partway down a quiet passage.

"These are the judge's private rooms. Hardly anyone comes this way when court is in session. See? My father's parlor is through that door, and *this* door leads to the Old Court. If I crack it..." She eased open a heavy door, and noise from the courtroom spilled into the corridor. "I can sit and take notes, and nobody minds."

She sank to a narrow wooden bench adjacent to the open door and withdrew a journal from her basket. Ethan stared at her, nestled in voluminous skirts, then looked up and down the passage.

"This is where you have Clementina observe from, when she's sweeping and whatnot."

"Through this very door."

"It's a lot of trouble to go to," he said, "to avoid asking for a man's seat."

"Depends on the man." She smiled humorlessly. "Really, some days it's no trouble at all."

"And some days it is?"

"Some days." She lifted one slim shoulder. "Some men."

She opened her journal. He glanced through the gap in the courtroom door and wondered which of the assembled spectators gave Belle Sinclair a hard time when her father was a sitting judge.

"Why do you keep returning?" He leaned against the wall next to her bench. "If it can be unpleasant?"

"Because I love the courtroom," she replied simply.

"Ah, yes." He gestured to the empty passage. "The courtroom."

"The atmosphere then," she allowed, the corners of her lips lifting. "I can't help it. I love being here with my father. I love watching trials...or listening to them. Mostly I love writing about them." Her smile grew wistful. "You don't stop doing something you love just because it's trouble some days."

"I suppose."

"Do you enjoy your work?" She peered up at him. "Not the penny blood, I mean. The work you *want* to do."

He rubbed his thumb over his bristled jaw. "There were some things I liked about the newspaper," he said slowly. "Going about the city, talking to people, reporting on issues that mattered. Given my editor's pompous aspirations, I can't say I was very keen at the end." He shook his head. "Maybe one day."

"Outside of the paper then?" Belle nodded encouragingly. "What do you enjoy when you *aren't* working?"

He hesitated.

"Your interests," she prompted. "Your pastimes? You know, how you spend an ordinary day."

At the implication he had opportunity to cultivate pastimes, Ethan couldn't help but laugh. "Earning a decent living doesn't leave much time for leisure, Belle." He nudged her bench with the toe of his boot. "On an ordinary day I work, I read the papers, I don't turn down whisky. That's about the sum of it."

He aimed for nonchalance, wishing to skirt this glaring difference between them. But Belle was still looking at him with doe-eyed assessment.

"I don't believe for a second that's the sum of it. You are a competent and enterprising man. Surely, there's *something* you find gratifying?"

He frowned pensively. It was becoming a damn nuisance the way she kept setting him to challenges he felt compelled to meet. In truth, she wasn't entirely off the mark. All week, he'd been struck by a renewed appreciation for print work—composing, pressing, assembling. It was satisfying, to build something from nothing, to put into the world what hadn't been there before.

"I suppose I enjoy making things," he said finally. "I like working with my hands. Printing suits me, and I missed it. If I can't yet establish my own newspaper, this, at least, is another kind of gratification."

Her mouth ticked up, a pretty, endearing curve.

"I enjoy making things too—though my creations only exist in my imagination." Faint color gathered in her cheeks. "Until you."

His chest instantly, unexpectedly warmed. Belle was the most inventive person he'd ever met, but she'd spent God knows how long whittling her pencil down to nothing, with nothing to show for it.

Until him.

"When did you start writing?"

"Oh, I've always done it." She looked down, rummaging through her basket. "I must have been about ten when I wrote my first story."

"Did it involve severed fingers?"

"That came later." She located a pencil and pointed it at him. "The first one was about Barnacle, a one-eared spaniel who stole aboard a haunted treasure ship."

"Barnacle." Ethan grinned, charmed by the idea of a tawny-haired little girl with ink on her hands. "Inspired. As the son of a wastrel-turned-sailor, I wasn't much taken with ships as a boy." He recalled his recent crossing. "Or as a man."

"Haunted ships are different," she assured him. "Though I moved on from Barnacle rather quickly. I found it more compelling to write about women than puppies."

"For good reason." His smile grew contemplative. "Though, it's odd, isn't it?"

"How so?"

He looked her over, once again perplexed that the woman who could produce tulips at a moment's notice could also write two pages about a bludgeoning.

"Well. You *do* write about ladies—Clementina, her clients—but your stories…"

"What of them?"

"Crime and gore." Ethan raised his eyebrow. "Not very ladylike."

Belle straightened, her expression growing sharp. "Crime and gore are the byproducts of high passion and high stakes, human conditions not exclusive to men."

Ethan opened his mouth, then realized he had no argument.

"Besides." She crossed her arms over the slight swell of her breasts. "Women aren't as innocent as men like to think. My upbringing was filled with ladies seeking legal counsel, and they always knew *so much more* than anyone gave them credit for. Why shouldn't a woman be the one to unravel secrets?"

"It does seem as though most of the secrets in your stories involve the demise of a man," he observed wryly.

"Well." Her smile slanted, a mischievous little flash. "Only if he deserves it."

There was a sudden clamor in the courtroom, the idle din turning expectant. Belle swiveled on her bench, peeking through the slivered door.

"That's my father," she murmured as a bespectacled man took his seat in the center of the bench.

Ethan studied the wedge of visible courtroom. In his dark robes, Justice Sinclair exuded a quiet command. From somewhere beyond Ethan's sightline, a clerk read the charge. It appeared one Mr. George Prescott was accused of attempting to abduct Miss Louisa Wortham, the daughter of his landlady.

"Damn." Ethan whistled softly. "We're getting straight to it."

Belle hummed her agreement, already writing with studious intent. A moment later, a gaoler brought in a wide-shouldered young man with gleaming red hair.

"*That's* the defendant?" Belle's eyes rounded as she peered through the cracked door. "Well. This just got interesting."

"How's that?" Ethan frowned.

"He's very handsome," she said, flipping over her page. Her pencil was flying, and Ethan craned his neck, trying to read as she wrote. "Notice how Miss Louisa is looking at him. Makes you wonder…"

"Wonder what?" He studied the defendant. The man wasn't *that* handsome.

"Wonder if the *mother* or the *daughter* is making the accusation," Belle said significantly. "Look at her. She's enamored with him."

In spite of his aim to resist, Ethan found himself gradually pulled into the proceedings of the ginger-haired giant. All the while, Belle scribbled away, transcribing the trial with alarming efficiency.

"Christ, you could be a court reporter," he observed, noting how many pages she'd filled.

"Absolutely not," she protested, shaking her cramped hand. "It's all too predictable. I guarantee when we read the full recounting in tomorrow's paper, the mother will be described as 'plain-of face' and the daughter as 'a pallid beauty.'"

"How would you have them describe the defendant?" Ethan squashed onto the bench beside her and swiped the journal. He glanced at her notes. "*A fire-haired Adonis*? Truly?"

She reddened. "It's for the serial."

"Hmm." Ethan flipped through her pages. "I see you made no mention of *his* beard."

"He doesn't wear it well," she said lightly.

Ethan didn't even try to hide his grin.

She looked away, her lashes lowering, her blush deepening, but just as quickly, she lifted her gaze back to his, catching him in a flare of unwavering hazel. It was that swift return that did him in—the blistering notion she couldn't look away, even when she tried. Heat shot through him as he silently coaxed her to keep that golden gaze on him.

The sound of the gavel rang from the courtroom, dissipating the thick air between them.

"Counselor." It seemed Justice Sinclair was directing his censure to one of the lawyers. "What do you mean, you have a note from Miss Wortham?"

"Just that, Your Honor."

Through the door opening, Ethan spied the defense counselor hurrying forward with a paper.

The judge read it once, closed his eyes, and drew a long-suffering breath. "Is this authentic?"

"My father is vexed," Belle murmured, her face alight with curiosity. She hastily turned a new page. "I can only imagine what that letter states."

The clerk cleared his throat.

"To call you my dear mother is impossible. I shall not correspond with you again. My husband—for yes, we sealed our union on the very day of my twenty-first birthday, thus freeing me from you once and for all—has told me the truth. I know you begged him to marry you, and when you learned he had pledged his troth to me, you vowed you would seek vengeance on us both. Jealousy drives you, Mother, and I hope it drives you to hell. Signed, Mrs. Louisa Prescott."

The courtroom erupted.

Ethan turned to Belle, who had a hand clamped over her mouth.

"Was *that* what you imagined?"

She started laughing. "I could not have imagined that if you gave me ten years to do so."

Inside the courtroom, the gavel banged again.

"Jealousy drives you, and I hope it drives you to hell." Ethan chuckled. "My God. The new Mrs. Prescott could put you out of work."

"Ethan, stop." She laughed harder, swatting him on the arm.

He instinctively caught her fingers and curved them around his forearm. He held her palm there, smoothing it on his sleeve, letting his fingers rest between hers.

"After the wedding," he murmured.

"Ah...what?" Her laughter faded as her eyes grew wide. Her hand tightened around his arm for the second time in an hour.

Ethan looked her over. They were sitting right against each other, Belle pink-cheeked from laughter, her pale skirts half covering his legs, and he realized they very much resembled a couple escaping a spring wedding breakfast.

"For the story title." He cleared his throat, reluctantly releasing her hand. "If you add this case to the serial, you could call it 'After the Wedding.'"

"Yes." She slowly withdrew her hand and set it in her lap. "That's quite good. I think I can change the—"

A chorus of voices sounded from the top of the passage, and Belle abruptly broke off. She looked past Ethan, her brow furrowed.

"We *are* permitted to be back here, aren't we?" he muttered, craning his neck.

"Generally," she said vaguely. "Perhaps we should go. I have plenty of notes."

He climbed to his feet, reaching first for her basket, then for her arm. They started back up the passage, and the voices grew louder. A small group of men came into view, caught in animated conversation at the foot of a staircase.

Two of the men wore the uniform of constables; the third—a tall, fair-haired man who had the others in his thrall—wore not a uniform but a dark coat. At the sound of Ethan and Belle's approach, one of the constables turned. His eyes fell to Belle, and he elbowed the tall fellow.

Belle stiffened, shrinking against the wall.

"Belle?" Ethan looked over his shoulder. "Are you coming?"

"No, you go on." She shook her head, a peculiar, closed expression on her face. "I—I've decided to wait for my father."

"Is everything—"

Before he could finish his question, she'd slipped back down the corridor and disappeared through one of the doors opposite the courtroom.

What in the devil?

He passed the trio of men, nodding with bland politeness as he wondered if he'd somehow offended her.

"Excuse me. Were you walking with Belinda Sinclair?" The fair-haired man stepped into his path.

"Ah." Ethan halted, taken aback by the brusque question. He considered lying, but what was the point? She was clearly a well-established figure around here. "Yes, I was."

"And you are?"

Ethan frowned. "That depends who's inquiring."

"Detective Inspector Lawrence Duncan," the man said in a tone that indicated he never tired of saying it.

Ethan stared at him blankly.

"Of Scotland Yard," Duncan prompted.

Ethan sensed he was meant to be impressed. "Ethan Fletcher," he said, mirroring Duncan's long pause. "Of Fleet Street."

"Are you acquainted with Miss Sinclair, Mr. Fletcher?"

Ethan's frown deepened. "Is there a problem, Inspector?"

"Not for me, certainly." Duncan looked at the constables, who both sniggered. "Possibly for you."

Ethan glanced back down the corridor where Belle had disappeared. "I'm due back at my shop, sir," he said. "If you don't mind?"

"You're American," Duncan observed, stepping fully into the passage and blocking Ethan's progress. "Have you been in London long?"

"No longer than this conversation." Ethan flashed an easy smile before he could be accused of impertinence. One of the constables chortled, but Duncan was still looking closely at him.

"Miss Sinclair is my associate," he finally relented, recalling what she'd told the guard earlier. "I can assure you, she's causing me no problems."

She was, in fact, causing him a number of problems, but he wouldn't share them with this peacock.

"Is that so? She's your business associate?"

"Something like that." Then, because he feared his ambiguity made this confusing conversation worse, he added, "She's…consulting. On a publication I'm printing."

"A publication." Duncan nodded thoughtfully, and the constables exchanged a knowing look. "She's nothing if not consistent. Until, of course, she isn't. I'm sure you'll learn."

At the man's tone, Ethan decided this conversation was concluded. "I don't make it a habit to talk behind a lady's back, Inspector." He eyed the man up and down. "Then again, a lady doesn't usually feel the need to turn hers on me."

Duncan's smile faded.

"If that's all, I really do need to be off."

After another long pause, Duncan finally stepped back and allowed Ethan to pass.

"Good day, Mr. Fletcher. Of Fleet Street."

Ethan left the courthouse, perplexed by the entire confrontation. The man clearly had an issue with Belle, and by the way she'd taken off down the corridor, Ethan could only assume the issue was reciprocated.

Not that it was any of his business what men Belle did and did not have issues with. He thought of the tulips she'd brought to the shop and felt a prickle of unease.

He grimaced, rubbing his hand over his beard. He was growing it because she clearly liked it. He couldn't decide if it made him a genius or a fool. When she looked at him, he could see a flicker of interest, but he didn't know if it was idle...or an invitation.

She's nothing if not consistent. Until, of course, she isn't.

He looked behind him at the brick exterior of the Old Bailey, and his discomfort dug deeper.

Hell. None of this mattered anyway.

Because setting aside the inspector's unsettling insight, the looming shadow of the Central Criminal Court reminded Ethan he did, in fact, know one thing for certain.

Belle Sinclair was a judge's daughter.

Her dresses matched her bonnets, she had a housekeeper to bake scones, floral arrangements enough to spare. She had *pastimes*, for Christ's sake. She was more than a world away from him, meant for a well-bred life in London. No amount of laughing together in the corridor would change that.

She's not for you. The rebuke scraped, bringing him back to himself. *Stay clear.*

Tonight, he would send the tulips home with the Porters. Perhaps Tobias could give them to his wife.

Ethan sure as hell had no use for them.

9

<u>Accounting Ledger of E. Fletcher</u>
Week of 22 April 1848
Secrets of the Old Bailey Vol. 1, No. 3
Earnings less expenditures—£5

Remaining debt owed—~~£93~~ £92 10s (corrected by B. Sinclair)

OVER THE FORTNIGHT following the first print run, Belle watched Ethan mark the passing days with careful notations in his account book, his green eyes assessing the calendar, taking their incremental gains in stride.

She was glad someone had a reliable way of keeping track, for her own sense of time was woefully skewed. Belle was living her days twice—first through the rapid blur of the printshop, and then again during the slow crawl of night, when she lay helplessly awake, recalling each interaction with excruciating detail.

Her mornings were interminable—waking far too early, agonizing over what to wear, picking at breakfast while staring at the clock. Then she arrived at the shop, and the sheer force of existing alongside Ethan hurtled her through the day. He was *every-where*—smelling of soap, whistling in the workroom, lifting her pen from her hand when he lost his. The days she went to the Old Bailey were easier to manage, but even so, his voice seemed to rumble from the margins of her pages, where she made notes of things she thought might make him laugh or scowl or rub his beard with grim consternation.

By evening, she would stumble home and force her head out of the clouds to the dinner table, half listening and hardly speaking until she could finally tumble into bed. If her family thought she was acting oddly, they didn't say, and Belle was grateful she had so many peculiarities to lean upon, for she had never in her life felt so peculiar.

Roll. Clank. Thud.

Slide.

She tapped her pen on the desk, trying to stay on task; she still had no motive for the villainous viscount. It wasn't easy, what with the goings-on in the workroom behind her. Tobias was inking, which meant the rhythmic rattle of the press came from Ethan. She could miserably envision the flex of his arms as he maneuvered the crank and lever. Every muffled thud of the platen evoked the beautiful ridge of muscle in his forearm, coiling and uncoiling beneath a dark dusting of hair…

Roll. Clank. Thud.

Slide.

"Miss Sinclair?"

"Oh. Hello, Sam." Belle smiled distractedly as Sam brought a tray of type into the office. "Are you coming to keep me company?"

"If you don't mind," the boy said, his deep brown eyes shining. "It's quieter in here."

"It is," she agreed, glancing at the workroom. "But not always better for concentration."

Just then, the sound of the press came to a halt. It was midday, and soon the Porters would go home for lunch. She could hear Ethan and Tobias in cheerful conversation as they came to the front office. The two men together could produce just over two hundred impressions an hour, a feat that was apparently cause for frequent celebration.

Ethan hadn't taken his own meal yet. She wondered whether he'd eat here with her, or if he'd stop somewhere when he went out for his errands. There was a tavern he mentioned sometimes. She imagined him sitting at a scrubbed table, giving that slow smile to a barmaid, and felt a familiar melancholy press upon her like a deep-seated bruise.

Belle turned back to her draft. Ethan could do whatever he liked; it was none of her business. Her business was here, on these pages. She absently jotted a sentence, tensing as he passed behind her.

"Belle, why is my accounting different?" He held the ledger she'd adjusted that morning. "You changed the amount of debt cleared."

"Yes." She didn't look up. She wouldn't engage in provocations today. "Your creditor came by earlier and—"

Ethan's voice was sharp. "Howe was here? With you? Without me?"

She snuck a peek at him. There was a flinty set to his jaw that thrilled her more than it should.

Belle set down her pen. She would engage in a small provocation.

"Yes." She rolled her neck; her shoulder was cramping. "Mr. Howe stopped in to chat about the serial. He said if Irascible Nell names a character after him, he'll dock half a pound from your debt."

"*The* debt," Ethan groused, looking disgruntled twice over. "I've told you already, it's not *my* debt. I didn't create it. It just…follows me around. Like a waif."

He shrugged off his leather apron and tossed it in the general direction of the coat rack. As usual, his waistcoat was unbuttoned. Belle gripped her pen, as if it could save her from the alarming stretch of his shirt.

"I was here," Tobias supplied. "Howe was just being friendly."

"Right," Belle said, gathering herself. "So in the spirit of friendliness, I need to devise something titillating for him—perhaps a railway magnate falsely accused of smuggling jewels?"

"That's good," Sam said approvingly. "What kind of jewels?"

"Rubies? I haven't done rubies in a while."

"Howe would be more likely to steal the jewels than be falsely accused," Ethan muttered.

"Hmm." Belle squinted at the page. "Actually, yes. That's quite good…I could have him acquitted, but *then*, after a fire at the foundry, they find the rubies in his possession."

"Mr. Howe won't like being a villain," Sam pointed out.

"I suppose not." Belle wrinkled her nose. "Fine, we'll invent a different smuggler."

"Would you ever write me in, Miss Sinclair?" Sam asked.

"Of course. Would you like to be a villain, victim, or hero?"

Sam thought it over. "A victim."

"*Really*?" Belle leaned forward, intrigued. "Sam, how grim of you!"

"It's unexpected." Sam grinned. "Abigail might feel sorry for me."

Belle swiveled to fully face him. "Abigail? Sam, do you have a sweetheart?"

"Not yet," Sam said with remarkable confidence.

"Oh, I'm sure we can fix that." Belle smiled conspiratorially, as if she knew the first thing about catching a sweetheart.

Sam snapped his fingers. "Maybe I should send her tulips, like the ones you brought in from Mr.—"

"Do either of you have work to do?" Ethan crossed his arms over the expanse of his chest. "I might remind you, this is a place of business."

"What, precisely, do you think we're doing?" Belle dipped her pen, already plotting Sam's downfall. "Sam is cleaning the type sorts. I'm writing. You're hindering us. This *is* business as usual around here."

"Must you verbalize every thought in your head? I can't concentrate on these accounts with you two prattling about burning foundries and Sam's misguided attempts to—"

"Do you suppose it's *easy* to write penny fiction?" Belle pointed her pen at him. "It took me half a day to figure out how deep a grave a laundress could dig, and you know it."

"It's not as though you're composing a complicated treatise that warrants constant consultation," Ethan said around the start of a smile.

"Wonderful." She tilted her head. "I'm glad you find it simple, because I'm in need of a motive for a murderous viscount. Any idea what could compel a man to act so wickedly?"

She'd meant it as a good-natured jest, but the moment the question left her lips, she regretted it. Ethan was staring at her in a way that made her whole chest burn.

"Are you ready, son?" Tobias lifted his coat from the stand.

"Cheers." Sam didn't need to be asked twice. "I'll finish with this tray when I return, Mr. Fletcher."

"Have a nice lunch," Belle said vaguely. "Give Mrs. Porter my best…"

The Porters left, leaving Belle and Ethan with the ghost of wicked motives between them. They looked at each other for a long time, and an unmastered thrill turned over in her belly. It was happening again.

It happened every time they were alone.

"You really don't mind writing Sam into the story?" Ethan finally asked. "Because if he's a bother—"

"Don't be a grouch, Ethan. He's no trouble."

Sam Porter was the absolute least of her troubles.

"You're very patient with him." Ethan moved to Sam's table. "It's good of you."

"Sam is a dear," Belle said fondly. "Here's hoping Abigail soon realizes it."

At the mention of would-be sweethearts, Belle decided it best to study her draft and not the handsome line of Ethan's profile. Even still, she felt the pull of his contemplative gaze.

"Is your mother waiting?" He began to methodically arrange the pieces of type Sam left scattered about.

"No. Not today."

Some days, Belle left at midday, too, because while she didn't require a chaperone, she was starting to feel she might need one.

"Have you told her what you're doing here all day? Or are we still masking the identity of Irascible Nell?"

"Actually, I arrived at a solution." Belle flashed him a wheedling smile. "I told my family I'm working on a literacy initiative."

"You told them what?" Ethan raised one eyebrow.

"That I'm participating in a charity to increase literacy of young men from the laboring class." She bit her lip. "If you think of it, it isn't *that* far from the truth."

He leveled her a look. "Depends how you measure distance."

"Sam told me his friend Paulie saves up every week to read it," she countered. "And you heard Tobias—the boys in their neighborhood love penny bloods, it gets them excited to read and *learn*—"

"You wrote about a laundress faking her own death."

"Well, now those boys know quite a bit about the limitations of an autopsy."

Ethan laughed, a wonderful, rich baritone. "Belle Sinclair, you are a marvelous puzzle."

A spark of confidence flared within her. Ethan never said things he didn't mean.

"You know, now that we're on the topic..." she started slowly. "I have an idea."

He was still smiling. "I'm sure you have."

"What if we were to lean just a touch more into the courtroom scenes? I could include more trial details and what have you. I certainly know enough, and I sense people find it intriguing."

Ethan considered. "It's an idea...so long as it stays fiction, no matter how real the inspiration," he warned. "We can't afford to print news."

"Of course," she said. "I always fabricate my court notes when I copy them over. If you're amenable, I think it could be an interesting angle. It would set us apart."

"Try and err and try again," he mused. "I don't see why not. You're right—folks seem to like the courtroom bits. At least as much as the…*inspired* ends your villains keep meeting."

She smiled, encouraged. "Do you think so? It's not too strange?"

"Oh, to be sure, it's strange." He looked at her in that stark way he had, as though he was seeing exactly what was in front of him. "But it's all right. You tell it well."

His compliment had her swaying a half step closer to his table. He was still deftly arranging the small cast-metal pieces of type.

"What are you doing over there?"

"Composing." He moved two more letters into place. "Old habit."

She peered at the indecipherable phrase. "You really can read the sentence backward?"

"You get used to it." He picked through the scattered sorts. "It has to be a mirror image."

She tried to reorder the small letters in her mind's eye. "I would never be suited to this," she admitted. The very thought threatened one of her headaches.

"I can show you, if you want to learn."

"Oh." She glanced at the desk, where her unfinished draft waited. "That's all right. I have my own work to complete…"

"You should know," he said firmly. "Seeing as this is your short-term line of business."

Curiosity won out. "I suppose I can try."

"Let's start with something easy," he said, moving aside so she could join him. "Your name."

She drew up to the table, and Ethan positioned himself behind her. Her heartbeat seized in an uneven stutter at the wall of heat against her back.

Good God. Surely, he wasn't about to—

Her thoughts evaporated, for he was already stretching around her, the thick ropes of his forearm circling her waist as he reached for the tray. Through her half-lowered lashes, she studied the strong flex of his wrist, the crescents of ink embedded in his short, neat fingernails. The scent of his soap was buried in his rolled shirt-sleeves, and she had to stop herself from turning around to press her face in the soft cotton of his shoulder.

Ethan methodically sifted through the tray, seemingly unaffected by their proximity and her rapidly approaching swoon.

"Here we are." He held up a letter. "*B*."

The single syllable drifted above her ear, and a slow shudder started at her scalp. The tingle spread, causing the skin on her arms to prickle.

"*B*." She rolled the sort in her palm—a small, solid little weight, still warm from his touch.

"Turn it over…"

His hand came around hers, and her eyes nearly closed.

If either of them gave an inch—if she stepped back, if he leaned down—she would be pressed to his chest, his beard dark against her hair. She couldn't even think of it, of how good it would feel.

She fumbled the letter, and he gripped her more firmly, the calluses on his palm stamping her knuckles. With patient assurance, he worked her fingers pliant. Together, they reversed the *B*, setting it at the right end of the table.

"*e*," he prompted, his voice very low.

She swallowed hard, reaching for the letter. Once again, Ethan moved her hand, his forefinger and thumb coaxing her own to flip the *e* and place it to the left of the *B*. His fingers were large and blunt yet so nimble, much more so than hers, now rendered useless in the capable cradle of his grasp.

Two *l*s followed in a squat little row, and she was grateful to see they were making *Belle* and not *Belinda*. She wasn't certain she could survive two more letters.

His breath moved across her neck, heat building at the small of her back. Her free hand tightened on the edge of the table.

"There," he whispered, his voice husky as they slotted the last *e* in line.

Her pulse slammed unevenly in her throat as she studied her name.

Belle—upside down, inside out.

She exhaled slowly, willing herself to settle.

"Was it difficult to learn?" she murmured, looking over her shoulder at him. "You said you started very young."

Slowly, Ethan stepped back, moving to stand beside her. The air instantly cooled, and she was grateful for the distance and the accompanying clarity.

"Yes, I was young. Too young." He looked at the small letters of her name. "My mother sent me to apprentice when I was hardly more than a boy. I left home sooner than I should have. And yet, not soon enough."

An image of a small, dark-haired boy surfaced, drawn from the anecdotes they'd traded over the last weeks.

"Did you miss her?"

"Constantly." He moved his gaze to her face. "She died after I left home."

"Ethan..." A heartrending chasm opened within her. "I'm sorry."

"You shouldn't be," he said in that straightforward way of his. "My mother was very unhappy."

"I'm sorry to hear that too."

He shrugged and resumed arranging type. "I come from a legacy of leavings. My mother left her family for a poor, philandering sailor, who emptied her coffers and broke her spirit. My father left her, and shortly after, she left me. And this may sound crass, but each leaving, I think, made things a bit better for whoever remained."

She studied him, struck by his candor. "Do you really think that's true?"

"I do now." He scratched his neck. "I didn't then. My work gave me a way to stand on my own two feet, and for a boy knocked down one too many times, that's a hell of a thing, Belle. If I'd stayed with my mother, I never would have learned my trade."

"Do you have any other family?"

She wanted to imagine there was someone who cared for him, who helped turn him into the forthright and decent man she'd spent the last weeks with.

"I had an aunt," Ethan said thoughtfully. "She lived near the sea. I visited her when I was a boy. When my father left for good, his relations seemed to fall away too."

"I've never been to the sea," Belle admitted. "And you've crossed one."

"I think you would like it," he murmured, unwinding a smile for her. "It's a bit like you. Entirely unpredictable."

She hummed with soft amusement, wanting to know more—wanting, specifically, to know if a woman waited for him. But she couldn't inquire, for it wouldn't be fair. If she asked too much about his past, he might ask about hers, and the prospect of allowing the specter of Duncan into this printshop was enough to turn her stomach.

Within these walls, she was just Belle—free from gossip, safe from scandal. For once, her reputation had not preceded her, and she wasn't keen on encouraging it to catch up.

"So." She shook aside her maudlin thoughts. "That's how you became a printer's apprentice."

"Believe me, it was nothing like it is for our friend Sam," Ethan said wryly. "I did all right for myself."

He nearly looked uncertain, and she wished she could take his hand.

"Ethan. You did more than *all right*."

"Hmm." He lifted the corner of his mouth in a gentle tease. "I didn't peg you for flattery."

"I mean it," she said sincerely. "It can't have been easy, but look —you have your own shop. You didn't let circumstances dictate where you landed. I aspire to be like that."

"Who says you aren't?"

"Circumstances tend to be a bit stringent for a woman like me," she pointed out. "Need I remind you, you just typeset a story written in the corridor of the courthouse?"

"Sweetheart, you're talking to a man who struck out to seek his fortune, only to find he was a hundred pounds behind the starting line."

She couldn't help it, she started laughing. His lazy smile stretched, then he was laughing too.

"We're quite the pair, aren't we?" She gestured to the small sorts he'd been arranging. "Just look, even with your help, I'm hopeless. I still can't figure out what this says."

"Let me get you a mirror." He reached behind him and produced a small brass mirror. "I have to check myself sometimes."

He angled the hand mirror for her, and finally the words shifted into place. She eagerly read aloud, then slowed, her heartbeat crashing as the partial quote registered.

"There is no exquisite beauty…"

She stared at the letters in the mirror, then at the man behind it. "This quote…"

"I didn't have time to complete it." Ethan's green gaze was soft. "Nor enough *ts* in this tray."

"It's from *Ligeia*." She looked up at him. "Edgar Allan Poe. I didn't know you were familiar."

"I'm not. You left it sitting out last week."

"You read it? Did you enjoy it?"

"Ah…" He narrowed his eyes, appearing to think it over. "Not… particularly."

She beamed, touched he'd even tried. "It's a bit odd," she acknowledged.

"Odd, confusing, terrifying." Ethan grinned swiftly. "I do like that line."

Her eyes pricked with unexpected emotion. She longed to move closer, to tilt her face to his. She longed for him to want it too, for him to see the steps she was trying to take, for him to step the rest of the way.

After one taut, confusing beat, Ethan cleared his throat.

"I need to step out for a bit." His tone was once more businesslike. "I'm due to deliver my next payment to Howe."

She looked down, very much hoping he wouldn't see the wound in her expression. She kept doing this—stumbling into the start of something, only to find a wall waiting for her. She was growing weary from fantasy, exhausted from constant proximity that was nowhere near close enough. Ethan was toeing an invisible line she had no idea how to breach.

"Will you be gone long?" She watched him shrug into his coat.

"A while. I imagine you'll benefit from peace and quiet. I've kept you from your draft long enough." He glanced up at her. "Don't forget, I need your final page by the end of the day."

"Yes. Of course."

He closed the door behind him, leaving her to her work, but she couldn't look away from Ethan's half-finished quote. Despite the abrupt reminder he quite obviously needed her for her pages above all else, Belle was unable to muster a prickly defense. Rather, her heart felt expansive and soft, as though it was taking over the rest of her.

She lifted the tray of type and carried it to the workroom, then found a composing stick at Ethan's table. She mimicked the way she'd seen him hold it—nestled in her left palm, her thumb marking her place. Carefully, she slotted in his letters. Then with painstaking slowness, she finished the quote, checking herself with his little mirror.

There is no exquisite beauty...without some strangeness in the proportion.

She looked at it for a long, long time.

Then she left the stick on his worktable and returned to her desk.

10

Secrets of the Old Bailey, Vol 1., No. 3
A Lucky Day for the Laundress

The problem with faking a death is sometimes a body is required. Not always—the Thames certainly had its uses. But the new Coroner's Officer had the unfortunate habit of seeing a task through. The laundress's vile husband was newly released from prison, a travesty which meant the laundress herself needed to disappear.

Fortunately, Clementina knew where they hid the bodies.

WHEN BELLE RETURNED HOME Tuesday afternoon, it was to find Lena and their cousin Cecily in the front kitchen garden. She spied them from the door and hesitated, debating whether she'd prefer to be alone. Then the pair laughed, their heads together, and Belle accepted she could benefit from a bit of conspiratorial advice.

Smitten.

She was smitten with Ethan Fletcher.

It was not lost on her that the root of *smitten* was *smite*, which evoked a possibly more accurate definition. If she wasn't yet powerfully afflicted by disaster, she had a feeling she was well on the way.

"Hello, dears," she called, mustering a smile as she stepped into the small, square garden.

"What a coincidence." Lena beamed from where she sat in the shade of the house. "We were just wondering where you were today."

"Belle." Cecily rushed to her. "My goodness, I haven't seen you in weeks."

Belle waved to a lounging Lena and bussed her cousin's cheek. At twenty-three, Lady Cecily Travers was as charming as she was irreverent. Tall and athletically lean with her father's gray eyes and her mother's dark hair, she treated the marriage mart like a game she only played when bored. Cecily was best suited for a caper, always good for gossip, and she'd pulled the Sinclair girls into more trouble than their father preferred. She was also their most steadfast friend.

"I've been busy," Belle admitted, sinking to the bench beside Cecily.

"Yes." Lena poured them all lemonade. "That's precisely what we were discussing."

Belle paused, wondering how much she could share. The thought of verbalizing her confounding attraction to her secret business partner was as embarrassing as it was tempting.

Much like the confounding attraction itself.

She opened her mouth, blushed, and closed it again.

"Belle?" Cecily tilted her head. "What is it?"

"With that blush, I'd say the better question is *who* is it," Lena teased lightly. "But we know Belle is steadfast in her loyalty to Doyle at the Old Bailey."

Belle mentally lurched to the courthouse with Ethan—his gaze hot on her face, his hand hot on her arm—and color stained all the way down her throat, to where all her words were stopped up.

Cecily watched her obvious fluster with interest. "Well, now I simply must know where you've been."

"Where you've been for *weeks*," Lena corrected before turning to Cecily. "Belle is disappearing more than usual…and considering she typically walks a well-trodden path between courthouse, garden, and her bedroom, I would say…"

"Mischief is afoot," Cecily finished.

"Mischief is *not* afoot," Belle said firmly. "Mischief is stalled. Mischief is, in fact, regressing."

"That's it." Lena leaned forward. "Who is he?"

"Who is who?" Belle picked up the pitcher of lemonade, realized nobody needed a refill, and held it on her lap. Like a shield.

"Whoever has you making that face." Cecily narrowed her gray eyes.

"I'm not making a face," Belle said quickly. It was a blasted nuisance, how badly she wanted to be seen and to hide away, all at the same time.

"Belle."

She looked between Lena and Cecily.

"He's a printer," she said despondently. "*Please* don't make a fuss—"

Her plea was drowned out by immediate and substantial fuss.

"Belinda Rose Sinclair!"

"You little minx!" Cecily scrambled to not upend her beverage. "What are you suggesting…there *is* someone?"

"We were only teasing." Lena looked as delighted as an aghast person could be.

"I *really* had no idea. Lena, did you?"

"No. I thought she was just off doing research she shouldn't be— a *printer*!"

"Do we need something stronger than lemonade?" Cecily all but clapped her hands.

"He's an American," Belle continued against her own wishes.

"What?"

"He's tall and kind and…his shoulders…" She pressed her cheek, as if to stop her rebellious mouth from moving. "He has a beard."

"Oh my."

"Definitely something stronger," Cecily instructed Lena.

"If you think I'm leaving this garden, you're mad," Lena said, rising and squishing onto the bench beside Belle. It wasn't made for three, but Belle was comforted by the familiar sandwich of her sister and cousin.

"I've been working with him on the…literacy initiative," Belle said haltingly. She looked up to find them both gaping like a pair of pretty fish.

"What do you mean *literacy initiative*?" Cecily asked.

"Never mind that. What do you mean *working with him*?" Lena's blue eyes were round.

"Just that." Belle sighed. "We're publishing something together, with the aim to…provide reading material for working-class boys."

She thought of Clementina's foray to the mortuary, and twisted her mouth closed.

"So that's where you're going every day. Off to some printshop, in your nicest dresses, wearing my rouge." Lena gave her a superior smile. "I'd recognize that shade anywhere."

"You can have your blasted rouge," Belle groused. "Because our professional association is the whole extent of it. His only interest is what I can write for him."

At this, both Cecily and Lena fell quiet.

"And you want something more?" Cecily asked cautiously. "Because you usually don't want…"

"I know," Belle whispered. She was perilously close to tears. Hell, everything was topsy-turvy as of late—including her detached reserve. "This is wretchedly confusing."

Belle sensed a rapid and silent conversation happening over her head, but she was too forlorn to care. "He made a poem for me yesterday," she admitted. "Well. Sort of. It was actually a line from a

Poe story, about a woman who was resurrected as her husband's new wife."

"Ah." Lena patted her hand. "That's…romantic."

"Maybe," Belle said. "I don't know what to make of it. I *never* know what to make of it. I suppose I should make nothing of it at all."

"Darling, we haven't heard you talk like this…ever," Cecily said slowly. "I don't think you should make nothing of it."

"You should make *something* of it." Lena sipped her lemonade.

"He might not even stay in London," Belle pointed out morosely. "He's focused only on this temporary project."

All three fell into contemplative silence.

"Well." Cecily was first to speak. "That's an idea."

"What's an idea?" Belle turned to meet her cousin's sly stare.

"A *temporary project*." She said it as though she were proposing something illicit, and a half second later Belle realized that's exactly what she was doing.

She slid her cousin an exasperated look. "I can only guess half of what you're insinuating, and I can tell you, I'm not doing…*that*. I wouldn't even know where to begin. I haven't tried to attract a man's attention…well, in years. Not really even before that. Duncan's pursuit was disingenuous, but he initiated it."

"You could, Belle," Lena said quietly, and Belle was startled to find her sister wasn't teasing. Lena's eyes flashed. "Why *shouldn't* you? You'll really let that louse keep you on the shelf forever?"

Belle looked down. She'd been the one to bring up Duncan, and now she deeply regretted inserting her past into this discussion of her present.

"It's not as though I have much choice in the matter." She heaved a confused sigh. "I *am* on the shelf. Spinsters don't take on *temporary projects*."

"Belle, don't say that. You aren't a—"

"Helena. Please."

She'd never so boldly stated the truth; it hurt more than she expected. She *was* a spinster—not nearly, not almost. She *was*. She was twenty-five years old and an indisputable outcast. For years, she'd endured rumors far more shameless than she'd ever been, quietly accepting them as her due. A future free of Duncan had a cost, and life in the shadows seemed a fair price to pay.

But these last weeks with Ethan had yanked back those gray curtains. Suddenly, *sunlight*.

Why couldn't she open the shutters the rest of the way?

"We're getting ahead of ourselves." Cecily was still scheming. "Let's focus on what we know. Belle is spending her days with someone who I can only presume is a handsome American—"

"Who quotes Poe," Lena added. "We mustn't overlook that."

Belle couldn't help but smile. She would never overlook that.

"We don't need to know how long he's staying, or what mysterious project you're working on, or anything so big and serious as what spinsters do and what they don't," Cecily said thoughtfully. "Why don't we just start very small?"

"How small?" Belle asked cautiously.

"Suppose you arrange to see him socially?" Cecily said. "Outside of his work. Something simple."

At the thought of intentionally seeing Ethan away from the shop, her stomach tightened with something frighteningly like anticipation. That's when she recognized how far gone she truly was, because Belle didn't anticipate seeing anyone, and she certainly didn't anticipate initiating it herself.

"For instance," Lena prompted, "the man eats dinner, I presume?"

Belle made a very small sound of defeat, and as one, Cecily and Lena's arms came around her.

They understood it was neither small nor simple.

"Excuse me, miss—watch yourself!"

Ethan glanced down to find Belle studying the street with ferocious intent. Since she wasn't looking ahead, he did so for her, firmly grasping her elbow to tug her out of the way of a pushcart barreling down Fleet in the opposite direction.

She seemed entirely unbothered by her near-capsizing, though she was certainly bothered by something else. She'd been like this the last few days—distracted and oddly quiet. He presumed it was due to her writing. She went through stretches when she withdrew, lost in private musings he wouldn't be privy to until they appeared in garish detail on the composing stick.

"Ethan…"

"Hmm?" He could drop her arm; there were no more pushcarts in sight. He decided it was better to be safe than sorry.

"Ah, if you have a moment, there's something I want to speak with you about."

"You mean other than helping you sneak into a crypt?"

"*I'm* not sneaking into a crypt," she admonished, meeting his half smile. "I'm simply verifying the general feasibility of sneaking into a crypt. I might add, I didn't ask you to help me."

It was Friday afternoon, and in a surprising turn, Ethan and the Porters were ahead with this week's production, which left him time to escort Belle on this short walk to St. Bride's. The nearby church was the site of an ossuary she wanted to use in an upcoming story.

"Of course I had to help you," he said lightly. "What good would it do for you to break your neck trying to hop a churchyard gate? I'd have to ask Sam to write next week's story."

"If anyone is hopping a gate, it will be you." She glanced down at his long stride. "There's not much trouble I can cause in my skirts."

Ethan gritted his jaw. *He* could certainly cause trouble with her skirts. But now was not the time to contemplate how far his hand could wrap around her thigh.

There would never be a good time to contemplate that.

"I feel this should go without saying, but nevertheless, skirts or no skirts, nobody is breaking into a crypt today."

"There should be a staircase to the ossuary inside the church," she said thoughtfully. "I think. If not, I can probably make do with a cemetery…"

Ethan decided to change the subject before she could extend this outing to include further gravesites.

"Listen, there's something I need to speak with you about as well," he said reluctantly.

She steered him down a narrow, cobbled passage to the church. The noise of the street was muted by tall buildings framing the churchyard. A pair of sparrows chirruped from their perch on the iron gate. Ethan wondered which was the male and if he was likewise in the thralls of the most intense and inconvenient attraction of his life.

He drew to a halt and reached inside his coat, withdrawing a stack of handwritten pages Belle had given him that morning. "I need you to rewrite this."

"What do you mean?"

"I'm not typesetting this." Ethan shook his head. "It's not ready."

"What's wrong with it?" She took the story and folded it protectively against her chest, as though it had ears.

He scrubbed a hand over his neatly trimmed beard and leaned on the stone wall surrounding the yard. Above him, the church's tiered spire pierced the sky.

"This story is intriguing and entertaining, but on the whole, it's a bit…tidy."

"Tidy?" Her mouth dropped open, and she jabbed the pages. "Ursula DeVry's chaperone was *garroted*."

"Well, yes, but Clementina solves a case every single week. It's getting a little predictable, don't you think? We might consider the benefit of more suspense. What if you drew out the scene in the dungeon, and then just…ended. And Ursula DeVry isn't saved until next week?"

"That means Clementina would completely overlook the invisible ink in the diary," she protested.

"Yes. Which works, if you move the diary to the scene with the glass-eyed caretaker."

It was a testament to Ethan's new line of work that these debates had become entirely commonplace. He used to write about the growing number of immigrants in Boston; now he was an expert on invisible ink and dungeon garroting.

"Last week, it worked well, didn't it? Your idea to add more trial details had us selling more copies than any issue to date. Let's try this too," he said. "Let everyone suffer more. In a theoretical sense. There's plenty of actual suffering, already."

"Hmm."

Belle joined him against the wall. She grimly studied her pages, and Ethan grimly studied her.

With the weather improving, she'd been getting more sun, aided by her maddening habit of pushing back her bonnet. It was inconceivable she could grow more fair, but there it was—the wisps at her temples gleamed gold, a bloom painted her cheeks, and a small constellation of freckles dusted the bridge of her nose.

Ethan stared; the freckles were a recent development.

He glanced mutinously at the bonnet trailing by its ribbons. The fact that she owned a dozen hats and couldn't be bothered to wear them correctly was proof of his rotten luck. Why *wouldn't* life hand him yet another problem?

At that inopportune moment, Belle reached for the pencil he kept in his coat pocket, her slender fingers unthinkingly brushing his chest. He was seized by a rapid and inflaming reverie—popping the buttons on her bodice, peeling back the soft muslin, baring her shoulders to the rough pads of his fingertips. He imagined angling her head, kissing a path up the smooth line of her throat, of all the places she would flush that had nothing to do with the spring sun…

Hell.

In light of all her covert freckles, he took a moment to remind himself of the other things he knew of her. She was a respectable lady, she had men sending her flowers, she had men chasing her out of the courthouse. She had time for *hobbies*—the serial was probably one of them, helping to fill her days until she married some limpid barrister and set up her own house with her own damn scones and her own damn tulips.

He grimaced. Only half of those things were true.

"Fine, yes. I see your point." She sighed, making a quick series of notations. "I don't like it, but I see it."

"I don't mean to be insufferable," he offered. "It's just good business."

"I know."

She fell quiet, apparently in no hurry to enter the church. Ethan looked about, wondering how long she meant to loiter.

"Did you want to go inside…or…?"

She looked up, and he was startled to see her expression was one of determined misery.

"What's wrong?"

"Ah…Ethan. As I mentioned earlier, I've been meaning to ask you…well, all week really."

He wondered if he should be as concerned as she seemed to be. "Yes?"

"I was thinking…if you aren't otherwise engaged…ah. That is, I noticed you didn't take your midday meal." She winced, color high on her cheeks. "And dinner is, you know…next."

He squinted, trying to parse if he'd been asked a question. "What?"

"Never mind," she said quickly.

He blinked, the fumbled invitation finally landing.

She was asking him to dinner.

Belle wanted to spend time with him outside of work.

She wanted to do it intentionally, because *yes*, there was intention in her blush, and now that he could see it, he couldn't see anything else.

Something inside leaped with golden, cheerful confusion, only to abruptly halt, as though a leash had tightened around his throat.

No. *No.* He had no idea what she was on about, but he would not be finding out over dinner. Whatever friendly feelings she elicited with her soft-smelling hair and thoughtful cleverness weren't useful for anything but the penny blood.

As for *other* feelings she elicited...those were for Ethan to untangle alone, at night, staring at the ceiling, his palm sliding over his aching—

Stay clear.

"I'm engaged for dinner tonight," he said quickly, hoping she would leave it at that. "Mrs. Porter invited me."

"Oh." She looked disappointed, which was probably for the best. And yet, he felt an irrational urge to put his finger on her wounded little frown and smooth it away.

Fortunately for Ethan's irrational urges, at that moment, a pair of women in elaborate hats strolled through the churchyard. Belle glanced at them once, then again, her hazel eyes growing wide.

"Blast."

She looked at Ethan as though assessing whether she could hide behind him. She stuffed her story behind him instead. Their hands briefly touched as she closed the papers in his fist, and then she was whirling around.

"Miss Sinclair? Is that you?"

Belle's bonnet was back on her head before Ethan could so much as straighten from the wall.

"Lady Beaumont." She looked at the church looming behind them. "My, what a surprise. Is...is this your parish?"

"Heavens no." The older woman scoffed. "My Thomasina and I are here to see about contributing to one of the charity schools."

"How nice."

Belle shot Ethan a look he didn't know how to interpret. He frowned; he was used to being able to read her moods. The two women were now looking at Ethan too—he could interpret their moods just fine.

"Lady Beaumont, Miss Beaumont, this is Mr. Fletcher."

Ethan scrambled for any notion of what to do—forms of address to aristocracy were lost on him—and decided on a nod. "Pleased to meet you."

Lady Beaumont's sniff indicated he'd got it wrong in one way or another. Likely all ways.

"Helena very much enjoyed your ball a few weeks ago," Belle said politely. "She was brimming with praise."

"Yes, well, the feeling is entirely mutual. Your sister is a lovely, accomplished young woman," Lady Beaumont said. "There's no doubt she's a credit to your parents."

Belle's smile shifted to something practiced and tight. "She most certainly is."

"It's a pleasure to host her," the matron continued. "And dare I say, my other guests would agree. I spoke with Mr. Turner just last week—he was quite *effusive*."

The woman trilled another laugh, and Ethan's frown deepened.

"It's nice to see you, Thomasina." Belle directed her attention to the young woman standing halfway behind her mother. "It's been a long time—"

"Forgive me, Miss Sinclair, we really must be off." Lady Beaumont jerked her chin at her daughter. "Thomasina invited friends for tea this afternoon. Perhaps your sister will join them next time. It's such a convivial group, I'm sure you recall."

There was a small, uncomfortable lull.

"I'm sure she would appreciate an invitation," Belle finally said.

"Good day, Miss Sinclair, Mr. Fletcher." Before either of them could respond, the woman and her daughter were hurrying away and disappearing down the cobbled passage.

Ethan stared after them.

"I'll take my papers back now," Belle said quietly.

He passed her the draft, which she'd nowhere to put, except back in his still-extended hand. He folded her story and tucked it in his coat pocket.

"Shall we go in?" she asked, pushing her bonnet back again. "I really am fine to go alone. If you want to ready yourself for the Porters."

"No, I'll come." And then, before he could think better of it, he added, "Did she say *Mr. Turner*?"

"What?" Belle looked at him with brief confusion. "Oh. Mr. Turner. Yes, he's—"

"The man who sent you tulips." Ethan hoped Tobias had a healthy dose of strong liquor at his house.

"Tulips? You mean the flowers I brought to the shop?" She gave him a strange look. "Those weren't for me. My sister received them after Lady Beaumont's ball. I merely thought they might brighten the place a bit."

It was Ethan's turn to stare.

"What?" She asked suspiciously.

"Nothing." He didn't know how to explain to her he'd never felt quite so much like an ass as he did right now.

He looked after the Beaumont ladies, hard-pressed to think of someone who was more superior company than Belle Sinclair. Hell, she'd spent a full hour yesterday helping Sam write himself into next week's story as the heroic victim of a vengeful heiress, all in service of impressing not-yet Abigail.

Belle was a good friend, but did she *have* any? She spoke often of her sister and cousin but rarely of plans outside the printshop. He'd assumed it was because she didn't want to make things uncomfortable between them.

Now he didn't know what to think.

"Belle…"

"You know, I've always liked this church." She resolutely looked at the spire overhead. It was plain she wished to change the subject, and Ethan figured the least he could do was let her.

"Why's that?"

"Legend has it, the four tiers on the steeple inspired a young baker to create a marvelous wedding cake for his betrothed. It's how tiered cake came into fashion."

Ethan studied the spire. "That's a nice story."

"Not all of my useless anecdotes are morbid." She exhaled a soft laugh. "Sometimes my notions are romantic…though still useless."

Even with the muffled noise of the street behind them, it was remarkably quiet here, standing with Belle outside the crumbling wall of a stone wedding cake.

"Not useless." He shook his head, ugly guilt moving through him. "Your notions are the most stimulating aspect of my life lately."

He stepped closer, near enough he could see the striations of amber in her hazel eyes. Her hair was mussed from her bonnet, one tendril slipping along her neck, needlessly calling attention to the pale curve that had been tormenting him since the first day in the garden.

Stay clear.

But she was standing beside him, with her pages in his pocket and a wash of freckles on her subdued face, and Christ, if it wasn't the *exact* formula to push him right into the damn middle of it.

"Your hair is coming loose," he murmured. And he reached for it, unable to resist twining the gleaming coil of golden brown around his calloused finger. He had no right to touch her, which made him want to do it all the more, to fit the scarcest lovely part of her around himself.

Just that, and only that—

There was a ruffle of feathers as one sparrow flew away.

"There." He tucked the hair behind her ear, soft upon soft, and his throat ached. "Sort of. It's the best I can manage."

Her wide eyes swept over his face, and it was all too sweet, too harrowing, and he suddenly wished he *did* need to break into a crypt, for he was itching to do something reckless.

"Ah. Thank you." She reached up, her finger trailing around the shell of her ear.

"Belle." He grasped the gate of the churchyard. "About before. When you very helpfully pointed out that dinner follows lunch—"

"Never mind," she said quickly. She averted her eyes, but not before he saw a flash of blunted hope. "It was nothing."

"Tomorrow," he said against every single one of his good intentions, "I have no engagements."

She startled, then smiled, a small slice of radiant relief, and he knew what was happening and wished he didn't know, wished he hadn't helped her along…but how could he not? This was a bad idea by every measure—except for the brightness on her face, which had somehow become the only measure that mattered.

"Tomorrow," she told his shoulder, "My housekeeper is making gooseberry fool."

There was a long, heavy pause.

"I like fools," he said, feeling exactly like one.

She blushed, a gorgeous disappearing of her freckles. "So do I."

11

Ethan—

Enclosed is my family's address; I sketched a little map of the most straightforward route. (I took the liberty of noting a possible point of interest—the site of the Duke of Bedford's botched beheading some two hundred years past. Four blows of the axe, can you imagine?)

While I'm on the subject of capital offenses, please note my house-keeper will expect you to use the boot scraper—you'll find it on the left side of the iron railing, near the front door.

A good-faith effort will suffice.

—B.

THE SINCLAIRS LIVED in a narrow brick town house on the northern edge of Lincoln's Inn Fields. It was hardly more than a quarter hour walk from 62 Fleet, but the minutes belied the true distance between where he and Belle each lived.

Ethan paused outside, feeling a sense of otherness—the neatly stacked rows of windows, the iron fence hedging a lush flower garden, the well-dressed passersby—and wondered what would happen if he just kept walking.

At that moment, the door opened, and a stout, iron-haired woman appeared, looking at Ethan as though she knew he was contemplating retreat, along with every other wicked thought he'd ever had. She ushered him inside, introduced herself as Mrs. Bowers, and took his hat.

"Well." She surveyed him dispassionately. "Good evening, Mr. Fletcher."

"Good evening." He glanced around, unsure if he was meant to chat. "Very pleasant weather—"

Fortunately, Ethan was saved by a door opening to his right.

"Thank you, Mrs. Bowers," Belle said hastily, hustling Ethan along. "In here, if you please, Mr. Fletcher."

She grabbed his arm and pulled him into a dark-paneled room, a pair of gilded oil lamps casting the rich wood in burnished light. Her father's study, no doubt. Ethan looked at the barely cracked door, wondering what Mrs. Bowers thought of this retreat.

"Your housekeeper is friendly."

Belle wasn't listening. "Before we go in, there are some things you should know," she said very quickly, eyeing him up and down. "Oh. You…" She blinked. "You look very nice."

Ethan squared his shoulders. He'd asked Tobias last night what the hell he was meant to wear to dinner in a judge's home, to which his pressman responded he couldn't imagine Ethan had a plethora of choices, so what did it matter?

Tobias was right. Ethan had only one good coat—the one he'd worn to those detestable society events on Beacon Hill—so he supposed it would do. Besides, Belle saw him every day. She saw him when the ink spilled, when the unsold papers were returned, when he smashed his thumb in the frisket of the press.

She could damn well see him in a dinner coat.

He cleared his throat. "You look beautiful."

She was wearing the dark green from the first day in the garden, and *beautiful* insufficiently conveyed the startling decadence of reliving that moment.

"Ah." She looked down, her lashes dark against her cheek. "Thank you."

Her blush came slowly, his smile came slower. That rosy stain was his glad affliction.

"Right." He pulled his gaze from her, taking in the study properly. "What do I need to know?"

She slipped to the cabinet in the corner and hefted a bottle and a glass. "Whisky?"

"Please."

There was something pleasurably domestic about the way she poured a measure and handed him the glass, as though she did this every night. He could imagine it all too well—Belle in the upstairs residence at 62 Fleet, curled beside him on the sofa, reading the paper and passing a single glass between them until the whisky was gone, and her hairpins were gone, and he was laying her back and making long, lingering work of it…

"Ethan?"

"Yes?" He drank his whisky, a vintage about ten times smoother than what he was used to, a forcible reminder he was in her father's study, in her family home, and her hairpins were doing their unfortunate job.

"First, don't forget my family doesn't know about the penny blood. I've told them you are an acquaintance from the publishing industry, unfamiliar with London, and I extended this invitation as a kindness. They believe we are part of a charity group working on a—"

"Literacy initiative," Ethan finished wryly. "I'm aware."

"Second, my parents grant some leniency, but this won't be anywhere as lax as the shop. While it's common for our dinner table to have an assortment of guests, this is still a little unusual. You mustn't call me Belle in front of them, only Miss Sinclair. The whole *associates* bit is rather dependent on formality."

"Noted." He raised his eyebrow.

"My father won't say much," she continued in a rush, moving past him to peer out the door into the corridor. "But he's listening—always—and not necessarily to what you're saying. My mother is more conversant, but she's unlikely to like you, so don't worry about that."

Ethan almost asked why Mrs. Sinclair wouldn't like him, but then he remembered he was an impoverished foreigner squirreling her daughter away on a secret project six days out of seven.

He rubbed his jaw, wondering if he should have shaved.

"My sister…will be a problem." Belle grimaced. "The more I think of it, everyone is going to act a little strange. I'm not quite sure why I invited you." She pinched the bridge of her nose. "This was possibly ill-advised."

"Why?" He knew why it was ill-advised—because he had one good dinner coat and it was worth less than Belle's flimsiest bonnet.

But he wanted her to be the one to say it.

"Because…" She lifted the whisky from his hand and took one resolute swallow. In the low light, her eyes flickered with unreadable emotion.

"Because?"

"Because I haven't invited anyone to dinner…" A faint tremor touched her cheek. "Since I ended my engagement."

A dozen replies fizzled in his throat.

He stared at her, his arm snapping forward to take back the whisky. He downed it, keeping his eyes on her. She held very still.

"What was that?" he finally said.

"I'll explain later," she murmured, breaking eye contact.

"You'll explain now." He was working a muscle in his jaw with intent to bruise. What in *hell* was she talking about?

Belle's breath turned shallow at the intensity on his face. "We don't have time—"

He flattened his palm to the door, halting her retreat. He stared at his hand, understanding his body was reacting in confusion and jealousy and some other reckless thing he couldn't wrap his head around.

"You invited me here, and you'll tell me what the devil you invited me into."

"I invited you to nothing more than dinner." Her voice was very low. "We are expected—"

"*Who* were you engaged to?" He looked at her fourth finger, as though a ring were still there. A ring *had* been there. A man had lifted her hand the way Ethan lifted her hand three times a day, but instead of jabbing a pen into it, he'd put a goddamn engagement ring on it.

"It doesn't matter." Her face shuttered.

Ethan bristled. He'd seen this immediate reserve crash on her before—

At the Old Bailey.

Understanding thudded into place. Her abrupt retreat from the knot of constables, his unsettling encounter with Detective Inspector Duncan. The way Duncan spoke about her. The way he wouldn't let another man move past him.

Some men, she'd said.

"The inspector," he growled, his stomach growing tight.

"What?" She blinked in alarm. "What do you know of it?"

"I met him once." Ethan scowled. "At the courthouse. He's…"

She flinched, and a terrible, terrible feeling came over him as he recalled Belle's name in the lousy prig's mouth. The oily, self-important *swine*.

Who she had never once mentioned.

"Yes," she said quickly, her fingers flitting to her temple. "It was him. It was *years* ago, Ethan."

He felt as though she'd bashed him over the head with the decanter of whisky. He'd spent nearly a month in Belle's company. They talked all day, about everything—they talked about things he'd truly had no interest in talking about before. And never once, in all her chatter, did she mention she'd nearly been *some other man's wife*.

Why hadn't she told him?

"You were going to *marry* someone? You were going to marry *him*?"

"Now is not the time," she said, interrupting the mutinous questions Ethan battled. "My family is in the parlor."

"Wait, Belle—"

But he lowered his arm, and she slipped past him to the corridor. He stared after her, his thoughts a stormy tangle. He badly wanted to pour more whisky but thought better of it.

It was expensive after all.

And she was costing him enough as it was.

"Belle, darling, is something disagreeing with you?" Mama frowned at Belle's mostly untouched plate.

She looked at Ethan, sitting across from her with a glower as dark as his coat. Something was most certainly disagreeing with her. And she didn't blame him. She'd blurted out her past with his whisky on her tongue and whipped down the corridor before he could so much as ask a single clarifying question.

"No." Belle picked up her wine, then put it back down. "I'm fine."

"Mr. Fletcher, tell us about the paper you worked for in Boston," Lena prompted cheerily. "Our father is intrigued by New England politics."

She offered Belle an encouraging smile. Her sister thought her reserve was due to nerves, not from the crumpled confession she'd flung at Ethan in the study.

"Is that so, dear?" Mama turned to Papa. "You've never mentioned New England politics."

"It seems I'm interested tonight," Papa said mildly. Nevertheless, he turned to Ethan. "I do find myself curious. Was it a political paper?"

Belle pushed her mutton across her plate as the conversation unfolded around her. She couldn't hear anything but her own stupid admission, hanging heavy in the air between them.

She'd meant only to warn him dinner might be awkward. Well... she'd seen to that, hadn't she? Because a warning required a reason, and she refused to lie to him. From the start, he'd been clear about his shortcomings—the debt, his obstacles. He never coddled her about the serial, always telling her, in his blunt way, when she needed to fix things, when he expected more of her.

He had earned her trust; he deserved her honesty, delicate and fractured as it was.

"The *Sentinel* wasn't affiliated with a political party," Ethan was saying, and Belle forced herself to rejoin the conversation. "It was a working-class paper, priced at a penny."

"A penny?" Mama sounded surprised. "I can't imagine it would be profitable?"

"There's no news tax in America," Belle murmured. She chanced another glance at him, then looked away, overcome.

She wasn't used to seeing him dressed so well. Every day, she was tortured by his ease—his sleeves rolled, his tie yanked sideways, his leather apron strapped across his chest. Sometimes, in the honeyed light of afternoon, his tie would come loose and reveal a smattering of dark hair in the open collar of his shirt.

It was *intimate*, the way she saw him at the shop. She hadn't realized just how intimate until she'd watched his approach from the study window tonight—tucked in his dark coat, so unreasonably handsome—and she'd wilted with longing.

She wanted all the versions of him. What he showed the world, what he didn't.

Was it so naive to hope he could want all the versions of her in return?

"The paper was meant to be produced for the masses," Ethan explained, swirling his wine. "Free of political influence, covering issues of import—abolition, worker's rights, women, immigrants— but the editor died, and his son took the helm, and somehow, the goals changed. I always counted myself fortunate to be a reporter until I stopped being able to report on very much."

"You know," Papa murmured thoughtfully, "there was a large unstamped press movement here, about ten years ago. A great many publishers were arrested in the thirties. It's why they reduced the duty from four pence to one."

"But newspaper prices are still abhorrent," Ethan said. There was a glint in his eye, a glowing purpose Belle hadn't seen before. "Not only does it keep people uninformed, it keeps them illiterate. If you want a population to read, you have to give them affordable material."

To Belle's surprise, Mama was now looking at Ethan with friendly interest.

"I agree, Mr. Fletcher. You know, some refer to stamp duty as a 'tax on knowledge,' and for good reason. I remember the frustration in my own youth. By virtue of my employment, I lived in homes that could afford books and newspapers, but when I was between households…"

Ethan was clearly caught unawares by this wildly unexpected anecdote.

"My mother worked as a governess," Belle explained. "Before she…married."

She fumbled the last word, and Ethan lifted his scalding gaze to hers.

"So that's what this *literacy initiative* is about?" Mama said, ignoring the tension blossoming between them. "You're producing reading material for the laboring class?"

"It's…a bit of that," Belle conceded, and Ethan thankfully did not elaborate.

"So if I may ask, what will you do here in London, Mr. Fletcher?" Lena inquired. "We don't have newspapers like the one you published in Boston."

Ethan set down his fork, looking away from Belle. "No, unfortunately, you don't, and it's a damn shame—ah, pardon." He glanced at the fine china in front of him, attempting to wrangle back both his grimace and his curse. "Truth be told, when my current endeavor is completed, I don't know what I'll do. If I can sell my shop, I'll possibly return to Boston. Or go to New York."

Belle froze. She tried to recall if this was new information. In a way, it *couldn't* be, for it made perfect sense, given his aims. And yet hearing him say it so casually…

Papa glanced at Belle. "Is that so?"

"Perhaps." Ethan raised a shoulder. "I have acquaintances there, men I knew from the printing chapels. We used to talk about establishing our own newspaper. We had a plan."

"You did?" Belle blurted. *A plan.* A plan was very different from a daydream…wasn't it?

"Yes."

"You never mentioned you had earnest designs to return," she said quietly. "I thought it was just something you said when you were feeling sore about London."

"There are many things that never come up in our conversations," he said. "As it turns out."

An inscrutable injury flashed across his face and worked its way deep into her chest.

This was her fault. She should have told him about Duncan sooner—but when? *How*? Her courage failed her, that day in the courthouse…though it seemed Ethan had run into him all on his own.

The inspector, he'd murmured in the study, his jaw so tight, it moved a muscle in his neck. She newly considered that Ethan had met Duncan, had *spoken* to him.

What must he think of her now? That she was unwanted, unwantable. A harlot of the heart, loose with her promises. Loose with everything else.

I'm not, she tried to tell him. The message was likely lost, seeing as she was staring at her plate. *I'm not those things. No matter what you heard, you've seen more of me than he ever did.*

Harriet, the housemaid, arrived to serve the gooseberry fool. Belle allowed her nearly untouched plate to be cleared.

"Now, Mr. Fletcher, you mentioned a printing chapel?" Lena leaned forward. Belle had to hand it to her; her sister was heroically conversant. "I must confess, I'm unfamiliar with your trade. I'm interested in learning more."

"It's not very refined," Ethan warned, but he reluctantly launched into a description of his apprenticeship. Mama and Lena were both quite taken with his explanation of typesetting, peppering the poor man with incessant questions.

"Does it take a long time to learn?"

"He taught me," Belle found herself saying. "It takes some practice, but it's not so different from any puzzle."

Her neck grew hot as she remembered his lesson—Ethan's palms curving around hers, his breath moving the hair at her nape, the prose she helped him finish. *There is no exquisite beauty…*

"You've always enjoyed unraveling puzzles, Belle," Papa said thoughtfully.

"She enjoys making them too," Ethan muttered, but his green eyes had softened.

She wondered if his thoughts, too, were back in the shop. She wished they were there now. She wanted to speak to him alone. She wanted to climb in front of this silent flush and take his hand and make him understand—

"What does it look like?" Mama wondered. "A typeset sentence?"

"Belle can show you." Ethan looked swiftly at her. "She's getting quite good."

She startled; he'd called her by her name. But if her family noticed, nobody said a thing, for now there was an experiment afoot.

There was a general commotion as plates were cleared and paper and pen procured. When everyone was settled, Belle wrote a few lines, right to left, carefully reversing each letter. She turned the paper to face her mother and sister.

"How peculiar." Mama laughed, now fully relaxed. Apparently, tales of working-class hardship and word puzzles were enough to charm her. "Let me see."

"*Dinner…*" Helena scrunched her nose, angling the paper. "*Dinner was lovely.*"

"Yes." Belle nodded. "Very good, Lena."

"Let's do another. Mr. Fletcher?"

Ethan took the offered pen and quickly scratched his own backward sentence, keeping his eyes on Belle.

She glanced at his scrawl and exhaled softly, relief lifting in small, hopeful sunbursts as she recalled their conversation outside St. Bride's.

"*Especially the fool,*" she read aloud.

He passed her the pen, his littlest finger nearly brushing hers. She hesitated, then laboriously wrote another sentence.

"These two words are the same," Lena pointed out, bending her head next to Mama's.

Ethan craned his neck, read the sentence, and looked sharply at Belle.

"Mr. Fletcher knows it," Lena smiled.

Belle stayed silent, watching his face.

There was a long pause.

"*Let bygones be bygones,*" Ethan murmured at last.

"Yes…though I now see I got the second *s* wrong." Belle's fists curled in her lap. "Even so, I hope the meaning is clear."

His hand tightened around his wine glass. "It's clear."

"You know, you two could have your own language," Lena said lightly, looking between them. "Everything upside down and backward."

"Indeed," Belle whispered, unable to look away from the profound urgency in his expression.

Upside down and backward, she most certainly was.

And she only hoped he could read her anyway.

12

<u>Accounting Ledger of E. Fletcher</u>
Week of 29 April 1848
Secrets of the Old Bailey Vol. 1, No. 4
Earnings less expenditures—£7

Remaining debt owed—£85

BELLE SINCLAIR WAS GOING to save his sorry neck, if she didn't kill him first.

So it would be the latter.

Her hopeful entreaty would be his undoing, the furrow in her brow a tiny grave for his resolve. He could hardly stand being around others, but he had no idea what he would do if he got her alone. All he could think through the entirety of dinner—with its fine china and expensive wine and tolerant, intelligent people—was that every good thing he had going for him was because of her.

And her confounding revelation was throwing all of it into turmoil.

Belle was still holding the pen she'd used to scrawl her earnest apology when a clock chimed somewhere deep inside the house.

Mrs. Sinclair looked up in surprise. "My, so late already?" She hesitated, studying her daughters before turning to her husband. "Gavin, you have an early morning, don't you, darling?"

Justice Sinclair regarded his wife. "Not particularly early."

"Early enough." She nodded thoughtfully. "I don't expect Mr. Fletcher or our daughters are quite so tired as we are. The vigor of youth and what have you." She placed her hand on her husband's. "Perhaps you'd like to read, and we can permit Belle and Helena to see Mr. Fletcher out."

At this pronouncement, a series of silent conversations unfolded around the table, chiefly between Belle's parents, which resulted in Justice Sinclair pushing back his chair and examining his pocket watch.

"For the next quarter hour, and not a minute longer, I will be in my upstairs sitting room, reading my overpriced newspaper." He stood from the table. "Thereafter, I will retire, and so will the women in this house."

He looked at Ethan for what seemed an inordinate amount of time before turning to Helena. "In the meantime, Helena, if you would like to sit with your sister and our guest, that would be fine."

Ethan glanced around the table, nonplussed. It appeared Belle's younger sister was about to be their chaperone.

The Sinclairs bid him adieu, and he grudgingly followed Belle and Helena toward the parlor, wondering how it was possible he could never catch a single goddamn break. It was unbearable, to be so close to her, unable to speak his mind.

In the lamplit corridor, Belle halted, peering anxiously between Ethan and Helena.

"Well," she started. "I suppose we could all play—"

"Belle," Helena said suddenly. "I just had a terrible thought. I never finished my letter to Leo." She turned gravely to Ethan. "Our cousin wrote to me last week, and I've been a beast about responding in a timely manner."

"Oh." Belle looked up at Ethan, who was by now roiling with agitation. "Well…"

"Would the two of you mind if I took a moment to finish it?" Helena smiled, honeyed and dangerous. "I expect it won't take more than…fifteen minutes." She paused. "I'll be in the parlor, and I unfortunately do require complete quiet for correspondence. Perhaps you two might wait in Papa's study?"

"Ah." Belle paled at the heat emanating from Ethan's gaze. "That's not—"

"Thank you, dearest, I appreciate your understanding." Helena squeezed Belle's arm. "Just watch the latch, you know." She glanced at Ethan with something akin to warning. "The study doesn't lock."

And with a rustle of skirts, Helena slipped away.

Belle eyed the door to her father's unlockable study. "I must apologize for my sister," she said. "I'll see you—"

Before he could think better of it, Ethan was pulling her into the study, he was closing the door, and he was estimating he had twelve minutes until Justice Sinclair could reasonably have him thrown in jail.

"Ethan! What are you—"

He spun her around to face him.

"*Why?*" he demanded quietly. He searched her face, his earlier aggravation clouded by something else, something peculiar and protective.

She didn't need him to elaborate. "Please understand, the betrothal is not something I usually discuss."

He clenched his jaw, newly wary. There was an edge to her expression, a downcast turn he didn't know what to do with.

"If you must know," she said haltingly, "I didn't say anything because I didn't want it to matter."

She brought her gaze only as high as his shoulder, that faint muscle bunching in her cheek.

"To you?" He stared hard. "Or to me?"

"Both. Neither." She released a small, unhappy laugh. "It certainly matters to everyone else. Gossip's claws cut deep. Outside this home, there are very few places where I am free of it." She finally put her eyes on him. "I'm free of it with you."

"Belle." His lungs constricted. He had a hundred questions, but none would form into any coherence.

"Did he…" *Hurt you. Touch you.*

"Do you…" *Care for him. Miss him.*

He shook his head, muted by confusion. What he could ask her, what he couldn't.

"I was twenty when he asked for my hand." She folded her arms over her stomach, speaking very quickly. "My mother and father warned me there was no rush. I didn't think I was rushing. I thought I was simply moving forward, the way one does. It's not as though I had other offers. I was always a bit of a wallflower. At least back then, I was in the room."

She looked down, and he had never wanted to put his fist into a man's face as much as he did right now.

"At some point during the betrothal, I realized I wasn't moving forward. I was staying still. He was holding me there, in place. He ruined my first manuscript—he called it an accident. But it *wasn't*. He was showing me what he thought of me. Thank God I *listened*. I heeded the warning with my eyes wide open. Unfortunately, everyone else listened to him too, but what they heard about me was nothing good."

"Belle—"

He was reeling, hit by a jab and hook of resentment and regret.

The women who snubbed her on the street…

Belle, alone outside her father's courtroom…

Goddamn it.

He should have *known*.

"I didn't intend to tell you this evening," she said, her face cast in wounded frustration. "At least not like that, not so abruptly."

"Then why the hell did you?" He grasped her biceps. Her skin was warm beneath the soft fabric of her sleeves, and he instinctively let go, raking his hand through his hair.

"I suppose…I was about to stumble into a lie, and I didn't want to. I thought of what you said, the first day in the shop, and I wanted you to understand."

His pulse pounded painfully in his neck. "What did I say?"

She held his burning gaze. "We could be honest with each other."

The swift, shallow hope on her face pierced him. She was trying to let him in. If she were smart, she'd bar the door.

He couldn't make things better for her.

He couldn't make *anything* for her.

"Ethan…" She trailed off. "I can see you're upset."

"I am."

"Don't be." She surprised them both by taking his hand and holding fast. Her eyes gleamed with unshed tears. "Don't be upset. Not you."

She opened his fingers and slipped hers between them, putting her smaller hand inside his. He tightened reflexively, twining their fingers together.

"I'm not upset you were engaged," he said gruffly, hating the hurt on her face, hating everyone who put it there, including himself. "The last thing I'm bothered about is your past."

Her heart was in her eyes. "Then what?"

My future.

"This isn't wise," he muttered. His eyes fell to the hand he wasn't holding. She was twisting her fingers in her fine skirts, and for a wretched moment, all he could see was his mother's knuckles, bleeding and raw from the hard life his father dragged her into.

Once more, the question rattled through him, born of confusion and ambition and shame. *What the hell was he doing here?*

"You told me there's no pretense between us." She cautiously stepped nearer, refusing to let him look away. "Is that not true?"

"Belle." His discomfort sharpened in flares of warning. "There is *so much more* than pretense between us. Hell, your father's whisky costs more than my monthly rent. Look at this study. Look at this *house*."

"What if…what if you don't look at the whisky?" she whispered. "What if you don't look at the house?"

"Belle…"

Her voice hitched.

"Ethan, what if you just look at *me*?"

His hand was lifting before he thought to lift it, reaching for her, cradling her beautiful face in his calloused palm.

"Do you think I'm not looking at you?" he breathed.

In a near fugue, he watched himself touch her, trailing his knuckles over the curve of her jaw, relishing the downy softness of her cheek. He stroked along the shell of her ear, and she gasped, her mouth falling open, and he put his finger there too, compulsively tracing the corner of her lip, taking in the sweet slackening, the way her bottom lip dragged against his thumb.

If she hadn't closed her eyes, he might not have done it.

But—*oh God*—she did, her lashes lowering on a sigh, such yearning, a wild possession cracking inside his chest. He couldn't tolerate Belle wanting for anything, even if she wanted a man as limited as him.

In something like apology, he found the curve in her neck and finally, *finally* put his lips to the tantalizing stretch of skin. She keened, and he did it again, sucking gently on her racing pulse for one perfect, wavering breath.

And then he was drawing his mouth up her throat, letting himself savor the full weight of this looming mistake.

"Belle," he murmured. "The entire damn problem is that I'm looking at you."

He brought his thumb to her chin. One slow stroke, tugging her mouth open—she moaned faintly, he would never unhear it—then he sealed his lips over hers.

The relief was instantaneous. Her lips were soft and pliant, and he kissed her as if they'd always been kissing, as if his mouth had been learning hers this whole time, a thousand exchanges, a hundred pushes, a hundred pulls. There was no hesitance, no coaxing. Ethan groaned—rough, low—his tongue moving against hers, his hand flexing in her hair, and it was exactly as sweet and punishing as he'd imagined it would be, yet nothing like he'd imagined at all.

He was burning, *burning*.

Belle moaned again, the prettiest plea, ruinous in her asking. He kissed a feverish arc from her swollen lips to the tender curve of her jaw, and she clutched his sleeve, stumbling into him. He found her hand and loosened her fingers from his coat, drawing her arm around his neck. And she was cleaving to him, pressing against the jagged ache inside him, and *Christ*, he had to keep her here. Helplessly, he planted his palm on the small of her back, holding her just so, for he was a grasping, selfish bastard and he *wanted* her. He wanted it all—her fantastical musings, her maddening fluster, her steadfast, hopeful heart.

He tilted her head, sensing the abrasion of his beard on her soft skin, but she only tunneled her free hand in his hair, accepting his searing onslaught, meeting him in turn. He couldn't believe how good her mouth felt against his, how every one of her gasps brushed damp and needy against his lips, like they belonged there.

"Ethan…"

She wrenched away, her ribs shuddering beneath his palm. She buried her face in his shoulder, blushing and breathless, and only then did Ethan realize he had a fistful of her skirts, that his thigh was between hers.

Enough—

Enough.

He braced one arm on the door above her, fighting to control himself.

"We can't," he murmured raggedly, his entire body rioting with arousal and guilt. "Belle, it's too far."

A lie; it wasn't far enough. But her family was on the other side of the door, and so were about eighty-five pounds sterling worth of reasons he needed to take a goddamn step back.

"Don't say that." Her voice was very soft; she held his face between her hands. Her thumbs lightly stroked his beard, testing the shreds of his self-possession.

He looked down at her, glassy and flushed, stubborn and afraid. His cock ached; his lungs ached. It was inconceivable that hardly a month ago, he'd thought her to be his good news, when in fact, she seemed likely to be his imminent downfall. In the span of a single evening, Belle had neatly, sweetly, torn their tenuous professionalism asunder, and though Ethan usually faced his problems head-on, he wasn't certain this could be fixed. He wasn't certain he *wanted* to fix it.

But he sure as hell had to try.

"Our work…" With forced effort, he put his lips not back on hers but just above her ear. Her hair was soft against his nose, and it felt so good, he closed his eyes. "Our work is vital. The serial *cannot* be jeopardized. We can't…Belle, we can't do this."

"Ethan."

"I'm sorry." Gently, gently, he smoothed her hair. He had to put her to rights, in case her father's clock was fast. "This was careless of me."

"It wasn't," she insisted. "I know what you're doing. Don't build this wall higher."

"Sweetheart." He laughed humorlessly. "I can't even afford the bricks."

13

———

SECRETS OF THE OLD BAILEY, VOL 1., NO. 4
AFTER THE WEDDING

Portia St. James claimed her tenant absconded with her impressionable daughter, but when the gaolor brought a fiery-haired Adonis into the courtroom, it was plain to anyone with two eyes Lydia St. James had left her mother's house on her own two feet.

Fortunately, Clementina had already located the banns and left them on the Judge's desk. Portia St. James wasn't pleased with the surprising turn of events, though Clementina wasn't convinced all the fuss was warranted.

The man wasn't that handsome.

❦

THE LONE SAVING grace after Saturday evening's calamitous encounter in the study was that the Sinclairs were expected at Fordham House on Sunday. Much like Aunt Cora and Uncle Nate's family, their residence on Upper Grosvenor was beautiful, warm, and the site of sustained havoc.

Needless to say, Belle very much hoped the outing would mask her fevered befuddlement.

Unfortunately, not even the chaos of her extended family could detract from the knots she was in. Belle was heated and distracted and quite possibly permanently useless for all endeavors aside from keeping her head above the tides of one restless daydream after another.

The door behind her, hard against her shoulders. Ethan before her, hard against her breasts. His beard dragging along her collarbone, his mouth everywhere—the side of her neck, the curve of her jaw, the corner of her desperate, desperate lips…

"Belle," Cecily called from the far side of Aunt Cora's sunny drawing room, where she sat with Lena, purportedly embroidering a baby blanket for Tess. "Belle, were you listening?"

"Hmm?" Belle's book slid from her lap, and she touched her collarbone, praying her flush stayed below her neckline.

Cecily tilted her head. "Did you sleep well last night, dear? You look a bit peaked."

Belle did not rise to the bait. She'd spent most of the visit pretending to read and avoiding Cecily and Lena's curious glances. She knew her cousin was itching to hear about her evening with the American printer, a wish Belle was in no hurry to grant.

"She looks perfectly fine," Aunt Cora interjected. "Though, Belle darling, you dropped your book." Belle hastily bent to retrieve it as her aunt admonished Cecily. "And you're hardly one to talk about sleeping well, Cecily Travers. Don't think I don't know you were up playing cards half the night."

"Papa wagered sapphire earrings." Cecily yawned. "I had no choice but to make a stand." She looked around. "Where is he, by the way?"

"Uncle Nate is waiting for Tess." Lena was making much better progress on her half of the blanket. "I hope you won the card game. Sapphires would be lovely with your hair."

His big hand gentle in her hair, his eyes wary as he smoothed the strands he'd tugged loose…

"Belle?" Her mother regarded her carefully. "You know, you do look a bit peculiar."

"I'm fine," she said thickly. "Just hoping Cecily bested Uncle Nate."

"Unfortunately not," Cecily groused. "One of these days."

"I expect the earrings will turn up regardless." Aunt Cora shook her head. "Your father is not known for restraint."

"As opposed to yourself," Papa commented dryly. "Cora, Lady Fordham, patroness of restraint." He looked over at his sister, halfway through addressing a bevy of invitations for a party she was arranging for Belle's eldest cousin, Leo, the ninth Viscount Dane. "That's quite a guest list Leo provided. Has *he* seen it?"

"Belle." Cecily would not be deterred. "I was wondering about—"

At that moment, Belle was granted reprieve in the form of a series of echoing shouts from the corridor.

"Oh!" Aunt Cora beamed. "That must be Tess and the boys."

"Bloody hell." Tess's curse entered the room before her. A moment later, fair-haired, blue-eyed, foul-tempered Lady Rockwell stormed into the drawing room.

"Hello, darling." Aunt Cora rose to embrace her daughter. "Did the travel not agree with you?"

"It most certainly did not." Tess flopped inelegantly across a chaise. "Three hours in a coach with three little hellions. Nathaniel nearly pitched out the window." She frowned at the small swell of her stomach. "*This* one better be a girl."

"Right." Cecily smirked. "Because *your* daughter is unlikely to be a hellion."

Mama patted Tess's hand and passed her a platter of lemon bars.

Aunt Cora looked about. "Speaking of Nathaniels, has your father seen the boys?"

"Indeed he has." Uncle Nate strode in, covered with small, tousle-haired ruffians. His little namesake sat on his wide shoulders, while Alexander and Raymond were glued to his legs. "And a finer troupe of gentlemen, I've never encountered."

"Says quite a lot about the state of the company you keep, Papa," Tess observed.

Uncle Nate winked cheerfully. "All right, boys, down we go." He managed to extract himself from his grandsons, who were shouting about a dead crow they'd seen on the roadside.

"Come here, my little loves." Aunt Cora swept up the boys, kissing three nearly identical heads in swift succession. "Have you been to the nursery yet? Last week, I found your mother's old storybooks. I thought we might have a look."

"Are there pages left in them?" Uncle Nate feigned surprise as the boys scampered off.

Tess's rude retort was mostly muffled by a lemon bar.

Uncle Nate laughed and joined Papa at the corner table, which was covered in enough newspapers to curdle Ethan's stomach should he catch sight of it.

Not that Belle wished to think of Ethan's stomach, or how obscenely hard it felt beneath her hungry hands when he held her against the door and plied her with one melting kiss after another, until she felt woozy and raw and thoroughly, deliciously *claimed*…

"If the boys are occupied, I suppose I should rest," Tess announced, interrupting Belle's delirium. "I know it's rude, but politesse was never my strong suit. As evidenced by the fact that I will be taking these with me." She hefted the tray of lemon bars and followed her boys out of the room.

"I wonder which of her storybooks survived," Uncle Nate contemplated. "I thought most of them were turned into maps."

"And ransom notes," Papa added.

Belle smiled, remembering their increasingly elaborate childhood games. She came by her imagination honestly.

Though she could do with a little *less* imagination right now.

"Now, Emilia." Aunt Cora finished addressing an invitation with a flourish and turned to Belle's mother. "Are you and Gavin ready for your departure to Wiltshire?"

Mama brightened. "Nearly. We're set to leave at the end of the week. Gavin has some business to finish at Westminster first."

Belle looked up in foggy surprise. It was a testament to her increasing distraction that she'd completely forgotten the assize courts were nigh.

Every year, judges were required to preside at circuit courts, and Mama had long made a habit of accompanying Papa for a few weeks in the countryside. When Belle and Lena were growing up, they'd stayed with their aunt and uncle's family, but in recent years, they divided their time between Fordham House and staying home with Mrs. Bowers. Belle had come to think of those brief weeks of increased independence as preparation for her future—helping run her mother's household, serving as her sister's companion, largely minding her own business.

But in prior years, her business didn't involve spending every day with Ethan Fletcher. She gripped her book, lest she drop it again.

"We've been over Lena's calendar." Aunt Cora reached for her diary. "I have her engagements noted, and it's my pleasure to chaperone." She turned to Belle with a warm smile. "Belle, what about you, darling? Shall we find something to do together while your parents are away, just the two of us? I could take you to the shops. Or the opera?"

"Don't bother yourself with plans for me, but thank you all the same." Belle was touched by her aunt's kind concern, even if there was less than no chance she could attend a society event like the opera. "I'm a bit busy these days."

"That's right." Uncle Nate spoke up from the table. "Cecily mentioned something about a new charity?"

Belle nodded reluctantly. If ever a day was to be rued, it was the one when she invented that blasted lie. Though...not *entirely* a lie. She stood by what she told Ethan—the penny blood *did* get boys reading. They just weren't reading anything especially virtuous.

"Belle is working with a charity to publish reading material for boys of the laboring classes," Mama explained, when it became apparent Belle wasn't going to elaborate. "We met one of her associates last evening. At dinner."

Cecily made a motion that might have been an attempt to grab Lena's hand.

"Indeed?" her cousin said, far too innocently. "How *was* your dinner?"

Papa lowered his newspaper again.

Belle paused. She imagined explaining the situation—that she blurted her engagement to Ethan with the grace of a butcher unloading a side of beef, that she let him *ravish* her in her father's study, that she watched him leave with confusion hanging heavy between them.

"Dinner was fine," she said instead.

There was a lull, and Belle felt her neck grow hot, wondering who knew what, if what they knew was better or worse than what they suspected.

"If you'll excuse me," she murmured, setting her unread book aside. "I'll be back in a moment."

She slipped from the drawing room and wandered a small distance down the corridor, willing herself to settle and maintain a measure of normalcy.

Her family's voices followed her down the passage.

"She's been out more than usual," Mama was saying, a note of caution in her tone. "Gavin is a bit uneasy about our forthcoming travels..."

"Come, Gavin." Aunt Cora's voice was firm. "Belle is older than either Emilia or I were when we were running households of our own. She can manage just fine while you're gone."

"I wouldn't worry, Sinclair," Uncle Nate added. "Belle stays clear of trouble, doesn't she? Unlike my brood."

"She likely won't even go to the courthouse without you there, Papa," Lena said softly.

Belle stiffened. This happened sometimes. She wasn't always in the same room as everyone else, which meant she occasionally stumbled upon gentle assessments from her loved ones. She considered herself through their eyes—reserved, unconventional, harboring wishes she was too trepidatious to share. They weren't entirely wrong about her...nor did they have her entirely right.

Sometimes she could be very reckless indeed.

"I should see if she's feeling all right." Her mother's voice floated from the drawing room, and Belle winced. She looked around, wondering if she could plausibly slip upstairs to see the boys. She could feign interest in their dead crow.

But Papa spoke. "I'll go, Emilia."

Belle closed her eyes.

She should have known.

PAPA FOUND her in front of Aunt Cora's rosewood hallstand. Afternoon light slanted through the windows, illuminating threads of gray in his dark hair. If it hadn't been combed so neatly, it would be as wavy as hers. She self-consciously reached up to check her hairpins, again reminded she was, in many ways, a messy version of her father. They were so alike in temperament, but her reality had always been far more tangled than his.

He came to stand beside her, watching in silence as she traced the ornately carved lip of the cabinet.

"I'm thinking of using a similar furnishing in my manuscript," she finally said, by way of unprompted explanation. "I'm trying to decide if it could reasonably include a secret compartment."

"Hmm..." Papa humored her. "Maybe a catch could fit here. Though it would have to be small."

"Yes." Belle touched the carving. "That's fine. It would hide something small." She refrained from mentioning further plans for the caretaker's glass eye.

"Belle, I want to apologize," Papa started. "It wasn't fair of us to make arrangements for Lena in front of you. I hope we didn't make you uncomfortable."

"Oh no." Belle shook her head. "It isn't anything to do with that. It was just a little noisy in there. You understand."

"Yes, of course."

He hesitated.

"Belle. About last evening."

She continued following the grapevine with her finger, keeping her face very still. It was an absolute travesty, at times, that her father earned his living by having a preternatural ability to see through bluster.

But she was not unprepared. She'd watched him work for years.

She knew silence was in her favor.

"Mr. Fletcher. You're friendly with him?" Papa's voice was mild, his expression sharp.

Yesterday morning, when she broached the topic of her hasty invitation at the breakfast table, she was asked this same question and had answered with near perfect honesty—*Someone I work with on occasion. Mutual interests in publishing. A friend, of sorts.*

Now…

She weighed how best to respond. All these weeks later, she'd come to treasure having the printshop for herself. She liked being Irascible Nell, who could write whatever she liked without Belinda Sinclair having to answer for it.

Her feelings for Ethan felt like that too—only for her, hidden and safe.

"As you've heard, I'm writing something new." Belle scanned her father's face. "It matters to me. And Mr. Fletcher is instrumental to that endeavor."

He nodded thoughtfully. "I must say, it gladdens me to see you with renewed purpose. I know your writing has been a struggle, as of late…" He paused. "I'll even go so far as to say I like knowing you have new acquaintances."

This comment was perhaps the frankest evidence to date her family worried about her. If Papa was willing to see strange Americans as a relief, Belle's social circle had grown horrendously small indeed.

"You know, Belle, the hardest aspect of these last years has been watching so many avenues close to you," Papa said slowly.

"Granting you some autonomy may not have been a conventional choice, but it was calculated. Encouraging you to carve some space in the world is perhaps the only gate I can still lift for you. So in that spirit, I won't ask you to pause your new project while I'm away."

"Thank you," she said softly, but Papa raised his hand.

"However—I will remind you of expectations." He gave her a pointed look. "The fact that you have proven yourself to be a good judge of character is not an excuse to forget your own. You are to apprise Mrs. Bowers and your aunt of your comings and goings. Above all, I ask you write to me while I'm away."

"Of course," she said sincerely.

Papa studied the carvings on the hallstand. "You know, I think you might be right about this." He tapped the curved rosewood. "It's remarkable, isn't it, all the places we can hide things? Even things that seem very small at first."

"Papa…"

He sighed. "I must admit that lately, I feel a bit adrift with you, Belle."

I feel adrift too, she wanted to say. She wanted to explain she felt so out to sea, the shoreline had become unrecognizable. The landscape was so much bigger and wilder than she thought possible.

"I'm not adrift. I'm right here." She took his hand, feeling tremendously peculiar and more than a little sad. "That's the thing, Papa. I've *always* been here, haven't I? Always, the same place."

"Belle." Papa squeezed her hand. "Do you know what I most admire about you?"

"No." She looked up in surprise.

"You know your own mind." He smiled suddenly, and his face looked much younger. "Wherever you are, I've taken comfort in the fact you must want to be there."

Papa touched her cheek. "I'll tell your mother all is well, but I wouldn't tarry much longer."

She nodded, and he returned to the drawing room.

She watched his retreat, then slowly turned to regard her reflection in the beveled mirror of the hallstand. From this vantage, she indeed looked the same as she always had.

But she didn't feel the same anymore.

She tugged down her collar, just a little. The bruise of Ethan's kiss was very faint. She touched it gently, then stroked up her neck, her fingers walking the same path as his lips. He could say he was careless, but she knew the truth.

He *cared*. Her body carried the memory of the rough and welcome force of his care.

Unyielding.

Undeniable.

Wanting her.

She watched her cheeks color, assailed by an ascendant swell of hope. Resistance was futile; she'd been soaring since the day she met him, caught in the rarefied orbit of a man who vowed he would make something of them both.

If only he would allow them to make it *together*.

Ethan said the work was vital; she agreed. The work *was* vital. But something astonishing was taking root between them, and he was too stubborn, too afraid to give them a chance to nurture it.

Well.

That was bloody unfair of him, wasn't it?

She readjusted her collar, prickling with indignation at the way he insisted on knowing what was best and getting it so perfectly wrong.

Was she meant to be patient and brave enough for them both? Because Ethan might think they could ignore what passed between them, but she wasn't capable of regretting him. And she couldn't withstand the torment of watching him try.

What a disaster. Belle wanted to laugh. Or perhaps cry. Papa believed she knew her own mind, but she'd never felt so muddled.

It might be prudent for her to retreat a bit. Give them both time when they had no choice but to act as the polite business partners Ethan pretended them to be. She could use the space to collect herself, and Ethan could…well, she wasn't exactly sure *what* he would do.

She supposed he would be happy. She was going to give him exactly what he said he wanted.

They might have to work together…

But he never specified *where*.

14

———————

Sunday, 30 April 1848
Mr. Fletcher,

*Please be advised that due to obligations with my family, I will
write from home this week and should not be expected at No. 62. Rest
assured that in my absence, I will revise my pages on the Ursula DeVry
story, per your specifications, and send them to you in a timely manner.*

*As you correctly intimated, our work is vital. I do not wish to cause
a delay.*

Sincerely,
Belinda Sinclair

Sunday, 30 April 1848
Miss Sinclair,

*Thank you for apprising me of your plans, but precedent indicates
revisions go most smoothly when we consult on them. Therefore, I will
expect you at the shop this week.*

I hope your family is well.

—E.F.

Monday, 1 May 1848
Mr. Fletcher,

> *No consultation necessary.*
> *Enclosed find my proposed revisions.*
> *You will see Ursula DeVry's fate is now uncertain.*

> *—B.S.*

Monday, 1 May 1848
Miss Sinclair,

> *Your proposal is fine, but I don't feel we had sufficient opportunity to consider the implications of a dramatic shift in narrative arc.*
> *I added notes.*

> *—E. F.*

Tuesday, 2 May 1848
Mr. Fletcher,

> *Yes, I saw your notes.*
> *I feel confident the arc is sufficiently concluded. Furthermore, during our conversation outside St. Bride's, you instructed me to prolong the suffering.*
> *I always do as I'm told.*

> *—B.S.*

Tuesday, 2 May 1848
Miss Sinclair,

> *That sound you heard rattling through your father's house was my emphatic scoff; I imagine it was audible all the way from Fleet.*
> *I maintain Clementina has drawn an unsatisfactory conclusion, given the established motive and evidence.*

> *—E.F.*

Tuesday, 2 May 1848
Mr. Fletcher,

I'm surprised you are unsatisfied, given the draft arrived at the conclusion you directed.

Perhaps you are in the habit of muddling motives and evidence?

—B.S.

Tuesday, 2 May 1848
Miss Sinclair—

I will once again suggest we might benefit from comparing notes, because in my mind, the evidence was pretty damn clear.

When might you return with your pages?

I'm working faster than usual.

It seems I've found myself with excess energy, and my press has taken the brunt of it.

Patience is not my virtue.

—E. F.

Wednesday, 3 May 1848
Mr. Fletcher,

Patience might not be your virtue, but nor is wisdom.

If you would like my pages, I suggest you focus more on your work and less on interrupting mine.

You see, every time the messenger boy comes, I need to set down my pen, leave my bedroom, and go downstairs to see to whatever you have decided you need from me.

You can expect my final pages for next week's issue by tomorrow afternoon.

(Enclosed please find licorice for Sam; see he gets it, if you wouldn't mind.)

—B.S.

Wednesday, 3 May 1848
Belle—

If you think I'm going to fall behind schedule because you're avoiding me in your upstairs bedroom, I advise you rethink your plans.

And if you want me to stop interrupting you via messenger, there is a solution to that as well.

—E. F.

Wednesday, 3 May 1848
Miss S—

I received the licorice you sent. Thank you for thinking of me.

Are you coming back this week? Mr. Fletcher has been—in the words of my mother—ruing the day. (Not that I know what that entails, just that he's acting the way I imagine it would look.)

Sam Porter

Wednesday, 3 May 1848
Sam,

I'm so glad you enjoyed the sweets. I'm caught up with some things and hope to come in when I am able. I also kindly ask that you remind Mr. Fletcher he will not be behind schedule, so there is no need to concern himself with what I'm doing in my bedroom.

Miss Sinclair

Wednesday, 3 May 1848
Belle—

I suppose you think I don't see you exchanging notes with Sam Porter and ignoring me. I assume it's because you're finishing your draft, not because you're enjoying the thought of me handing over my few coins to the damn messenger boy.

You know I'm pressed.

Thursday, 4 May 1848
Dear Tobias,

*As promised, here are my final pages for next week. Please inform
Mr. Fletcher he does not need to have me approve the galley—whatever
he thinks will be fine.*

Sincerely,
B. Sinclair

Thursday, 4 May 1848
Miss Sinclair—

Thank you for sending your pages.
*Mr. Fletcher would like me to extend his gratitude and also ask if
you will deign to grace us with your presence soon? (In truth, I'm
paraphrasing quite a bit. He can be much more creative with his adjectives than either of us suspected, but I will not be committing any of
them to writing.)*

Sincerely,
T. Porter

BY FRIDAY AFTERNOON, Ethan was tense enough to snap. He felt like
a caged animal as he went out on his errands, stalking a well-worn
path—to the bank to withdraw his hard-earned money, to Howe's
office to hand it over, then back to the shop to glare at his ledger.

Reviewing the dubious state of his affairs was akin to rubbing
salt in the wound of his mediocrity. Still, he'd prefer to stew over his
accounts than over Belle's empty chair.

Empty. All week.

And all because he'd overstepped and still fallen short.

Not that he had any idea what he'd say to her if she were here.
When he thought it over, late at night, too deep in his whisky with
his hand flat on his stomach, he landed somewhere between an

apology and an appeal. *Don't give me more unless you want me to take it, sweetheart.*

"Twenty pounds in five weeks, Fletcher," Tobias said, drawing Ethan's restless focus. The pressman's tactic this week had been complete refusal to acknowledge Ethan's piss-poor temper. "Every increased run sees a higher return. Think we can clear five thousand Saturday?"

Ethan stared at the numbers. They were selling well—the longer story arcs and enhanced courtroom intrigue were working in their favor—but he wasn't convinced they could move five thousand copies this week. Unfortunately, if they didn't reach those kinds of numbers in the next fortnight, he was unlikely to make it. He'd be halfway through his repayment terms and nearly out of his store of paper. He had a real fear of the looming cost to purchase more.

"Maybe four and a half," Ethan muttered. "Not five, not yet."

"What happened to *other penny bloods do it every week*?" Sam asked as he carried a crate of assembled serials to the front office.

"Other penny bloods aren't written via messenger boy," Ethan groused, pacing over to his Columbian.

Sam would not be deterred. "Miss Sinclair's projections say—"

"It doesn't matter what her projections say," Ethan snapped. He hefted a leather inking ball and smeared ink on the prepared frame. "Projections don't matter. Reality matters. We can't clear five. We're going to be behind."

Sam shook his head. "You could stand to be a bit more optimistic, Mr. Fletcher."

"He's just out of sorts, Sam," Tobias said.

"He's not," Sam countered with a grin. "I cleaned the sorts this morning."

Ethan ignored them and slapped paper into the frisket before sending the type form juddering down the carriageway. He yanked the lever hard—*too hard*—knowing by sound and feel the impression was poor. He growled in frustration at his lack of restraint. The plate should gently kiss the frame, sealing ink to paper with a soft, sticky sigh. He reversed the crank, stared at the ruined page, and crumpled it up.

Another kiss he'd misjudged.

All week, he tried not to take Belle's absence personally as he glowered at the letters delivered by a fat-pocketed messenger boy. Her notes were written in an elegant script on heavy stationery; he imagined her writing them at a desk in her bedroom, which in his mind was directly above the study where he'd pinned her to the door as he sucked on her neck.

Then he summarily tossed her letters aside, because of course it was fucking personal. They were, inarguably, the worst partners in the world. The only thing they had to do was work together, and clearly, they *couldn't*.

Not with her wanting things she shouldn't want.

Not with him wanting to give them to her.

At that moment, the door creaked, followed by the faint jangle of the newly reinstated bell. Ethan paused as the outside came in, the warm afternoon breeze curling into the shop, making its slow way to the workroom.

A soft voice greeted Sam, a slim shadow crossed the floor.

Instantly, his heartbeat slowed, then surged, then stopped somewhere in between.

That was all it took—the faintest suggestion of her, the barest murmur of her voice—and all he could see was the intolerable longing in her face as she reached for him. All he could hear was the gorgeous fracture in her sigh as she pressed his name into his throat.

It was insane—absolutely senseless—how badly he wanted to hold her. All of his blood ran hot, and he was temporarily immobilized, unable to believe how attuned to her he'd become, unable to believe how much he *missed* her.

Tobias cleared his throat. "Fletcher?"

Ethan snapped his head around. "Did you say something?"

"Only that I'm going out to the alley to see to deliveries." Tobias shook his head. "I'll likely be at the Bull after that, if you need to come round."

Tobias went to the office, where he greeted Belle and collected Sam. Ethan's fist wrapped around the lever of the Columbian as he heard them exchange pleasantries, then the door softly thudded as the Porters departed.

He wavered, wondering if he should speak first, what he should say, if she was standing in the office, caught in the same tense confusion.

But the only sound to come was the scrape of the chair as she settled behind the desk. He heard her open her basket, arrange her things, and then—his vexation mounted—the faint scratch of her pen.

She was writing.

She was *writing*. Just as always. As if this was a normal day. As if she hadn't been gone for a week. As if he hadn't kissed her like she belonged to him.

She wasn't even going to *acknowledge* him.

Good.

An ungenerous relief ripped through him. Her nonchalance made things a hell of a lot easier. He couldn't be soft with her, but he could be irritated. He would do it *gladly*.

"How fortunate you could finally join us," he called as he strode through the workroom with aggravated intent.

"Hello, Ethan," she said cautiously.

So it was Ethan again. In spite of how good his name sounded in her mouth, he held fast to his fight.

He swung into the office. She was perched behind the desk, wearing a dusky purple dress, her tawny hair in a tidy coil at her nape. He inhaled sharply—that damn soft mint—and his fight threatened retreat.

She looked exactly right—too pretty for her own good, certainly too pretty for his. Ethan needed one of them to be good, and he was fairly certain it couldn't be him for much longer.

"Was your messenger boy busy today? You had to deliver Sam's licorice in person?"

"Absolutely not." Her eyes glinted in warning. "If you're itching for an argument, look elsewhere."

She saw right through him, as always, and the thorns in his chest wound tighter.

"Are we not going to acknowledge the fact that you haven't been here for five days?"

She slid him a neat stack of pages. "I can't imagine it set you back. I sent you a revision, as well as the next issue's pages, and here's the outline for the week after. Just the same as I would have provided if I'd been here."

"But you *weren't* here," he challenged. "You were instead running me *ragged*."

He stepped closer. She looked pale, a faint fatigue clouding her countenance. It seemed he wasn't the only one feeling ragged.

"You told me we had to work together," she explained, maddeningly patient. "I agreed. I judged it might be more productive to our business endeavor if I kept my distance."

Her eyes moved over the general state of him. "I see my decision was the right one."

He flattened his palms on the desk, and it lurched a bit. The damn thing was still wobbly; he should have fixed it properly. It must be even more noticeable to her after a week writing at home, at a real desk, likely one her mother picked out especially for her, something that overlooked the garden and didn't have a stack of rotting newspapers holding it up.

"Yet, you're here now."

She looked at his hands, then her gaze drew all the way up the length of his arms to the tight set of his jaw. In the afternoon light, her eyes were the color of whisky.

"I did wonder if it might be best for all parties if I continue to write at home and send in my pages, but I really do need to be here for revisions." She looked away. "Which means we need to find a way to be professional."

"I can be professional," he growled.

"Yes. I can see that." She nodded somberly. "You're acting like the consummate business associate at the moment, what with all your stomping about and staring at the neckline of my bodice."

His eyes snapped away from the delicate lace, how it hugged the shallow curve of her breasts. Every part of his body was suddenly on fire. And now his irritation had increased tenfold.

Because she was right.

"Go on. I'd love to hear more about your assessment of professional behavior," he grated. "I suppose disappearing for a week is on the list?"

She exhaled sharply, wincing as she reached up to knead the side of her neck.

"What's wrong?" He narrowed his eyes, suddenly cognizant of the stilted way she was holding herself.

"A headache," she muttered, rolling her right shoulder. "It will pass. Nothing to concern yourself with."

He wavered. "You shouldn't be here if you don't feel well."

"Please." She shot him an exasperated look. "You wasted half your remaining paper demanding I return."

"I need to know I can rely on you," he said flatly. "This serial is my livelihood—"

"I *know* that." She folded her arms. "Are you so obtuse you can't see that by now? Ethan, of course I know what this means to you. I would think you know what it means to me too."

He was acting like a boor, and he couldn't stop it any more easily than he could stop a seething locomotive. Her placid expression had caved to something fierce and wounded, and he was glad of it. The wall between them had turned as unsteady as the desk, and he needed her to shore up her side.

"I was simply trying to remind you this is a business," he gritted out. "This is *my* business. Not all of us have the luxury of dabbling."

"Believe me, your message is clear." Her eyes were very bright. "Fear not, you'll have what you need from me. I won't upset you by offering so much as one iota more."

He knew damn well she wasn't talking only about the work, and he felt sick with shame and longing.

"Don't…" *Christ*, he hated this. He hated it.

"I'm here, like you wanted. I'll write, like you wanted," she said softly. "But right now, I prefer to do it alone."

"Belle." His voice scraped low.

"I'm trying to compromise, Ethan, and I very much need you to let me." She finally looked away. "Perhaps you should go join Tobias."

He stared at her, entrenched in a battle he couldn't possibly win. He'd thrust their work between them, used it as an asinine defense, but the bald truth was there were no defenses to be had. Every letter in his workroom was cast-metal proof of their shared endeavors. Over the last weeks he'd strung thousands of her sentences, weaving her words until her voice was all he could hear.

Now there was a new story, hanging heavy in the silence.

If he could stretch her over the desk, unbutton her bodice, bare her smooth stomach to the sun-streaked windows, what words could he roll in ink and press between them? He could write a whole damn story on her skin, all the things he longed for, all the things he feared.

Mine.

Yours.

Ours.

But even ink wouldn't make it true.

"Fine." He heaved a sigh, raking his hand through his dark hair. "I'll go. I'll leave you to it."

In a way, it was its own kind of blessing, to finally give her something she wanted.

15

Secrets of the Old Bailey, Vol 1., No. 5
The Fallen Hero

"As this is my Confession, I suppose I should begin with how I became a woman smearing rouge on her cheeks not five minutes after smashing half of her good teacups with her husband's heirloom sextant. I was close, you see, so close to having it all.

And if it weren't for that terribly clever, tragically heroic young Samuel Porter, I would have got away with it altogether."

It was true the headaches were unpredictable, but not always. Her mother believed they stemmed from tension, an assessment confirmed by the random, angry flares of the strained muscles in her right shoulder. Conditions of Belle's own making could bring them about—too much writing, poor posture, fitful sleep.

She hadn't fared well this week, and she shouldn't have come to the shop halfway to a headache and fully ill-tempered.

And now…

She groaned, digging her fingers into her hair, kneading a spot in her scalp where pain bloomed like a rose.

Bloody hell.

She should have left as soon as Ethan stepped out. Her parents departed for the assizes yesterday, but she could have gone home to the care of Mrs. Bowers or to Fordham House and her aunt. She could have taken a spoonful of laudanum and hoped to wake with a clear head and a reasonable heart.

But now she *couldn't* leave. She'd been determined to finish her revision, and the revision was going badly, and somewhere around page five, she realized her head was in her hand, a band steadily squeezed her temples, and she was two pages past the point when she could have managed to get herself home.

She whimpered, lowering her forehead to the desk. Her pen rolled to the floor with a splatter of ink, but she couldn't be bothered to care. The wood felt cool—that was good—but the surface pressed cruelly against her brow. Imagining her skull collapsing like a sad little soufflé, she queasily turned her head, resting her cheek on the desk instead.

Better.

She drew a breath, willing herself to sit up, to gather her things. She couldn't bear the thought of Ethan finding her in this state. He was already in a beastly mood with her, and that was before she'd ordered him out of his own shop.

For the sake of her fragile feelings, she needed to leave before he returned. She couldn't absorb any more pain tonight.

Stand up…lock the shop…find a cab…

She closed her eyes.

One more moment…

A scrape, a click, a key turning in the front door.

Please be Tobias.

Her heart leaped with sickening hope at the tinny chime of the bell. She took stock of herself—her hair was loose, her cheeks streaked with tears and ink. But Tobias wouldn't judge her.

"Belle?"

Ethan's voice carried through the office. There was a series of scuffles, then the flare of a lamp. The light surprised her. She must have fallen asleep at some point, for she hadn't realized how dark it was, how many pages she'd strewn about.

"What the *devil* are you still doing here?"

"I'm sorry." Her mouth felt heavy. "I meant to finish…before you returned." She tried to swivel away from him and nearly cried out at a searing spasm in her neck.

"Hell."

"I think you will need to find a cab for me." She rubbed her forehead, desperate for counterpressure. "Please."

"Are you…" His tone had changed, the earlier challenge bleeding first to surprise, now to something different altogether. "Belle, what's wrong?"

Heavy footsteps, a long shadow, the scent of soap and ink.

"Are you hurt? Did something happen?"

"My head…"

She thought he might dismiss her, but when she managed to look up, Ethan's face was drawn. He sank to his haunches, kneeling beside her. She closed her eyes against the scald of the low light.

A tug on her bicep, gentle but insistent. "*Shh.* Come here, sweetheart."

She weakly protested into her own forearm as he pulled her chair away from the desk. His arm came around her, gathering her against him, and then she was on the floor, in his lap, and he was so warm, and she hadn't even known she was cold.

"My God, you're limp as a rag."

He lifted his hand to her brow, sweeping away the mess of tangled hair. Somehow or another, she'd loosened the pins, but the pain wasn't in her scalp. Her right shoulder burned, and she reached blindly behind her, digging into the taut stretch of muscle along her neck. She moaned faintly, trying to find the deep-seated knot of tension.

"Is that where it hurts?"

"Yes," she half whimpered.

And then—*oh mercy*—his hand was there too, stroking gently along her temple, down behind the curve of her ear, all the way to the sweat-damp hair at her nape. She pitched forward, curling into an ecstatic swell of relief as his thumb pressed hard at the base of her skull. Her forehead hit his shoulder, nestling instinctively into the broad, solid shape of him, and she drew her knees into his lap.

"*Shh.*"

His thumb worked in widening circles, and she twisted her fingers into his shirtsleeves.

"*Shh.* There we are…"

"You're angry with me," she weakly tried to remind him. "I told you to leave."

"Furious." But his voice was soft against her brow. "You're wildly inconvenient, Belle Sinclair."

"I'm sorry," she murmured.

"Don't you dare apologize," he said grimly. "Not when it's my turn."

The center of pain moved with each press of his thumb. She closed her eyes, imagining the force of his hand blunting the ache, smoothing it away until it was small, smaller, smallest.

"I am though," he whispered. "I'm sorry. I know you aren't dabbling, Belle. I know how hard you work, how much you care. You pushed yourself tonight—for weeks now—because of me. I'm so sorry I dragged you into my mess."

She mumbled into his shoulder.

"What's that?" he asked, ducking closer.

"I said you didn't drag me." She swallowed thickly. "I leaped."

His laugh rolled across her cheek. He found a spot that markedly dissipated the pain, kneading deep, relieving strokes. Her sigh was nearly carnal, so hungry was she for the gradual slack of tension, the way it funneled to her shoulder before ricocheting through her skull.

"God." She buried her pallid cheek in his neck. "Don't stop. Don't ever do anything that's not this."

His arm tightened around her waist and halted her restless shifting.

"I know you're in a world of hurt," he rumbled in her ear. "But I need you to be fractionally less vocal about it."

Her pitiful laugh was muffled by his shirt. The fabric was soft and thin, a frugal mask for the warmth of his skin and the springy mat of hair blanketing his chest beneath her cheek. She nuzzled into the hard wall of soft linen, and her eyelids grew heavy, lulled by his firm caress.

"Breathe...that's it..." His hand moved to the tight muscles between her shoulder blades. As he descended, the immediacy of his fingers was blunted by the thick cotton of her corset. "Is this bothering you?"

"A little," she admitted, rolling her forehead against his collarbone. "It doesn't usually, but..."

He found the buttons on her bodice and hesitated.

"It's all right," she murmured. "You can loosen it."

He slipped free the fastenings until her bodice gaped. A swift series of tugs, his palm beneath the busk of her corset, lifting it free, leaving her only in a chemise.

"Oh God..." She exhaled shakily. Her corset wasn't usually painful, but right now, everything was painful, every measure of relief more profound.

"There," he murmured. "That's better, isn't it?"

His hand moved easily now, pushing deeply on either side of her spine. Up and down, steady and soothing, and like everything else he did, exactly right for her.

"You'll put me to sleep."

"That's fine." His free hand drew lazy circles on her arm. "You can sleep a little. I can't send you home in this state—you'd topple over in the street."

"Or retch all over a cab," she admitted. "It will pass soon, I think. Then I can take my medicine."

"All right," he reassured her. "We'll take care of it in a bit."

She hummed a soft assent, already drifting.

"Belle." His voice was warm at her temple.

She loved his voice. She loved that nobody else she knew spoke the way he did.

"Mmm?"

His lips brushed her ear. "I missed you."

She tried to look at him, but her head was heavy on his shoulder.

"I hated you being away. I should have told you sooner, but I'm telling you now. You, sitting in that wobbly chair at the damn wobbly desk—it's the steadiest I've felt in my life."

She exhaled a soft, sad laugh. "Me in the wobbly chair—"

"You *anywhere*." His nose moved against her temple. "Anywhere, Belle. It's not our work. Our *work* is not what's vital. I made an excuse. I let my guilt take the reins, because I'm so goddamn unprepared for this."

The wound in his voice pierced her mounting fatigue. She took a deep breath, bringing the scent of him inside her.

"You shouldn't feel guilty for wanting something good, Ethan," she murmured. "I want something good too."

He was quiet for a long time. She finally lifted her head, and her heart fractured at the raw yearning on his face.

"Wanting is not the same as having." His green eyes burned in supplication. "At least not in my experience."

"It could be." She dropped her forehead back to the warmth of his shoulder, his vulnerability beckoning hers. "For once, it could be. We could want each other. We could *have* each other."

She felt close to tears, and she wasn't certain why. Her pain was easing, but she wanted him to keep holding her.

"Now's not the time, Belle," he said quietly. "You need rest. Can you sleep for me?"

His arm tightened around her, bracketing her securely against him, and she was flooded with a heavy sense of relief.

"What...about you?"

She found his hand, and he braided their fingers together.

"I'm fine, sweetheart."

He always called her that.

But this time, it sounded different.

BELLE AWOKE SOMETIME BEFORE MORNING. A cool gray shrouded the shop, casting everything in shadow. She blinked, woolly-eyed and warm.

She was still on the floor, still sideways in Ethan's lap, her head burrowed between his shoulder and his neck. In the night, he must have eased them back so he could lean against the wall, twining them in an easy embrace.

From her vantage, nested within his arms, she felt her headache had lifted. A dull twinge radiated from the back of her head, the pain no more than a shallow discomfort.

She drew a long inhale, her body singing with relief, and his breathing changed with hers.

Ethan was awake.

His thumb moved very slowly along the small of her back.

She was afraid to move; she was afraid not to move.

In her half-roused state, it all floated back to her, golden and hopeful, and so like a dream, it took her a moment to realize it hadn't been.

Last night, a new bridge had formed between them, crafted of soft whispers and careful hands—and so long as it wasn't fully daylight, Belle sensed they needn't look ahead or below or side to side.

They only needed to cross it.

She shifted, just a bit, feeling the solidness of his lap, the hard expanse of his chest.

And then, in the dusky margins of the breaking day, she pressed her lips to the warm skin of his open collar and kissed his neck.

His thumb stilled on her lower back, and she did it again. Soft, insistent kisses along his neck, the hair dusting his collarbone.

Gently seeking his jaw, the brush of his beard on her face. She opened her mouth, trailed back down, and she felt all her rising tension slacken and go into him, for he was now holding her tight as a vise, his body reacting to her, his breath growing shallow.

"Belle." His voice was deep and gravelly, and it was doing delicious things to her. "Your head—"

"My head is fine." She nuzzled his throat. "My head is clear."

His groan vibrated against her lips. He raised his hand to her hair, smoothing the tousled curls.

"I've been trying to be careful with you," he rasped. "I'm *barely* hanging on. Do you understand why this shouldn't happen? There's not a single promise I can make to you. My future is entirely uncertain—"

"I've lived with uncertainty for years," she whispered. "Uncertain is hardly the worst thing a future can be."

He swore, very soft. His gaze was soft too.

"I promise, Ethan." She pressed her cheek to his palm, willing him to climb over the blasted wall and come to her. "I don't need anything, except for you to want this too."

All the things he told her of his life. *A legacy of leavings.*

Those leavings brought him here, to *her*—a woman who did, in fact, know her own mind.

"Tell me to stop," she murmured, opening his collar wider. She pressed an openmouthed kiss to the hollow of his throat. "I'll stop. I'll do whatever you tell me to."

Another kiss. Another. Everywhere but his mouth.

His body was taut all around her, one hand still tangled in her hair, and she numbly realized her breath was catching, her lashes were wet.

She felt dreamy and brazen and so deeply sad. This was it. This was the farthest she could go without him.

"You never lie to me, Ethan." She touched his bottom lip. "If you tell me you don't want me, I'll believe you. If you tell me I'm alone in these feelings, I'll believe you—"

"Stop." His voice grated in her ear. "*Stop*."

She froze instantly, her fingers still twisted in his collar.

His hands fell to her waist, and with a strong pull he guided her to straddle him.

"Belle." He put his lips right against hers, slowly pressing each word upon her. "Sweetheart. You were *never* alone."

He prolonged the last kiss, and at the sound of her pleasured sigh, the last vestige of his sleep state crumbled away. In an instant, her mouth was opening, his tongue stroking hers, exactly like she wanted. She closed her eyes against the burn of tears, losing herself to him, unable to believe it was happening again, unable to believe how good it was.

He hummed low in his throat and planted his palms on either side of her face, breathing as hard as she was.

"It stops now, Belle," he muttered. "This torment, we're ending it."

"Yes." She gripped his wrists.

"I mean it." His voice was husky with untold emotion. "I'm done—I'm *finished* withholding from you. I'm not a saint, and there is no benediction in this world or the next worth allowing you to think I don't see you, to think I don't *want* you."

He pressed his forehead to hers. "If your eyes are open, so are mine."

He kissed her again, *again*. She accepted the onslaught, she relished it, digging her fingers into his shoulders, helping him want her.

An ache was building between her thighs, and he found it, lifting his hips until she felt a muted rising beneath her skirts. He was growing hard for her, she was affecting him. And then he was rocking her slowly against that length.

Hard and soft, the tender, searing press of his kiss, the dizzying friction of his arousal working against hers.

His hand slipped into her bodice, still gaping where he loosened it last night. He dragged his knuckles against her chemise, drawing beneath the small, plump curve of her breast. She gasped, willing his fingers to move higher, to find the sensitive bud of her nipple.

"Ethan…"

"I've wanted to touch you for so long." He closed his eyes, hissing a moan that sent her heartbeat pulsing between her legs. "So long. My God."

He tugged her bodice down and pressed his face to the soft linen covering her breasts. She whimpered and arched her back, desperate for relief.

"Yes," she urged him. "*Please.*"

"Belle…wait." He groaned, seeming to master himself. "Wait."

"What is it?" She was hot, everywhere—but now a little cold too. *No more waiting. Please, no more waiting.*

"I don't know what you know of this. When you were engaged…" He looked over her, his gaze dark and glassy. "Have you been with a man?"

She froze, suddenly fearful of the real cost of her choices. She hadn't slept with Duncan, but she'd let him go further than she should have.

And now she was ruined; everyone said so. Ethan might think so too.

It was unbearable to think he might not accept what she so badly wanted to give him.

"No." Her eyes glittered. "I haven't, but Ethan…I'm not entirely innocent. I would understand if you—"

"I don't give a damn who's had you before," he breathed. "I'm having you now. But I'll take you easy this time. Is that all right?"

"This time," she repeated, feeling faint.

He smiled his slow, *slow* smile, the one that made her follow him from the garden and hand over her plans, her pages, her heart.

"The thing about letting a wanting man have…" He stole another drugging kiss. "He doesn't easily reverse course."

He finally brought his hand to her breast. He unhurriedly circled her nipple through her chemise, drawing a tight, eager pucker to his fingertip. The featherlight touch seemed to reach every part of her. A moan caught in her throat, a ragged sound she hardly recognized.

"Lay back," he murmured. He reached for his discarded coat, balling it beneath her head. "Shh…there. Are you certain your head is all right?"

"Yes." She pulled him down by the loose ends of his tie. "That's not where I'm aching."

"Poor thing." He stretched above her, bracing himself on one arm as his thumb stroked a smile to her lips. "You're having a hell of a time, aren't you?"

"Terrible." She gasped as his hand slid beneath her petticoats.

He played with the hem of her drawers, tracing the crease of her hip through the flimsy layer, stroking her thatch of curls, and then— *oh God*—he firmly pressed one long finger along the damp split seam. Her eyes fluttered closed with the thick, relieving pressure.

"Mmm…" She squirmed, he swore. Perspiration beaded between her breasts. She was impatient and needy, knowing he would be good to her, knowing it was coming.

Oh, please, please, please…

"Lift your skirts," he muttered, helping her raise her bottom. She tried to gather the heavy swaths of fabric for him, then his thigh was separating hers. In one fluid motion he dropped his head and raised his knee.

And there was nothing but the wet tug of his mouth on her cotton-clad nipple, nothing but the hard line of his thigh pressing her aching sex.

Belle cried out; she'd never felt so thoroughly mastered. She rocked helplessly against him, her drawers sticking, the pressure divine, and it wasn't until he was answering her that she realized she'd been asking.

"Shh, shh…I'm going to give you more." His eyes were hooded. "I'd say nothing could be as lovely as this, but I've yet to see you come apart."

In a fog, she looked down, treated to the obscene view of him bent over her straining breasts. Her skirts were twisted around her waist, and his dark trousers looked so good between her splayed thighs, it set her pulsing anew.

She rose to her elbows, pulling the ties of her now-sheer chemise. Ethan groaned, yanking the useless garment down her stomach. He cupped her breasts and again drew his tongue over the stiff peaks, nudging her nipples tighter and pinker until her back arched in a responsive curve.

His beard tickled; his teeth scraped. A guttural, bitten-off sound hit her ears.

If he touched her between her legs, if he parted the slit in her drawers and traced her wet cleft with his fingertip, she would unravel. She'd touched herself enough to know; she thought of him as she did it.

But this—*this* was frightening, how fast, how forceful, how wild, the strength of her feeling.

"I'm—so—close," she panted, putting her thumb to his bottom lip.

"I know." Ethan stroked her hair away from her face. "I don't mean to tease, but you have no idea what a luxury it is to *savor*."

And then—yes, *yes*, he was loosening her drawers, he was tugging them down and shifting her, baring her as much as he could with half of her dress still between them.

He put his hand around her knee, a slow squeeze up her thigh, his palm curving so close to where he'd turned her aching and slick.

"Please…please…" She lifted her hips, faintly hysterical. "*Please*, Ethan—I'm begging you…"

His hand moved higher, pressing her wider, and he was dropping between her spread knees, the span of his shoulders forcing her wider still. Everything was laid open. She was sore for him—*oh God, yes*—he was right, it was its own terrible luxury, to want and want and want again.

He kissed her thigh, his lips warm and tugging, his beard keeping her on the wrong side of tender.

"Never beg me," he murmured. "You'll have everything you want. Tell me you know that…that I can give it to you."

She mumbled something crumbling, incoherent.

"Belle." There was no reprieve. "Tell me you know."

"I know." She wove her fingers tightly through his hair. "Ethan, I know."

He looked up at her—then, finally, *yes*—he laid his tongue to her heated flesh. Her breath caught at the first teasing lash, then he was nuzzling her, finding a firm, melting pressure that had her digging her heels between his shoulder blades.

He groaned, the sound moving against her. He yanked her close, desperation in the bruising force of his fingerprints, as if he were as ransacked as she was. His tongue worked relentlessly—now stroking, now circling—and Belle half sobbed, her hands over her face.

"Are you with me?" He dragged his cheek up and down her thigh. "If you don't care for this, I can use my hand—"

"Your mouth," she managed.

He grunted his agreement as he cradled her bottom. The air burned around her. He was lifting her hips to his mouth, her back sliding against the floor. She wondered what she must look like right now—her breasts bared, her thighs spread, her hair everywhere, her skirts everywhere, and Ethan's head between her legs. She nearly pleaded again, but instead, she bit her fist, understanding he wanted to provide…

But oh God—*oh God*—

"That's it," he praised, building bliss beneath his tongue. His fingers flexed into her bottom, helping her rock against his face. "Take what you need."

"Yes," she moaned. Her nipples tightened, a tingle ignited at the base of her spine. He shifted, and then—*oh*, unspeakable pleasure— his tongue entered her, moving with small strokes.

She hazily imagined it was his finger, his cock, all the ways she wanted him to take her, a series of hot and half-formed fantasies, born entirely of the ache between her legs and the steady lave of his tongue.

"I need…" Her words lifted on a gasp, floating between them. "You."

He moaned, lush and low, then his finger was inside her. He pushed hard, filling her in a stretch so exquisite, it had her crying out—his tongue pressed flat, and the white-hot glow finally consumed her, taking her apart in a long, hard rush. Ethan was ruthless, pushing her further, extending the wave until her throat hurt, her thighs hurt, and her legs fell closed around his head.

"So good," he murmured, sagging back and pulling her to him. "So fucking gorgeous. My God. Belle, sweetheart."

He kissed her mouth, her temple, her wrists. His shirt was loose, and she buried her forehead in the damp hair of his chest, both of them breathing heavily. She could still feel him, how hard he was beneath her, but Ethan seemed completely at ease. He rubbed his palm up and down her spine.

It was ridiculous he thought he couldn't care for her, that he had nothing to offer her.

But before she could tell him, there was a shout, followed by a pummeling fist at the door.

"Fletcher! Mr. Fletcher!" The voice belonged to a young man, and then, just as suddenly, another voice joined.

She froze, Ethan's arms still tight around her.

"Is he in yet?"

"I don't know."

Slowly, Belle lifted her head. They were behind the desk, at the back of the office, and thankfully, the windows were grimy enough to provide cover.

Bloody hell.

"We're out already at Roberts's."

"Nelson's as well. He sent me straight away for more. Fletcher?"

Nelson, Roberts.

Numbly, she pieced it together.

Newsagents.

Another voice, another.

"Have you seen Fletcher?"

"Not yet, but Roberts wants at least a hundred more, if he has stock."

"Ethan." Belle scanned his face, her heart crashing in her chest. It was Saturday. *Publication* day. "What's happening?"

His hand stilled in her hair, his beautiful green eyes widening in something like shock.

"I don't know." His voice was scratchy. "But it sounds a hell of a lot like a sold-out serial."

16

Accounting Ledger of E. Fletcher
Week of 6 May 1848
Secrets of the Old Bailey Vol. 1, No. 5
Earnings less expenditures—£15

Reprint 9 May 1848
Earnings less expenditures—£4 10s

Remaining debt owed—£65

~

"DESCRIBE CLEMENTINA BLOOM." Victor Marks, aspiring illustrator of penny bloods, stared at Belle with rapt attention. "I want to capture her *essence*."

Ethan stood next to Belle's chair, his arms crossed over his chest. There was no chair for him, as Victor Marks was sitting in Ethan's chair with a sketchbook on his lap. He didn't mind standing at Belle's shoulder; not only did it give him considerable height over the long-haired artist, it gave him an advantageous view of her neckline.

Ethan was trying not to stare—he was, in fact, a professional—but it required effort.

The trouble was, he could claim blissful ignorance no longer. He now knew precisely what awaited him beneath the floral muslin of her bodice. How sensitive. How soft. How pink her nipples turned when he—

"What does our heroine look like? On the outside, on the *inside.*" Marks leaned forward, and Ethan nearly put a hand on Belle's shoulder to stop her doing likewise.

But of course he couldn't touch her right now.

He had to *wait.*

He was always waiting. Over the last few days, despite the frenzy of the serial, Ethan felt he was in some sort of purgatory—waiting for Belle to arrive early at the shop, waiting for the others to step out. Waiting to get his hands on her whenever he could, however he could.

Waiting, most of all, for an elusive stretch of privacy when he could finally, *finally* make love to her, with no threat of workmen or newsboys or interruption from sundown to sunup.

"Clementina is quiet." Belle pondered. "She's discreet. She prefers to slip in and out, never stand out."

"Marvelous," Victor Marks murmured. "An *enigma.*"

The artist's charcoal was flying, and Belle eagerly craned her neck. Ethan frowned. He'd set up this meeting to appease her, but he wasn't keen to hire an illustrator. He'd already had to grasp the nettle and bring on a new compositor this week. At this moment, George Newburn, a wiry, straw-haired fellow possessed of preternatural concentration, was setting type in the workroom. Ethan didn't welcome paying two additional salaries, but Belle was right. Illustrations would keep *Secrets* relevant, and they couldn't lose momentum now.

He couldn't believe he was doubling down on this penny blood, but it had somehow become what they'd scarcely dared to dream.

A *success.*

Saturday's print run had caused absolute mayhem—Ethan sent

Belle scrambling upstairs with her corset in her hands while he tucked in his shirt and bellowed to the newsboys to give a man a minute. Once he looked plausibly presentable, he quickly ascertained at least half a dozen stalls were already sold out of *Secrets of the Old Bailey*. When Belle reappeared with her dress buttoned and her hair tidy, she sat at the desk like the queen of her kingdom, beaming and taking slips from cheeky newsboys, never letting on that she herself was the mysterious Irascible Nell.

By the time the Porters arrived, Belle's tallies made clear they would benefit from a midweek reprint, and for the first time since he arrived in London, Ethan had standing orders for coming issues.

Somehow, someway, they were pulling the damn thing off.

Now Ethan cleared his throat and widened his stance to remind Victor Marks of his role as the publisher of this operation, a man far too busy to entertain a bohemian artist's failing attempts to seduce Belle Sinclair.

He had more important things to do.

Namely, to successfully seduce Belle Sinclair himself.

Surely, she sensed his impatience. She *must*, for she had started to trace the side of her neck. Up, down, over her collarbone. Her thumb slid over a loose lock of hair, and she looked up at him, devilishly wide-eyed.

God help him.

"What do *you* think she looks like, Mr. Fletcher?" Belle inquired, a faint tease edging her smile. "On the outside, on the *inside*."

God help *her*.

Before Ethan could wrangle a response, Newburn, his new and alarmingly efficient typesetter, appeared in the doorway with a satchel over his shoulder. "Fletcher? I've finished the next two frames. I'm taking my meal."

Ethan eyed the clock. Newburn was stepping out; the Porters had gone to the type foundry and weren't due back until early afternoon.

Finally—a damn window.

He just needed to get Michelangelo out of here.

"It doesn't matter what Clementina Bloom looks like," he said brusquely. "Make her look however you like. Make her a silhouette. Show her from behind. Use any face at all—"

"Just a thought, Mr. Fletcher." Marks eyed Belle. "If she's modeled after Miss Sinclair, for instance..."

Belle blushed prettily, and Ethan wondered if he could reasonably snap the damn charcoal in two.

Marks was now sketching with intent. "I don't know if anyone has ever told you, Miss Sinclair, you're a very beautiful woman."

"She's been told," Ethan rumbled, placing his hands on the back of her chair. "She's aware."

She half turned, meeting his eye, a flush gathering in her cheeks. He'd told her she was beautiful just last evening, after Sam and Tobias had packed up for the day and he lifted her to the desk and teased his thumbs beneath the tops of her stockings.

Ethan shifted, glancing significantly at the artist.

"Ah, I think that's all for today, Mr. Marks," Belle said, licking her bottom lip. "You may leave your sample for us. We'll use it while making our final decision."

"*If* we make a decision," Ethan clarified. "We have a number of deliberations as the serial expands."

"Of course," Belle said pertly. "It would be irresponsible if we didn't leave room for growth."

Her eyes flicked over Ethan, and he nearly thickened on the spot.

"And, Marks..." He hastily marshaled his wayward thoughts. "Regarding Miss Sinclair's involvement. Nobody outside the shop knows she's the author of *Secrets*. I expect you to keep it that way."

Belle nodded, silently confirming her wishes.

"Of course." Marks looked at her appreciatively. "*Fascinating*. An enigma, indeed."

"Oh!" Belle's exclamation cut off Ethan's growl. "I nearly forgot. We also need our illustrator to assist a bit with assembly. Folding and stacking the papers and what have you. It's become an all-hands situation."

"Certainly." Marks tilted his head. "My hands are at your disposal—"

"Right." Ethan circled the desk and yanked back Marks's chair. "Here you are—all your papers, don't leave anything behind. Your pencil too. And your payment for today."

A moment later, Ethan had all but shoved the artist and his overeager charcoal out the door. Before the shingle stopped swinging, he was hauling Belle to the storeroom and pressing her against the shelves.

Ten minutes. He only needed ten minutes alone with her…

"Ethan." Her smile was wide as she slid her arms around his shoulders and pushed away his coat.

"Mmm." He settled his mouth against the plush curve of her lips. Kissing her was intoxication, a drunken, languid ecstasy. He wanted to kiss her everywhere. He reached around her back, seeking the fastenings on her bodice, hungry for the sensation of her pebbled nipple on his tongue.

"You were rather rude to Mr. Marks," she breathlessly admonished him, twisting to loosen her corset.

"I'll be nice now," he muttered. "How many petticoats am I fighting today?"

"Three." She gasped as he fisted them in one hand. "But no drawers."

"You're so good to me." He pulled her into another long kiss, drawing his palm up her thigh.

"Did you find…" She blushed. "Ah. You know…"

He knew. "No, I have not managed to procure a condom in the last two hours." His fingers moved between her legs, playing in her soft, damp curls. "I will."

"There are other ways to prevent a child," she said weakly, spreading her legs wider. "My mother instructed me on measures, when we were preparing for my wedding. I could use a sponge. I have one, actually—she told me how to use it, said it might be more comfortable than other…ah, strategies…"

"Do you have it with you?" He couldn't believe he was considering bedding her while George Newburn was at a tavern.

"No." She moaned as his finger lightly circled her. "I don't. You could withdraw…"

"I don't want you worrying about that." He gently sucked her bottom lip. "Soon, sweetheart. I promise."

"I just…I wish you would make love to me."

He saw black. "Christ, Belle. You can't say things like that."

"Why can't I?" She unknotted his tie, opening the collar of his shirt. She practically purred as she stroked the hair on his chest. "I think about it all the time. I imagine it, you moving inside me."

She was so damn earnest; she was making him insane, *insane…*

He had her petticoats over one arm, making room for his other hand to cease teasing. He pushed one finger inside her, stretching her a little, and she cried out.

"Go on, then." He pressed his forehead to hers, stroking deeper. "Imagine it."

Imagine it. He imagined it too.

He imagined he was a different man, a man with prospects, a man who could give her the expansive life she deserved, instead of close, stolen moments.

But *God,* what glorious theft.

"Harder," she pleaded. He drank in the helpless demand on her face and ground the heel of his hand into her quim, adding a second broad finger to her soaked channel.

"Yes…" She sighed, her head sinking back onto a shelf. "Yes."

He leaned into her, unable to stop from rocking his rampant arousal against her. The many layers of broadcloth and wool and cotton between them were sobering torture. He was so hard, even the faintest brush of her body against his trousers was enough. He spread his legs to either side of her, until he could drag his covered length back and forth along her stomach. He would spend if he did this much longer. He wanted to. It would feel so good, to release against her, with her mouth open under his, her desire all over his hand.

He closed his eyes, sucking her damp neck, and let himself pretend for one sweet minute he was lifting her, settling her on his cock, all her wet heat around him. She would take him like a dream, of this he was certain. He rocked into her one more selfish, delirious minute, then groaned, pulling his hips away, even as his fingers thrust harder.

Her face was drowsy with pleasure, but she noticed his shift.

"Ethan," she murmured. "Open your trousers. I...I can help you."

Stop her. He would have to pull his hands from her body to do so. Her eyes were glazed and determined as she unfastened his trousers, freeing the jutting weight of his arousal.

His tip was wet and he wanted her thumb on it and he *couldn't* make her stop.

"If you tell me what to do..."

She followed the rigid line of his cock with one rounded fingernail. He inhaled through his teeth, his need so sharp, anything would blunt it.

"I want to touch you, Ethan."

"Hell."

The relief of her slender fingers sliding around his heated flesh was indescribable. He'd been taking himself in hand every night, half-mad with memories of her spread legs, of how sweetly she asked for him...but *this*—her skin, so soft...

Hesitation was beyond him.

"Put your hand to my mouth," he muttered, still working her with his fingers. She moaned, and he licked her palm, wetting it.

"Make a fist," he managed, closing his eyes against the sound of her pleased hum.

"Ethan?"

"Yes...good, Belle, that's good. Move slow."

She began to stroke him, following his hoarse directions. He felt her quiver against his hand, and blood rushed to his cock.

"You like it slow." She gasped at his ministrations, which were anything but.

"You like it fast." He half laughed, groaning at how good she felt wrapped around him.

He kissed her forehead, and she tilted her face, wanting his mouth.

He gave it to her.

They moved together, a fierce tangle of lips and hands. The sensation gradually changed, more than lust, more than desire. Making love, in its own way.

Giving. Taking. Selfless, helpless, pleasure-seeking.

He couldn't keep her; he couldn't ask her for that.

But maybe just a bit more, a bit longer.

He could give her this.

"Are you going to come, sweetheart?"

"Are you?" She moved her fist faster, chasing the rock of his hips.

"Yes." He nudged her head back, brushing his lips over hers. "I'll come for you."

"I will too." She closed her eyes, laughing on a moan.

If Charles Howe were to walk in and promise to forgive every cent of the debt so long as Ethan stepped away from her, he could not, with any certainty, say he would do it.

ON SATURDAY, Belle woke in a quiet house. She slipped her wrapper over her night rail and wandered down the sunny, silent corridor with nary a soul in sight. Lena had decided to spend weekends at Fordham House, and Harriet and Mrs. Bowers were at the market.

She had the place to herself.

She made a cup of tea and took it to the small kitchen garden. She curled up on the little iron bench and tucked her bare feet beneath her, watching an enterprising bumblebee drift through the lavender. Her hair was braided over her shoulder, the end of her plait tickling her wrist as she raised the teacup and blew at the steam.

When she was a girl, Belle had wanted a little garden just like this, should she ever find herself mistress of her own home. She used to imagine herself sitting in the morning sun, writing, while her husband puttered inside, shaving and dressing and paying a messenger for his morning paper. She would cut a posy of flowers for the breakfast table; she would pour her husband's tea and fasten his cuffs; she would send him on his way and once again pick up her pen. She'd imagined her life to fit around his.

That idle daydream changed many times over the years, shifting in ways painful and unexpected until it brought her back to where she'd started—her parents' house with the provisions they'd made for her.

And now the daydream was transforming again.

She sipped her tea, considering.

The residence above the printshop had no garden, but she would settle for a window seat overlooking Fleet. She could buy flowers from a stall in Covent Garden, but she suspected Ethan rose earlier than she did, so it wouldn't be much of a surprise. He wouldn't need to shave, only trim his beard, and he drank coffee, not tea. The paper he read would be the paper he published, though she would stock two more to make sure he had something to complain about. After he finished grousing, he would pull her into his lap and lift her plait and kiss her neck while she read him her latest chapter. And the two halves of their lives would fit right next to each other.

I cannot offer you anything. She knew he believed this. She understood when he balanced his accounts, he weighed his shortcomings highest of all. She didn't mind. Her scales were tipped quite differently. They were already fixed with hope.

She slipped today's issue of *Secrets* from the pocket of her wrapper, the first copy with Victor Marks's etching. Her nom de plume winked from the title page, her scrambled name above the drawing of a loose-haired young woman tucked into the shadows of a morgue.

Thousands of copies of this installment were at bookstalls around the city today. The quantity thrilled but so did it reassure. If those copies moved, it would be another twenty pounds sterling. More than half of Ethan's debt would be repaid, with higher returns every week.

It was *working*. They would keep making it work. She envisioned the sum evaporating, turning thinner and smaller until she could blow it away as easily as the steam from her tea.

She went inside and readied for the day, dressing and packing her basket. She penned a letter to post to her father, then jotted a note to inform Mrs. Bowers she was stepping out this morning.

Having accounted for her physical whereabouts, she set off for the shop, her mind slipping to her latest draft. She had a responsibility now to maintain their readership. Ethan was right— expanding story arcs over multiple issues was a canny business decision. But it meant each case needed *more*. More intrigue, more scandal, more—

"Excuse me, Mrs. Fletcher?"

Belle drew up short. A stout young man was looking at her expectantly. It took her a moment to place his bright red jacket—the postman who walked up and down Fleet a dozen times a day.

"Oh. I'm not..." Her voice was dry; she hadn't yet spoken aloud today. She cleared her throat. "May I help you?"

"I have Mr. Fletcher's mail here," the letter carrier said, digging in his sack for a tidy bundle. "I was heading to the printshop, but I saw you and figured I'd ask if you know of any vendors along this way that might have a copy of *Secrets of the Old Bailey*?"

"Yes." She frowned. "There should be a few places quite close. Mr. Roberts carries it, and two of the bookstalls on the Strand as well."

The postman sighed. "I've been to all three with no luck."

"No luck?" Her pulse quickened. "They haven't *any* copies?"

"All gone already," the young man grimaced. "I was itching to know what happened to that countess's chaperone."

"Contessa," she corrected vaguely. "She married a lesser Italian count."

"Right." The postman handed over Ethan's mail. "Between us, I wouldn't know the difference."

Belle badly wanted to explain the geographical significance of Ursula DeVry's malevolent husband but refrained from revealing herself as the author. She instead accepted Ethan's mail, promising she would take it to the shop.

"Oh," she added as the young man turned away. "Wait—I have one copy of the issue." She dug through her basket. "Here you are. I would perhaps just take note of Count Fulco. His proximity to the Adriatic Coast is rather important."

"Thank you kindly, Mrs. Fletcher." The postman waved genially and continued on his way.

"It's Miss Sinclair," she explained to his retreating back. She didn't say it very loudly.

She continued on, sorting through the mail as she walked. Invoices, an updated promissory note from Mr. Howe, a letter from…

She halted, surprised by the number and variety of stamps.

New York City.

Her finger slid over the fat envelope. She flipped it over, but the wax seal was unadorned. Only a name and address across the top— *The Daily Sun, Park Row, New York City.*

A newspaper.

"Miss Sinclair!"

Belle looked up to see Sam rushing toward her from the opposite end of Fleet, waving his arm above the crowd. She stacked the envelope with the other letters and put the lot in her basket.

"Sam, where have you been?"

"Checking in at the bookstalls." He grinned. "*Gone.* Two weeks in a row. Paulie is right sore he didn't order more."

"The postman said the same," Belle said, hurrying alongside Sam. "He couldn't find any. I gave him my own copy."

They rounded the corner, and there was Ethan, standing outside No. 62.

Waiting for her.

"Ethan," she called, excitement blooming as she pushed down the street. "The serial, it's—"

"Sold out!" His grin flashed easy and bright, and he raised his arms wide. "*Again*. Not a fluke, Belle. We're the genuine article."

"It must be the heirloom sextant." She laughed, covering her mouth with her hands. "The bloodied compass, pointing directly to the portrait of the murderer." She waved away her own jest. "I'm only teasing. It was the illustration, of course, just as I knew it would be."

"Damn right, it was the bloodied compass." He strode up to her, dropping his palms to her arms. "Come here, you morbid little genius."

"Ethan! You *can't*..." She gasped, incredulous as he tugged her closer. "People will see. I'm standing in the middle of the street—"

"Lucky for the street."

His arms came around her, strong, encircling, lifting her clear off the ground. He whooped, spinning her in circles. His hat fell off, toppling into a puddle, and the harried passersby threw them an assortment of affronted looks. Belle only laughed harder, holding on to her bonnet with one hand.

Joy.

Oh, this was never meant to be hers, such unfettered, unbothered acceptance. She was suddenly greedy for it, for *more*, to become more and more herself, for Ethan to keep embracing the enormity of exactly who she was.

"We need to celebrate," Ethan announced, setting her down and winking at Sam. "Tonight. Sam, spread the word—I'm buying everyone a drink when we finish today." He turned to Belle as Sam cheered and swung into the shop. "Can you join us? Where is your sister staying tonight?"

"Lena is at my aunt's." She bit her lip. "I can tell Mrs. Bowers I'll stay there too. She's supposed to visit her daughter anyway. I won't have any trouble being neither place I ought to be."

Ethan slowly cocked his eyebrow, and her stomach spun out. "Aren't you a wicked thing."

"Not yet." She meant to play coy, but fervent anticipation tore through her.

"Pretty damn close," he rumbled, his gaze hot with intent.

Her heart pounded as Ethan bent to rescue his hat from the mud. He shook it off with a grimace and surveyed the street.

"Hell. Do you suppose I need to burn this?"

I love you.

The words floated within her, as light as the dust spinning above her desk in the close air of the printshop. Invisible to the eye until a slice of swollen sunlight slanted just right, illuminating what was already there, setting hidden truth stark and sparkling.

She was in love with him.

She'd supposed, if it ever happened to her, it would be the result of some grand declaration, some poetic gesture. Surely, such a cataclysmic realization would be sweepingly romantic, heralded by a moment of shattering significance.

Surely, it wouldn't happen because of good luck and a muddy hat.

She'd been wrong.

It happened like this—*just like this.* In the middle of the morning, in the middle of the street. With a pencil behind his ear, with her story in his hands, with so much promise between them.

"Shall we?" Ethan offered her his arm, lifting the corner of his mouth, right where she wanted to put her lips.

I love you.

For years, Belle had been saving her words.

But in the end, she only needed three.

17

———

Secrets of the Old Bailey, Vol 1., No. 6
The False Chaperone

Ursula DeVry had been missing for months, but when questioned, her lady's maid maintained she was abroad, reuniting with Count Fulco, her estranged husband. She had taken Captain Howe as her chaperone.

Of course, this assertion was called into question when the real Captain Howe was brought into the courtroom, with no Contessa in sight.

"I SHOULD HAVE ASKED to be a villain after all," Sam crowed in a corner of the workroom, where Ethan spied him holding court over a trio of newsboys. "A recurring character, if you see my meaning."

"Your mother appreciates that you made a one-time appearance," Tobias said dryly as he lifted the glass from his son and took an experimental sniff. "Besides, I don't know what anyone here has to do with it." He gave Sam a heavy look. "*Irascible Nell* is the author."

"Who is it *really*?" Paulie, one of Roberts's newsboys, tossed a roasted nut in the air and spectacularly missed catching it. "The author."

"Paulie, if you can't handle your liquor, you damn well better handle your nuts," Ethan barked. "Pick it up or pack it up."

He leaned in the doorway, surveying the chaos of his shop. As it turned out, the Bull and Crow would not serve Belle, and the Compass wouldn't serve the Porters, so when Belle suggested they return to No. 62 to devise an alternate plan for the evening, it seemed harmless enough. But somehow over the last two hours, the printshop transformed from the site of *planning* to the site of *happening*.

Ethan looked around at the cramped revelry. What had started as the six denizens of 62 Fleet—he and Belle, Tobias and Sam, George Newburn and, unfortunately, Victor Marks—had nearly tripled in number and noise. There was Newburn's brother, Roger, who played the accordion with the same enthusiasm with which George set type. A pair of Marks's fellow artists, who had appeared with a dusty crate of clinking bottles. A group of pressmen Tobias was friendly with. And Sam's loyal band of newsboys. Everyone knew someone who wanted to toast to the author of *Secrets*, who was apparently enjoying a bit of mystery-fueled celebrity in the neighborhoods along Fleet.

Unbeknownst to the crowd of devotees, Irascible Nell was much nearer than they realized. In fact, she was arranging a plate of ham sandwiches and slices of current cakes she'd sent Sam and Paulie out to purchase from a street vendor when it became clear the contents of the artists' dusty bottles would go down easier with sustenance.

"To Nell!" Roger Newburn launched into a polka on his accordion, and bottles were handily passed. "Whoever he is, may he be irascible no longer."

Ethan drew nearer to Belle. He glanced behind him at the jovial group, then swiftly dropped his hand to her hip. "How much do you regret your choice of pseudonym?"

He was only half teasing—given their crashing success, he'd

started to wonder if she might want to stake her claim as the author. But Belle balked at attention, always assuming it would be negative. As long as she was content with her alias, Ethan would keep inking it.

"I don't regret it half so much as Sam is going to regret that second bottle," she said, leaning briefly into his hand. In the low light of the oil lamps, her face was flushed—but she, like Ethan, had drunk little more than a half glass of champagne.

He felt intoxicated anyway.

Sometime in the late afternoon, Belle had gone home, ostensibly to tell her housekeeper she was joining Helena at their aunt and uncle's home. While she was there, she changed into a simple dark blue gown that had him by the throat. He couldn't look away from the sweeping neckline, the elbow-length sleeves—so much bare skin, all dewy in the stifling air of the shop. Her hair had stopped behaving at least an hour ago, so she'd given up with pins and instead wove her tresses into a long, thick plait. The hair around her face was curling in the heat, and he wanted to put his hands in her damp, messy waves, to draw her face to his.

He settled for slowly trailing the back of his knuckles along the impossibly soft skin of her forearm.

"Are you enjoying yourself?" He lowered his voice and kept his back to the room. He slid one foot behind her skirts, shifting infinitesimally closer to block the gradual traverse of his fingers along her wrist.

She sighed, her hazel eyes flicking up to him. "You shouldn't."

"I know." He curved his palm fleetingly over hers. "Any minute now, I'll remember why."

He reluctantly stepped back, and not a moment too soon, for their ragtag group of celebrants had started to call for a toast.

"To Fletcher," Tobias boomed, raising the mug he'd lifted from Sam. "For keeping us at work."

"Hear, hear!" The men whooped and stamped, which was wholly unnecessary, seeing as Ethan only kept a fraction of them at work.

"To Miss Sinclair," Sam called. "For keeping us in line."

Ethan had no choice but to raise his own glass to that.

Belle looked up from rearranging the platter of refreshments; all eyes were on her. Ethan rubbed his jaw, watching closely. If she shirked from the attention, he would step in.

But to his immense pride and pleasure, she accepted Newburn's hand and climbed onto her own desk chair.

"To all of you." She lifted her half-drunk champagne. "For keeping me company."

The men cheered and clapped, and she beamed, her eyes bright. Ethan's heart clenched. She looked perfectly at ease, and he wished every man in her father's courtroom could see her now, holding court of her own. He took her hand to help her down, but she remained standing on the chair beside him.

The shop grew quiet, everyone waiting expectantly.

"To dreams," Ethan finally said, his eyes on Belle. "For keeping us bold."

"Fletcher, if you have a moment?" Tobias drew up beside him, clapping him on the shoulder.

Ethan turned away from the card game one of the artists had started—not that he had been playing. He preferred not to bet on anything but himself.

"I have a moment."

Tobias jerked his chin toward a trio of men crowded around the worktable. "Thought I might make an introduction."

Ethan followed him to the corner, passing behind Belle, who was attempting to teach Sam the polka. "You're not so much leading as dragging." He heard her instructions as Sam hauled her through a turn. "Sam, that's my foot—"

Crushed toes aside, she seemed to be enjoying herself. Which was too bad, because Ethan was ready to bring this party to an end.

He didn't want to share her any longer.

"Fletcher, this is Hawkins, Smith, and Ferguson." Tobias pointed to his fellows, and Ethan nodded to each man in turn.

Ferguson, a silver-haired fellow with a weathered face, looked to Ethan in interest. "Porter says you worked on a paper in America. A penny daily?"

"I did."

"In what capacity?"

"First at the press, then the pen." He thought of the passion Belle brought to her work, and his own subsequent appreciation for publishing. "Though I'm far better at the former than the latter."

Ferguson tilted his head. "That your aim here? To start a paper?"

"Ah." Ethan cracked his knuckles. "Aims are a bit obsolete at the moment. I arrived here with one firm plan, and it was promptly wrenched sideways. Currently, my only concern is getting things straight again."

The men chuckled, and Ethan glanced over to Belle. He did, in fact, have aims aplenty, but all of them depended on wrangling a reliable business.

"Ferguson was heavily involved with the unstamped press movement about ten years back," Tobias explained. "Now he keeps the rest of us apprised of the work underway to abolish the newspaper duty."

"You should come round with Porter sometime," Ferguson said. "Learn about our efforts. We don't have anyone with experience with a penny paper. Could use your insight, Fletcher."

Ethan slid Tobias a questioning glance.

"I thought you might like to know what's happening here, on a larger scale than the serial," Tobias said casually. "In case it's ever of interest to you."

Before Ethan could respond, Belle appeared at his elbow. She was pink-cheeked and panting and so damn pretty, he felt an idiotic grin start at the corner of his mouth.

"I didn't know the polka was so dangerous," Tobias observed as she held the table, rotating her ankle.

"None of us did." She winced.

"You're kind to show him, Miss Sinclair. My wife thinks nigh on seventeen is too young, but…"

"The point of young love is to be young," Belle teased warmly.

"Seventeen," Ethan mused. "Not so young. I had a girl when I was just a bit older."

Tobias boomed a laugh. "So did I—my wife."

Ethan smiled wider. The Porters were a rare breed indeed.

Belle tilted her head at Ethan in curiosity. "Who was she, then?"

He looked over to her, hoping she wasn't bothered; he didn't think she was. It was a very long time ago. And Belle, of all people, knew the past was past.

"Her name was Rachel." Ethan sat on the edge of the table. "She was the daughter of a butcher. I was infatuated, she decidedly less so."

Belle hummed sympathetically. "What happened?"

"I wasn't ready." He shrugged. "I was a new journeyman, a long way from establishing myself. I don't blame her for not wishing to wait for me."

"Aye." Tobias nodded. "Those are hard years, and a long wait."

"Indeed." Ethan moved his eyes across Belle's watchful face. The past *was* past, but it nevertheless nipped at his heels, reminding him how far he still had to go.

"I suppose it depends on what you're waiting for," she murmured.

Her shy smile might as well have branded him for all the heat he felt at her sweet promise. He was going to kiss her in the next five minutes, the men in this printshop be damned.

"Porter!" Marks and Newburn waved from the card game. "Do you want in?"

Tobias ambled over to join the others, and Paulie the newsboy immediately replaced him.

"All right, Miss Sinclair. If you're done with Sam, I'll take a turn." He winked. "Fear not. Your ankles are in good hands."

"Oh…" Belle looked faintly alarmed.

"Her ankles are going nowhere near your hands," Ethan warned. "At least not if you want to keep them intact."

"You know, Paulie, I think I need to step outside for a spell. Mr. Fletcher, would you mind escorting me?"

Gladly.

He eyed Paulie as he followed her out of the noisy shop into the cool spring evening. A lamplighter had worked his way down Fleet, sending pools of light into the gathering darkness.

"Ah…" She tipped her head back as the breeze teased the flushed line of her throat. "That feels heavenly."

Ethan drew her around the side of the shop. Even in the alley, he could hear the raucous noise of the accordion vying with a barrage of shouts. It seemed George Newburn was losing at cards to one of the artists.

"This has been wonderful, Ethan. I know you're not keen on having everyone in the shop, but it's nice, isn't it? All these people we've somehow collected?"

She leaned against the brick wall, and Ethan braced one arm above her. She looked up at him, her face half-hidden in shadow.

"I wouldn't go so far as saying a full shop is *wonderful*," he murmured. "I had a slightly different agenda for the evening."

"Did you? How enterprising."

"Always," he promised her, his mouth tilting. "I'll give them another quarter hour before I clear everyone out. Starting with Paulie."

She smiled and reached forward, stroking the lapel of his coat. "Does that include me?"

"I love how you make me say it." He stepped into the space she'd made for him. "To think, Sam toasted you for keeping us in line, when the truth is, you're dragging me *right* over it."

"Oh, that reminds me." She pushed him fractionally away from her. "All this talk of keeping things in order…" She reached into the concealed pocket of her skirts and withdrew a sealed envelope.

"You're ruthless," he muttered. "I'm a hair's breadth from

stealing a kiss, and you decide now is the time to play letter carrier?"

She ignored him. "I meant to tell you before, but everything's been so busy. On my way to the shop this morning, the postman stopped me with your mail. I put everything in the top drawer of the desk." She hesitated. "Except this."

She handed him the letter, her hazel eyes searching his face.

"I didn't open it," she added quickly. "I just didn't want it to get mixed in with your other correspondence. It seems…important."

He took the letter, lifting it to the small circle of light from a nearby streetlamp.

"Park Row…" He licked his lip, glancing at Belle. "Newspaper Row."

She was silent.

Ethan slid the letter, unopened, into his coat pocket.

"Wait," she blurted.

"Precisely my thought." He stepped closer, once more backing her to the wall. "The letter can wait. God knows we have."

His lips fell to the exposed curve of her neck. It was his weakness—and hers. He sucked gently, just a little, not enough to leave a mark.

"Don't…" She sighed, angling her head for him. "Don't you want to open it?"

"Not right now, I don't," he murmured. "I want to open something else."

"Ethan…"

"I want to take you to bed, sweetheart." His mouth moved up, teasing beneath her jaw. "Would you like that?"

A slow shiver rolled through her, and she breathed a soft laugh. "Would I?"

"Yes." He drew one fingertip lightly over her collarbone. "You would."

She inhaled, her lips parting, a honeyed invitation.

He kissed her slowly, his tongue playing with hers. She tasted like champagne. He found the end of her hastily woven plait, and he played with that, too, imagining how good her soft, heavy hair would look splayed across his bed.

He pulled away, his voice husky. "But only if you want it."

She slid her palm over his chest. With his waistcoat between them, he couldn't feel the heat of her skin. Always, *always* a barrier. It was unbelievable he had yet to strip her bare, to put his body against hers.

"I want it." She was breathing very fast. "I want it, just as you said."

"I have a condom." He hesitated, needing to temper her expectations for the stiff sheath. "They can sometimes be a bit coarse, Belle. If you don't care for it, I'll—"

"It's all right." She stared at him, her eyes glowing in the faint light of the streetlamp. "I brought what I need from home, and I would prefer to use that."

"Are you certain?"

"Yes." She gently stroked his chin. "You needn't worry. We can take good care, Ethan."

Good care.

It touched him in a deeply unexpected way, that she wanted to help him care for her. That she was caring for him in kind.

He couldn't remember the last time someone had taken care of him.

"Belle." He caressed her cheek, seized with the urgency to make himself explicitly clear. "I meant what I told you. I can't offer you anything but myself, for the time I'm here. I *know* how insufficient it is—"

"Stop." She touched his mouth. "You are *not* insufficient. Never."

He kissed her again, cradling her face, angling her closer. He wanted nothing between his abraded palm and the soft expanse of her body. He wanted to hold her in his arms and feel no guilt or censure.

He wanted them to be ordinary people, skin and bones and two hearts beating together.

So not very ordinary at all.

18

Autumn, 1843

To my daughter Belle, on the occasion of her betrothal to Lawrence Duncan —

Mark this book well but mark my words better. I promise to answer any questions you have with honesty and discretion. Embarking on a new life can be uncomfortable in many ways, but this should not be one of them.

> *— Inscribed by Emilia Sinclair inside*
> *Every woman's book, or, What is love?*

THE PARTY WAS OVER, the revelers long gone. Beneath Belle's feet, the printshop was quiet. The fierce thrum of her heartbeat was anything but.

Ethan had lit the fire in his bedroom and brought her close, unfastening the small hooks at the back of her bodice. Yearning turned her tender; tears threatened at the careful way his hands shaped around her shoulder blades. He kissed her neck and told her to take her time, then he returned downstairs to ensure all was well.

There was no need. She'd already helped him tidy the shop.

Ethan was giving her a moment, and it seemed to her a profound intimacy.

She turned down his counterpane, and the scent of his soap lifted from his bedsheets. Soon she would be in this bed, in his arms, and she tingled with expectancy as she finished undressing—gown, corset, petticoats, stockings. Her linen shift she left on, the fabric soft as it skated over the sensitive tips of her breasts.

She opened her basket and lifted the small jar she'd brought from home. Recalling her mother's long-ago instructions for a wedding night that never came, she carefully maneuvered the delicate sponge, placing it as directed. It was a relief, to be ready for this evening in more ways than one.

Finally, she unwound her plait until her hair fell loose down her back. Having no brush, she ran her fingers through the long waves, trying to smooth them. She couldn't see what she looked like; she didn't know where Ethan kept his mirror.

No silk, no lace, no trousseau. Even so, devotion kept her calm. These were the preparations a wife would make, how she would anticipate her husband.

"I'm ready," she said softly, sensing a shadow behind her.

She looked over her shoulder and took him in as he leaned in the threshold of his bedroom. Ethan's shirt collar gaped open, his tie loose around his neck. His eyes glittered in the firelight as he stretched one arm above the door.

"You are so goddamn lovely."

At the hoarse conviction in his voice, she colored instantly, everywhere. Her nipples puckered as he drew near. She glanced down at her shift, trying to stem a sudden wellspring of nerves.

"I should have brought something finer," she whispered.

He reached for her, sliding his thumbs over her straps and peeling her shift away. His arms were around her before the linen kissed the floor.

"There is *nothing* finer."

His mouth grazed hers, lingering there, gentling her upper lip until she opened for him. He deepened the kiss, the assured caress of his tongue sending a moan from her chest to his. His palm smoothed over her bare skin, and she arched her back for more.

"Please keep touching me," she murmured.

"Keep touching you? I won't be able to stop." His mouth followed her blush over the small rise of her breasts. "This flush has cost me sleep. I'm putting my hands all over it."

"You make me flush." She lifted his shirt, lightly scratching his stomach. "You pull it from me. *You* do this to me."

"Christ, you've no idea," he groaned. "A flush is the very least of what I'll pull from you."

He kissed her again, thumbing her nipples until a syrupy heat settled low in her belly. Every teasing stroke heightened her anticipation, until she was thoughtless, airless, empty. She wanted fullness. She wanted *more*. More of this, more of *him*, the firm press of his body, the hungry slide of his tongue, the intoxicating scent of ink and soap.

"What can I give you?" Sweat beaded in her hairline, and he nuzzled there, groaning faintly. "My fingers? My mouth?"

"I want *you* inside me." She kissed his neck. "Just that."

"Not yet." He brought her hand to his trousers, forming her palm around the growing length of his arousal. "Let me settle you."

He stood back, shucking his shirt, dropping his trousers.

She drank in the firm slope of his shoulders, the tapered ridge of his collarbone, the way the firelight licked shadows on his skin. The broad expanse of his chest was forested with dark hair stretching down the thick muscles of his stomach. His cock jutted hard and dusky in his hand.

Her throat grew dry. *So beautiful.* All of him, all for her.

She reached for him, kneading the warm muscle of his chest as his palm curved over her bare bottom. An agonized craving tore through her as the rough pads of his fingers found wetness between her thighs.

She spread her legs, clinging to his biceps, dimly aware his bed was right there. She should lie down, she should be doing something for him.

"The bed," she whispered. "Should I…how do you want me?"

He pushed a finger inside her—oh *God*, the stretch—then withdrew, circling her, stroking again. His other hand wrapped around her thigh, urging one leg up and over his hip as he teased and thrust. His cock was trapped between them, the hot press against her stomach eliciting a rush of desire that had her shamelessly arching her back.

"Don't worry about the bed." He put his mouth against her ear. "We'll get there. Once you come apart for me, I'll lay you back, we'll see about the bed."

She moaned as he pulled her into another long kiss. His hand continued its unhurried torment, but she found his wrist and held him where she wanted him.

"That's it," he muttered. His fingers filled her, stroking hard where she pulsed. "You can be selfish with me. I want you to be."

She was quivering around him, the first faint flutter.

"I could never…be selfish with you," she breathed, her voice slurring in his chest.

"Let me have it then," he urged. "That's it, sweetheart. Let it feel good."

Her head fell heavily against his shoulder as she wound tighter, *tighter*, tight enough to unspool in a long, welcome release.

"Ethan," she gasped, gripping his arms.

He was already lifting her, easing her to his bed. She stretched, sluggish with pleasure, as he stood over her. He raised her leg, pressing her foot flat against his chest as he moved his fist over his straining cock.

"Do you feel better?" His eyes were hooded, his handsome face lazy with satisfaction.

"Yes," she sighed. "And no." She lifted her arms for him. "Come here."

He moved up her body, taking his time, and she was sated enough to let him.

In a dream state, sensations rolled together, building her back up. The brush of his beard along the inside of her knee, his thumb at the crease of her hip, the slow lave of his tongue over her damp, aching sex. All the while, his warm, deep voice floated to her, telling her she was good, she was precious, he would take care of her.

Finally, his hands came around her thighs, and she shifted, letting him settle between her legs. She reached for him, stroking his shaft as he'd shown her. His fingers joined hers, helping notch his cock to her.

"Easy, Belle," he coaxed, breaching her with a shallow, patient thrust. "It's going to take me a moment. We'll go slow."

She stretched around the slight rock of his hips, pulling tight and thin, eager to accept him, knowing it would be good, *so good*, as good as everything else he gave her.

"You'll tell me if it's too much." He smoothed her hair. "Yes?"

She nodded, her forehead brushing his. It wasn't too much; it was just as much as she wanted. She'd never felt higher than this, so certain of herself, so right in her body and mind. Ethan lifted her, wrapping his arms around her, holding her close to his chest.

"Beautiful girl."

He dropped his hips, sinking deeper now.

"Gorgeous girl."

An enormous pressure, a breath-clutching sting.

"My sweetheart."

The pain briefly grounded her before sliding away, turning as blurry as the rest of her. He spread her wider, his thumb finding the tingling apex of her sex. And then he was moving, slow, nudging thrusts, waiting for her marginal slackening, holding back until she yielded, her hips following his in mindless obedience.

"So easy, isn't it?" He kissed the corner of her mouth. "So right. I knew it would be." His voice was husky. "It always is with us."

"You thought of this." She cradled his jaw, stroking his beard. "Of being with me, like this?"

"Mmm." He kissed her again, moving faster, his cock throbbing within her. "Every fucking night since the garden."

"Me, as well." She tilted her hips, taking him deeper, craving more of the rigid pressure where she was already tender. "Ethan, it's better than I invented—"

"No invention," he breathed. "No fantasy." He slowed his movement, his eyes searching her face as he laced their fingers together. "Only us."

"Only us." She squeezed his hand. "It's always been enough."

His thrusts grew longer, a sublime friction that had her free hand clutching his shoulder hard enough to leave a mark. She wrapped her legs around his waist, drawing him close to her, luxuriating in the sheer force of him—the hard plane of his abdomen, the mat of hair on his chest, the sweat streaking his corded neck.

He was still holding her hand. She turned her head, staring at their entwined fingers. *I love you*, she imagined telling him, the words lifting in her throat. *I love you.*

"You can let go," he whispered. He was watching her watch their hands. He tried to loosen her grip. "If you need to."

"Ethan. I'm not letting go."

A sound escaped him, a low, soft keen, and his control slackened. He hitched his hips, stroking harder, his thumb again playing at her clitoris.

"Please," she gasped, seized by a violent jolt of pleasure. She was quaking, a veiled release flitting nearer, licking over her in waves, each surge tempting her to succumb.

"Yes." He drew their still-twined fingers over her head. She was strung as tight as a bow, her arm stretching, her thighs spread, Ethan over and around and inside her.

"I'll follow you, Belle."

With his reassurance, her pleasure crested. She pressed her face to his arm as she met the next wave head-on, crying out as it dragged her under. Her climax came hard—she was shaking—she couldn't let go—

"Belle," he murmured into her hair. "Breathe."

She was still in pieces when he shifted her, gently rolling her to her side. He curved around her, his cock still hard. She foggily understood he hadn't yet spent. He lifted her thigh in his palm, easing into her from behind. She shivered, clutching his forearm. She wasn't certain how much more she could take.

"Ethan…my God."

"I won't be long now." He kissed her shoulder. His thrusts grew very small, very deep, grinding a circle inside her. Her eyelids fluttered; the pressure was overwhelming. She let him move her, and in a daze, she sensed herself climbing again—or she hadn't yet come down.

"Are you giving me another?" His breath turned shallow, his chest pressed against her back. His fingers moved her sweaty hair off her neck, and he kissed her there. "You are."

"I don't know…" she panted. She couldn't stop convulsing. She didn't know if it had ended or started. His hips rolled, his hand pressed flat on her stomach and—*oh God, yes…*

"There it is." His voice, so low. "*Yes*, sweetheart. That's it."

She couldn't take in his words, only the way they moved through her, stirring a final flare, her body gasping as the quell of a candlewick. She had scarcely stilled when Ethan withdrew on a shudder, spending in a warm rush over her hip.

He groaned and collapsed back on his pillow, pulling her with him.

"Fucking glorious." He pressed his cheek to hers, and she felt the wide stretch of his smile. "I'm not as deft with adjectives as you are."

She couldn't move. She could hardly breathe.

"No," she managed after a long pause. "*Fucking glorious* captures it quite well."

Ethan laughed and rolled to find a handkerchief, gently cleaning her bottom and thigh before settling the counterpane over her. She sighed, curling into him. Soon, she would need to rise and see to her ablutions, but right now, she only wanted to lay with his warm body against hers.

"How do you feel?" His hand was on her back, seeking tension in her shoulders.

"I feel..."

Fine. The word nearly slipped from her, born entirely of habit. She always said she was fine whenever she was asked. How strange, that *fine* had seemed the most reasonable thing she could aspire to be.

She pressed her sleepy smile into his forearm. "I feel *wonderful.*"

BELLE AWOKE in skin-warmed bedsheets with Ethan's mouth moving slowly down her spine. She rolled to her stomach and buried her morning fog in his pillow, letting him pull her out of one dream into another.

Through heavy lids, she watched the morning find them. The gradual advance of dusty sunbeams—breaching the windowsill, stretching down the wall, lengthening across the floor—echoed their own lazy awakening.

By the time daylight spilled golden over his bed, Belle was newly drowsy and Ethan uncommonly cheerful.

"It's Sunday," she observed vacantly. She was sprawled sideways, her foot braced on his stomach. He hummed his agreement, and his muscles moved beneath her toes.

"You won't have to work, will you?"

"What do you suppose I was just doing?" He rotated his head to look at her. "Was that not ambitious enough?"

"Well. It was rather—"

She squealed, laughing as he lifted her foot and kissed the sensitive arch. "Ethan, no...*don't*—"

"I would very much like to know how you were going to end that sentence." He wrapped his hand around her ankle. "It was rather what?"

He kissed her again, his beard damnably tickling, and she wheezed, trying not to kick her beloved in the face.

"I suppose it was ambitious," she relented, gasping for breath.

"You *suppose*." His smile was dangerous. "Give me half an hour, and I'll show you ambitious."

She propped herself on her elbows, savoring his dark tousled hair, the beautiful curve of his bicep, flung behind his head. She'd never seen him so at ease.

"A whole half hour?" She smiled, feigning relief. "What a generous reprieve. I might even have time for a cup of tea."

"Now she wants tea." He gently lowered her foot and swung his legs to the floor. "Tea in bed, on a Sunday morning. Has pleasure turned you indolent, Belle Sinclair?"

"I don't need tea in bed." Belle stretched. She did feel rather indolent today.

He leaned over her and kissed her slowly. "You can have anything you'd like in this bed, including tea."

"You spoil me." She bit her lip as he crossed the room, taken by the strong line of his thighs, the flex of his shoulders, the taut globes of his buttocks.

Spoiled, indeed.

She could hear him whistling as he moved about the kitchen, a sound so perfectly intimate, it had her smiling like a fool. She sat up properly to survey his bedroom, which had become a mess of clothing. She should tidy up. He hadn't many garments; she didn't want them to wrinkle.

Belle climbed from bed and set about folding his trousers, wondering how they might spend the day. Perhaps a steamer to Greenwich Park? They could stroll beneath the old trees. If they didn't see anyone they knew, she could even take his arm…

She lifted his coat to hang it on a peg. As she did so, she heard the rustle of paper.

Her stomach jolted.

The letter from New York.

Waiting in his pocket, where he'd tucked it away.

Slowly, she slipped her hand inside his coat, withdrawing the still-sealed envelope. She climbed back into bed, drew up the counterpane, set the letter on her lap.

She stared at it.

"Belle?" Ethan approached the bed with a steaming teacup on a mismatched saucer. When he saw what she'd rediscovered, his expression turned somber. "Ah."

"*Newspaper Row,*" she said quietly. "That's what you said, isn't it? Last night in the alley?"

"Yes." He sat on the bed beside her. "It's what they call the street —it's a publisher's haven, of sorts."

Haven implied safety, though Belle felt certain this letter contained only hazard.

Silently, she handed him the envelope.

He slid open the seal and unfolded the contents, holding it so they could read together. There was a long note and a few sheets that appeared to be a contract.

"Who is Todd Eamon?" She glanced at Ethan.

His face was very still. Only his eyes moved, up and down the page.

"Man I knew in Boston," he finally said. "The desk manager at my old paper, though his brother is a publisher in New York."

Belle licked her lip, drawing her gaze back to the letter.

Left the Sentinel…secured the necessary capital…establishing our own paper…We both thought of you…

"He's offering you a position." Belle folded her hands very tightly in her lap. "He wants you to be his editor."

"So it would seem."

He lifted the second set of pages, examining the terms of the offer, his jaw working so hard she heard a faint pop.

"Are the terms agreeable?" Her voice sounded remarkably normal.

"Ah." He nodded once. "Yes."

"When?"

It was the only question that mattered.

He scrubbed his hand over his beard, scanning the contract. "I would need to be in New York by July. They've secured passage from Liverpool." He paused. "Departing the seventh of June."

Belle stared at him as he folded the letter. "Who would have guessed the month of June would be so portentous?"

Her forced levity did not land. Her voice no longer sounded normal.

"Belle."

"You'll take this." She directed her words to the teacup he'd brought her. "The offer. In New York."

She'd never given much thought to New York. It was unfair so faraway a place could be such a direct and immediate threat.

"I don't know that I will."

She snapped her gaze to his face. His expression was grave.

"Of course you'll take it. You *must* take it, Ethan. This is a sure path to what you want. Not like here, where you have the debt to pay, no paper to publish even if you do pay it off—"

"I have the serial." He studied her closely. "*Secrets* is successful. It's selling. And I promised you I would see you through a ten-week run."

"Yes, but—"

He took her hand. "Belle. We have a partnership."

She shook her head. His words clarified her confusion. She glanced at the letter on the bedside table, gradually understanding what was happening here, or what might happen very soon.

Because this—*all of this*—hinged on their mutual need.

She'd known it from the first day outside the newsagent's stall—the flaw in their plan was the resolution. The serial was a *means* to his end; the serial *was* her end. The first time she realized this, she'd felt foolish.

Now…

Now she was *terrified*.

"But ours is not a true partnership, is it?" she said slowly. "You shouldn't be limited by it."

"I don't understand." He looked at her sharply.

"If I walk away…" Her breath hitched uncomfortably. "If *I* walk away, *you* would be fine. You could hire another writer, and the worst it would cost you is the expense. You don't need me in the way I need you."

"That's not true." His voice was firm.

"You will be fine, Ethan," she insisted, giving voice to her wretched fears. "Don't pretend otherwise. Don't pretend we're even. We're not, and we can't ever be. It has nothing to do with where I live or my father's profession or whatever self-flagellating game you play inside your head. The reason we aren't even is that you are a man, and you have options. Your options don't need to include me. They *shouldn't* include me—"

"*Stop*. Stop talking like this."

She snapped her mouth shut, shocked into silence by the blazing look on his face.

"I gave you my word, which is one of the very, *very* few things in my possession to give. I would ask you not to dismiss it so easily."

She swallowed, chastened, and his tone softened.

"I told you I would publish you for ten weeks, and that hasn't changed." He grasped her shoulders. "I'm not responding to Eamon's offer yet. There's no need. We're making strides, and we still have nearly four weeks to get where we're going."

"Are you certain?"

"I wouldn't say it otherwise." He gently touched the tangled ends of her hair. "My options include you, Belle. They're *because* of you. The way I see it, we're building something together. And I'd very much like to see what it looks like when the time comes."

She clutched the counterpane. She didn't know how to speak around the enormity of her hope.

"Do you believe me?" He raised his forefinger to her chin. "Yes?"

"Yes," she whispered, releasing the bedsheets and reaching for his hand. "Yes. Ethan, I'm sorry."

She kissed his knuckles, an uneven reassurance settling over her. *When the time comes.*

"And Belle…" His voice lowered with urgency. "Never again say I don't need you. That I will be fine." He shook his head roughly. "I wouldn't be fine."

His face changed before her eyes, his wary self-governance yielding to boyish, unmasked longing. Her nerves fell away, straight into the tender cracks he opened for her.

She knew what he wanted.

It already belonged to him.

"Ethan, I want to tell you something, but I don't want to frighten you."

He put his palms on either side of her face. His hands shook, just a bit, until his fingers wound through her hair.

"Sweetheart, I already know. And believe me, I'm already frightened."

He exhaled slowly; his eyes were very, very green.

"God help me, Belle, I love you too."

He pulled her into his lap at the same moment she kissed him— as ever, two halves of the same story. He embraced her for a long time, his arms winding tight, his chest moving against hers. She let him draw her into his cadence, until she could anticipate each breath before he expelled it. There was a space there, between the catch and the release.

That space was hers.

Finally, he pulled away. "Will you stay with me today?"

"Yes." She kissed him again. "I'll stay."

But she wasn't the one who would go.

19

____

Accounting Ledger of E. Fletcher
Week of 13 May 1848
Secrets of the Old Bailey, Vol. 1, No. 6
Earnings less expenditures—£20

Remaining debt owed—£45

N.b.—paper stock low

"YOU WERE RIGHT, PORTER," Ethan remarked around a mouthful of bacon. "You estimated by mid-May, we'd run through our store of paper, and damn if you didn't hit the mark."

It was Wednesday morning, and all around them, the coffee-house thrummed with efficiency as working men traded publications and good-natured barbs over steaming cups of piquant brew.

"Good God, Fletcher, are you even chewing?" Tobias remarked, wrapping his hands around his own coffee as he watched Ethan's steady progress through his plate.

Ethan grinned as he tore a thick slice of buttered bread and piled it with eggs. He was, in fact, famished. Helena Sinclair had been at a ball until the early hours, an excuse Belle had rallied behind when making her own arrangements with the housekeeper. Of course Mrs. Bowers did not know Belle wasn't attending to her sister and cousin, but rather was being attended to by Ethan in his bedroom above the shop.

He'd been up half the night making love to her, only to rouse her just before dawn. In the quiet shadows of his bedroom, he was sleep-rumpled and slow, kissing her palms, her eyelids, the curve of her shoulder. When the hour came to see her home, he'd pressed his lips to hers, beckoning the first sweet tilt of her mouth. The sunrise on her face was far brighter than the one breaking through the window.

"Fletcher?"

Ethan swigged the scalding coffee.

"Careful. You'll burn your mouth," Tobias warned.

"It doesn't bother me," Ethan assured him. "The hotter, the better."

"Speaking of paper." Tobias stared as Ethan loaded up on ham. "We need to send our purchase order to the paper mill. You're right. The forthcoming issue will use the last of our reams."

"The mill in Kent?"

"Fifteen miles from London," Tobias confirmed. "Not the closest we can do, but…"

"So long as it's the cheapest. And pulp paper." Ethan frowned. "The paper duty is a goddamn travesty."

"It is," Tobias grimly agreed. "But we don't have a choice."

"You don't have a choice *yet*." A gruff voice interrupted them.

Ethan looked up to see the grizzled mane of Ferguson, Tobias's publishing acquaintance from Saturday's party at the shop.

"May I?"

"We're due at the shop soon, Ferguson," Ethan said, gesturing to the empty end of the bench.

"I only need a moment. Heard you breakfast here." Ferguson slid a small pamphlet to him. "Thought I'd stop by to give you this."

Ethan glanced through what appeared to be a political pamphlet, promoting peaceable means for working-class reform. There were remarks on the expansion of voting rights, calls to remove property qualifications to stand for election, and above all, wider public access to the news. There was nothing in here Ethan was opposed to, but now was not the time to take up causes.

"This is intriguing…" He lifted one shoulder. "But I'm not looking for a political party. I don't even know if I have a permanent residence here yet."

"If you care about cheap press, this is a group you'll want to look into." Ferguson rapped his knuckles on the table. "Radical but nonviolent, and their work is catching notice. It may not happen soon, but happen it will. An abolition of the tax on knowledge."

"You think?" Ethan appraised the man. "A repeal on the newspaper duty?"

"Mark my words." Ferguson eyed Ethan significantly. "One day, Fletcher, you could turn your penny blood into a penny paper. Come round some time, when you aren't printing fiction. There's work to be done, and we could use your help doing it."

Ferguson shook his hand and took his leave.

"Hmm…" Ethan showed Tobias the pamphlet. "You suppose there's any weight to this? A repeal?"

Tobias shrugged. "Suppose you'll have to stay around to find out."

"Believe me," Ethan muttered, "I'm working on it."

"And you're succeeding," Tobias said bracingly. "Think of it this way, Fletcher. We wouldn't need to purchase more paper if we hadn't used up our supply. We've made more strides in the last few weeks than anyone has any business doing. Over fifty pounds, paid."

Forty-five pounds still to go.

Ethan's appetite soured.

"Buying paper means our profits are about to contract." He pushed his plate away. "Significantly."

"We should still be able to make it." Tobias sipped his coffee. "It will be tight, but…"

"No margin for error," Ethan finished his friend's thought. *"None.* I looked at the accounts yesterday, wondering if adding Marks and Newburn was ill-conceived. But we need them to move the numbers we need to move, and we need to move those numbers *every single week."*

"Do you have any of your own funds to contribute?" Tobias asked. "If you get close enough to close the gap?"

Ethan heaved a sigh. "Not anymore. My savings were meager to begin with, even before my passage here. I need to retain at least some funds, or else I can't—" He broke off, flushing.

He never flushed. The sensation was so unfamiliar, it took him a moment to recognize the vulnerable heat for what it was.

"True," Tobias said casually. "Very true."

"What's that?" Ethan's neck prickled uncomfortably. Surely, there was no way Tobias could see how red he'd turned. Hell, half his face was covered by his beard and the other half with a scowl.

"It makes sense you'd want to keep a little savings at the ready." Tobias stole a piece of Ethan's toast. "Marriage doesn't come cheap."

Ethan glanced at him sharply. "Nobody is getting married."

Not yet, at any rate.

Because Tobias was right.

Clearing the debt was only the first Herculean effort in a long, looming series of them. The penny blood was a shovel, meant to dig him out of the ground. Once he was standing on his own two feet, he still had so far—*so damn far!*—to go. Even if he managed to stay in London, things would be very difficult.

He hadn't appreciated how truly precarious his situation was until he'd seen another sort of beginning reflected in Belle's golden gaze. There was promise there—and hope. Which meant the stakes had never been higher. She dreamed of writing a novel, not penny fiction; he, too, had ambitions beyond the serial.

He needed to turn a temporary arrangement into a solvent business—real outlay, real capital.

A foundation they could build upon.

Tobias leaned forward. "Something on your mind, Fletcher?"

Ethan unwillingly thought of his bedside chest, where the letter from Todd Eamon was tucked inside a drawer. A generous, unexpected offer, including travel arrangements for a steamship out of Liverpool in just over three weeks.

He should feel relieved. He could forfeit the shop and its financial noose and be in New York publishing a newspaper by midsummer.

And yet, here he was, sitting in a coffeehouse, sourcing paper and joining up with tax reformers.

"I've been offered a position." Ethan pinched the bridge of his nose. "Editor of a paper. In New York."

Tobias nodded slowly.

"Belle says I should take it."

"Editor of your own newspaper?" Tobias raised an eyebrow. "She's not wrong."

"I haven't responded," Ethan clarified.

"Why haven't you?"

Ethan shook his head. "I don't want to take the offer. Nor can I afford to turn it down. I *clawed* my way to that offer, years and years of work…I can't discount that."

"Nor should you."

"I have to keep that door open, in case it ends up being the only door left."

"Perfectly reasonable."

"Hell." Ethan exhaled in sharp frustration. "Nothing about this is reasonable. All my choices feel half-formed. The loose ends are strangling me."

"So what will you do?" Tobias watched him closely.

"Forge ahead, I suppose." Ethan frowned. "The serial has been selling so far. There's no reason to think it won't do exactly that for the next few issues. I'm not surrendering hope that for once, I'm going to end up on the other side of something good."

Tobias looked at him for a long time.

"What?"

"I feel compelled to ask you a frank question."

Ethan waved him on. "Please, by all means."

Tobias slowly folded his arms. "I don't know the extent of what's transpired between you and Miss Sinclair—nor do I want to know, let me be clear—but I know a moon-eyed man when I see one. I'm living with one. Hell, I *am* one."

Ethan smiled.

"Miss Sinclair is a fine lady, and I don't say that only because of her family—though in this case, I mean exactly that." Tobias hesitated. "I'm sure you're aware she likely has a portion set aside. I imagine it would be some help."

"We aren't there yet," Ethan warned. "I'm weeks away from knowing where I stand and what it means for Belle and me."

"But if you were?" Tobias prompted. "I know you, Fletcher. This is what you do. You solve problems. You can't tell me you haven't considered that she can go some way to solving yours."

Ethan gritted his jaw.

He *had* considered it. But while a dowry might provide temporary relief, it wasn't a long-term solution. Just look at his mother— she'd come from some small means, and it hadn't been nearly enough to offer any measure of real security.

He'd once thought Belle would save his neck, but he'd never meant like this. She deserved a man who didn't rely on her.

He deserved a chance to be a man who could rely on himself.

"I can't." He shook his head. "I can't do that. I don't want to be a kept man, taking handouts from others, depending on my wife and her family. It turns my stomach in more ways than one. Look at the mess I'm in right now, because of an inheritance. A boon that came with a load of shit attached to it."

Tobias regarded him. "You once told me you weren't a proud man—do you remember that? I told you there's no prestige in penny fiction, and you laughed me off."

"I remember."

"This isn't about penny fiction, is it?"

"No," Ethan said quietly. "It's not."

He spun his empty coffee cup in his hands, mulling it over.

"Ever since I was a boy, I've been under someone else's thumb. Buffeted by their whims. Reliant on them. Damaged by them. There's such wretched uncertainty in being tethered to that kind of life." He rubbed the back of his neck. "Am I a proud man? I suppose I'd like to be. I'd like to have something I'm proud *of*. I'd like to build something that can't be taken away."

I'd like to build it with her.

Tobias leaned back in his chair. "Then my last piece is this—I wager you can relieve yourself of at least one concern where she's concerned."

"What's that?"

"Miss Sinclair isn't the girl back in Boston who refused to wait for a journeyman," Tobias said bluntly. "She'll wait for you. I'm certain of it."

Ethan stared at him, his chest constricting.

He knew Tobias was right.

Belle *would* wait.

But that's not the promise he wanted to ask of her.

20

———

Secrets of the Old Bailey, Vol 1., No. 7
The True Chaperone

Clementina could not rest on her laurels, nor could she rest on the prophetic bloodied sextant. She knew who had not absconded to the dungeons with Ursula DeVry.

And with the trial date approaching, this was decidedly less useful than knowing who had.

"So if I use the silver theft from Friday's trial for number nine, I'll need to go back and revise the entire thief-in-the-attic arc for this week. It's repetitive, isn't it? Besides, I think the butler is too obvious."

It was Sunday evening, and Ethan was walking Belle home from the shop. They were taking their time in the pleasant weather, the mild breeze an unnecessary reminder that June was nearly upon them.

Ethan looked down as they strolled along her street. He wasn't touching her, and the price of respectability was gouging him. There were two inches between the swish of her skirts and the dark line of his trousers, and he watched the gap sway back and forth as she bubbled on about her draft.

"See?" Belle waved her burgundy journal under his nose. "Look at this part, here—"

Ethan drew to a halt, examining the passage in question. A lamplighter was making his way along Lincoln's Inn Fields, sending circles of light into the dusk. Belle stepped closer, anxiously watching his face as he read. He'd already finished the passage, but when he felt her skirts brush his knee, he read it again.

"I see your point." He handed over her journal. "Though I think the problem isn't the butler, so much as I'm not convinced an oyster fork could cause this much damage."

"Depends where you stick it." She winced as she rolled her shoulder. "The fork is fine. The real issue is we need a new villain, someone *worse* than the butler. I'm worried this isn't enough, Ethan."

A stab of guilt hit him at the shadowed anxiety on her face. She, too, was feeling the pressure. And he hated it.

"We had another successful day yesterday—number seven sold very well," he reassured her. "We're holding steady at the new numbers."

"But you've started buying paper." She bit her lip. "Unsold copies cost more than nothing now."

"We don't have any unsold copies."

"But—"

"No more writing tonight," he warned her. "Your head is bothering you, and you know it. You're bouncing between drafts for two issues at once, and it's wearing you out."

"We can't fall behind," she argued. "We only have three Saturdays left. Besides, I don't have a proper headache yet."

He lifted his hand, as if to put it on her shoulder. If they were alone, he could sink his thumb into the knot of tension that liked to burrow at the base of her neck. The little plea on her face nearly had him doing it.

"Not on the street." He shook his head. "I'm sorry, sweetheart."

"I wish I could stay with you tonight." Her eyes gleamed in the flickering lamplight.

"I know."

"Ethan…" She looked pained, but not from her head. "My mother and father are returning in a few days. We won't be able to steal time so easily."

The calendar had somehow become his greatest nemesis. It seemed to contain nothing but a series of ill-fated dates.

"I know," he repeated, leaning a scant inch closer. If it had been daylight, he would have been able to see the freckles dusting her nose. "I'd prefer you stay too, but your sister and your housekeeper are waiting tonight."

She sighed.

"Besides," he pointed out. "If a headache is nigh, you need your own bed. I want you to rest."

"And I won't rest in your bed?"

"Historically, sleep has not been our favored pursuit."

"I sleep very well next to you." Her smile turned beautifully devious. "I certainly *wake up* very well next to you."

"You're quite a little swindler, you know," Ethan said. "Hiding your wicked mouth behind your lilac bonnet."

She laughed, clearly delighted. "I've been told I'm a bit of a puzzle."

He imagined pulling her into the circle of his arms and sliding his finger beneath her chin for one long, leisurely goodnight kiss. And then, because his beloved was the sweetest of scoundrels, he imagined taking his leisure in other ways entirely.

He grudgingly resumed their walk up her street.

"Which window is yours?" he asked, nodding across the green to the ivy-laced bricks of the Sinclair residence.

She pointed him in the right direction. "Top left."

"I'll stay until you light your lamp," he promised. "Then I'll know you behaved and took your medicine and went straight to bed."

"You mean you want to loiter while I undress in my bedroom," she teased, letting the back of her hand brush his knuckles. "Bad man."

"You said you needed a new villain." He grinned.

She pretended to think it over. "A ruinously tactile tradesman… it has some merit, I suppose."

"If you want me to be a bad man, you can tell me what you're going to do when you slide beneath your bedsheets in your pretty white nightdress."

Even in the dusk, he could see her blush.

"I have a headache, remember?"

He boomed a laugh.

"I love you." His little finger wrapped its way around hers. "So damn much, Belle."

She hummed happily. "I love you too."

Heavy footfalls sounded behind them, and Ethan reluctantly released her hand. He turned to see the approach of what appeared to be a night watchman. He looked vaguely familiar, his face illuminated by the arc of his raised lantern.

"My, my," the man drawled. "What have we here?"

Ethan placed the voice a half second after he saw the flash of revulsion on Belle's face.

Not a night watchman.

"I saw a couple prowling about and thought I'd best ensure nothing unsavory was going on." Detective Inspector Lawrence Duncan lifted the lantern higher. "I have to say, I find myself thoroughly unsurprised."

"'Prowling about'?" Ethan asked skeptically. "Can one really *prowl* at half past eight?"

The inspector ignored him and stepped closer. "Belinda."

Ethan's hackles rose at the way Duncan said her name.

"Good evening, Inspector," she said stiffly. "And it's Miss Sinclair."

"Of course." Duncan nodded. "You're not married. We can't forget that."

Belle fell silent, but Ethan could see the muscle in her jaw tightening. Tension rolled through him. He needed to put a quick end to this encounter and see her home.

Duncan turned to Ethan. "Fletcher." He tilted his head. "Of Fleet Street."

Ethan stepped forward, placing himself between Duncan and Belle. Maintaining an air of indifference, he looked the inspector up and down. They were nearly the same height, but Ethan was broader.

Unfortunately, he was also less qualified to place someone under arrest.

"Is there a problem, Constable?"

"Inspector," Duncan corrected. "You tell me. From where I stood, it looked as if you were exhibiting threatening behavior toward this woman. Justice Sinclair's daughter, no less."

"Oh please," Belle said indignantly. "He was doing no such thing."

"Pardon my ignorance." Ethan folded his arms. "I'm still learning the many intricacies of London, but I wasn't aware inspectors were on night watch?"

"I've had my men observing the vicinity between the Fields and Fleet." Duncan flicked a speck of lint from his dark coat. "Thought I might take a look for myself."

"In other words, you're having me watched." Ethan scoffed. "For how long?"

"A good thing I have," Duncan countered smoothly. "It seems to me, you need watching. I could bring you in for indecent assault."

"Nonsense," Belle muttered.

"Not to mention last week," Duncan continued. "You were seen at Croom's Coffeehouse meeting with a radical."

"I took a pamphlet." Ethan shook his head. "I wasn't planning a riot."

"Even so, perception and whatnot. Rumors can be quite

damaging to a reputation." Duncan looked to Belle. "You recall, Belinda."

She made a small sound that opened a chasm inside Ethan, and the wound on her face filled it with fury. He was moving before he could think better of it, before he could think anything at all, and nothing but the soft pull of her hand on his bicep could have stopped him from doing something cataclysmically stupid.

Such as slamming his forearm into Duncan's throat.

"Speak to her like that again, and I'll turn the key in my own damn prison cell," Ethan gritted.

"Don't," she warned.

He lowered his arm but didn't back away.

"Or do," Duncan said lightly. "I'd be happy to take you off the street, Fletcher. Though from what I've heard about the state of your business, you might need to make yourself comfortable out here."

Ethan coiled tight enough to snap. But Belle was right; he couldn't afford to go to prison. Especially not at the hands of pigeon-liver like Duncan.

"Fortunately..." Ethan widened his stance. "I'm the sort of man who's comfortable anywhere."

A tense silence stretched between them.

"As you can see, Inspector, I'm quite well." Belle's voice was quiet. "There's no need to concern yourself."

Duncan didn't move. Ethan glanced at Belle; she was pale in the lamplight.

"Fine." The inspector shrugged, feigning disinterest. "Then move along, Fletcher. Miss Sinclair, if you need an escort, I'm obliged to see you home."

"The hell you will," Ethan said curtly. He reached for her again, tucking her close to him.

Duncan looked between them, finally shaking his head with a laugh.

"I have to say, Belinda, I didn't think you could fall any further." He started to turn away, his lip curling. "I'm of half a mind to collar him anyway, but I don't feel inclined to do either of you any favors."

Ethan instinctively stepped into the street, blocking Duncan's sour retreat.

"Go ahead then." Ethan raised his hands. "Take me in. I'll go gladly, if only to watch you tell your men the reason for it."

"Oh?"

"I'm sure they'd love to know the woman who dropped you picked up a Yankee—and you *can't stop* thinking about it." Ethan's mouth tilted with firm assurance. "I wonder if they'll pity you? They should. I find myself hard-pressed to think of anything quite so pathetic."

Ethan shook his head. *Pathetic* was right. This had nothing to do with Belle, and everything to do with an arrogant man's need for the final say. Duncan's mouth twisted, but Ethan must have struck a nerve, for the inspector huffed in disdain and finally strode away.

Ethan watched the lantern disappear in the twilight, his pulse racing from the hostile confrontation. He shook out his unfortunately unused fist and turned to Belle. "Christ, if he couldn't throw me in prison, believe me, I would have *throttled*—"

To his utmost surprise, she was beaming.

"You're wonderful," she said, her hands on her cheeks. "Oh. That was *tremendously* satisfying." Improbably, she spun in a happy little circle. "I'd kiss you, but I'm afraid he would arrest you, after all."

"Are you certain?"

"Oh, to be sure. You hit Duncan where it hurts—he values *nothing* so much as his own pride. Do you know, I think I found my new villain."

"No—I meant are you certain you can't kiss me?"

Her irrepressible smile widened, and he took one step closer. But no, they had to be careful. Doubly so, with Duncan about.

Ethan groaned softly. "I suppose I really do need to see you home now."

She sighed. "I know."

They walked the short distance in silence, mindful to keep far more than two inches between them. When they arrived outside her home, he fell back as she climbed the few stairs to the lacquered front door.

"Belle."

She paused, turning to look at him. He stuffed his hands in his pockets.

"Stealing moments in the dark," he said gruffly. "It can't go on forever this way. Something will have to change."

"Not us." Her gaze brushed his face. "Everything around us."

His favorite thing about her was the way she always said the good part for him. He wasn't adept at sentimentality, but Belle saw him so clearly, it was easy to be hopeful with her.

"If I tell you that one day, we'll walk through our own front door together, you'd believe me, wouldn't you?"

"Of course I would." She smiled, beatific in the lamplight. "Darling, you've never lied to me."

She pressed her fingers to her lips, then turned and slipped inside, closing the door with a soft, decisive click.

Slowly, he ambled across the green and leaned against an iron railing to wait for the faint flare in the top left window.

He was still there, long, long after her light went out.

21

---

23 May 1848
Papa,

Secure in the knowledge I will see you in a matter of days, I will keep this letter brief, so you can anticipate hearing more upon your return.

Helena has been aflutter with activity; as to be expected, Aunt Cora has been an indefatigable ally to her social calendar. I've been busy in my own way—writing my stories and trying very hard not to get ahead of myself.

I miss you. I hope you and Mama are faring well, and your weather has been agreeable. You'll find you are returning to London on the cusp of summer.

It's very hard to believe June is a week away.

> *Love from your daughter*
> *—B.*

THE FORDHAM HOUSE breakfast room was quiet Tuesday morning. Belle sat alone with a heaping tea tray, though she was more focused on her story than her stomach. Two different sets of notes were spread before her; she'd just started a revision of her latest draft, much improved by Clementina's foiling of a swell-headed detective inspector.

What she had *not* improved was the state of her journals. She frowned at the mess, shaking out her wrist. Ethan was right—she had too many stories going at once. The breakneck pace of the serial was catching up to her, but she couldn't slow down.

Next week marked the beginning of June, and soon, Ethan would have to determine once and for all if he was going to decline the New York offer. Things *looked* promising, though still very tenuous. If only she could race ahead to the finish and report back, reassuring him all was well, he could keep the shop, they could be together…

Unfortunately, her assistance was limited to finishing this blasted draft by day's end.

"Oh, Belle, there you are." Aunt Cora's voice drew her attention. "I didn't realize anyone else was awake."

"Well it *is* half past nine." Belle forced a smile as her aunt came into the room. "Not so very early."

"Not for some of us." Aunt Cora shook her head in amusement. "Already at work, darling? I hope I'm not disturbing you. You seem rather…caught up."

Belle looked at her piles of papers, feeling the exact opposite of *caught up.* "I was just finishing something."

"Hmm." Aunt Cora sat beside her, pouring them both tea. "Did you sleep well?"

"Very."

Belle had lingered with Ethan last evening, arguing over the proof for number eight until they'd resolved their differing opinions to their mutual satisfaction. She hadn't arrived at Fordham House until after Aunt Cora and the girls departed for their dinner party.

"Mrs. Bowers wasn't expecting you?" Aunt Cora said lightly.

"No." Belle sipped her tea. "I told her I would be here."

"Ah." Aunt Cora smiled. "I must have been mixed up with Sunday."

"I was at home on Sunday," Belle said, thinking of the standoff with Duncan and the lonely night in her own bed.

"Of course," Aunt Cora allowed. "My mistake. It's so very hard to keep track of your comings and goings. Especially when there have been so many…goings."

Belle stilled, forcing herself to meet her aunt's hazel-blue gaze.

"Your new endeavor is keeping you very busy," Aunt Cora finally said.

Belle managed a nod.

"I imagine a new project involves new people." Aunt Cora paused. "Perhaps a new…friend."

Recognizing this confrontation for exactly what it was, Belle stiffened. "Is it such a marvel I would have a friend?" she asked quietly.

"You tell me, darling." Aunt Cora studied her carefully. "Does it feel like a marvel?"

Belle's feelings were on her face, and she knew her aunt could read them. The two of them had always been close, doubly so in recent years. Aunt Cora understood all too well what Belle had narrowly avoided with Duncan, for she herself hadn't been so lucky. Her first marriage had been arranged, horrendously unhappy, and resulted in near-catastrophic consequences for her small family.

Now Belle recalled the evening after she broke her engagement, how her aunt had arrived at the Sinclair residence with a bottle of amber liquor in hand. Belle curled on her bed while Aunt Cora sat at her dressing table to pour them each a healthy measure. When Belle morosely asked what they were toasting, her aunt had gently replied that in her experience, the first thing a woman does when she sheds an onerous man is raise a glass to her future.

"Yes," Belle said softly. The truth spread through her like sunshine, immediately improving her strained mood. "It does feel rather marvelous. To have a friend."

For a long moment, Aunt Cora was quiet, studying the floral pattern on her teacup.

"Belle, perhaps you might permit me a bit of retrospection this morning?"

"Yes. Of course."

Aunt Cora busied herself fixing a plate of eggs. She set it in front of Belle.

"When I was married to my first husband, there was a great deal of unhappiness in my home. Even after he died, loneliness was inescapable." She watched Belle closely. "It was a very bad turn, darling."

Belle nodded.

"When your Uncle Nate came around, it was an explosion of light. Every corner of my home was filled with him. It was intoxicating—to be loved so freely after all the horrible restraint. It was bigger than me, bigger than my worries, bigger than my good sense. I was very fortunate he took good care with my heart, with my future."

She reached for Belle's hand.

"You know, Belle, sometimes…after a bad turn, anything that's *not* bad seems good. That's a thing to be careful about, darling. The temptation to settle for less can be very real—especially when the lesser part was all that was offered."

Belle knew what her aunt was trying to warn her against, just as she knew there was no need for it. Ethan was her very own explosion of light.

"What happens the other times?" Belle asked. "When something that seems good *is* good? When something turns out to be so much more than the lesser part?"

"You count yourself very fortunate." Aunt Cora finally smiled, wide and lovely. "And you hold on to it with both hands."

At that moment, voices sounded in the corridor, followed by Cecily, Lena, and Uncle Nate, apparently in the midst of dissecting the soiree the ladies attended last night.

"Good morning," Belle called, smiling at her sister's and cousin's wan countenances. "Late night?"

"They're all late nights." Lena yawned, kissing Belle on the cheek. "You look bright today, dearest."

Belle blushed, looking at her dress. She was wearing the pale yellow Ethan seemed to favor.

"Now, what happened after that final hand of hearts with Henry St. James?" Lena asked Cecily as she accepted a cup of tea. "You weren't really going to go through with a kissing forfeit, were you?"

"That isn't something *my* daughter would do." Uncle Nate turned to Cecily, his handsome face sharp with inquiry. "Would she?"

"Hmm?" Cecily busied herself by selecting a pastry for her father. "Jam, Papa?"

"Don't distract me with biscuits." He raised one eyebrow. "I invented that trick."

"I wasn't going to lose." Cecily waved aside his concern. "And I certainly wasn't going to kiss him. Now if Henry *Sullivan* had been playing—"

"Wait." Uncle Nate looked between Lena and Cecily. "I thought you *were* playing with Henry Sullivan."

"No, I was playing Henry *St. James*," Cecily corrected.

"Which one is—"

"Henry St. James is a clodpoll, and Henry Sullivan is a cad," Lena explained.

"Ah." Uncle Nate picked up his paper. "So glad we sorted that out."

"Good morning, ladies." A smooth, deep voice sounded from the threshold. "Father, I see you remain a thorn amongst roses."

Belle looked up to see her cousin Oliver amble into the breakfast room. Lord Travers was still wearing evening clothes but appeared as irrepressibly handsome as always—tall and broad, with dimples he wielded like weapons. He was the picture of his father, and unfortunately, he knew it.

"Good morning, Ollie." Lena grinned. "Or should I say goodnight?"

Oliver winked and shrugged out of his coat.

"I sincerely hope it's not goodnight." Aunt Cora pointed a finger at twenty-seven-year-old Oliver, who towered over her. "You're meant to escort me to Mrs. Everett's garden party, and I expect you to at least pretend you want to be there."

"Fear not." Oliver kissed his mother's hand and widened his smile. "Nobody will be looking at me so long as you are on my arm."

Aunt Cora beamed.

"I invented that too," Uncle Nate said dryly.

"Invented it? You secured the patent," Aunt Cora teased, and Uncle Nate turned a smile on her that put Ollie's dimples to shame.

Cecily grimaced. "Not today, I beg you."

Oliver slung his coat over the chair next to Belle. She scooted her knee away from the fine wool; it reeked of smoke and liquor.

"How was *your* evening, Cecily?" he asked. "Sullivan asked after you."

Belle hardly heard Cecily's animated exclamation. She was too distracted by Oliver's rumpled coat.

He'd left it folded, the lining visible, and from the interior pocket peeked the top right corner of a publication.

Belle stared.

She *knew* that top right corner.

She knew every word in the top right corner…and in the other three corners too.

Those words shouldn't be *here*, in front of her, at breakfast.

How…

She tilted her head, trying to get a better view, as though if she looked hard enough, the type would rearrange itself into the *Times* or *Standard*.

But no. There was no question.

Oliver was carrying *Secrets of the Old Bailey*, No. 6.

Her belly flipped several times in rapid, unpleasant succession, and each rotation seemed to funnel more heat to her cheeks.

"Oh, Belle." Oliver noticed her staring and plopped next to her.

"I nearly forgot. I saw this at my club, and it reminded me of some-thing you might like."

He pulled the serial from his coat and tossed it to the table.

'The False Chaperone' stared at the ceiling. Belle looked up, too, as if a hole would appear and suck her right up from the breakfast table.

How on earth had Ollie found it? They didn't distribute the serial in Mayfair. They didn't distribute anywhere *near* Mayfair…

Oliver was looking at her expectantly.

"Thank you, Ollie," she managed. "This is…"

"It's not erudite, that's for damn sure." Oliver grinned. "I thought you might have fun with it. I know you like horror, though this is more horrifically dramatic."

A strange but certain discomfort crept over her, seeming to steal her words and breath in one swoop. No matter how long she looked, she couldn't make this situation make sense. It was entirely incongruous—an etching of Clementina Bloom holding a skull… beside Aunt Cora's third-best breakfast china.

"Belle can like what she likes," Uncle Nate cut in. "I'll put my vote of confidence behind any paper that has *you* actually reading."

His tone held a faint warning; he thought Oliver was making fun of her reading selection.

No, Uncle, she thought dully. *Just my writing.*

"I…" She faltered under a crushing weight of awkwardness. How to explain? She wasn't prepared to reveal her secret today. "This…was at your club?"

"It was mixed in with the other papers." Ollie took the scone Cecily had tried to ply her father with. "I thought the woman looked a bit familiar, so I picked it up."

Belle was torn by brief vindication that the illustration was, in fact, doing exactly as it ought and outright horror that Victor Marks had put her face on Clementina's.

She quickly pulled the paper into her lap.

"A penny blood?" Aunt Cora blanched, glancing at the folded

publication. "She doesn't want to read that, Oliver. Aren't they rather...scurrilous?"

"What do you know of penny bloods, love?" Uncle Nate tilted his head toward his wife. "I didn't know you were in the habit of perusing street literature."

"Mama, I would do something drastic to see you read that." Cecily leaned forward. "I'd give you my new lace gloves."

"She would only make it to the second page," Oliver predicted. "There's a garroting. It ends *quite* badly."

"Garrotings...don't usually end well," Belle said haltingly.

Her throat was very dry. In her mind, her stories had seemed wonderfully sensational, but that was before her family analyzed them over breakfast. It was undeniably jarring to have her two worlds collide in such an unexpected way.

"Belle, perhaps you should give it back to Ollie." Aunt Cora looked worried. "Your father won't want you reading this—"

Lena curiously craned her neck, and Belle folded the serial. If Lena saw the name Clementina Bloom, she would instantly know Belle had written it.

"Papa won't mind," she found herself saying as she scooted back her chair. "I'm at the courthouse half the day anyway. I can't imagine anything in here would upset me."

"Besides, from what I've heard, her novel is highly shocking." Lena grinned.

"She won't let anyone read it," Cecily added. "Believe me, I've tried."

"My manuscript," Belle corrected, "is not yet published."

"That's right. Belle is a *novelist*," Aunt Cora said decisively. She looked at Belle, her expression warm and proud. "Stop feeding her drivel, Oliver."

Belle's smile froze in place as her aunt came around the table to wrap her in a fierce embrace.

"I'm not...a novelist," she mumbled into the gathered pleats of Aunt Cora's shoulder. "Far from it."

"Oh, darling." Her aunt touched her cheek. "Don't discount yourself so easily."

"I'm not." Belle fumbled over an explanation she wasn't prepared for. "That is…I'm not a novelist. But I'm not discounting myself. I…"

Everyone was looking at her.

Tell them, a brave corner of her mind spoke up. *Tell them you wrote this. Tell them thousands of copies of this are spread all over the city. Tell them you are in love and halfway down a wildly unconventional path with a wildly unconventional man, and you plan to keep walking it.*

Tell them.

Belle's face heated. There was nothing for it. She was facing the prospect of what she feared and reviled most in all the world—scrutiny.

So she did what she always did.

"If you'll excuse me…" She cleared her throat. "I need to ready myself for the day."

"Belle?" Lena looked concerned. "Oh no, stay. We didn't mean to upset you. You don't need to read it, really."

Belle folded the serial in half and stuffed it in her basket, wishing she could just as easily set aside her family's reaction to it.

Instead, she carefully schooled her features.

"I'm not upset." She forced a smile. "I'm perfectly fine."

BUT BY LATE AFTERNOON, it was clear that Belle was not, in fact, perfectly fine.

She was uncharacteristically irritable, unable to concentrate in the noise of the printshop, unable to write more than a few sentences at a time, unable to find what she needed in these *bloody piles* of jumbled notes—

"So then I was talking to Paulie about my story—you know, with the heiress who poisoned me—and he had a great idea."

Sam had been pacing in front of her desk for the last quarter hour, and while Belle usually enjoyed entertaining Sam's creative notions, she couldn't match his enthusiasm today.

"Where is my research journal?" she muttered, sifting through a stack of old revisions. She hissed in impatience and tossed the papers aside.

As soon as she had time, she very much needed to reorder her notebooks. These last few weeks, she'd been writing so much, so fast, that instead of keeping her court notes in one journal and her stories in another, she'd fallen into grabbing whichever notebook was nearest and making do.

It was becoming a rather untenable operation. Her handwriting had taken on a slightly manic slant, and her journals were bursting at the seams with shorthand notes and half drafts. Last week at the Old Bailey, she'd been so inspired by the proceedings of a trial for a silver theft, she penned half her story right there alongside the court transcription.

Come to think of it, she still needed to revise that fair copy for Newburn. She'd added the untimely end of the greedy banker but had yet to alter the trial details.

Blast, there was too much to do.

"You know how Varney the Vampire keeps being resurrected? Well, what if we bring *me* back from the dead too? I could haunt someone."

"Sam." Belle pressed her temples.

"My first thought is the heiress, because it would only be logical, but I can leave it to you, Miss Sinclair, and I told Paulie—"

"You told Paulie what?" she snapped, sitting up in alarm. "You told him I'm Irascible Nell?"

"No." Sam looked flummoxed. "I told him I'd *talk* to Irascible Nell about it."

"More like Irascible Belle," Victor Marks observed. "You've been tetchy since you arrived, lovely."

"I just don't think we need to include supernatural elements, that's all. I don't suppose we could stand to take ourselves a bit seriously? My aim was to write about trials, you know, but of course, why not add vampires and ghosts and hauntings, and be just like every other penny blood on the corner stand. We haven't baked anyone into a pie yet, why not try that next?"

She flung her pen into the workroom, watching it sail through the door, instantly regretting it but too mortified to retrieve it.

Marks made a small sound of interest, his charcoal moving quickly as he studied Belle.

"And *stop* drawing me, if you please." She snatched the artist's latest sketch. "I don't want my face all over the city."

"What the devil is going on in here?"

At the sound of Ethan's deep voice breaking over her shoulder, Marks and Sam exchanged a look of patent relief, as though they were boys being saved from an angry school-mistress by the arrival of the headmaster.

Belle's neck heated. She was already feeling combustible; she did not need to add a stern Ethan Fletcher to the mix.

"You dropped this."

Her pen appeared before her, dangling idly from Ethan's fingers.

She pressed the heel of her hand to her eyelids. *Heavens*, she was acting beastly, wasn't she?

"I'm sorry." She looked worriedly between Sam and Marks. "I must apologize for my outburst. It seems I'm having some difficulty today."

Ethan jerked his head toward the door. "Give us a moment, gentlemen."

The pair evaporated to the workroom.

"Well?" Ethan looked at her expectantly. "What's got into you today? I haven't heard you snap at anyone except me in the last two months."

"I do feel a bit like a pot boiling over," she admitted, pushing her hair off her forehead. "My papers are disordered, my stories are vulgar, my parents are set to return day after next, and I'm expected to spend the rest of the week at home with them, which means I won't see you, and I'll miss you, and I can't help you—"

"Who says the serial is vulgar?" Ethan shook his head. "And

missing you aside, I'm not concerned about the work. We're on schedule—your draft of number nine is nearly finished. We'll print it this week to distribute next Saturday, and you'll be back in time to revise number ten."

She bit her lip, still uneasy.

"Look." Ethan raked back his dark hair and glanced at the clock. "We're almost done for today. I think you ought to go home and clear your head."

She followed his gaze to the clock and cursed. "Damn. I'm meant to help Lena ready for the opera."

"Go. Help your sister. I can't afford for you to break any more writing instruments," he pointed out wryly.

She sighed in frustration, accepting he was right. Her agitation had stifled her productivity today. She couldn't stop revisiting breakfast at Fordham House, hating the way she'd frozen, besieged by an uneasy swell of doubt. What if she was ruining her future—or worse, *his* future? Ethan was pinning all his hopes on her.

If *Secrets* couldn't pull through for him...

If *she* couldn't pull through for him...

She swallowed a small, painful lump.

"Belle." Ethan's tone was firm and kind, breaking through her rising nerves. "Leave me your fair copy, sweetheart. I'll handle the rest."

Grateful for a task she could complete, she gave him her journal.

He easily hefted the notebook in his palm, as if it belonged there.

And then he pressed her fingers to his mouth, as if they belonged there too.

22

Accounting Ledger of E. Fletcher
Week of 20 May 1848
Secrets of the Old Bailey Vol. 1, No. 7
Earnings less expenditures—£20

Remaining debt owed—£25

   N.b.—expenditures now include purchase of paper, inclusive of tax

ETHAN STARED at Belle's lacquered front door. It was early evening, and there was nothing overtly wrong about him coming to call. Except he hadn't been invited. If he were a gambling man, he would wager Mrs. Bowers did not take kindly to unannounced guests.

But Belle hadn't left him much choice—nor, as it turned out, had she left him the correct draft when she departed the shop earlier.

He sighed and wrapped two fingers around the door knocker. The resounding clang seemed louder than it needed to be.

There was a long pause.

He rubbed the back of his neck and raised his hand again.

The door swung open. To his surprise, Belle's face appeared in the crack.

"Ethan?" She looked thoroughly perplexed. "What are you doing here? Is something wrong?"

"You tell me." He raised an eyebrow. "You left the wrong journal, and Newburn needs your fair copy first thing tomorrow."

"Are you certain?"

"I went through it all." He shook his head. "But I didn't see anything for number nine. The silver theft, isn't it?"

"Yes." Belle frowned, opening the door wider. He could now see she was wearing a pale pink wrapper. "Come in. It must be upstairs. My notes are all over the place…"

Ethan hesitated. It was very hard to look away from the smooth expanse of her collarbone. "Where is your housekeeper?"

"She's with her daughter tonight." Belle motioned him inside. "Her grandson is colicky. I told her to go see the babe, to take Harriet to help. It's only me here tonight. Lena already departed for my aunt's."

Her gaze turned velvety. "I was going to come to you later, but I've been a bit distracted."

"Yes," he acknowledged, following her inside. "I noticed. I thought I should check on that too."

She reached behind him to close the door, and Ethan ran one finger down her spine. He might not be a betting man, but he liked his odds that she wasn't wearing a corset.

"Did you say your journal was upstairs?"

She slid him a look. "Come on, then. Though be warned, my bedroom isn't fit for company."

"I promise I haven't looked at a single thing since you opened the door half-dressed."

She led him up the stairs and down a hall to an airy bedchamber. Everything was dark wood and ivory lace. A polished desk sat in front of her window, just as he'd always imagined.

But the most notable feature of Belle's bedroom was that it was a complete disaster.

All over the bed, draped over both upholstered armchairs, and spilling from an adjacent door was a mess of clothing—gowns and shawls and ribbons and jewelry scattered in a glittering tableau.

"Belle?" His lustful urges were momentarily waylaid by the shock of such clutter. "What in hell—"

"I was helping Lena." She winced and set about gathering armfuls of rustling fabric. "She wanted to wear my bronze shot-silk, but it didn't quite fit, then she wanted *me* to try it on, because I never get to wear it…and then things got a bit out of hand. Not all of this is mine," she added, depositing a pile in her small dressing room.

He was silent, looking about, taking in all of her fine, fine things. He picked up a pale blue gown, rubbing the satiny fabric between his calloused fingers.

"I wore that to my first ball." Belle lifted the bodice from his hands and held it in front of her, moving to stand in front of the gilded mirror over her dressing table. She swayed slightly, the skirts swirling around her shins. "It's pretty, isn't it?"

"It's very pretty." He joined her at the mirror. "I can't imagine how beautiful you must have looked."

In truth, he could imagine it all too well. A cloud of silk, her radiant face. Something heavy pressed upon him, and the weight of it hurt.

She draped the gown over a chair. "And I wore this." She lifted a delicate necklace from a tray on her dressing table. "A gift from my aunt. Sapphires and seed pearls." She gently fingered the string of tiny jewels. "You know, I can't remember the last time I've worn it."

"Why not?"

"I haven't had a reason to wear it," she told their reflections, a wistful little smile playing on her lips. "I don't go anywhere that calls for anything so splendid. But I like knowing I have it."

"You could wear it for me."

An odd tangle of defeat and determination knotted inside his chest. Never in his life could he give her jewelry like this, but he could give her a reason to wear it. It mattered in a way he couldn't explain, that Belle had someone to dress up for, should she wish.

She shook her head. "It's silly…"

"I'd like to see you wear it." His palms fell to her shoulders.

"All right." She blushed and raised the necklace to her throat. "You'll need to help—the clasp is finicky."

"I've got it."

He slid his fingers along her collarbone, then around to the back of her neck. Her hair was bound in a loose knot that left her nape exposed. He gently stroked her skin as he fastened the clasp of her necklace.

"There." He looked up, his green eyes finding her hazel in the mirror. "You can't tell me you looked better than this the last time you wore it."

She reached behind her, wrapping her arm around his neck. Her reflection grew heated at the lazy intent in his gaze.

Then she blinked, seeming to return to herself. "The notebook," she said hastily, turning from the mirror. "I nearly forgot."

"Don't worry about it right now," Ethan muttered, trying to draw her back to him.

"No. I forgot once already." She moved to her desk, found the journal, and held it aloft. "I can't let you leave without this."

She frowned as she brought it to him. "Goodness knows, it's distracted me enough today."

"Is this what made you so prickly this afternoon?" He flipped through the journal. "If you were having trouble with the draft, you could have told me."

To his own surprise, he'd come to truly enjoy playing the foil in her machinations. It brought him untold satisfaction that Belle could invent scenarios as outlandish as she pleased, safe in the knowledge he'd rein her in when needed.

"Not the draft." She shook her head.

"What then?"

"The serial as a whole, I suppose." She sank to her desk chair, sitting on top of a paisley-printed shawl. "This morning, my cousin Oliver brought a copy of *Secrets* to my aunt's house."

"In Mayfair?" He'd never been to Mayfair, but he'd gleaned enough of London in the last two months to know Clementina Bloom would be an unexpected visitor.

"Someone was reading it at his club, and he picked it up for me…and now, my whole family has seen it."

He nodded slowly, starting to understand the shape of her odd mood. "I see."

"My aunt was worried about it being inappropriate. She didn't want Oliver to give it to me. She was…a bit embarrassed, I think." Belle looked at her hands. "She made sure to note my manuscript is far superior to a penny blood."

Her expression grew pained, and Ethan felt a dull discomfort move through him. *Right.* Her manuscript. The one he couldn't publish for her.

"What did they say when they found out you're Irascible Nell?"

"Oh." She bit her lip. "They didn't find out. I didn't tell them."

She looked up at him, a faint uncertainty in her hazel eyes, and Ethan's agitation sharpened.

"You didn't tell them?" He lowered his brow in consternation. "So you…what? Pretended you didn't write it?"

"I couldn't. I wasn't ready. I still need to find the right opportunity…"

He regarded her, staving off a faint rankling. He was used to scrambling her name every week, hiding her identity in spite of their sensational success, but he hadn't thought she would flat-out deny what they were working on when confronted with the chance.

"I don't usually make assumptions," he said slowly, "but I can't help but assume the paper falling onto your breakfast table might have been an opportunity, sweetheart."

"It's not so easy for me." Her face was racked with nerves. "You know good and well how I get stopped up. Those women on the street, the evening with Duncan—I'm not good in the middle of a moment. I take four drafts to do anything for a reason, Ethan."

He folded his arms. "You're fine with me."

"I'm many things with you." She peered up at him, her forehead creasing in concern. "Are you upset with me...for not telling my family?"

"I don't exactly relish the notion you feel the need to hide what we're doing."

What had he vowed, the very first week? *I can make something fit for her name.* It's what he'd promised himself, even before he wanted to promise Belle anything. His nostrils flared, a fight working its way up his spine as he considered the prospect of battling her shame.

"You said your aunt seemed embarrassed, but given your reaction, I can't help but wonder if she was the only one. I'm well-aware of all the many ways I'm holding you back. God knows, your writing shouldn't be another."

"I'm *not* embarrassed," she said firmly. "I really do believe that, because I thought about it all day—at the expense of nearly every other thought. But it doesn't mean others won't find it embarrassing. You must understand, me writing a penny blood would be a tremendous scandal in some circles. And it wouldn't be my first."

She looked down.

"Whether or not I'm Irascible Nell, I'm always going to be Belle Sinclair. I've chosen to manage that by keeping things separate. Today, they nearly collided, and...it was unsettling."

He understood what she was trying to say, but he could clearly remember when she *hadn't* been so quick to keep things separate. He strode to her window and looked out, spying the railing he'd leaned against two nights ago.

"When we first met, you wanted to publish under your own name," he said. "You shook my hand and told me you were the author of your manuscript. You were proud of it."

"I did." Belle was still eyeing him carefully. "When I was trying to publish a novel, yes, I wanted to use my name. But I'm not writing a novel anymore. I'm writing penny fiction."

"For me." Ethan felt compelled to say the obvious, necessary thing. "You're writing penny fiction…because that's all I can offer you."

"Yes." She lifted her chin. "That's true. You couldn't publish a novel, so we didn't. It's not a judgment on you. It's what happened. I can mourn something I never had at the same time I embrace something I do." She rose and drew nearer to him. "You're acting obtuse, and I don't know why. Don't you sometimes miss publishing the news?"

He worked his jaw. "Yes."

Her color flared high as she put her hands on her hips. "How is that different? Neither of us planned to write a story paper. We're compromising, we're seeing what comes of it. I *like* what I see. But not everyone will, and that is a challenging prospect."

He expelled a helpless groan. "You still can't see it, can you? Belle, I *cannot compromise* when it comes to you. I cannot bear to watch you do it for me."

He cast his gaze about her bedroom—the finery splayed on her bed, the beautiful desk where she no longer wrote her novel. Everywhere was evidence of what their compromise cost her.

"The last thing I want is for you to settle for me," he said roughly. "If I ever find I'm holding you back—"

"Holding me back?" She breathed a soft, incredulous laugh. "*You're* the one who pushes me. Two months ago, I was half of the woman I am now. Because of *you*."

"Belle…" His voice caught as her words landed.

"Enough."

The fight was leaving him and finding Belle. Her eyes glittered in the slice of sunset falling through her window.

"I see you, Ethan. Allowing a pile of disordered ballgowns and discarded jewelry to put you on edge."

She swayed closer, keeping her eyes on him.

"As if *anything* in this room could hold a candle to you."

Closer still.

"As if anything in this *city* could hold a candle to *you*."

In an instant, his blood turned thick as honey. He tracked her, riveted, as she stalked across the room to the pile of gowns on her bed.

"Do you see this?" She snatched up a shimmery green bodice. "I wore it the last time I attended the opera. I dressed myself with such care, only to overhear a group of matrons say the most wretched things behind my back." She raised the dress for his inspection. "Do you think *this* matters to me?"

"No." The air in his lungs grew heavy. "No, I don't."

She threw the green aside.

"Here—" She flung a length of yellow silk toward him; he caught it one hand. "I wore that shawl to my engagement soiree. Duncan told me it didn't suit. And you know, I stopped wearing it, even while I kept wearing his damn ring." She raised her chin. "Should I care about that?"

"No." His pulse slammed in his ears. "*Hell* no."

He tossed aside the silk and stepped toward her.

The sharpening of her usual reserve whetted his own primal response.

Belle was offering him every one of her beautiful edges.

He knew *exactly* what to do with them.

"And this one..." She grasped an ivory lace bodice. "This was to be my wedding gown. Can you imagine *anything* less important than this?"

"Not a damn thing," he said huskily, closing the gap between them.

She dropped the gown at his feet. He held her blazing stare, his chest straining in tempo with the rapid rise of her breasts.

"I'm sick to death of you acting like you can't offer me anything, Ethan." She slid her palms up his shoulders. "I want *you*. Only you. Always you."

"You mean that." His voice was raw with conviction. He wasn't asking her a question—she meant it, and *yes*, he knew it.

"I mean it," she whispered hotly.

He put his hands in her hair, angling her face to his. "Why?"

"Because I love you. Because you make me mad in more ways

than one. And because you are the only person on earth I can use even half of my words with."

She was incendiary, sparking something blistering and uncontrollable within him. She was about to find out how *shatteringly* good she made him feel—

As if he were the biggest man in the world.

"Then do it." He inched her back, and she gasped, her glazed eyes reflecting his own mounting fervor.

"Do what?"

"Use your words with me."

Another step.

Another.

Her breath came fast against his throat.

"I want all of your words, Belle."

Her back hit the door of her dressing room, and he lowered his lips to her ear.

"Remind us both why nobody in this entire goddamn city can hold a candle to *me*."

Her sigh hitched as she wrenched him down, dragging his mouth to hers. He groaned at her unmastered assertion, her gentle nip at his lower lip. *Christ.* He stroked the hungry press of her tongue and she yanked him closer still, winding his loose tie around her fist.

"What do you want right now?" he rasped, nudging his nose against hers. "Anything...I'll give it to you."

Her chest heaved as she leaned against the door. He braced his arms on either side of her, caging in her blossoming demand. He was in thrall to her boldness, greedy for her greed.

"I want you to undress me," she whispered.

He was already opening the tie at her waist. Beneath her wrapper, she wore nothing but the sapphire necklace and a pair of lace stockings. He took her in—rosy and ready—and his cock pulsed.

"I'm going to take such good care of you." He eased his thumbs over her stiffening nipples before dragging her wrapper to the floor. "Tell me how."

"Ethan..."

He sank to his knees, nosing the soft curls between her legs. She was wet, as wet as he was hard, and he groaned as he wrapped his hand around her calf.

"You want these stockings off, sweetheart?"

"No." Her cheeks were pink. "Leave them on."

He licked his lip. "Yes, ma'am."

He spread her thighs, his palms pressing wide, and waited.

"Your mouth on me." She squirmed against his hands. "Please."

God, yes.

"Do you want me to make you come?" He kissed the crease of her hip. "Or just play a little?"

Her flush found the tips of her breasts.

"Make me ready for you," she panted.

He loosened a gravelly moan and slipped his tongue over her swollen, eager bud.

"And then?" He looked up at her, kneading his fingers into her bottom. Her expression was glassy, her hair spilling from its knot. He compulsively dropped one hand to his trousers to palm his straining cock. "Tell me, Belle. It's going to feel so good."

"I...I want you to handle me." Her voice was ragged as he nestled his mouth between her shaking thighs. "Don't be delicate. Show me you understand this is *real*, that you're exactly what I want, that you can have whatever you want of me."

She drew a breath.

"Then I want you to take it."

A powerful, alien sensation tore through him as he held her legs open and licked a long stripe.

They moaned in tandem.

She was so wet, it was turning him senseless, and he licked her again...*again.* Lips, mouth, teeth—he angled her closer, his fingers digging proprietary crescents into the skin of her thighs.

She wanted to come with his cock, she was telling him this, her pleas desperate in his ears, but he was lost to the intoxicating desire sliding beneath his tongue. For the first time since he met her, he was going to deny her.

"Ethan, I'm ready," she gasped. "You can—"

"*You* can," he ordered, his throat burning. He pressed his mouth back to her. He couldn't stop—all sugared softness, all for him. "You've put me on my knees, Belle. For the love of God, let me stay here."

"Yes, *yes*." A shiver tore through her, her fist tight in his hair. "Don't stop."

He dragged her leg over his shoulder, widening his access, tonguing the slick of arousal on her thigh. She heaved a faint sob when he settled his lips back around her clitoris, and he chased the sound, circling hard, soaking up her crumbling cries until she was pulling him closer, shuddering above him, coming undone under the demand of his mouth.

Her calf slid limply along his back, and he opened his trousers with one hand, seeking relief, any relief. His cock jutted hard against his stomach, and when she saw it, she moaned softly.

"Now." She tugged at his shoulders. "I swear to God, Ethan…"

He was already on his feet, yanking off his shirt.

"You still want me to handle you, sweetheart?" He needed to be sure.

"You'll have to withdraw," she managed. "But yes, I want this." She bit his earlobe, and he slipped into some sort of haze. "I *need* it."

And *yes*, she did, she loved this, he could see it all over her. He pressed her more firmly to her door, and his cock thickened to the point of pain.

"You asked me if I know what's real," he muttered. "I *know* what's real." He tweaked her nipple, and she moaned into his chest. "This." She spread her legs, so good for him, and he fit his palm against her. "*This*."

"*Yes*. It's yours, *please*…"

"What else is real, Belle?" His hands fell to the back of her thighs, and he lifted her, holding her to the door as she wrapped her legs around his waist. "What else?"

"You," she gasped. "You—"

"Me," he confirmed, dragging his length along where she was wet and hot and so gorgeously needy. "*Me* inside you."

He sank to his bollocks, his back rigid with pleasure. Her arms twined around his neck, and the glorious drag of her stiff nipples along the hair of his chest sent him momentarily spiraling.

He gripped her hips and lengthened his thrusts. Ruthlessly claiming, roughly reassuring, deep-seated plunges rattling the door. Her hair tumbled loose, sticking to her neck, and he buried his face in her glossy strands and salty skin.

She clutched him as he pinioned her to the door, the prettiest gasps urging him on.

Deep, deeper, more.

He filled her, stretched her, nearly splintered within her, but no— *not yet*—not until she felt him everywhere, not until he took care of her, his brilliant girl…he'd do anything for her, anything, *anything*.

"I feel it." She dragged her bottom lip over his chin, to his mouth, taking his half-rendered promises on her tongue. "You're there, Ethan. *We're* there."

He swore, forcing himself to steady, even as the bite of her fingernails channeled straight to his cock. He hissed an agonized exhale and angled his hips, working hard against a spot that had her keening into his neck—

And then—*oh God, thank God*—she shattered around him.

She sagged as she spiraled, her cries blunted by his shoulder. He moved on instinct, he had to withdraw, he had to do it *now*…

He set her on her shaky feet and pulled from her, slamming both his open palms to the door above her head.

"Belle—"

He kissed her, and she grasped him, bringing him to release with the slick friction of her fist. In a fog of black relief, he spilled onto her stomach, shuddering with the brutal force of his climax.

She burrowed her face into his chest, her ribs shaking beneath his hand.

"Holy *hell*," he muttered, pressing a hard kiss to her hair.

He eased her to the floor and tugged her into his lap, pushing aside her crumpled wedding gown. He found a handkerchief and cleaned her stomach as she stared at the ceiling, dazed.

"I love you too," he whispered, not exactly sure when she'd said it, just that the words were ringing softly in his ears.

"I know. Blast, I'm going to miss you this week."

She lay her head on his shoulder, gently scratching the hair on his chest, pulling them into a lull.

"I'll write to you," she murmured. "And I'll come to the shop… as soon as I can…"

She went on, something or another about what she would be doing with her family, but Ethan was only half listening.

He was instead staring down at the soothing pass of her palm over his chest.

At her beautiful, unadorned left hand.

My God.

In an instant, his clarity was pristine. He could see straight through his misguided principles, to where Belle was waiting, steadfast and certain.

He kept insisting—*insisting*—he couldn't promise her anything.

But he damned well *could* offer her a promise.

With dazed resolve, he reached for his trousers. He thought he might have…*yes*. He had cut a length of twine from a bundle of serials earlier, and there it was, still in his pocket.

"I can come by Tuesday," Belle was saying. "Possibly sooner. It depends if…Ethan? What are you doing?"

"Something incredibly ill-conceived but wholly necessary."

He lifted her hand and wound the twine around her fourth finger, measuring the length.

"Ah…" She looked up at him in question.

"One day," he said hoarsely as he began to loop the twine. "I'm going to own the shop outright."

She watched his face as he tightened the knot. "All right."

"I'm going to find a tenant for the upstairs residence." He

checked his knot. "Then I'm going to lease the worst house on the nicest street I can afford."

She let him turn over her palm, gentling her fingers between his.

"I'm going to fix our broken desk and set it in front of a west-facing window. I'm going to come home every night to find you sitting there, half-covered in ink and half-formed ideas."

He looked up, caught in the warm relief of her hazel eyes.

"And you will see me Monday." He was loosening, reckless with devotion. "Because that's the day I'm going to speak with your father."

He slid the twine back around her finger.

She grew still, aside from the steady bloom of her smile. "You are?"

"I am." He kissed her palm once, then again. "If you would like that."

"Yes."

And it seemed to him she was answering many questions at once.

"*Yes*, Ethan."

"I'll do better than this when I can," he said, rubbing his thumb over the little circle of twine from the printshop. "Unfortunately, a ring is about tenth on my list."

"I wouldn't go to too much trouble." She kissed him, her lips tilting into his. "We've already established I have little use for jewels."

"It will be a long wait, Belle," he warned her. "A long, long wait. Longer than the repayment of the debt. Do you understand that? I need to have something of my own first." He shook his head, his throat tight. "My circumstances haven't changed, only my heart."

"I understand." She was beaming. "I'd rather wait for your circumstances than your heart."

In his darkest days, he knew he would return here, to this moment.

Anticipating the rest of their lives.

Knowing it was all still possible.

23

———————

The Mistaken Inspector —

…Charles Lennox and William Barnaby maintained they'd arrived in Belgravia with the intention of attending a watercolor exhibition. Clementina thought swindling a crate of the host's heirloom silver was its own kind of artistry—the thieves left behind a splatter of paint, which anyone with any sense could see contained the imprint of a boot.

The Inspector paid her no mind. The first of his many mistakes.

—Excerpt from Secrets of the Old Bailey, Number 9 (Draft)

∿

"WHAT DO YOU MEAN *TODAY*?"

The last Monday of May found Lena lying sideways across Belle's bed, her flaxen hair unspooling to the floor. She was staring at Belle with her face upside down, but even from this vantage her blue eyes were round with surprise.

"Just that. Ethan's coming today," Belle repeated, beaming at her own sunny reflection as she brushed out her waves. "He's going to speak with Papa when we return from the courthouse later."

"Does Papa know?" Lena asked excitedly. "Wait. Does *Mama* know?"

Belle frowned, trying to recall what Ethan had told her of his plans. As predicted, she'd been busy with her family in the days since her parents' return, but according to the letters he'd sent, all was well at the shop. They'd printed a record number of copies of number nine, all bundled and assembled for the weekend. Ethan estimated that so long as sales held the next two weeks, they would be nearly there.

He hadn't elaborated on *nearly*, and Belle had chosen not to press.

She hadn't actually seen Ethan—except for a covert hour in the Inner Temple Garden, but they hadn't done much talking. He'd pulled her to their secluded bench, now hidden behind abundant blooms, and kissed her with heedless abandon until she felt as wild and carefree as a girl running down a sloping summer hillside.

"Belle?" Lena waved her hand back and forth. "Did you hear me? I asked if Mama and Papa know you are about to be whisked away into a life of typesetting and working-class reform?"

"He said he would write." Belle resumed the long strokes of her brush. "Do you suppose I should pretend I don't know?"

"I'm still trying to understand what *I* know." Lena sat up, flipping her hair over her head in a voluminous cloud. "Because nary a month ago, you sat outside with Cecily and me, bemoaning you couldn't get him to look at you twice."

"Well." Belle cocked an eyebrow at her reflection. "He's looking now."

Lena squealed and threw a pillow at her. "You know, you should give up writing crime stories and start an advice column instead—*How to Secure a Betrothal from A Handsome Tradesman Despite Never Leaving the Courthouse for Four Years.*"

"Yes." Belle reached for a jar of Pear's Almond Bloom. "Unfortunately, *Spinster's Quarterly* isn't currently accepting submissions."

Lena howled with laughter, pressing her face into the sole pillow remaining on Belle's bed. At that moment, a brisk knock sounded, and Mama poked her head in.

"What's all this?"

Lena was still curled on the bed in some sort of fit, so Belle rose from her dressing table, taking Mama's hands and pulling her into a twirl; she proved a much more proficient partner than Sam.

"Your father and I leave for three weeks, and suddenly, you're dancing in your night rail?" Mama laughed. "Why so sunny, darling? Did you receive word about your manuscript?"

Belle wondered how she must seem right now—pink-cheeked with glee for the first time since…well. It had been a very long time, hadn't it? Her family must have a rather somber view of her, if a joy so small as a morning waltz surprised them.

"Not my writing…" Belle paused, nearly telling them her writing, too, was a source of unexpected happiness. But there was no need to digress from a pleasant topic to an awkward one. "It's something else." She squeezed her mother's hands. "It's *someone* else."

"Oh?" Mama tilted her head. "Mr. Fletcher then."

"Yes." Belle's heart skipped.

"What do you know of Mr. Fletcher?" Lena looked faintly rabid for news. "Did he write Papa?"

Mama looked bemused at Lena's excitement. "Which of you is he coming for?"

"Belle, of course." Lena raised her finger. "But I would like to bear witness."

"To what?"

"Just…him."

Lena looked devious, and Belle laughed.

"Is he really so handsome?" Mama pondered. "Even with the beard?"

"Yes." Lena and Belle answered as one.

"The beard is rather part of the effect," Belle added, and Lena bashed her with the pillow again.

"Your father informed me Mr. Fletcher sent word," Mama finally admitted with a small smile. "He's coming to call. He'll offer for you?"

"Yes." Belle slid her finger through the twine ring, which she wore on a long, thin chain around her neck. "He will. Are you…is Papa…"

She felt a sudden crush of nerves. It occurred to her that when Duncan spoke to her father, she hadn't any idea until after Papa told her. Mama folded her arms, her lovely face placid and unreadable. Belle tried hard not to picture the very different expression on her mother's face four years ago.

She put her hands on her mother's shoulders. "It's different this time."

"Is it? Mr. Fletcher is not a rising man who requires a well-connected wife?" Mama narrowed her eyes.

Belle blinked. In her mind, Ethan was so dissimilar from Duncan, it was laughable to suggest they had anything in common. She gathered up a heavy handful of her hair and twisted it off her heated neck.

"You know, Ethan really is very talented, Mama. Very enterprising. It takes remarkable character and fortitude to build something out of nothing…and he's done it over and over, his whole life. He knows how to take care of himself. He knows how to take care of me—"

"Belle," Mama said lightly.

"Moreover, why should he have to take care of me?" Belle's voice rose with atypical passion. "Why shouldn't *I* take care of him in turn? He needs someone, too, and—"

"Belle. Enough." Mama raised a hand, but her face had softened. "Your points are well-taken, and you can rest your defense. Besides, it's not my decision."

"Papa doesn't make any decisions without you," Belle protested. "If you're upset with me, or with Ethan—"

"I'm hardly upset. Cautious, perhaps, but not upset." Mama cracked a sly smile. She had a single dimple in her left cheek, which had the effect of making her appear rather impish at times. "How could I possibly be? You're in love."

Belle's blush brightened. "I...I never said that."

Mama laughed. "Darling, you don't have to."

WHEN BELLE and her father entered the din of the Old Bailey at half past ten, it was immediately apparent the Old Court was busy today.

"The gallery might be full already," Papa remarked as he and Belle crossed through the crowd toward his chambers. "We're arriving a little later than I wanted." He slid her a look. "My companion was part of a very involved tête-à-tête for half the morning."

Belle laughed, tucking her hand through Papa's arm. "You could have joined us," she teased.

"I'm of the mind that information is not necessarily beneficial when it comes to raising daughters," Papa mused. "I prefer a stratagem of plausible deniability."

"Mama tells you everything," Belle pointed out.

"Hmm." Papa slowed his steps. "She does actually."

He opened the door to the judge's rooms, ushering Belle inside.

"Speaking of," he said slowly as he lifted his heavy robe from the wardrobe. "I believe we are both aware I have an appointment later this evening?"

"Yes."

She lowered to a chair opposite his desk and set her basket on her lap. She rifled through it, once again futilely looking for her court notes. Though she'd made progress this week in reordering her papers, she was still missing one of her journals. It was either at the shop or Fordham House, and she kept forgetting to ask. *Drat.* She'd have to make do again today.

"You'll be nice to him, won't you, Papa?" Belle tilted a wheedling smile at her father. "He's a dear, you know."

"No, I do not know," Papa said soberly. "But I'll hear him out. I'd like to hear you out first."

Belle stood, straightening Papa's cravat, which had twisted with his robes.

"You don't need to worry this time," she said softly. "I would very much like to marry Ethan."

"You're certain?"

"I'm certain." She held her father's blue stare. "*Most* certain, Papa."

He nodded slowly, polishing his spectacles on a handkerchief.

"As to any other business the two of you need to conduct, I'll stay clear of it," Belle said in a rush. "But you should know, he takes great pride in his endeavors. He values security above all else—though he's rarely experienced it, and never at the hands of anyone else." She paused. "He will be very uncomfortable with your conversation. I ask you not to hold it against him."

She sat down and arranged her recent draft in front of her.

"Thank you for informing me," Papa said thoughtfully. "I'm looking forward to our discussion."

"You are not." Belle chuckled.

"Well," Papa said with a small smile. "It's the sort of thing one says."

A clerk knocked briskly. "Justice Sinclair, we're ready."

Papa turned to her. "Will I see you inside?"

"I'm going to stay here for a bit," she said, digging for a pencil. "I want to finish this scene…unless you have something titillating coming up?"

"Up first is sentencing in the Lennox case," the clerk said, looking at his list.

A small, cold prickle tugged at her.

Her pencil stilled.

Lennox…

"Remind me of that one?" Papa asked, flipping through his briefs.

"The silver theft at the banker's house out in—"

"Belgravia," Belle said at the same time as the clerk.

An uncanny sensation of familiarity seized her so tightly, her skin broke into gooseflesh.

She stared at her hand, wrapped around the pencil, and had a near visceral recollection of that same pencil forming that same name.

"Did…" She blinked at the clerk. "Did you say *Lennox*?"

"Yes." The clerk squinted in concentration. "Trial was ten days ago. May—"

"Nineteenth," Belle said faintly. "Friday. May nineteenth. Chadwick Lennox and William Barnaby."

"That's right, Miss Sinclair." The clerk's face cleared. "Good memory, you have."

Belle murmured a vague assent; she *did* have a good memory.

For instance, right now, she was remembering with perfect, terrible clarity sitting in the corridor of the courthouse on May 19th, hastily scribbling notes about a pair of swindlers who finagled their way into an artist's exhibition at the home of a wealthy banker, only to make off with heirloom silver.

It was excellent fodder for a story—and she'd written down all the details in her court notes.

Word for word.

Her hand pressed her chest. Beneath her palm, her breath was coming in odd fits and spurts.

She kept a separate journal for court. *Always.*

But no.

Not always. Not lately. She had too many stories going. She'd taken to drafting in whatever notebook was nearest…

Charles Lennox and William Barnaby.

She'd used their trial for inspiration for number nine. But now a dreadful urgency gripped her, a snag in her recollection, and something wasn't right…

The clerk was still talking, Papa was still nodding, but Belle was desperately trying to conjure the image of her fair copy.

Had…had she *changed* the names?

She must have.

Hadn't she?

Her stomach plummeted.

"Excuse me," she said abruptly, already on her feet. "I need to..."

"Belle?" Her father looked perplexed. "Are you leaving?"

"I'll be back," she mumbled, her head spinning. "I'll be back... later."

She bolted down the passage, her body moving on instinct, her brain already bearing down on the horrifying prospect.

She needed to get to 62 Fleet. She needed to find her journal, to put her eyes on her fair copy.

Because if she *hadn't* changed the names, if she *hadn't* altered the details...then Ethan hadn't printed a penny blood...

He had printed *news*.

And every single one of those assembled serials would be liable to stamp duty.

Oh God.

She pushed through the courthouse, her progress slowed by the blustering constables and self-important barristers blocking her exit. In a fit of impatience, she elbowed through, not caring about the muffled curses following her. She skirted past the crowd in the street, her petticoats in her fists, her lungs aching as she hurtled round the corner of Ludgate Hill.

What notebook had she given Ethan when he came to her house? She'd lifted it from her desk...his thumb turned the pages...her pages had been such a mess. She'd been in a strange mood, distracted and worried and...

She couldn't remember.

She flung open the rickety door to the shop, blowing straight past a befuddled Sam Porter as she raced to her desk and rummaged through an assortment of papers.

"Belle?" Ethan looked up from the Columbian, his green eyes sharp. "What in hell?"

"The fair copy," she managed. Her corset wasn't tight, but she wasn't breathing properly. "Where's the copy…for nine?"

"We've finished with the fair copy," Tobias said. "We printed it days ago."

She was already pushing past him, tearing into the storeroom. Sam had the serials stacked and ready for Saturday, thousands of them—*oh God*, so much paper. She dropped to the dusty floor, her skirts pooling around her as she heaved a bundle into her lap. Her fingernails dug into the twine binding, the same twine as the crude ring on a long chain around her neck.

"Belle, what are you doing? Those are assembled." Ethan filled the doorway of the storeroom, casting a long shadow that matched the cooling of her blood.

"I meant…I meant to revise my draft…" she said thickly, scrabbling with knots, scrabbling with recollections. "The silver theft. I needed to alter the details. I was working on it the morning my cousin brought the serial to breakfast…I was so ill-tempered…I was so distracted…"

"I remember." Ethan knelt beside her. "Belle, you're worrying me."

His hand came around hers, trying to stop her.

But he couldn't stop her.

And he *should* be worried.

"I—I don't think I revised it." She pressed her hands over her eyes; her head was blazing. "Because when *would* I? I gave you the journal that day…" She swore, half turning, reaching for his coat. "Christ, Ethan, I need your pocketknife."

Seeming to sense she couldn't be trusted with the blade, Ethan reached around her to slice through the binding. A pile of *Secrets* slid into her lap.

She stared at the opening sentences until the words blurred, willing the names to change, to scramble like her own name on the title page.

Then she ripped through another copy.

Another.

"Belle?"

Surely, one of these *wouldn't* say Lennox and Barnaby.

One of these would have the wrong details.

One of these wouldn't read like a *bloody court report*.

"Ten pounds," she muttered. Her thumb sliced open on a ragged edge of pulp paper, but she hardly noticed the sting.

"What?"

"Ten pounds, this week and next, would get you nearly where you need to be," she repeated his own letter as she continued rifling through the pile like a madwoman. "That's what you said."

"Belle." He lifted to his haunches, his eyes darting between her and the papers he hadn't yet realized were worthless. "Stop. Your thumb. Sweetheart—"

"How much is the news tax?" She heard herself asking the question, a touch of hysteria audible to her own ringing ears. She knew the answer, but she wanted to be wrong. "Ethan, how much is the news tax?"

"A penny per paper." His voice seemed to come from far away. "Why?"

A penny per paper.

An entire week's profit.

Every Monday, she watched him tally. Everyone knew Ethan could not afford a setback. Not *any* setback. Let alone twice over—lost expenditure, lost profit.

An anguished sob tore through her. She'd let him down. He needed this business. He needed this *chance*.

"*Belle.*" His hands were on her shoulders. "You need to tell me exactly what's happening right now."

"This shouldn't have been the fair copy."

It hurt to look at him.

"Ethan. I…I gave you the wrong journal."

"What are you saying?" There was a cast to his expression she'd never seen before.

She reached for another stack, then another, unable to stop, even though every one of these useless papers was patently identical.

"These are real people in here. Authentic details." She jabbed the nearest serial, and her bloody fingernail left a bright smear on the page. "It's news. We printed *news*. We…we can't sell this as fiction."

She felt numb.

"We can't sell it *at all*."

Ethan's face was pale and thunderous as he took in the mess she'd made of herself and the storeroom.

It was only then she realized he was wearing his nicest coat.

His nicest coat to speak to her father.

"Everything…was supposed to be fine." She swallowed, pressing her snagged fingertip to her face. "Ethan. *We* were going to be fine."

She loved him even then, in the midst of ruining his life.

24

―――――――

<u>Accounting Ledger of E. Fletcher</u>

1 June 1848

Secrets of the Old Bailey Vol. 1, No. 9 — CANCELED

Inclusive of expenditures, profit loss —£20

~~Remaining debt owed—£20~~

Remaining debt owed—£40

When Ethan was made reporter at the *Sentinel*, his first story had been about the opening of a local medical surgery. He'd spent a morning in the grimy operating theater, observing unspeakable horrors, and his main takeaway was that it was a beastly business that seemed to mostly revolve around knowing what could bleed for the longest.

He could bleed for the longest.

So the agonizing pain in his own chest would have to come last.

It had been four days since Belle stumbled into the printshop, breathless, begging for her fair copy. In rising horror, Ethan watched her claw through one serial after another until he finally understood enough to lift her away from the carnage. As she pressed her tearstained face to his knee, he'd sluggishly understood he would need to begin cauterizing wounds.

First, Belle. He bandaged her thumb and ordered Sam to take her home. Only after the shop was clear of her heartbreaking sobs was he able to turn his attention to everything else. He'd painstakingly restacked the useless copies of number nine. He poured a strong drink for Tobias and Newburn and a stronger one for himself. Then late into the night, he'd paced, working through the accounts, curtailing his panic with any semblance of action.

By the following morning, it was plain they had to halt production on number ten. Ethan had lost more than twenty pounds on expenditures for an issue they couldn't sell. He couldn't piss more money at the walls until he knew if the walls were worth saving.

Now he surveyed his empty, silent workroom. Everything about it felt *wrong*. Tobias and Sam and Newburn and even Marks should all be in various stages of production. Belle should be at the damn broken desk, hoarding adjectives like jewels.

But nobody was here, and he hadn't seen Belle since Sam took her home. He'd written to her father to apologize for missing his appointment, and he'd written to her to tell her he was sorting things out and would call on her soon. It was the most demoralizing series of letters he'd ever exchanged—and that included the letter he'd missed from Gabler, informing him he'd inherited a debt-ridden printshop halfway across the world.

A mistake.

After all their work—every gain, every stride, every hope they'd nurtured in this godforsaken shop—it came down to a fucking *mistake*.

The door clanged, and a grim-faced Tobias strode in with a small stack of newspapers rolled in his hand.

"Well?" Ethan tensed. "Did you find anything? How deep is the shit we're standing in?"

They'd been keeping an eye on the news, trying to discern how well-publicized the Lennox trial was. A very real part of him wanted to believe Belle had the entire thing wrong.

"The *Standard*." Tobias tossed down a newspaper. "And *The Guardian*. Roberts scrounged them from the week of May twenty-first, and yes, the Lennox trial is in here. We likely didn't notice because we hadn't started production on number nine yet. At any rate, last week's news from Parliament crowded out most other stories, so the trial was buried several pages deep. I wager that's why we didn't recognize the names we were typesetting."

"So it's genuine news." Ethan scrubbed his face. "If we used her court notes, I already know she got the details right. It's what's made us popular, the authenticity."

"Yes."

Ethan swore, raking back his hair. "All right. Let's go through it again, Porter."

He couldn't stop revisiting number nine, because there were thousands of copies sitting in the storeroom, and there had to be *something* he could do with them.

Problems had solutions. Every problem had a solution. He could find it. He was the physician in the surgery; he had the sutures, the scalpel, the dressing.

He refused to believe it was too late to use them.

"Fletcher."

"Again, Porter." Ethan pressed his palm to the Columbian, in his mind, the second-most beautiful resident of his printshop. "Because if I'm about to send for an auctioneer, I need to be damn sure selling the Columbian is my *only* option. If I lose this press, we're down to one, and it's going to be an entirely new set of problems."

"Fine." Tobias cracked his knuckles. "Go on."

"We can't pay the tax *and* sell it as a penny blood," Ethan started.

"We'd be nearly worse off than we are now," Tobias agreed. "We can't pull a profit when stamp duty is the same as the price. And people won't pay more than a penny for it."

"We can't sell it as a newspaper and charge five pence accordingly."

Tobias shook his head. "It's *not* news. The case is real, but nothing else is. Plus the title, the illustration…there's plenty of fiction in it."

"Right." Ethan closed his eyes. He pictured a set of scales, tipping against him, one tax at a time.

"We *could* do nothing," Tobias said bluntly. "Pretend this never happened and distribute the same as any other week. Nobody has to know it contains news. Our readers can't afford the news."

Ethan hesitated. He'd had this thought too. But no.

"I can't risk it." He grimaced. "That damn inspector is watching us. He's already holding it over my head that we took a radical pamphlet at the coffeehouse. If we attempt to sell news illegally—"

"Christ, yes. You're right. You'd be fined." Tobias closed his eyes. "Fined, certainly, if not jailed. We could lose the business."

I might lose it anyway.

Number nine had somehow become more of a puzzle than Irascible Nell had ever been. Too factual for a story paper, too sensational for a newspaper.

It was worthless.

Ethan stopped pacing and looked at Tobias.

"Selling the Columbian is the right decision, Fletcher," Tobias said, his voice low. "It will set us back in the short term, but we only need to get through a few weeks. Once you own the shop, you can recoup over time. You'll still have the serial. *Secrets* sells. You said it yourself."

Ethan dropped his head to his hands, growling in frustration. If he lost one press, he would have to scale back weekly production. Their profits would diminish; he'd have to cut Newburn loose.

And he'd have to wait even longer to stand on his own two feet.

But it hardly mattered. Every one of his dreams and desires were bound up with Belle. If retracting was the way to keep them moving forward, he would do it.

"Fine. We'll auction the Columbian. We'll use the profits to bolster what we lost from this week. We'll resume work on number ten." He sighed. "In the meantime, I'll pray Justice Sinclair is an understanding man."

There was a sudden loud knock at the shop door. Tobias crossed and swung it open, and in stepped Victor Marks with a gray-haired fellow Ethan didn't recognize.

"Marks…" Ethan shook his head. "Didn't you receive my note? We're holding on number ten. I don't have a commission for you yet."

He would have to cut the illustrator loose too.

"That's why I'm here," Marks said, jerking his thumb to the man next to him. "Might have a solution for you, Fletcher."

Ethan glanced at Tobias, who shrugged.

He turned to the gray-haired man. "Fletcher. And you are?"

"White." The man nodded. "Gregory White. *Illustrated Metropolitan News.*"

Tobias and Ethan turned to Marks as one.

The artist raised his hands. "I do some work for them from time to time. When I was at their offices this week, White mentioned a new story he's working on, but he needs information. And he's willing to pay for it."

White patted his pocket, withdrawing a notebook. "You publish a penny blood, Mr. Fletcher?"

"I might," Ethan said suspiciously. "What's it to you?"

Some would call the *Illustrated Metropolitan News* a newspaper; Ethan considered it a scandal sheet. The coverage was always melodramatic and often unfavorable. He didn't trust White any further than he could throw him.

"Did you know there is a contingent at Scotland Yard positing that penny fiction is related to rising crime among the laboring class?"

"*Penny fiction?*" Ethan scoffed. "As opposed to inhospitable living conditions, poor working hours, disease, starvation—"

"My source believes boys who read such ruthless stories are more likely to commit theft and assault." White angled his pencil. "It seems susceptible young minds are ripe for undue influence. I'm writing about the looming moral panic sure to be caused by the glorification of crime and bloodlust."

Ethan stared. "You are aware that's utter rubbish from top to bottom?"

"Are you willing to make a statement to that effect?"

"No, but I *am* willing to turn you out of my shop."

White tilted his head. "Now wait, Fletcher. This is going to be published whether or not you're involved, but I'd very much like to include a counterpoint in my article series. *Motivated*, if you will."

"Motivated, are you?" Tobias crossed his arms. "And it's a series now?"

White ignored him.

"My intent is to speak to your author."

Ethan's misgivings sharpened their claws. "Absolutely not."

"I want to find out more about the creators of these *controversial* tales," White continued. "*Secrets* is a bit different from other penny bloods, wouldn't you agree? Irascible Nell has proven *elusive*. A mystery author for a mystery paper, eh?"

Ethan's throat went dry.

Marks leaned closer. "He'll pay, Fletcher. For a statement. For a *name*."

White slid Ethan a note. He glanced at the offer, a sick leap rocketing through him.

"Do you expect me to believe you'll pay this much for my author's name?"

White chuckled. "You have a very narrow understanding of how hungry people are for gossip, Fletcher."

"You said Scotland Yard." Ethan narrowed his eyes. "That's your source, is it?"

Duncan after the last word, of that he had no doubt. He should have crushed the man's arrogant windpipe when he had the chance.

"You aren't the only one who isn't revealing sources," White said. "Suffice to say, I was encouraged to look into you. And once I started looking, my interest was piqued."

"It's a healthy sum, Fletcher," Marks cajoled. "You need this money."

He stared at the note in his fist. He *did* need this money.

But there was no way in hell he would betray Belle. She'd been so adamant that day when her cousin found the serial—she wasn't ready. She wanted to be a serious novelist; she didn't want to be tied to a penny blood. It was her choice, even if he wished things were different.

It was *her* choice.

God, he couldn't give her anything, but he could give her that.

"I'm not giving you a name. I'm not giving you a statement," Ethan said roughly. "That's final."

"*Nobody* is giving you a name," Tobias added, looking at Marks with heavy warning.

White looked disappointed but shrugged. "Then you should know I'll have no choice but to default to the information provided by my other source. I imagine it won't take much to get him to share his suspicions, but I did want to offer you the opportunity first."

Ethan's fists clenched as a divot of helpless rage pressed upon him. He couldn't buy Belle's name. He had *nothing* to buy it with.

And then just as quickly, the flare retreated.

Ethan wasn't angry; he'd never been an angry man. He had always, *always* understood the only aspect of his life he could control was his own willingness to face each day head-on. For a long time, he'd managed it.

And he was so damn *tired*.

It felt as though his whole life had taken place in the middle of an unfortunate story. Until one day, there was Belle. His ray of light, his stroke of fortune, his *one good thing*.

He would not—he *could* not—let her be his collateral.

"What do I have to do for you to keep *Secrets* out of it entirely?"

White's smile widened.

"Well. That's an interesting question, Fletcher." He looked around the shop. "Our operation has been looking to expand. We're on the rise, you see, and could use additional space. Rumor has it, you only have these premises until June fifteenth."

He poked his head into the workroom, glancing about with interest.

"Suppose we exercise discretion regarding your publication, and in turn, we'd be much obliged if you had Charles Howe arrange a private sale."

And there it is.

Ethan thought again of the long-ago surgery, wondering if the men on the table recognized the fatal blow for what it was. He sure as hell did.

He couldn't keep the shop without *Secrets*.

He couldn't keep publishing *Secrets* without a shop.

And he refused to keep *any* of it at Belle's expense.

Tobias cursed, but Ethan could only summon a cutting sense of recognition. He'd tried to make this work. He had *tried*. But he was nearly out of options, nearly out of time. He was holding his hands over too many damn wounds.

He had to finally accept what he'd been trying to avoid this entire week—this was a bleed for which he had a bandage.

No. He had *tourniquet*.

A last resort, to stop the hemorrhage.

He'd lose the shop but only in service of salvaging the rest.

A safeguard for his prospects, a safeguard for her name.

It looked like a newspaper in New York City.

25

The question I pose, then, to your Esteemed Publication: what is to be done about this letter-press offal? Hundreds of boys line up each week to put their penny in the pockets of monstrous purveyors of this street literature—if it can even be called such. Corruption at the corner stand, day after day. And all the while, the presses run.

—Excerpt, Letter to the Editor, Illustrated Metropolitan News

YESTERDAY WAS the first of June, which meant the days she'd been dreading were finally upon them. All week, Belle felt time slipping between her fingers, even as she sat at home, idle and afraid. Ethan had written that he was working on things and would call when he was able, but she couldn't stop thinking about the twin hazards looming ahead—a fortnight until his debts were due, a week until his New York colleagues expected him on a steamship. She felt like Odysseus, bearing down between Scylla and Charybdis.

She tried to remember how the Greek hero managed it, but she was fairly certain it involved a number of sailors meeting their untimely end.

When a knock sounded at the front door, Belle was curled in the parlor, ignoring a dinner tray in lieu of catastrophizing. She lifted her head as Mrs. Bowers answered the door; she didn't think they were expecting anyone tonight. At the sound of a deep American voice floating over the threshold, her listless, heartsick limbs jolted to life.

"Ethan."

She skidded down the corridor, her loose hair tumbling down her back. At the sight of Belle's disheveled state, Mrs. Bowers pursed her lips and swept off to fetch Papa.

"I didn't know you were coming," Belle exclaimed when they were alone. "My God, I *missed* you. Are you well? Is…is everything…well?"

She reached for him, but Ethan imperceptibly shook his head, raising a hand to stop her from drawing any closer.

"It's all right," she reassured him. "Only my father is here, and he's upstairs—"

"He's here to see me, Belle."

Papa's voice sounded from behind her, and Belle hastily took a step back.

"He is? You are?"

She turned to Ethan. She now realized his expression was tense; if she didn't know better, she would say he looked nervous. Her pulse ticked faster as she worked through it.

He was here to see her *father*.

"Oh. You *are*."

She understood why he'd canceled his appointment Monday; of course he had, his life was in an abject chaos of Belle's making. But he was here now, which meant he must have worked out a solution. He'd fixed the problem. They were back on course, just as they'd been that night in her dressing room, when he told her the best story she'd ever heard.

"I'll…leave you to your business." She looked significantly at her father, hoping he would remember to take things easy with Ethan. He was going to loathe going through a marriage settlement.

Oh, her darling man, so grouchy and stubborn—

"No," Ethan said abruptly. "Belle, you should come too."

"Mr. Fletcher." Papa glanced at Belle. "I would counsel against that. These conversations can be rather awkward for all parties. It might be best if Belle—"

"I only want to say this one time, and I need both of you to hear it," Ethan said firmly.

Perplexed, she followed Papa and Ethan to the study. It was strange to be here again, with the shadow of their first passionate embrace still haunting the threshold.

Papa sat at his desk, Ethan and Belle in the two chairs across from him.

"Well then, Mr. Fletcher." Papa steepled his fingers; he looked exactly as he had when he'd practiced law out of this room. "What can I help you with this evening?"

"I need to apologize on two counts, Your Honor."

Belle looked at him quizzically, but Papa's face remained inscrutable.

"First, for not meeting with you Monday," Ethan said. "There was an urgent matter with my business, and it has required my attention all this week."

"These things happen," Papa said. "I hope all is well now."

Ethan's jaw moved beneath his beard.

"My second apology is that I have misled you about my intention for meeting with you tonight."

"Oh?"

"Justice Sinclair, I am not asking for your daughter's hand at this time."

What?

Belle's smile slid sideways as she pivoted to face him, suddenly worried for his wellbeing. He'd been alone in that shop all week, likely drinking and bruising his fists on something; who knew what he'd done to himself. *Something* must be wrong with him, for he wasn't making sense.

He'd *already* asked her to marry him.

"Ethan?"

He glanced at her, a swift yearning moving over his face before he forced his attention back to her father.

"I'm here to give you—both of you—my word. I *will* ask for it one day." His jaw clenched again, this time so hard she could hear it pop. "I wish, very much, to make Belle my wife, but I have to make something of myself first."

"Ethan." She shook her head. "We've discussed this."

She had his twine ring on a chain hanging from her throat. They were going to wait a long time, then live in the worst house on the nicest street. He was going to fix her desk, and she was going to pour him whisky while he complained about London.

"I'm departing for New York," he said quietly, still looking at her father. "My ship leaves in five days. I have an offer there—an offer I *cannot* lose. I didn't want to take it." His voice cracked as he turned his gaze to her. "Belle. You know I tried very hard to not take it, but it's our last chance."

He was saying more things, explaining the terms of the offer, answering Papa's questions. A newspaper, an editor, something steady, something reliable, something about settling and coming for her later. Numbly, Belle swung between Papa's frank concern and the misery on Ethan's face, but her ears had stopped working—they couldn't take in any more words.

All the words hurt her.

"No. This isn't happening."

Her voice, when it came, dropped between them like a stone in a pond. She watched the ripple, her words stoppering all the horrid discussion of enterprising men and what they could build and where.

"You aren't leaving me." She turned to Ethan, then to Papa. "He's not leaving me."

She felt around her neck, her fingers grappling with the thin chain.

"Belle." Ethan looked physically pained.

"Mr. Fletcher, if it's a matter of funds..." Papa frowned, looking at Belle. She couldn't begin to imagine what her face looked like. "I feel obliged to make clear, there would be a marriage settlement. Belle's portion—"

She shook her head as Ethan's hand closed around hers. His fingers were warm where hers had gone very cold. She knew, of course, this was the very last thing he wanted.

"Justice Sinclair…" Ethan was speaking to her father, but he was looking at her. "That's not what this is about. I don't need to own a printshop. I need to own my *prospects*." He exhaled tightly. "I need to rest secure in the knowledge I finally have something that can't be taken away. Not because it was given to me, but because I *made* it."

"Belle?" Papa was still looking at her. "Is that what you want?"

"I…" She blinked away from her father to find Ethan's beseeching gaze. Her eyes burned with tears. Since he was a boy, he'd been chasing what was finally in front of him. How could she deny him?

She'd promised him—she *promised* him—she would wait for his circumstances.

"I…yes. I want him to have choices," she said haltingly. "I want Ethan to have a chance to make his way. It's the very least I would hope for any man, let alone the man I love."

Ethan's hand spasmed around hers.

"Well." Papa nodded slowly. "I take this to mean—"

"I'm going with him," Belle said.

"No." Papa and Ethan spoke together.

Belle was already pulling her hand away and pushing up from her chair.

"Yes." She looked between them. "Yes, I am."

"You are *not*." Ethan was standing too, his face blazing. "Are you *mad*?"

"Yes." She put her hands on her hips. "I'm mad. I'm furious—"

"Belle." Her father's placid temperament evaporated. He was looking at her with blatant alarm. "Surely, you understand I cannot permit you to go with him."

"Why shouldn't you permit it?"

"Because you aren't *married*." Papa braced his hands on the desk. "And because he doesn't want it. Belle, weren't you listening? He wants to go, he wants to get settled. He wants to make something of himself. He wants you to *let* him."

Drawing breath was painful. She felt more out of control than ever in the face of her father's grim rationality. He made it sound so simple. He had no idea Ethan was doing this because of her error. She'd driven him to take the only chance he had left.

And now he would be *alone*.

"May we have a moment?" She grasped her father's arm. "Please, Papa."

Papa's face was tight, but he seemed to sense that of all the things he was denying her, a private conversation was perhaps the least damaging. He took his leave and closed the door behind him.

"This is because of what happened this week," she whispered fiercely the moment they were alone. "This is because of *my* mistake."

"Yes," Ethan said. He stepped forward, coming to stand before her. "I will admit number nine was the catalyst."

"Then why—"

"*And* it's because I need to sell my Columbian to pay my men's wages. It's because I've been pushing you all past the limits of what is reasonable."

"I'll do better. It won't happen again."

"No, it won't happen again." He sighed, looking unbearably fatigued. "Because that's the other problem, Belle. The serial *can't* be published anymore."

She startled, her blood pounding hard in her temples. "I don't...I don't understand. We only missed one issue."

"The *Illustrated Metropolitan News* is about to print an article listing us among the penny bloods causing moral panic—unless I have Howe broker a sale of the shop. It's the final nail in the coffin. There's no business left to build, even if we somehow clear the debt."

"What?" She covered her mouth. "It can't be published anymore?"

"Not unless we want to be dragged through the mud." Ethan pushed back his hair. "I told you I didn't make this decision lightly, but it's *too many things*, Belle. We've been on a tightrope, and we looked down…and now it seems damn near impossible we ever balanced in the first place."

She stared at him, desperately trying to absorb this information in a way that didn't feel like she was being pummeled from within.

"We won't be apart forever," he murmured, touching her cheek. "But for now, I need to take this opportunity. It's a *good* one. Editing a paper, it's a solid start for us, Belle. I could never do that as things stand in London. And you…you can keep writing—anything you wish, no more penny bloods, no more hiding—"

"I can't." She clutched his wrists, certain that until right now, she'd never felt truly frantic in her life. "I cannot do this without you."

"You can write without me," he argued. "You can—"

"I cannot do *life* without you." She could hardly speak over the force of her rising sobs. "Don't ask this of me. You can't just offer me all these big, messy dreams, then *leave* me alone with them. We can be happy together…"

He gripped her arms, his handsome face etched in an agony she felt had been carved by her own hand.

"Do you understand what it means to start a life from the ground up? Do you understand that the money we've made is nothing, it's *nowhere*? It was only ever going to get me to the very bottom rung. I haven't earned a single red cent. I'm hemorrhaging my savings to stay."

"Then go. Go, and *I will go with you*. I don't need all this." She waved around the study. "Over and over, I've told you, I don't need this house, this life—my father's study or my mother's draperies or whatever you've fixated on—"

"What about your mother?" The splinter in his voice was brutal. "Do you need *her*? Belle, I know you would go with me, but I'll never, ever repeat my father's mistake. My God, I don't even have a residence in New York. I want to give you *everything*, sweetheart, but I can't yet put a roof over your head. I need to ensure the new paper is viable, I need to make things stable, I need to make things *safe*. And until I do, I will not allow you to leave the people who love you."

Oh God—her family. Her parents. Lena. She couldn't...she *couldn't...*

She was spiraling with sorrow. How had this happened? How had it come to this? Somehow along the way, she must have asked for too much. She hadn't thought she had. Only to take up a small space.

Only to do it alongside him.

"It's going to be all right." He drew her close, putting his lips against her hair. "I'll send for you. I'll come back. I swear to God—I swear to *God*, Belle—I will make it so we can be together."

She couldn't breathe. She'd lived in the half light until she met him—her person, made for her, meant for her—and now an entire ocean and how many months or years between them. *So long, so far.* She might never see him again. She might never touch him or hold him or hear the voice she loved best in all the world—

"Belle." His thumb stroked her tears away. "I've never lied to you. I never will."

"What if I've lied to you?" She didn't recognize her voice; she wasn't even sure he could understand her. "I must have. Because I'm not as brave as you think I am."

Her fracturing seemed to pull him into focus. Ethan's anguish cleared; he thrummed with resolve. He found her fingers, linking them. She stared at their hands, remembering the first time they made love, how she couldn't let go.

"No, sweetheart. You've been my beautiful puzzle since the day I met you. And while you keep me guessing nearly all the time, this much I know for certain—you can abide this." He stroked back her hair. "I *know* you can. Somehow, all this time, you've acted as though love is a given."

He pressed his face to her shoulder, and her arms came around him. He crushed her against his chest, and she knew he was burying his composure in the curve of her neck.

In that moment, she understood that if she let him, Ethan would break himself for her.

She had a duty not to let him.

For a long time, she held him, considering what he was asking of her.

Abide.

To bear patiently.

To endure without yielding.

To await with anticipation.

"I act as if love is a given because it *is,*" she finally whispered. "I gave it to you, and now it's yours to keep."

She drew a shuddering breath and held his face to hers.

"So when you dock in New York Harbor, you can rest easy, for you have something that cannot be taken away."

The sob started deep in her chest. He must have felt it coming, because he was already kissing her, and it was agony and bliss, it was determination and devotion.

It was *Ethan.*

And yes.

Yes, she could abide it.

---

4 June 1848
Porter—

> *As discussed, enclosed is a letter of recommendation for you. It's likely the most effusive I'll ever be—but I mean every damn word. I regret losing the shop for many reasons, but significant among them is that it affects you. I sincerely hope your next place of employment is a sounder operation than mine.*
>
> *I'll write from New York with my new forwarding address.*
>
> *And Tobias, if you happen to see Belle, you'll have both my envy and my gratitude. I know she, too, considers you a friend.*
>
> *—Fletcher*

TODD EAMON HAD ARRANGED Ethan's passage on the *Empire*, sailing from Liverpool on the seventh of June. Ethan reluctantly determined it best to depart London two days prior; he couldn't afford unexpected delays.

The shop he left in the hands of Tobias, who would close out their operation before the deed was signed over to Howe. Tobias was to sell what he could—the presses, the paper, the ink—and use the profits to pay their outstanding salaries; the remaining funds he should keep for his family. Ethan deeply regretted putting the Porters out of work, but a successful auction should see them through until Tobias secured new positions for himself and Sam.

But none of that, of course, would replace what Ethan was really losing—his friend. Tobias had been a stalwart companion, measured and competent and kind. Ethan hoped Belle would still see him. He drew painful comfort in the thought of their little band carrying on without him.

On his last evening, Belle came to him. She didn't say what she'd told her mother and father, and Ethan didn't ask. When she knocked on the door of the shop, the sun was low in the sky, and he was waiting for her.

He led her inside, up the stairs, to the residence they would never share.

Days had been hurtling by, but there, in his bedroom, Ethan determined time would slow. They undressed each other in increments, lingering over each small intimacy. There are things a man might forget—the heavy swing of her hair along his stomach, the stretch of his bicep above her head, the way her sigh met his.

Ethan wouldn't forget.

He put her hands everywhere he wanted his memories; he put his mouth everywhere he wanted hers.

He moved within her, letting her quicken his pace, their hushed promises tangling in the slivered air between them.

When she came apart, he hooked his arms beneath her shoulders and slowed, holding in his mind's eye the exact shape of her breathless smile, of how she lit up for him.

He kept her as long as he could, and then a little longer.

When he finally walked her home, it was very late. He saw her to the door, he crossed the green, he waited for the top left window to darken.

It never did.

THE NEXT MORNING, Ethan departed for Liverpool. When he arrived in Euston station, once more carrying his own trunk, he couldn't help but think how far he'd come, how little he'd traveled.

He was right where he'd started—the same locomotive, the same shit-covered boots, the same empty pockets.

Yet nothing was the same at all.

Somewhere in the middle of all the London fog, Belle's lamp was glowing.

27

THE SHINGLE HANGING above 62 Fleet was crooked. Belle reached up, tracing the faded paint. GAINES PRINT WORKS. How odd, that the business was still called that. They'd never managed to change it.

Instead, they changed everything else.

The door swung open, and Tobias stuck his head out. His dark eyes were creased in concern. "Miss Sinclair? What are you doing out here? It's raining."

She stared at him, feeling as vacant as she probably looked. It *was* raining; she'd barely noticed. Nor did she have any clear sense why she was here. When she left Ethan's residence last night, she hadn't planned to return this morning.

But her feet brought her.

"I'm sorry," she finally said. "I don't know why I came. Should I leave?"

"No." Tobias shook his head. "No, come in, out of the wet. We were just tidying up, taking inventory…"

He ushered her inside the shop. She walked through the office, her skirts trailing a wet puddle across the floor.

She let Tobias take her shawl, and he hung it on the coatrack. Belle was the only one who ever used it; Ethan tossed his things wherever he liked. Unthinkingly, she turned to the bench where his coat was most often slung.

"When?" she asked quietly.

"He was gone before I arrived," Tobias said. He checked his pocket watch. "His train will have already departed for Liverpool."

Gone.

"Oh." Belle clenched her jaw, tight enough to focus her pain. The sear was a welcome change from the empty ache in her chest. "Is… there anything I can help with?"

She needed to be busy. She couldn't stomach the thought of sitting at home with her family's worry. They'd been treading lightly for days, and today was bound to be the worst of all.

Tobias must have sensed her aimlessness. "We're cataloging supplies. I'm arranging for an auction, and I could use another pair of hands."

"I can do that."

"Sam's in the workroom. Perhaps you could help him distribute the sorts."

Dully, she set her basket on the desk, then followed Tobias to the workroom. She paused next to the Columbian, recalling Ethan's practiced efficiency. She touched the eagle counterweight; it was such a beautiful press. She hated the thought of somebody buying it, of it being disassembled and carted away.

She joined Sam, her melancholy heightening tenfold in the quiet workroom. How had Ethan endured this all week? It must have torn him to pieces, trying to plan, knowing his hard work had come to nothing.

"We're sorting type, Miss Sinclair," Sam instructed, only too happy to put her to work. "The uppers are all mixed in with the lowers, so if you can just make a pile for me..."

She absently set about her task, hardly noticing when the door to the shop creaked open. There came the soft jingle of the bell, followed by the voice of Victor Marks, calling to Tobias in greeting.

Belle plucked a *B* from the case and engaged in a self-sabotaging recollection of Ethan's hands around hers, showing her how to typeset her name.

She put the *B* on the table, flipping it upside down.

There is no exquisite beauty...without some strangeness in proportion.

She wished she'd printed the quote for him. He'd never shown her how to work the press. She asked him once, and he had only laughed his beautiful big laugh and told her if she could write, type-set, *and* print, she'd have no use for him. *It's my own brand of security, sweetheart,* he'd teased, kissing her temple. *I need to make sure you need me.*

She passed Sam the *B*.

"I'll have your final pay by week's end." Tobias's deep voice drifted from the office. "I'll see you get what you're owed, Marks."

"It would have been a fair bit easier if Fletcher hadn't played white knight and just accepted the payment on offer," Marks grumbled.

Belle lifted her head, caught by the mention of Ethan's name.

"What's done is done, and he had his reasons," Tobias said sternly. "The *Metropolitan* is a racket, and you know it."

"A racket that would have kept this door open." Marks sighed. "Alas, what the heart wants..."

Belle frowned. *What are they on about?* She left Sam's table to slip back to the office.

"Miss Sinclair." Marks offered a chivalrous bow. "Regretful turn of fate for us all. I shall miss having you as my muse."

"Yes," she said distractedly. "I'm sure you'll find another." She looked to Tobias. "What was that about the *Metropolitan News*?" She bit her lip. Ethan had said something about a story lambasting penny bloods. "Is it related to that article?"

"The article?" Marks shook his head. "There is no article. That's precisely my point, *ma cherie*—"

"Marks, you're from Derbyshire," Tobias barked. He turned to Belle. "There was *going* to be an article, but you needn't worry. Fletcher took care of it."

Marks looked doubtful. "I suppose that's one version of what happened. Because he chose to let it happen."

"I don't understand." She was exhausted and cold and her boots were wet from the rain. She had no patience for unraveling mysteries right now. "Might you speak plainly?"

"Miss Sinclair..." Tobias said carefully. "What exactly did Fletcher tell you?"

"Ah..." Belle wrenched herself back to her father's study. "He was fighting a losing battle on too many fronts." She rubbed her forehead. "He was forced to stop printing, because there was going to be an inflammatory article...we were too behind on the debt, and he has real prospects in New York..."

Tobias and Marks glanced at each other, and Belle had the distinct sense she was missing something. The conversation with Ethan was a blur. She'd been overwhelmed by grief; he'd been miserable and resigned.

"I can't recall him saying anything about a choice in the matter," she finished uncertainly.

"Likely because to him, it *wasn't* a choice." Tobias sighed.

"What do you mean?"

"They wanted a name," Marks said, leaning against Belle's creaky desk. "*Your* name, specifically, lovely. It was meant to be the pièce de résistance in their article to stir up melodrama about a moral panic. And he was willing to pay Fletcher for the information."

"What?" Belle whirled to Tobias. "Is this true?"

"Yes," he replied reluctantly. "Marks came by with one of their correspondents. He was aiming to get a statement from Fletcher, and a meeting with his writer."

Her stomach fell somewhere beyond the dusty floor of the shop.

"Say it again," she rasped.

Tobias looked at her with palpable concern, and it was no wonder—she was half-bedraggled and hadn't slept in two days.

"Say all of those things again but say them differently…because I don't understand."

Resigned, Tobias repeated the story with the patience of a father speaking to an unreasonable child.

And from a fog of fear, Belle understood what had happened, what Ethan had done.

For *her*.

He could have taken the payment, he could have continued publishing, he could have kept the shop from being sold.

Ethan wasn't the one with his back to the wall.

Ethan's back was shielding *hers*.

She stared vacantly into the workroom, at the table where they'd worked together, remembering what he'd told her. *A legacy of leavings.* Each leaving made things better for those who remained.

"Miss Sinclair?" Sam was at her side, his face close and worried.

She blinked, trying to clear the clamor in her head.

"The article," she said, her voice sticking oddly. "Have they written it yet?"

"Not that I've seen."

A terrified conviction unlike any she'd experienced started in her boots and rattled all the way through her. The happiest she'd been in half a decade had been these last months in the printshop. The serial was affirming. It was challenging and interesting and successful. It wasn't drivel. She wasn't ashamed of it.

It was *theirs*.

"We can save it." She stared at Tobias with woozy determination. "We can save the shop for him."

"What?" Tobias looked at her as though she might be ill...which was the only correct way to look at her right now.

"We could publish number ten," she said in a rush. "You just said it was Ethan's choice to stop producing the serial—and he only did so to keep me out of things. What if I *wasn't* out of things? What if we moved forward? We could pay off the debt, Tobias. No forfeiture to Mr. Howe. No sale to anyone."

Belle looked at the men for a confirmation nobody seemed keen to give her.

"Ah..."

"That's not—"

"I already have it written," she insisted. "We only need to print it."

"But Miss Sinclair..." Sam looked nearly sorry for her. "Mr. Fletcher is already gone."

Everyone fell silent as Sam's words dropped into the middle of her aching heart.

"He's gone." Belle managed to keep her voice steady. "But he's not gone forever. We can give him something to come back to. We can keep running the shop for him, we can keep publishing the penny blood. And then if things go wrong in New York, or if he wants to return, he will have the *option*, Tobias. He never has options. I can give him that...can't I?"

She was pleading, and Tobias seemed to waver.

"Well...we can't run it *well* without him. Not at the capacity we've been doing. But some version of it, I suppose."

"All right then." Belle twisted her little twine ring. She felt anxious and afraid, which was far better than feeling helpless and sad. "Then I say...we make a go of it."

"Hold, Miss Sinclair." Tobias looked grave. "Your aim is earnest, but there's still the problem of actually clearing the debt. We can't bring enough in on number ten. It's just not feasible. Fletcher and I looked at those numbers more times than I care to recall."

She raced over to the tabulations, still tacked on the wall.

"It's the fifth of June," she said. "We have ten days. If we start production today, we could exhaust our paper supply. That's... what? At least fifteen thousand copies."

"A penny a piece..." Tobias shook his head. "It's not enough."

"We can charge more in Mayfair..." Belle's thoughts were scrambling, but she was growing sharply clear on one point. "We can charge *triple* in Mayfair. Three pence is *nothing* there."

Tobias frowned. "We don't have an audience in Mayfair. High society doesn't read our penny blood."

Belle straightened. Every sickening, embarrassing, lonely experience of the last four years revolved around her in a panorama show —all the people who looked at her askance, who stopped hiding their whispers, who shut her out of their homes. The men who sidled too close at the courthouse, as if they couldn't decide if she was too ruined or not yet ruined enough. The friends who no longer wrote to her. The weddings she missed, the children she hadn't held.

Enough.

She didn't need *one* of those people to ever look at her again. The only eyes she wanted on her were Ethan's, and he was *gone*, trying to salvage what was left of her reputation. But her efforts to maintain separate lives had only torn her life asunder. *And for what?* So she could be taken seriously one day, so her dreams were still on offer?

But her dreams weren't worth more than his. They were worth the same. They *were* the same.

She gripped Tobias's hand in white-knuckled resolve.

"Society will read it if they know who writes it."

"*Hell.* No." Tobias looked pained. "Don't even think of it—"

"What, exactly, is happening?" Sam glanced between his father and Belle.

Tobias shot her a warning look, but Belle was too far gone.

Because this mattered. It *mattered.* Ethan deserved to have someone helping him.

"I'm going to give my name to the *Metropolitan News*," she said, whirling to face Sam. "I'm going to make them pay handsomely for it. Then we're going to give society what it loves best—a scandal. The judge's disgraced daughter penning drivel and gore. Once they've said their piece, we'll publish number ten. The circles I grew up in won't be able to help themselves."

"Diabolical." Marks looked impressed.

Tobias, meanwhile, looked sick.

She laughed humorlessly. The article practically wrote itself. *But what of it?* The people who cared about her would still care; the people who didn't, never would.

Sam looked at his father. "So should I reassemble the composing case?"

"Yes," she said decisively. "What do we have to lose?"

Tobias hesitated.

"Tobias," she whispered. "*Please.*"

He swore fantastically. Belle blinked in surprise at his uncharacteristic outburst.

"God help us. Sam, grease the press." He nodded to Marks. "You need to fetch Newburn. We need a compositor."

"I can start typesetting." Sam's brown eyes were surprisingly grave. "Until we find Newburn, that is."

"Sam…"

"Mr. Fletcher's been teaching me," the boy said, more resolute than Belle had ever seen him. "I'm slow as can be, but I can do it. If it would help." He looked to Belle. "I'd like to help you, Miss Sinclair."

"Of course." Belle's throat felt tight—more tears were on their way. "Sam, that would be a wonderful help. But you need to come with me. I need to get you the draft—the *correct* draft—and then you can get started."

"Where will you go?" Tobias looked worried. "The offices for the *Metropolitan*? I can't let you go alone."

"No," Belle said, her heart lurching. "Not until after I speak to my family. I cannot move forward with any plan until I tell them what's happening…what's *been* happening. It affects them too."

"Fletcher wouldn't want this," Tobias said, his face etched in concern. "He wanted to keep you out of it."

"It's not just for him." Belle's eyes were bright. "It's for *me*. It's time. It took me long enough, as it were."

She looked at the desk, the crooked leg still secured by Ethan's rolled up newspaper.

"It's for us."

28

———————

On the first day of Spring, Barnacle, the one-eared spaniel, decided being a one-eared spaniel was rather limiting, in the grand scheme of all the things one could be.

And so he set off to have a great Adventure.

—Excerpt from "The Pirate Dog," written by Belle Sinclair, aged ten,
transcribed by her Father to ensure correct spelling and whatnot.

THERE WAS A VERY good chance Belle Sinclair was ruining her life, but she would be damned if she were doing so in vain.

The morning's rain had eased, and glittering puddles studded the Strand. Belle's boots were wet, her hands cold, but purpose warmed her.

Purpose and nerves.

"Papa..." The nearer they drew to their destination, the more prickly she became. "Are you certain? Are you *certain* you harbor no reservation of your own?"

"Belle." Her father's voice was quiet in the bustle of the street.

"You've asked me thrice already. Are you certain you don't *want* me to harbor reservations?"

She grasped his arm more tightly. She might, in fact, wish he had a reservation. It would be nice if *somebody* did, if something could slow time, for the afternoon had whipped by with alacrity. Suddenly, her abstract notion in the printshop was about to become a glaring, permanent reality.

When she returned home and upended a basketful of penny bloods on her mother's sofa table, feeling every bit a black cat dropping a dead mouse in the middle of tea, it had taken her family nearly half an hour to understand what Belle was telling them. What she'd started with Ethan. What it had become.

What she planned to do next.

Mama had paled when Belle shared the numbers. *Thousands.* Tens of thousands of readers over the last nine weeks. It was remarkable to say it aloud, to consider all of it had stemmed from handing Ethan her journal in a garden where neither of them was meant to be.

After the initial shock settled, her mother took the news in stride. "It's unexpected, but we'll manage. The dust will settle. It always does. Nobody ends up free of dust, anyway." The brisk assessment had been a welcome reminder that Mama didn't come from society, and she didn't care about it more than she had to. "But I don't understand why you felt the need to hide from us, darling."

"Because naming myself will reignite gossip." Belle twisted her fingers. "This isn't a proper novel. It's not really proper at *all*. It took me far too long to know if the serial was an endeavor worthy of garnering another black spot."

"And now?" Mama studied her.

"It *will* be a black spot. But I'm proud of it anyway." Belle looked around the parlor. "I know it's just a penny blood, and if you wish for me to keep silent, I will understand, but I cannot live half a life anymore. If I can't be myself here, I want to follow Ethan. He did this to protect me. I know he's gone, but—"

"We don't want you to live half a life either." Mama gripped her hand. "We've never wanted that for you. If we had, we would have expected you to see through your betrothal to Duncan. This is a lot to take in, darling, but it's also you. It's *you*, Belle. And who you are is never something to keep silent about."

Papa had remained quiet, listening with inscrutable composure, but Belle was most worried about Lena. Her sister was gaping at issue number one—it was difficult to say if she was more horrified by the magistrate's severed finger or the fact that Belle wanted to take credit for it.

"Lena?" Belle asked cautiously. "What do you think of this? Of me giving my name to the papers?"

"Me?" Lena glanced up. "Why would it matter what I think?"

"You're out in society," Belle murmured. "I loathe the thought of jeopardizing your chances of making a match. People might say..."

She couldn't say aloud the things people would say. *Have you heard about Sinclair's daughter?*

"Belle." Lena took her other hand. "For years, I've watched you diminish yourself. The last few months, you've been different. You're *happy*. What does it matter to me if you do something unconventional? And why on earth would I marry a man to whom it matters?"

"You'll have to explain—"

"That my sister is an author of gothic fiction."

"You would say that?"

"Why wouldn't I?" Lena looked indignant on her behalf. "It's true." She paused. "Moreover, you're all but engaged, aren't you? Writing aside, you're doing the thing most people expect of you. I don't see it will reflect so much on me in the end. Especially if you're on the arm of a strapping American."

Belle laughed, wiping her eyes. *Oh God*, she could only hope. This would all be more bearable if she were able to hide her face in Ethan's real shoulder, not his metaphorical one.

Now, as they made their way along the Strand, she turned to her father and searched his face. "Of course I don't *want* you to harbor reservations, but you hardly said anything this afternoon, except that you would take me to this meeting."

Papa sidestepped a puddle. "If you have no reservations, then neither do I."

She smiled sadly. It was the reverse of what he'd told her the night before she broke her engagement. *If you have reservations, then so do I.*

"Because I know my own mind?" She looked down. "Are you certain you wish to keep allowing that?"

"Belle. Allowing you to know your own mind is the entire point of raising you."

He slowed his steps. "Here is something I've never told you before."

"Oh?" She glanced at him quickly.

Papa was quiet for a moment; she could see him picking through his words.

"Your mother said today we've managed before—she wasn't only referring to you. We've been a black spot ourselves, you know." He lifted the corner of his mouth. "The day I proposed marriage to your mother was the very same night I told a Serjeant-at-Law in the Court of Common Pleas he could eat rot."

Belle nearly tripped, temporarily distracted from her woes by this bewildering account. "You did *not*."

"I did. I was quite the up-and-comer back then, under consideration for a promotion. But instead of doing as I was meant to, I prosecuted my fellow's philandering son against a woman he'd hurt. And, if I may say, I skewered him." Papa shrugged. "It set me back for some time…and then, eventually, it didn't."

She looked up, meeting his dark blue eyes.

"I won't rise to a position higher than the one I'm in," Papa said candidly. "I'll never be made Common Serjeant or Recorder of London, the way some judges are, nor do I aspire to that. I'm *excellent* at my work, but I don't pander, and I never have. Do you know why?"

Belle shook her head.

"Because I built my legal practice around helping women who were oftentimes used as the pawns of men. I vowed the day I held each of my daughters, I would give you what choices I could. And…" He paused significantly. "I would not allow your choices to hurt me. Your mother and I already made our way. We built what we wanted. We did it the hardest way possible. Who's to say you and Ethan Fletcher can't do the same?"

"Papa." Her eyes swam with tears. "I don't know what to say."

"I suggest you find something to say rather quickly." Papa smiled tightly. "Because we've arrived."

She glanced at the painted sign above the brick edifice.

The Illustrated Metropolitan News

"Do you know how you're going to handle this?" Papa's voice turned businesslike. "This is, perhaps, your sole chance to control the story."

"I know I used that literacy initiative as a silly excuse." Belle chewed her lip. "But I've been thinking about it. Penny bloods are readily available to the masses, and people can't learn to read if they don't have anything to practice with. You heard Ethan when he came to dinner. Most Londoners can't afford a newspaper, but they *can* afford the serial. People need something to read. They deserve something to read."

"But it's not the news." Papa narrowed his eyes. "They *are* rather sensational, Belle."

"I know these stories are garish and melodramatic—they're supposed to be—but that doesn't mean they're worthless or harmful." Her voice rose earnestly. "They offer hardworking people distraction, and in a way, it keeps them informed. Every issue of *Secrets* includes a trial. There's courtroom politics, prison reform, advances in forensics…"

She smiled shyly.

"It's damn good fun, Papa. And I'm *damn* good at it."

"Well." Papa contemplated her words. "That's a decent angle. I would, however, counsel against using expletives when you're trying to prove your points."

He touched her cheek and nodded, and Belle understood it was time to do the blasted thing.

Her fleeting humor retreated. "I'm afraid," she said abruptly.

"That's all right," Papa murmured. "Just don't let them see it."

"It matters how I walk in there?" Her brow creased. "I suppose you're always having to tell me that."

"I know." Papa squeezed her hand. "But it's because I believe you can walk so many places."

And then he opened the door for her, and before she lost her nerve, she strode inside, mustering a polite smile for the desk clerk.

"My name is Belinda Sinclair," she announced softly. "I would like to speak with Mr. White."

"Regarding?"

"His story on penny bloods. I'm here as a representative from *Secrets of the Old Bailey*."

"In what capacity?" The man dipped his pen.

Belle imagined Ethan's face in the garden. She held it there, in front of her, willing him to once more turn her brave.

"I'm the author."

29

———

Agent's Record, CUNARD STEAMSHIP COMPANY

Inward Second Cabin
Ticket No. 31040
Prepaid

For Passage on the Steamship Empire
To Sail from Liverpool, 7 June 1848

Name of Passenger
Ethan T. Fletcher, aged 29 years

～

"WELL?" Ethan collared his impatience as he appraised the massive steamship squatting in its berth in Liverpool's bustling harbor. "Is the *Empire* sailing today?"

The weathered dockhand folded his arms. "Aye. Looks like she'll finally go. I wouldn't wander too far—embarkation will be a crush after all this wait."

Ethan's jaw ticked. He didn't need to be reminded of the wait.

He'd arrived at his hostelry in Liverpool four days ago, and he *should* be two days into an Atlantic crossing.

Instead, there had been a delay in readying the *Empire* and her crew. Which meant it was now June 9th, and Ethan was nearly wrung dry from a slow twist of idle agony.

Around him, the dock teemed with passengers anxious for news. Luggage was stacked everywhere, foreshadowing the manner in which travelers would soon be stacked in their cabins for two hellish weeks.

Belle should set a story on a steamship. The thought came sudden enough to make him smile, before he resettled in an unwieldy melancholy.

He was going to be *so damn far away* from her.

Last night, he'd lain awake on his hard pallet in the hostelry, staring at the ceiling until the cracks became her curves. It made him sick with want and regret. *This*, right here, was the nearest he would be to her for months—and months, at the *soonest*.

His only pale, certain comfort was that Belle was fine. She had her family, she had her writing. She would be living a life much too small for her, but he would fix that as soon as he could.

He just needed to get the hell out of here to get started.

"I'll be at the coffeehouse," Ethan muttered to the dockhand. "Doesn't seem as though embarkation is nigh."

"Give it an hour," the man advised.

Hefting his trunk—he wasn't about to commit the entirety of his possessions to the bedlam of the dock—Ethan muscled through the crowd and crossed the bustling street.

He entered the coffeehouse, paying the requisite shilling for entry, coffee, and a paper. Incredible, really, how accustomed he'd become to the way of things here. He found an empty seat on a bench near the window and raised his finger to the harried proprietor.

A moment later, a steaming cup appeared, nearly sloshing over the slew of publications on the table in front of him.

"Might you have anything more recent?" Ethan asked. As far as he could tell, these papers were all at least a week old. If he was going to be stuck here for another afternoon, he at least hoped for some legitimate news.

The proprietor plucked through the pile. "This here is just from London," he offered, thwacking a copy of the *Illustrated Metropolitan News* in front of Ethan.

Ethan started to tell the man the *Metropolitan* was the shovel that buried him, but he couldn't tell him that.

He couldn't tell him anything.

Because Ethan was rendered utterly voiceless by the headline in front of him.

PRETTY BLOOD?

Judge's Daughter Wields Gruesome Pen

A crescendo of terrible confusion mounted as his gaze shifted from the title to the etching of a woman sitting at a desk. She had long loose hair and wide eyes and looked exactly like the love of his life.

"What in *fuck*?"

He was on his feet fast enough to upend his coffee. Hastily, he snatched the paper from the scorching spill, then instantly regretted it.

He wanted to burn this paper to ash.

But no.

He had to read it.

He *couldn't* read it.

A deep, painful pulse started somewhere behind his eyes. *Who had done this?* If that goddamn inspector had named her, Ethan would kill him. As his fists clenched around the paper, he feared it wasn't hyperbole.

Christ—*Belle*.

What must she be thinking right now? Her family…they still didn't know. *Nobody knew.* They had made sure of it. Ethan was sitting in the middle of godforsaken Liverpool to make sure of it. He'd *left* her to make sure of it.

And now, because he was gone, she was *alone* in the aftermath.

"Sir?" The proprietor was looking at him in alarm. "Do you need…"

Ethan realized he was on his feet, that he'd made a mess of his coffee, that he was twisting the paper as if to strangle it.

"I'm fine," he lied.

He scraped his hand over his face, forcing himself to read the article, to bear witness to whatever the hell had happened.

Many of our Loyal Readers are all too familiar with the increasingly popular story papers that litter our streets. But while some claim penny bloods warrant eradication befitting any vermin plaguing our City, other voices opine a different view. To that end, we ourselves have spoken to one so-called poison-publisher, namely, the Author of the popular new crime serial, SECRETS OF THE OLD BAILEY, who, in a shocking turn, is none other than the daughter of a renowned Judge who sits at the very same titular Court…

Ethan rapidly skimmed the article, sick with fury at the nasty insinuations—*prurient horrors…pestilent trash…low-minded gallows literature*—until his eyes locked on the closing.

"If the esteemed readers of the Illustrated Metropolitan News would like to discern for themselves the possible value of my writing, I urge them to procure a copy of the next issue of our serial, which will be available next week," Miss Sinclair stated.

There you have it, Readers. Dare I say, the gauntlet has been thrown?

It took him another two passes to look past the blistering commentary and properly absorb the article's counterpoints—*affordable to all… drawn from authentic trials…an opportunity to take leisure and learn.*

And from a great distance, Ethan realized Duncan hadn't done this.

Belle wasn't merely named.

She was quoted.

And she'd turned it into a goddamn advertisement.

What in the *devil* was she thinking? It was clear Belle and Tobias were publishing number ten. They were going ahead with it, trying to sustain what Ethan had been willing to set aside.

And she set fire to her own reputation to do it.

Holy…*hell.*

"Sir," a white-haired gentleman tapped Ethan's arm. "You were waiting for the *Empire*, were you not? They've begun embarking."

Ethan whirled around, craning his neck to see out the window—a swell of commotion now surrounded the steamship.

Christ.

"I can't…"

Ethan was decisive in all matters—always—but he couldn't make his brain and boots move together.

"I can't embark yet."

"I wouldn't tarry," the proprietor urged. "They'll start with the lower cabins."

Ethan drew a breath, a dozen concerns walloping him from all sides like musket fire. In a fog, he lifted his trunk and pushed out of the coffeehouse, crossing straight in front of a shouting stream of carriages and cabs.

His ship was finally leaving. If he boarded as planned, he would be in New York by the end of the month. He could pull a good salary, he could bring Belle to him. Or he could save, return, and establish a business in London. Either option required patience, but the payoff would be a steady, secure life for both of them.

All he needed to do was get on the boat.

He paused at the berth.

Get on the boat, Fletcher.

He stared at the steamship, now alive with activity, then looked out over the river. The sight of the sun on water pulled him straight through time, back to his boyhood, visiting the seashore—the gray waves, the whaling ships, the empty widow's walks.

Who would wait for a sailor? Now Ethan reconsidered those women, studying the horizon, holding their lamps aloft. He'd thought it the stuff of romantic legend. Yet here he was, living it.

He'd left a woman with her light on.

People jostled him, everyone rushing to and fro, Ethan standing still.

"Are you going?" A sailor was pushing a cart, waiting for him to move.

"Yes," he said, snapping his gaze away from the water. "Yes. I'm going."

His feet were finally moving, his thoughts racing to catch up. Her snubbing, her isolation. It would be all she'd already endured, tenfold. Not abstract, not theoretical. The article was *published*. It was already happening to her, which meant patience and steadiness were no longer viable options.

"Oy—the dock's the other way!"

"I don't need a ship," Ethan gritted. "I need a train."

He moved through the tide of passersby, muscling upstream to the line of cabs opposite the docks. He called to a driver and hauled his trunk into an empty seat, coiling with tension as he pulled away from the harbor. Every lurch of the cab moved him further from his plan.

To hell with it.

His plan didn't matter; it was in service of building a life he and Belle had been building this entire damn time. She was holding fast to that life.

He refused to let her hold it alone.

For months, he'd viewed her as something precious—beautiful and brilliant and far beyond his reach. He was a goddamn fool. Belle *wanted* to be reached. *Look at me,* she'd pleaded.

He'd been so afraid of letting himself give in, he hadn't seen how fearlessly she gave.

Belle might be the finest aspect of his life, but so was she his partner.

His helpmate. His friend. His one good thing.

And God help him, *he wouldn't leave her.*

"Lime Street," the driver called as the cab drew to a halt at the rail station. Ethan was already swinging to the ground. He hefted his trunk and shoved through the crowd.

"I need passage to London." He nearly barked at the baleful clerk at the booking office window. "Your next train, your cheapest fare."

He reached for his wallet and realized the newspaper was still rolled up beneath his arm. He tossed it to the clerk as he dug for coin.

He was already sifting through everything that needed done—shield Belle from repercussions, push production on number ten, capitalize on the *Metropolitan* article…so much work, so much *impossible* work—

And six days to do it all.

"Your paper, sir." The clerk wrinkled his nose at the etching of Belle, which enraged Ethan anew, because if nothing else, she looked beautiful in the stupid picture.

"I don't need it," Ethan muttered, taking his ticket. "You can give it away."

He started to turn away, to find his platform.

Then he froze.

Give it away.

He whipped back to the window, staring at the discarded paper.

He was again possessed of a ludicrous notion—and the thought somehow cheered him.

He could do hard things. He'd done them before. And now he had good people to help him.

He might have only a matter of days, but so did he have *thousands* of pages of free advertising.

All of it sitting in his storeroom.

30

"THE POST, MISS SINCLAIR." Sam appeared in the door of Ethan's small parlor, where Belle had been working the last few days. At her behest, Tobias and Newburn had moved the desk up here so she could have privacy. The shop had been aflutter with activity since the *Metropolitan* article was published three days ago.

Some of the clamor was welcome and exciting, but other visitors were far more disparaging. Everyone agreed it wasn't productive for her to work downstairs. But quiet was only part of the reason she made the request.

She was increasingly heartsore, and it was easier to breathe up here, in Ethan's space.

It was the tenth of June, only five days remaining. And despite the upper-crust booksellers who were, indeed, placing overpriced orders, Belle was starting to fear she didn't have the wherewithal to pull this off without Ethan.

It had been a rather…exhausting week.

Her work on number eleven was slow-going, what with the frequent interruptions from the letter carrier. The post was now her constant source of dread—she was as likely to find an order from a newsagent or bookseller as she was to find a letter from an irate matron or a disapproving moralist. She was trying to harness her nerves, but it was daunting to never know if she would uncover exciting success or bruising admonishment.

Except for the note from Paulie, the newsboy, asking if he, too, could have his own character like Sam, and also if he might call on her now Mr. Fletcher was gone. She appreciated Paulie's gumption, so she tacked his letter to the wall.

She could use all the gumption she could muster.

"Thank you, Sam." Belle smiled tightly, accepting the small stack as the boy raced back down the narrow stairs.

She scanned the letters, quickly sorting the curds from the whey. Three newsagents—one on Piccadilly—wanted to carry next week; that was a boon. But her spirits were decidedly dampened by a letter from Mrs. Nicholas Pendergast, who colorfully described the many ways Belle was a nasty, ineligible perversion of propriety.

Wonderful.

She crumpled the letter in her fist, then opened it up again, of half a mind to take down the address and assure Mrs. Pendergast that while she might be improper, she *was* engaged to be married… at some unknown point in the future…to a man who was, at present, a partial ocean away.

She crumpled the letter again and tossed it in the growing pile.

Belle sank to the chair behind her desk, pressing her fingers over her eyes. She had known to expect this. This was part of the whole coming into herself bit, wasn't it? The good and the bad, all together.

No more separate lives.

She just very much wished she wasn't coming into herself by herself.

Footsteps sounded on the stairs.

She hastily stood and turned her back to the door, wiping at her cheek. The footfall was heavier than Sam's, and Tobias had already found her crying twice this week.

"I'm fine," she called, hating the thick cast to her voice. "You needn't worry about me—"

"I thought there was no pretension in this shop."

She stilled.

When she was a girl, she'd been instructed in the principles of magnetic attraction. The way one pole could direct its opposite, helpless to do anything but cleave to its pair.

A dull ringing pierced her, moving slowly from one ear to the other. It tightened her neck, rotated her body. She had a blurred sense of a long, broad figure—dark coat, dark beard—then she put her eyes where they belonged.

Impossible.

"Oh God." He dragged his hand over his mouth, staring at her. "That's it. All I wanted."

She was rooted to the spot, but it mattered not, for he was already upon her. Ethan wrapped her in his arms, lifting her up and against him. She inhaled sharply, ensnared by the heated plane of his body, the heated look on his face.

"Sweetheart."

And then he was kissing her, a tender appeal, the barest brush of his lips on hers. The sensation of his firm, familiar mouth was all it took to burst her wonder, to scatter her surprise and confusion like stars. Instantly, she deepened the kiss, stroking open his mouth, both of them grappling and desperate with gratitude.

He kissed her until her lips burned, until her lungs burned, and even then, at the edge of a swoon, she could scarcely pull away. He groaned, his hands in her hair. She was clinging to him, she couldn't let go. He was *here.*

But *no*—no. He *couldn't* be.

He couldn't possibly be.

"What…what is happening?" She wrenched away, half-blind with shock and tears. "Ethan, I don't understand. You're meant to be aboard a steamship. You're not meant to be here."

His lips skated over her cheek, his beard a soft, reassuring brush against her skin.

"I could ask you the same thing." He was breathing hard. "You're meant to be *out* of the goddamn newspapers."

"The news—" She shook her head in confusion. "You can't mean the article?"

"I cannot believe you, Belle."

"No, you couldn't have seen it." She felt fuzzy from joy and bewilderment. "It wasn't published until the day you were to sail."

"The ship didn't depart as scheduled. I've been detained in Liverpool, barely able to resist dragging myself back here. Until yesterday, when I saw the article."

Dread crawled up her neck.

"Oh no, Ethan. Don't tell me that's why you came back."

"Your name, your illustration, the statement you gave—"

"It was my choice," she said rapidly, grabbing his shoulders. She needed him to understand, even though it was too late. He was here; he missed his boat. "I realized what you'd done, and I realized I could undo it."

"Belle, what were you thinking?"

"Ethan, no. I didn't mean to press your hand," she protested fearfully. "I thought you were gone. But I heard what happened with that reporter, what he offered, what you turned down. I had to do *something*."

"We had a plan—"

"I didn't like the plan." She shook her head. "I wanted you to have something to come back for. I didn't *want* to give up on the penny blood. It's what we made together. I want to keep making it."

"Belle—"

"I wasn't going to let some tawdry publication keep me out of my own damn story, Ethan." She crossed her arms. "They can't threaten my reputation anymore. It's all in the open. It's done."

He stared at her in disbelief. "You're patently mad, you realize that?"

"I think I must be." Belle felt about ten steps behind him. She put her hands to her cheeks, riddled with confusion. "I can't make sense of this. What about New York? What about your offer?"

"I'm not taking it."

"*No*. All your aims—"

"I'll rework them. I'll come at them from another angle. Right now, I'm taking the win."

Her heart seized in panic. He misunderstood her.

"The article didn't sway business that much," she whispered. "There's still nothing here. We don't own the shop yet. We *haven't* won."

"I'm not talking about the shop." His voice turned scratchy; his eyes grew bright. "The shop isn't all that matters. It's not even *most* of what matters. It's sure as hell not what I came back for."

He cradled her face.

"For all my life, I've been grasping. *You* are the only thing that has ever held on." His thumb moved gently over her lower lip. "That's not the kind of love you wait for. It's the kind of love you *live* in."

She clasped his arms, her chest heating with wonder.

"Belle, I was so focused on preparing for our worst days, I forgot some days aren't bad. Some days are merely ordinary." His smile tilted in a gradual curve. "And some days are really damn good."

"Yes," she breathed, taut with hope. "Some days really are."

"I mean it." He kissed her again, deep and slow. "I want to live in the ordinary days. I want to marry you now. Or as soon as now can be."

"What happened to waiting for your circumstances?" She found his hands, curling her palms over his. "I can wait, Ethan—"

"You shouldn't have to," he said. "For many reasons I assure you are deeply romantic, and one that's by necessity. My circumstances haven't changed, but *yours* have. You've put your whole weight behind me this week, and you can't tell me you're not taking a beating for it."

He shook his head, glancing at the pile of crumpled-up letters.

"I expect you need a husband, sweetheart."

"Yes." She smiled ruefully, thinking of her most recent correspondence. "You know, a husband would actually be quite useful."

He softened, but Belle grew serious.

"Truly, Ethan. I need your help. Things have improved since you were last here, but we're still behind. I don't know what else to do."

His expression sharpened.

"You're right." He strode to the desk and hefted the account book. "We have to harness this disaster once and for all. Tell me where we stand."

She launched into a rapid recounting of what had happened this week—the article, the aftermath, the sales, the censures.

"This is a hell of a start." He flipped through the purchase orders. "Your wild little stunt has been a boon for business—and I assume the *Metropolitan* compensated you for your remarks?"

"It's been accounted for," she said. "There, on the second page."

Ethan made a notation. "Closer…closer still."

"Not close enough?"

"Possibly." He looked at her. "You know, the article changes things in more ways than one."

"What do you mean?"

"Our association with *Secrets* is public now. It's legitimate in a way it wasn't before. If you're keen to continue writing it, I'm determined to keep publishing it. As long as we like, until we're ready for something new."

"Yes," she said swiftly, having already come to the same decision. "Yes. I want to keep going."

"Not a newspaper, not a novel. But perhaps that's all right." He laughed softly. "Somehow or another, we're pretty damn good at this, and while I think we'll be good at other things, we can't possibly plan for it now."

"It's not just about the debt anymore," she said, realizing where he was going with this.

"It *is* about the debt, but it's also about momentum." He closed the account book. "If this isn't temporary, we need longevity. I think your society gamble will pay off, in the short term at least. But I'd like to see if we can build our readership and really make a go of it."

He was right. Gossip was moving papers right now, but God willing, she wouldn't be the center of attention forever. They needed something more stable than overcharging bored matrons and the fair-weather friends who had spurned her.

"How?"

"When I was in the train station, I had a notion. Your idea for free advertising planted the seed."

She blanched. "I can't stomach another article."

"God no. Not that." He cocked an eyebrow. "I'm thinking about number nine."

"What about it?"

"What if we *give* it away?"

"What? For free?" Belle wrinkled her nose. "Ethan…I don't see how that would possibly help."

His eyes gleamed with excitement. "We can't sell it, Belle. But we can *give it away*. Think about it—just like the beginning, eyes lead to sales. We can take it to train stations, the dockyards, places with passersby."

Her breath staggered. "Constabularies. Post offices. Oh, Ethan!"

"*The Old Bailey*," they said in unison.

"Yes." She laughed, her pulse skittering. "That's *brilliant*."

"If we can lure readers who wouldn't normally pick this up, coupled with you wringing far too many pennies from the laden coffers of Mayfair—"

"We might have enough sales from number ten," Belle finished.

"Yes." He nodded. "Belle, I really think we can. You've already closed the gap on what we lost on nine."

"Shall we tell Tobias?"

"Yes. We'll need hands to help distribute." Ethan frowned. "I could pay the newsboys, Paulie and the like."

She refrained from mentioning Paulie was already offering her his services.

Ethan went to make a note, then paused, glancing about as if taking stock of his residence for the first time.

"What's the desk doing up here?"

"Oh." She winced. "I found it preferable to work up here. The shop has been quite busy…and not everyone stopping by is polite."

Her eyes filled with tears, but this time, she didn't try to hide it.

It was too much—everything that had happened this week, for better or worse, had pushed her past the point of endurance.

"Belle?" His green eyes narrowed with concern.

"It's been…a very hard few days," she admitted, drawing a shaky breath. "You weren't wrong. I've taken a bit of a beating."

She gestured to the pile of nasty notes, and his face darkened in understanding.

"That's ending now." He grasped her biceps, turning her away from the crumpled letters. "Everything comes to me. I don't want you to see another letter from a supercilious prig."

"Don't read them," she warned. "Ethan, you *really* shouldn't see what they say."

"Let them talk. Let them say whatever the hell they please." He tilted her chin. "It doesn't matter. I'll tell you the good news."

Relief washed through her, warm as a bath at the end of a long, cold day. They had so much to do, but it felt so good to stand in the circle of his arms. She pressed her face to his shoulder, and yes, from this vantage, it was easy not to hear anyone but him.

"Would you tell me now?"

His lips moved against her brow. "Always." He kissed her palms, her wrists. "As often as you need."

He brushed her mouth.

"And sometimes, when I need it too."

31

Secrets of the Old Bailey, Vol 1., No. 10
In Plain Sight

Some might say an oyster fork makes for an unconventional weapon. Judging by the scene awaiting Clementina at the safe house near the docks, Mrs. Parker was able to wield it just fine.

"Well," Clementina thought as she studied the fork, "at least it was a patterned carpet."

The Inspector, predictably, searched for the murder weapon late into the night.

It was no matter; Clementina had never needed to prove anything to anyone but herself.

❧

"If it makes you feel better, you can tell me the story of the prison spikes again," Ethan offered as they approached the Old Bailey. "I know how horrific facts soothe you."

"You tease, and yet, you did, in fact, retain the lesson." She glanced up at him. "*And* you came around on London."

"You're right. It was Newgate that convinced me."

"Truly, Ethan, you didn't have to accompany me." She tightened her grip on her basket. "I know you have a dozen other places to distribute today. I can manage here on my own."

Her confidence was undermined by her galloping nerves. She was, truthfully, grateful for Ethan's company. She hadn't been to the Old Bailey since the *Metropolitan* article.

"I know you can. But it didn't take as long as I expected at the railway stations today." Ethan frowned. "Deptford wasn't interested, but Euston's bookstall took a substantial stack. Might be something there. We'll see how Tobias fared at Paddington."

"Do you suppose it's working?" Belle gestured to the number nines in his crate. "Giving it away?"

He shrugged grimly. "It's not *hurting*. Orders have been picking up, between the article and free papers. I'd feel a hell of a lot better if we had one big push."

He opened the door for her.

"All right," she said as they entered the bustling din. "If you go through the gallery, you can pass out copies to the spectators…and the jury. They have to sit through all the trials this session, so they might like something to read. Counselors will be at the round table in the center—place some copies there too."

"And you?"

She swallowed hard at the thought of all those eyes on her, what they knew before, what they knew now.

Let them talk.

She resolutely reached for a stack of serials. "I'm going to circulate out here. Plenty of folks will pass by."

"I'll be back soon." He indicated Doyle, the guard. "If anyone is bothering you, send Doyle to find me."

Hefting his stack, Ethan strode into the Old Court.

Right. Circulate the serial. The one she'd written about the place she loved best. She could do this. If Ethan could haul copies to every port and train station in London over the last two days and still manage to come here with her, she would do her part too.

"Aye, Miss Sinclair." Doyle came to stand beside her.

"Hello, Doyle." She sighed, marginally cheered by the company of her old friend.

"Been a while since I've seen you about."

"Yes, well. I've been maintaining my privacy," Belle admitted. "I'm not presently a welcome face in some circles."

She stuck her arm out to stop a trio of junior barristers she knew belonged to Gray's Inn. "Gentlemen." She forced a smile. "Might I offer a bit of reading material?"

"A penny blood?" One fellow grimaced. "I'll decline. I don't read stories written by hacks."

"*She* wrote it." Another elbowed the first. "Justice Sinclair's daughter."

Three pairs of eyes grew keen.

"I did." Belle kept her face as placid as possible. "About the Lennox trial, but with a more...*surprising* outcome."

One man waved her off and went inside, but the other two took copies.

"Much obliged," she called. "The sequel comes out tomorrow, you can find it on the Strand..."

"There." She looked at Doyle. "That wasn't so bad, was it?"

"You needn't be so nervous," he advised. "I read it, you know."

Belle blinked. "You do?"

"Even before I knew you wrote it," Doyle said gruffly. "It's good. Too gory for a lady."

"Doyle." She beamed. "That's quite kind of you to say."

A gaoler walked past, and Belle thrust two copies upon him, urging him to take one back to Newgate. He paused to flip through the serial as two barristers walked out of the Old Court. One glanced her over, nudging the other. He whispered audibly, and it wasn't kind.

Belle ignored them.

The gaoler came back. "This the one that lady wrote?"

"Ah, yes." Belle said. "She did."

He shook his head and gave back the paper. "That ain't right."

A court reporter wandered over. "Number nine? I thought I'd missed it."

She handed it over, reflecting on its factual contents. "You missed less than you might think," she assured him.

The time passed quickly. For every one man who snubbed her, there was another interested in taking a *gratis* copy. Given that scowls couldn't hurt their accounts, Belle thought they were faring well, all things considered.

"See, Miss Sinclair?" Doyle said when the gaoler returned to begrudgingly take a copy after all. "Gossip grows stale quick."

"If anyone would know, it would be Belinda Sinclair," a voice drawled behind her. "She does insist on cooking up a continuous batch for herself."

Belle immediately stiffened. She turned around to see Duncan and a constable approaching from the Newgate passage. She clutched her last few papers and instinctively cataloged her appearance—hair was neat, skirts were smooth.

And then she stopped.

He wasn't worth her neat hair or smooth skirts, and he certainly wasn't worth her care.

She looked at her stack, realizing she only had two papers left. The rest had all been taken. She felt the stirring of pride—and the pride stiffened her spine for an entirely different reason.

"Inspector," Belle said, looking straight at him. "What brings you to the courthouse on such a fine summer day?"

"I found myself with a free moment." Duncan looked her over. "I'm sure you can sympathize, given that you've taken to playing costermonger."

Belle squared her shoulders. "And here, I would expect you'd have no time for leisure, seeing as you've been so busy dallying with the *Illustrated Metropolitan News.*"

"I couldn't possibly know what you're referring to." Duncan adjusted his coat.

Belle inhaled sharply. "Don't you?"

He looked at her like he always did, as if he were deciding the best way to make her small. He fully expected her to keep quiet and let him do it.

Well, that was just another of his many mistakes.

Because Belle wasn't so small, and she was no longer so quiet. And above all, she was *furiously* in love with a man who made her feel invincible.

She glanced at the constable. "I don't believe we've had the pleasure." She smiled. "I'm Miss Sinclair. You've possibly heard of me. I'm the wicked woman who ended an engagement to Inspector Duncan to pursue my own endeavors."

Duncan smirked, but his mouth tightened as the constable pivoted to look at him.

"In spite of the poor terms on which our association ended, Inspector Duncan has been so kind as to remain a great supporter of my writing," she informed his colleague. "So much so, he went very far out of his way to facilitate an advertising opportunity for me."

"That so?" The constable gave him a dubious look. "I wouldn't have expected it to be any of his business."

"Nor would I. It came as a great shock, that he would still have anything to do with me at all. I must assume it's because we've found ourselves treading in similar circles." She turned to Duncan, her gaze steady. "I can't imagine there will be any *continued* business between us?"

"I'm sure I don't know what you mean, Belinda."

She felt the warm press of a familiar hand at her waist a half second before his deep voice moved past her.

"If you can't discern what she means, you're as lousy a detective as you are a man."

Belle bit back a smile as Duncan's cheek twitched.

Ethan went on, unperturbed. "My fiancée has a very polite way of saying we don't give a damn about you, Inspector. You might as well give a few less damns about us. And if you don't, you'll have me to deal with." He gently squeezed her hip. "Though I'd argue she's the far more frightening one—and I'd guess about fifteen thousand readers a week agree."

The constable laughed, and Duncan glared.

"And it's Miss Sinclair," she added. "I'd ask you to remember that."

"Or don't." Ethan grinned. "In a fortnight, she will be Mrs. Fletcher."

"Cheers." The constable raised his serial, and Ethan tipped his hat in a way that would be infuriatingly smug if it didn't also make her want to be Mrs. Fletcher at this very moment.

Duncan rolled his eyes, but without a willing audience, he was a cat without claws.

The image broadened her smile.

"Shall we?" Ethan offered his arm.

But maybe she had one last damn to give, because Duncan had, in fact, dragged her through it, and all because she saw him for exactly who he was.

It was high time she made him see *her*, in turn.

"Here you are, Inspector." She pressed her sole remaining copy upon him. "It's your good luck, because that's my very last one. I know you were quite upset a few months ago, when you couldn't find my story anywhere." She nodded at the serial, now limp in his hand. "I don't expect you'll have much trouble anymore. Though you have to look for it early—we tend to sell out."

And with that, she linked her arm through Ethan's and let him lead her away.

They had work to do.

"WELL, Mr. Fletcher, the day is upon us." Charles Howe strode into the printshop like a man who might, in fact, own it. "June the fifteenth, my good man."

Ethan no longer had a desk in the office, seeing as his intended had situated it in the front window of his parlor. He didn't begrudge

Belle moving his shabby furniture around. God knows the blasted thing likely wouldn't withstand another relocation anyway.

But he would have preferred not to take this meeting over his composing case.

Beside him, Mr. Gabler, his perpetually anxious and generally useless solicitor, bounced on his heels.

"Well, then. Do you have my final payment, or do you have my deed?" Howe smiled genially, as if it didn't matter one way or the other.

"Believe me, Howe." Ethan shook his head at the blustery creditor. "I cannot believe it came down to this."

The preceding days had been a blur. So much work, everyone pitching in—taking orders, making plans, fearing it wasn't enough.

Doing it anyway.

"Don't be hard on yourself, Fletcher." Howe looked nearly sympathetic, and Gabler flinched. "Your uncle took out this loan two years ago to the day. In all that time, he hardly managed to pay a third of what he owed. You got close, my boy."

Ethan reached into his coat pocket and lifted a banknote, holding it aloft between his first two fingers. "You're damn right I did."

It had been a day and a half since Ethan realized they were going to make it, and even still, he'd nearly missed the moment altogether. When the June 13th two o'clock post was delivered, containing three withering letters and two purchase orders, Ethan hardly registered its arrival. The mail had been much the same all week—an assortment of censures and sales.

It was only later that day when he finally had a spare minute to look over the post. He made swift work of burning the letters before turning to the orders, ready to note another incremental gain. Indeed, the first had been from a fancy hotel in Mayfair, placing a request for a dozen copies, which Ethan was only too happy to gouge them for.

But the *second* order was from a new bookstall at Euston station.

Ethan had silently passed Belle the note. He drank in the exact instant she understood, her hazel eyes round in wonder. She looked at him, a buoyant thrill crackling between them—and then the moment passed. He returned to his press and she picked up her pen, because for them, success would never be completing a job. It would always be continuing one.

Especially now they were under contract with the railway for *two thousand copies a week.*

A wall of utter exhaustion and euphoria hit him, and Ethan started laughing, even as Gabler and Howe stared. But he hadn't appreciated it until this moment—extending his hand and passing Howe the money that had been his very last shackle.

He didn't owe a goddamn thing to *anyone.*

Howe examined the banknote. "I'll be." He tucked it in his pocket. "Unfortunately, you're six pounds short, Fletcher."

"I know." Ethan raised his palms. "I haven't received payment for all my outstanding orders yet."

He slid his account book to Howe. "Here you can see, this whole column is standing orders. Every week, Howe. I'm good for it. It's just a bit too recent to have all the funds in hand."

Howe gave him a pitying look, and Ethan's stomach turned over once. He reminded himself he'd known this would likely happen, and he and Belle had come to an agreement. They were to be married in two weeks, and while they wouldn't need to rely on her portion, they could certainly borrow six pounds from it.

Still, Ethan couldn't help feeling just the slightest bruising of his pride. *Damn…*he'd nearly made it, hadn't he?

Just then, a handful of sovereigns landed on the worktable.

Ethan looked up to find Tobias at his side.

"There's the last six pounds." Tobias shrugged. "No fathers-in-law necessary."

"Porter." Ethan shook his head. This was a month's pay for the pressman. "No. I can't possibly—"

"Consider it a loan," Tobias replied. "You just said you're good for it. And I certainly know where to find you."

Ethan experienced a poignant tug of gratitude.

"Pardon my interruption, gentlemen." Howe collected the

coins and made another note in his account book. "Whatever you're considering is no concern of mine, so long as your money is."

He slid Gabler a document as he pocketed the funds.

"That's the last of what I was owed by your uncle's estate, which means after you sign, we have no further business, Fletcher." Howe signed his own initials with a flourish. "You're free and clear. Unless, of course, you run into trouble."

Ethan grunted noncommittally. He signed the paperwork, staring at his signature. Relief funneled from the pen to his fingers, until his entire body buzzed with it.

"Good for you, Fletcher," Howe called as he took his leave. "You know, I really didn't think you'd make it."

When the door closed behind him, the air in the shop felt different.

For the first time in his life, Ethan was standing in a room he *owned*.

He was under no man's thumb, no man's direction. He could do whatever he damn well pleased.

"Not a loan," he said abruptly, turning to Tobias. "That is, of course, I'll repay you. But it occurs to me, I'd much prefer to think of it as an investment."

"Oh?" Tobias frowned.

"Yes," Ethan said, alight with conviction. "Tobias, you've kept this shop running—before I came, after I left. You helped Belle, you helped me. You shouldn't be my pressman. You should be my business partner."

"I thought you already had one of those." Tobias nodded to where Belle was currently arguing with Newburn in the office.

"She's about to promote me." Ethan grinned, thinking of his looming wedding day. "So I'd say I could use all the help I can get around here."

Tobias smiled in return. "I only paid six pounds. I think that makes me a poor shareholder."

"Six pounds?" Ethan clapped his friend's back and laughed.

"Porter, right now, you've officially brought in more money than I have."

"Truly, Fletcher?" Tobias grew serious. "I appreciate the offer, but it's unnecessary. You hardly require an official associate…the operation isn't so big as that."

"Not yet," Ethan countered. "It's not big *yet*. We have no idea what's next, do we?"

"I suppose not."

Ethan turned to Gabler. "We should sit down this week and draw up a business contract."

"Oh." Gabler looked apologetic. "I don't usually work with those sorts of documents."

"One day, Gabler, we're going to find your specialty," Ethan promised him. "So far, it hasn't been debt mediation or mailing letters. I have a good feeling about this one."

Ethan looked about the shop—Belle in the office causing someone a headache, Sam whistling in the storeroom, he and Tobias at the press. They might not know what was next, but Ethan had an idea it would be something pretty damn special.

"You know, Porter, maybe it's time I meet with your publishing colleagues at the coffeehouse," Ethan said thoughtfully. "Seeing as I'm now the owner of a business in this infernal city, I might as well start improving the place. Starting with the godforsaken news tax."

"You and your penny paper," Tobias groused good-naturedly.

"Perhaps one day." Ethan lifted his shoulder. "We've had more ludicrous notions than that, haven't we?"

Belle poked her head into the workroom, smiling in a way that meant her problem was about to be his. "Ethan, darling?" She lifted her chin, doubling down on his many weaknesses. "Might you please inform Newburn I do, in fact, require full use of my adjectives?"

"Tell Newburn I'll typeset your fair copy today," Ethan replied, striding to her with casual confidence.

"Is that so?" She had ink on her cheek and the stirrings of an argument on her face. The intoxicating nearness of her had Ethan on the cusp of a kiss.

"Assuredly." He smiled slowly, just the way he knew she liked it. "I'm in the mood to handle something fine."

He waited for her reprimand; betrothed or not, they were in the middle of the shop. But she merely raised her brow in challenge and pinned her draft to his chest with a fingertip. In a flash, his hand was on top of hers, holding her palm against him.

And then he kissed her, swift and sweet enough, she couldn't regret it.

After all, it would be a shame to waste such a damn good day.

32

MARRIAGES

At St. Bride's Parish, on the 26th day of June by the Rev. C. Braxton, Mr. Ethan Thomas Fletcher to Belinda Rose Sinclair of London.

—*Excerpt from the* EVENING STANDARD

THE WEDDING-CAKE SPIRE OF ST. Bride's church seemed to wave in greeting as Ethan wrapped Belle's hand around his forearm and led her through the churchyard. Her family and their friends from the shop waited in a small, cheerful cluster.

Ethan withheld a groan. To be sure, he was happy to see them, but he wasn't in the mood to loiter.

"Be nice," she admonished, looking up at him with a smile. "You knew to expect this. We went over the schedule yesterday. Twice."

"The only part of the schedule I'm interested in," he murmured, "is what happens in the half hour between the church and the wedding breakfast."

"Ethan!" Belle blushed. "Goodness. You might consider not being a brute on our wedding day."

"Apologies." He leveled her a look, watching the freckles across her nose fade in the prettiest wash of pink. "I must have misheard your sentiments the other day. I could have sworn you enjoyed me playing a brute, though my hearing was a bit restricted by—"

"Mama!" Belle pivoted abruptly to embrace her mother but not before stepping on his boot with surprising force for such a small, satin-slippered foot.

Emilia Sinclair wrapped Belle in her arms, which immediately had both women crying. Ethan decided he wouldn't be offended by this. He was confident he'd secured Mrs. Sinclair's good graces. Last week, he invited Belle's mother to the shop, and she seemed to take great delight in watching them work. It was hard to say what she appreciated more—Newburn's explanation of typesetting, or Marks's proclamation that he'd found a new muse.

Helena hugged her next—more tears—and because Ethan did, in fact, know today's schedule, he knew he was meant to stand back and be patient as the small crowd of finely dressed women—her mother, her sister, two cousins, her aunt, Mrs. Porter—greeted his bride.

Belle was resplendent, her untamed curls pinned beneath a wreath of flowers, her gown the same soft yellow she'd worn to the courthouse the day he first put her hand on his arm and imagined what a fine pair they might make. *After the wedding.* He'd had the right idea that day, because he did, in fact, intend to sneak her away. Lady Fordham was hosting what she'd assured them was a small and simple wedding breakfast—so simple, in fact, it apparently involved ten courses and required him to wear a cravat.

It was no matter. Despite playing grouchy for Belle's delight, Ethan was in the finest spirits of his life.

He just needed a moment with his wife.

Justice Sinclair approached. "Felicitations, Fletcher."

"Sir." He shook hands with his new father-in-law.

"Your men came by for Belle's last things."

Ethan laughed. His *men* were Sam and Paulie the newsboy. "I noticed. I can't currently see the floor of my residence."

"We can store what you need." The judge smiled. "As long as you need. It's all right if it takes time."

"Thank you, sir." Ethan regarded him. "I mean that sincerely. I know things aren't as stable as either of us would like—"

"They're exactly as stable as I'd like," Justice Sinclair said mildly. "My daughter married a creative and enterprising man—"

"Hardly."

"Who makes her very happy," Sinclair finished. "So perhaps I should be thanking you."

"Suppose we call it even." Ethan grinned. "I've about had my fill of debts—even ones of gratitude."

Belle appeared at his side. "Come, darling. Everyone wants to congratulate you."

He looked over her shoulder, to the little group of women watching him expectantly.

"The beard *does* suit," a willowy brunette remarked as Belle hauled him over.

"Cecily!" Helena Sinclair admonished.

Belle beamed. "It's all right. You can be honest with him."

"ETHAN, we really don't have very much time." Belle laughed as her new husband tugged her inside the shop. "We're supposed to be—"

His mouth descended, hot and eager. He leaned her against the door, reaching behind her to turn the lock with a decisive click. The small sound was somehow as erotic as Ethan's soft groan.

"It's been three weeks, Belle."

"Well..." She gasped, letting him angle her neck. She was wearing her sapphires and seed pearls, and his tongue slid over the jewels. "The banns, you know. I wanted to do things properly."

"As do I." His green gaze was dark. "Upstairs, sweetheart. I have a wedding present for you."

"A promising start," she teased, tugging at his collar.

Ethan evidently wasn't in the mood for banter, for he was

already pulling her up the staircase, his fingers twined with hers as they tumbled into the small parlor.

"Right." He dropped a lingering kiss on the back of her neck. "Sit on the desk."

"Ah." She eyed the wobbly desk. "Perhaps our bed, darling—"

"I feel insane when you say that," he muttered.

"I know." She kissed his jaw, unwinding his cravat. "I feel insane when you say anything."

He lifted her, crossed the room in six long strides, and unceremoniously dropped her in a pile of pale skirts on the narrow surface of the writing desk. Before she could so much as gasp, he was kissing her with furious intent, his tongue moving roughly against hers as he worked open the tiny buttons on her bodice.

"What about my present?" she managed when he finally released her lips in favor of the swell of her breasts. She moaned softly, instantly needy at the sensation of his mouth against the edge of her delicately embroidered chemise. "Never mind…"

"This *is* the present." He braced his arms on either side of her hips, his palms flat on the desktop.

"Yes," she agreed foggily, running her hands down the broad plane of his chest. "Indeed."

"No." He kissed her again, slower this time. "The desk is your present."

He shook the desktop, and she preemptively wound her arms around him, bracing for the lurch.

The desk remained sturdy beneath her bottom.

"I made it steady for you." He grinned proudly.

"Oh!" She leaned back, rocking a little, acutely aware of the way his hooded stare tracked the sway of her breasts. "Look at that. Darling, it's wonderful."

"Such a menace," he breathed, inching her skirts up her legs.

"I adore it, Ethan." She kissed him soundly, gratitude warming her all the way through. "It's exactly right. It's just what I imagined."

He spread her knees, moving to stand between them.

"You imagined this?" He slid his hands down the small of her back, fitting their hips together. "Being ravished on a sturdy writing desk?"

"No." She laughed, unfastening his trousers. "I mean, I imagined our life here, above the shop."

His face grew tender as he drew her flush against him.

"Tell me," he rumbled in her ear, "about an ordinary day."

"Waking later than you," she whispered. "Fixing your tie. Watching you yank it sideways…"

She arched her back, sighing as he lifted her bottom and seated himself in one slow stroke.

"What else?"

She pitched under the strength of her hopes and desires, even as he sated both. The life she yearned for, *here*, in her arms, filling all the space inside her.

"Your feet on the stairs. Writing at this desk. Making something together." She touched his mouth, breathless. "Not having the faintest idea what it will be."

She was hardly making sense, but he groaned, moving languidly within her. He captured her mouth, lazy and unmeasured, helping her take what she needed until what she needed was him.

"Yes," he murmured. "Let's do that."

There were many things about their circumstances they wished to improve, but not this. *This* was the one thing, perhaps, they'd managed to get right.

By some turn of providence, he had stumbled upon the right bench; by some miracle, she had allowed him space there.

And somehow, together, they had turned a stack of damaged paper into an entire story.

One day, they would look back from some great vantage and see the page.

For now, they only needed to join hands—

And turn it.

EPILOGUE

July 1855
London

FROM FOURTEEN DAYS AFTER THE PASSING OF THIS ACT it shall not be compulsory…to print any Newspaper on Paper stamped for denoting the Duties imposed by Law on Newspapers, and no Person shall be subject or liable to any Penalty or Forfeiture for printing, publishing, selling, or having in his Possession any unstamped Newspaper.

—Excerpt from the Newspapers Act, 15 June 1855

"Good afternoon, Mrs. Fletcher." Paulie, erstwhile newsboy, called to Belle from his bookstall across the Strand. "Dare I say, the summer agrees with you."

Ethan glanced at his wife. Her pinned hair gleamed in the late afternoon light, and her cheeks held the sunny blush that always reminded him of their first bright months together. Paulie was right, but he could stand to be a little less confident about it.

Ethan tilted back his hat. "The summer is about to disagree with *you*, Paulie, if you keep waving down my wife."

Belle laughed merrily and reached up to readjust his hat. "I would expect you to be in a better mood today, darling."

Paulie ignored Ethan's glower and raised a jar of colorfully striped sweets. "I have pulled sugar sticks, if the little ones like."

Thomas tugged at Belle's hand. "Mama, may we?"

"No we may not," she said briskly. "We're expected at the shop, and we can't be late."

Thomas looked over his shoulder, giving his sister a pointed look. Ethan felt a small hand slide into his.

"Da?"

He made the mistake of looking down. Marina's elfin face stared up at him with the same doe-eyes as her mother.

"May I please have a sweet?"

Ethan frowned between his children. The twins were nearly five years old, which meant they knew precisely who was their strongest soldier and what was their parents' weakest defense.

"Fine," he sighed.

"Ethan," Belle warned. "Everyone is waiting for you."

"It will only take a moment. Besides, why shouldn't they get a sweet? It's been pandemonium this week, what with me working all hours."

He moved into the street, stopping a cab and ushering his family safely across. The children raced to Paulie, purveyor of unwelcome flirtations and unnecessary sweets.

As Belle passed Ethan, her hand slipped into his coat pocket, deftly grasping his wallet. Her little finger grazed his waistcoat. "Is everyone getting a treat today?"

"Try that again and find out," he breathed.

She smiled wickedly and trailed Marina and Thomas to the bookstall.

"One piece each." She placed her hands on their curly heads.

As the children selected candies, Belle and Paulie drifted into conversation, and Ethan took the opportunity to survey the book-stall's offerings. The latest installment from Dickens was prominently featured, a recurrence that irritated Ethan to no end. He checked over his shoulder—Paulie was taking a coin from the twins—then quickly swapped out *Little Dorrit.*

"Really?" Belle shook her head as she sidled up to him. "Must you do that every time?"

They looked at the novel he'd placed on display.

CLEMENTINA BLOOM AND THE STEAMBOAT SABOTAGE
A Novel of Crime, Mystery, and Intrigue
Written by B. Sinclair Fletcher

"It's not even new," she protested. "*Steamboat* released last summer."

"Well, Paulie is sold out of *The Arson Affair*, so I made do."

"Sold out?" She frowned. "I suppose we'll have to take it up with my publisher."

"Indeed." Ethan laughed. "It's times like these, I'm grateful that's no longer me."

But Belle had her attention on their children. "I said *one*, Thomas Gavin Fletcher. One means one. Put that back. There will be cake at the party." She turned to Paulie. "Will you be joining us at the shop?"

"I'll come after I close up," Paulie said cheerfully. "I never miss a chance to drink to Fletcher."

"You never miss a chance for me to pay for your drinks," Ethan said wryly. "I'm glad you're coming. It will be good to have the old crowd there."

"Congratulations, sir. I mean it sincerely. You and Porter—you really did it, eh?"

"I suppose we'll find out tomorrow." Ethan ran his hand over his beard. "And I would say Parliament actually did it, when they repealed that damn tax. Porter and I were just ready to step in."

"Oh, come now." Belle beamed at him. "You needn't be so modest."

"I'm realistic." He pointed out. "It's a useful thing to be when starting a brand-new business venture."

"Hmm." She tilted her head. "I wouldn't know."

He called to the twins. Marina and Thomas waved politely, and their little foursome set off again. They passed through Temple Bar, and the Strand gave way to Fleet, where the old shop waited for them.

"It's odd, isn't it?" Belle mused as their children ran ahead. "I doubt they'll even remember it being a printshop. Only a newspaper office."

"I don't mind what memories stick," Ethan said. "So long as they're good."

He watched them—all coltish limbs and messy curls—and felt the profound satisfaction of knowing his children slept in their beds without a worry in their heads. He could buy them sweets on the street, he could use his old Columbian to print little stories they made up at the breakfast table. He could rest assured they would never see their mother's hands marred by anything but the ink stains she put there herself.

In the end, his prospects hadn't been as important as his purpose —to be a good man to the good people who loved him.

"Are you ready for tomorrow?" Belle asked softly. "Your first issue. It's all right if it feels peculiar. It's a big step, Ethan."

"I'm ready. It's been a long time coming. Though it will be strange to split my time between here and the new premises," Ethan admitted as they drew nearer to No. 62.

"Tobias will oversee the print works," Belle reminded him. "He's been itching for those new rotary presses."

"Don't I know it," Ethan said. "Even still, I don't want to be holed up in an office all day."

"If *you* want to run the new presses, you can just admit it," Belle teased. "If I have to hear one more time about how many papers you can push a week—"

"Here they are, the guests of honor." The door to No. 62 swung open, and the twins raced to greet Sam Porter, who hefted a small child in each big arm.

Ethan chuckled. At four and twenty, Sam had grown into his height and remained as cheerful as ever. Likely in no small part due to the recent nuptials to his longtime love, Abigail.

"Now that you two are here, you can tell your parents to go celebrate on their own," Sam winked.

"It's Da's party," Thomas explained. "For the paper. He has to be here, and we have to wear our coats."

"Oh, of course, my mistake. We can't toast to the *Weekly Register* without the publisher. Or our coats."

Sam set the children down, and they ran inside.

"Sam, it's kind of you to have us," Belle called as they approached. "You don't mind all of us stomping around the place?"

"Sixty-two Fleet still belongs to you, Mrs. Fletcher." Sam grinned. "But Abigail and I appreciate you letting us rent the upstairs."

"It's a good place to start out." She smiled. "You two take all the time you need."

Ethan tucked Belle's arm in his and reached up to straighten the shingle. They entered a shop full of faces old and new. Belle's family was there—Helena was already sneaking the twins more sweets—but seeing as they were staying with their grandparents tonight, Ethan decided to let it be the Sinclairs' problem. Tobias and his wife were caught up in a knot of folks from the early days. And all mixed together were Ethan's new employees and Belle's new publishers and their neighbors and friends.

Layers of life, all in his shop.

Sam was pouring a champagne toast, and the workroom gradually grew silent, everyone looking to Ethan. He had a speech to make, but his throat felt unexpectedly tight.

His family, his friends, his business.

His wife.

What could he possibly say?

He'd once thought life happened in sudden, cataclysmic shifts. The wrong correspondence from a solicitor, a journal passing hands in a garden. A delayed steamship. A returning train. Finite moments, setting life in motion.

Now he understood the shifts could be very small. Sometimes, life felt more akin to the way he typeset a page. Incremental progress, gradual gain. No isolated word or phrase made a difference—but together, *yes*, together, eventually, the creation became more possible than not.

"Thank you all for being here," he said, raising his glass. "Thank you for having *been* here."

He looked around to find Belle. "You all may not know this, but the second time I met my wife was the day we agreed to a madcap scheme that somehow led us to this moment…and every other moment along the way." He smiled at her, her face so bright, she might as well have been the only person in the room. "We had nothing between us, other than a press and a journal, but I still maintain it was the richest day of my life."

He paused, cocking his eyebrow.

"Until, hopefully, tomorrow."

There was a loud chorus of whoops and cheers, but before anyone could raise their glass, Belle cleared her throat.

She reached for his hand, steadying herself as she swiftly mounted a nearby chair. He looked at her, seized by the memory of the long-ago night when they first celebrated in this shop—her radiant face, her messy plait, her slender fingers raising a chipped mug.

"To my husband," she announced, lifting her champagne. "You are the finest man in London, Ethan Fletcher. Much to your eternal chagrin."

He laughed and kissed her wrist as another excitable chorus sounded. Belle leaned down, touching his cheek, her eyes soft and golden and always, always on his.

"I mean it, darling. Wishing you good luck—and good news."

"Thank you, sweetheart." He grinned and tugged her down, bringing her mouth close to his. "But I sense we'll be just fine."

Belle's hand tightened in his.

And Ethan held fast.

AUTHOR'S NOTE

"The duty on paper is heavy in England, which, added to the specific news-tax of one penny, or two cents, upon every sheet, amounts to a terrible burden upon the newspapers. Every newspaper in the kingdom must pay into the coffers of the government two cents for its every sheet. This makes the risk of those who attempt the publication of new journals exceedingly great."

—David W. Bartlett, in London by day and night; or, Men and things in the great metropolis (1851).

In many ways, *The Finest Print* is a very small story, which is strange, because it feels so expansive to me. I had to scale everything down for this book—country estates shrank to a shabby printshop; lavish ballrooms were traded for a hundred-pound debt. The villain of this book is *taxes*. I was so inspired by the very ordinary struggle to make life *work*. Ethan's earnest striving against his limitations became the impetus for this book, and Belle's steadfast belief they could do it was its heart.

The Victorian period saw many technological innovations and social shifts that transformed the publishing landscape, but it's estimated that by midcentury, many printing firms were quite small and still doing most of the work by hand. Through writing this book, I gained an appreciation for the exquisite care and craftsmanship inherent in the print industry, and I made the utmost effort to authentically describe Ethan's trade while servicing the story. One of the most important takeaways from my research was a deeper understanding of the ways in which the production and dissemination of information has been a driving force for change.

Printing enabled people to *read*.

What can be more powerful than that?

Evidently, some people were well-aware of the ramifications of an informed public, and made every effort to put up roadblocks to that effect. The so-called taxes on knowledge were egregious and effectively barred the working class from accessing the news. Newspapers had an easier time in America—penny papers started circulating in the 1830s—but in England, publishers faced a decades-long struggle until the taxes were repealed (1853 for advertising, 1855 for news, 1861 for paper).

It brought me so much creative joy to situate Belle and Ethan at the cusp of the social, cultural, and economic shifts ushered in by the stratospheric growth of print media. Here, I'll share some of the research that informed their story. As always, I'll include some of my references, if you wish to explore any of these topics on your own.

The Penny Fiction to Newspaper Pipeline

The Finest Print is a story that is a tiny bit true.

While Ethan Fletcher is decidedly his own man, his professional trajectory was partly drawn from a real Victorian publisher—Edward Lloyd, a prolific purveyor of newspapers, periodicals, and serialized fiction.

I can't speak to Lloyd's personal life or ideologies; it was his business endeavors that captured my interest. Lloyd wanted to publish an affordable newspaper, but the taxes were every bit as punishing as Ethan found them to be. Lloyd, however, was an industrious and experimental person. He employed all manner of strategies to circumvent taxes and increase sales, including, but not limited to, plagiarizing Dickens (to be fair, he wasn't the only one, and *Oliver Twiss* is a winning title!); publishing an illustration-only paper only *depicting* the news, not reporting it; and establishing sham newspapers that fictionalized current events.

Fascinating stuff, to be sure, but here is where Ethan comes in— Lloyd's earliest success was in *penny fiction*. In fact, Lloyd was the publisher of Sam Porter's beloved *Varney the Vampire* (yes, this was a real serial and it was a pretty wild ride). Lloyd also published what is arguably the most famous penny dreadful of all—*The String of Pearls*. You might not recognize the title, but I'd bet you've heard of the main character: Sweeney Todd, the Demon Barber of Fleet Street. (My husband wants to know how many of you sang that. *I* want to know if you caught Belle's nod to Sweeney Todd in Chapter 21.)

With the capital provided by his story papers, Lloyd established a legitimate weekly paper in 1842, but his newspaper prospects remained unstable for another decade. When the "taxes on knowledge" were abolished, he was finally able to reduce his prices and thereafter enjoyed immense success. On February 16, 1896, *Lloyd's Weekly Newspaper* became the only newspaper in nineteenth-century Britain to sell more than a million copies.

When I discovered Lloyd's story, I was in the midst of sorting out how to reconcile Ethan's newspaper aspirations with Belle's writing. You can imagine my utter delight to find there was a precedent for *this very journey!* How exciting to think the same publisher who brought us Sweeney Todd went on to be a key player in the Victorian newspaper industry. I like to imagine Ethan and Belle enjoyed similar smashing success.

A Literacy Initiative

Penny bloods—more popularly known today as *penny dreadfuls,* though that term was not in common use until the late 1850s— emerged during the early Victorian period as an affordable alternative to other forms of fiction. Story papers sold for a penny and regaled the masses with tales of the paranormal, crime, murder, adventure, mystery, and romance—let's be honest, they sound pretty damn fun. And they were *wildly* popular. Some scholars have compared the rise of penny dreadfuls to the popularity of twentieth-century comic books. Contemporary accounts describe working-class folks pooling their money to purchase the latest serials, reading them aloud on the streets, and generally alleviating the monotony of long hours with the escapism fiction can provide.

But penny bloods were more than simple entertainment. As Belle says—first as an excuse, later with conviction—penny fiction contributed to the spread of literacy. Though it's difficult to parse the precise role played by these stories, its growing popularity was certainly contemporaneous with the expansion of charity schools and public education. Indisputably, the Victorian period saw unprecedented numbers of people learning to read, and those people were hungry for affordable material. Some historians have posited that the desire to keep up with the latest adventures of beloved characters in chapbooks and serials was its own incentive to acquire literacy. After all, penny bloods reached their peak popularity for British teens before primary education became compulsory.

Penny bloods were not without their detractors. Story papers *did* cause a serious moral panic, not unlike today's arguments for censoring certain forms of media. Authors were called, as in Belle's case, "poison-publishers," and moralists disparaged penny fiction as a scourge to society.

But these concerns did little to stop the genre from veritably exploding. Between the 1830s and the 1890s, penny bloods reached millions of readers, heralding mass-media publishing as a viable route for professional success. Popular serials could circulate as many as 30,000 copies each week, and some of their creators went on to have long, successful careers.

If penny bloods are of interest, you can actually read them online! *The Dictionary of Victorian London* is a veritable trove of primary sources from the period, and popular serials such as the *Mysteries of London* and *The String of Pearls* have been digitized. (Unfortunately, Belle Sinclair Fletcher's *Secrets of the Old Bailey* survives only in excerpts.)

The (True) Secrets of the Old Bailey

As much as I wish we could visit the courthouse frequented by Clementina Bloom, the Central Criminal Court presided over by Gavin Sinclair no longer exists (the present building is from 1902). To bring the Old Bailey to life, I used artwork, contemporary descriptions, and historical floor plans. But by and large, the most useful source I found was the *Proceedings of the Old Bailey* website, which in addition to containing excellent contextual information, includes digitized transcriptions of the entirety of the *Proceedings*, published from 1674 to 1913.

It was from *Proceedings* that I found inspiration for the trial Belle and Ethan overheard at the courthouse. William Burton Newenham was accused of removing Frances Louisa Wortham from the home of her mother, only for Frances to (dramatically) reveal she willingly ran away with William when she learned her mother wanted to marry him instead. Unfortunately for literally everybody involved, Frances had not yet reached the age of majority, and her new husband was convicted for two years.

Stranger than Fiction

Last but not least, I would be remiss if I didn't share a little bit about a topic that is really important to me—the use of contraceptives in this book. I knew from the outset Belle and Ethan would utilize contraceptives, or "conception checks" as they were called. I also knew I had a perfect storm with Belle—she'd already been engaged, she had daily exposure to real-world issues at the courthouse, and her mother was a no-nonsense feminist. It seemed entirely natural she would receive an era-appropriate sexual education.

The book given to Belle by her mother was Richard Carlile's *Every woman's book, or, What is love?: containing most important instructions for the prudent regulation of the principle of love and the number of a family* (published 1826). In his writing, Carlile discussed a variety of birth control methods, but what drew my attention was this passage:

> *If, before sexual intercourse, the female introduces into her vagina a piece of sponge… it will be found a preventive to conception, while it neither lessens the pleasure of the female nor injures her health.*

Interestingly, Carlile wasn't the only one advocating for sponges and pessaries as conception checks in this period. In *Fruits of Philosophy* (first published 1832), Charles Knowlton likewise espoused this method. In these manuals, the authors explain that withdrawal was risky, and condoms could be uncomfortable, expensive, and ineffective. At this point, I was not liking my options for Belle and Ethan. But a sponge, as Carlile wrote, "is the female's safeguard." When I realized Belle could plausibly be aware of a birth control method that centered female pleasure, I knew I had to seize the opportunity. Ethan prioritizes Belle's agency in all aspects of their relationship, and I wanted to reflect that in their intimacy, too.

But most surprisingly of all, there was an additional facet in *Every woman's book* that had me grinning from ear to ear—its title page. You see, it wasn't until *after* I finished my first draft that I went to grab the full citation. And you'll never, *ever* guess where Carlile's offices were located in the 1820s.

That's right: *62 Fleet Street.*

Sometimes, we really *can't* make this stuff up.

Further Reading

Carlile, Richard. (1828). *Every woman's book, or, What is love? : containing most important instructions for the prudent regulation of the principle of love and the number of a family*. London.

Oats, L., & Sadler, P. (2007). Securing the repeal of a tax on the 'raw material of thought'. Accounting, Business & Financial History, 17(3), 355-373. https://doi.org/10.1080/09585200701609562

Oliver Twiss and Martin Guzzlewit – the fanfiction that ripped off Dickens. (2019, June 25). The Guardian. https://www.theguardian.com/books/2019/jun/25/oliver-twiss-twist-charles-dickens-rip-off-edward-lloyd

Price One Penny - Cheap Literature 1837-1860. (2020). http://www.priceonepenny.info/about.php

The Proceedings of the Old Bailey. (2024). https://www.oldbaileyonline.org

Rose, J. (2008). *The Intellectual Life of the British Working Classes.* Yale University Press.

Springhall, J. (1994). "Disseminating Impure Literature": The "Penny Dreadful" Publishing Business Since 1860. *The Economic History Review, 47*(3), 567–584. https://doi.org/10.2307/2597594

The String of Pearls - The Original Penny Dreadful Featuring Sweeney Todd, The Demon Barber of Fleet Street. (n.d.). https://www.victorianlondon.org/mysteries/sweeney_todd-01.htm

ACKNOWLEDGMENTS

Like many authors, I've come to learn that writing doesn't happen in isolation. In my book, Belle Sinclair is fortunate to surround herself with people who challenge her and believe in her, and I know exactly how she feels.

This book would not exist without my talented, insightful, and extremely patient critique partners and beta readers. Anjor, thank you for making my draft my happy place. Thank you for looking at my original outline and saying "...No." Thank you for making me keep Ethan's beard (friends, many moons ago the draft had him shave his beard in Chapter 6 and *never grow it back*). And thank you, most of all, for believing I could do this again.

This story started as a series of completely chaotic messages to Sarah T. Dubb and took a hundred detours along the way—thank you for being in the passenger seat for all of them, my dear friend. I couldn't do *any* of this without you. Silly Geese all the way (even though sometimes we have to be Serious Geese).

Lindsay Barrett, Celine Oliver, Amy, and Tzip: every one of you made this story better than I thought possible. I'm so fortunate to be on the receiving end of your feedback, guidance, and absolutely delightful commentary. It's a joy to share my words with you and to know you will take good care of them.

As always, I'm so grateful for my editor, Rachel Shipp. Your expertise in clarifying my writing and ideas has been invaluable, and it's because of you I love this story more than I ever thought possible. And many thanks to my agent, Jessica Alvarez, for making it possible for *The Finest Print* to have an audiobook release. I'm still in a bit of shock that my words have new life in new formats, and I appreciate all of your work to make it happen.

I would also like to thank Erin Dameron-Hill for my stunning cover, and Kelsey Bowman for creating such a gorgeous print wrap. Kelsey also designed the *most* fun and beautiful graphics and tie-ins (including a cover for Belle's penny blood)! Thank you for bringing my story to life in such fun and refreshing ways.

I'm so very grateful for the writing community I get to be a part of. The SF2.0 Discord continues to be a wealth of insight, knowledge, support, and hilarity. Alexandra Vasti–I still can't believe that two years ago I left you the first unsolicited message of my life and it's resulted such a wonderful and supportive friendship. I remain in constant awe of your talent and kindness! I also have to thank Liana De la Rosa, who I still credit with helping me sort out my publishing journey; it's been a true honor to watch you soar. And Gissane Sophia–thank you for believing in me from before the very start. I'm so proud of you and your words, my friend.

I was fortunate to take a very special trip to the Cincinnati Type & Print museum to learn all about nineteenth century printing. What I *didn't* expect was to learn about how prolific the print industry still is today. Moreover, the Type & Print Museum is a mission-driven organization that seeks to train printers and promote career opportunities in print media. I deeply appreciate the Museum for giving us a hands-on look at historical printing as well as illuminating the ways print work promotes social change.

I also want to thank Jennifer Arnold for dialoguing with me on my representation of Belle's headaches and providing excellent feedback. It was important to me to ensure I was describing Belle as suffering from mild-to-moderate tension-type headaches, which are not the same as migraine. Your considerate care helped me clarify my ideas and Belle is all the better for it.

I would be remiss, of course, if I did not thank my family and friends. I'm so lucky to have such wonderful people filling my cup and cheering me on. I have the best parents, sisters, children, and community around me. Thank you for keeping me grounded, distracted, and smiling.

Pete, there is no part of this book that exists without you. Thank you for listening, reading, scribbling down ideas as I shouted them from across the house. Thank you for creating an actual formula to calculate the cost of printing and disseminating a serial in 1848 (and to keep fixing it when I messed with it too much). Thank you for giving me time to write; thank you for giving me courage to write. Thank you for doing life with me.

Finally—an entirely insufficient "thank you" to my readers. I've said it before, and I'll say it again: writing was never the plan, only the dream. I thought *Forever Your Rogue* would be the only story I ever told. The outpouring of faith and support you have put in me and my characters has been an astonishing source of joy. Thank you for choosing to spend time with my books. It's been a beautiful privilege to share them with you.

ABOUT THE AUTHOR

Erin Langston is a historical romance author who crafts stories with heart, heat, and humor. A librarian by trade, Erin lives in the Midwest with her husband and two children. When not working, writing, or mom-ing, she can be found outside, drinking wine, buried in a book, or attempting to home-improve. A not-insignificant portion of her first novel was plotted in the preschool pickup line.

ALSO BY ERIN LANGSTON

Forever Your Rogue

A Day Until Forever

Some Winter's Evening

For book information and bonus content visit

erinlangstonwrites.com